Andrew Killeen

THE KHALIFAH'S MIRROR

Dedalus

Andrew Killeen gratefully acknowledges the support of Arts Council
England in the writing of this book.

Published in the UK by Dedalus Limited,
24-26, St Judith's Lane, Sawtry, Cambs, PE28 5XE
email: info@ dedalusbooks.com
www.dedalusbooks.com

ISBN 978 1 903517 97 0

Dedalus is distributed in the USA by SCB Distributors,
15608 South New Century Drive, Gardena, CA 90248
email: info@scbdistributors.com   web: www.scbdistributors.com

Dedalus is distributed in Australia by Peribo Pty Ltd.
58, Beaumont Road, Mount Kuring-gai, N.S.W. 2080
email: info@peribo.com.au

First published by Dedalus in 2012
The Khalifah's Mirror copyright © *Andrew Killeen 2012*

The right of Andrew Killeen to be identified as the author of this work has
been asserted by him in accordance with the Copyright, Designs and Patents
Act, 1988.

Printed in Finland by Bookwell
Typeset by Marie Lane

Prologue

From The History of the Prophets and the Kings, *by Abu Ja'far Muhammad ibn Jarir al-Tabari:*

When God cast Adam down from the Garden, He set him on the summit of the mountain called Abu Qubays, and laid out before him the whole world, saying,

"All this is yours."

But Adam asked,

"How, oh Lord, am I to know what is in it?"

So God made for him the stars, and told him,

"When you see this star, it means this, and when you see that star, it means that."

In this way Adam came to know the world through the stars. Then he lost that knowledge, so instead God sent from heaven a mirror in which Adam could see everything on earth.

On Adam's death, at the age of nine hundred and thirty years, a devil called Faqtas stole the magic mirror. He shattered it, and on top of the pieces he built the city of the east called Jabirat. When Sulayman ibn Dawud, King of the Jews, inquired about Adam's mirror, he was told of the devil's theft, and summoned Faqtas before him.

"Where is Adam's mirror?" he asked.

Faqtas the devil said,

"It is buried under the foundations of Jabirat."

"Bring it to me," Sulayman commanded.

"Who will tear down the city?" asked the devil.

"You will," answered the King.

So the devil destroyed the city, and retrieved the mirror, which he brought back to Sulayman. The King put the pieces back together and bound it round the edge with a strap. He looked into it every day until the day he died.

Once again the devils pounced on the mirror and carried it off, but they left a shard behind. The Children of Isra'il passed the shard down from generation to generation, century after century, until the Age of Islam, when it came into the possession of the Resh Galuta, their leader in exile. The Resh Galuta wished to gain the favour of the Khalifah Marwan ibn Muhammad, the Commander of the Faithful, so he gave him as a gift the shard from Adam's magic mirror. The Khalifah polished it vigorously and set it within another mirror. What he saw therein, though, so horrified him that he hurled it to the ground and had the Resh Galuta beheaded.

A slave girl was ordered to clear up the shattered mirror, but she took the magical shard of glass, and wrapped it in cotton, concealing it under a stone. When al-Mansur the Victorious became Khalifah, he asked what had happened to it, and was told that a woman had it. He ordered a search of the palace, and the shard was found.

Al-Mansur, too, polished it and set it in an ordinary mirror. And when he looked into it, he could see the man he had been searching for... It is said that the mirror showed him who was his friend, and who was his enemy.

I

The Khalifah Harun al-Rashid, the Righteous One, Commander of the Faithful, Successor to the Prophet of God, settled himself delicately on his cushion, and winced. It seemed that no amount of gold could purchase relief, that no down was sufficiently soft, no silk so smooth, as to save him from discomfort. If God had chosen al-Rashid to lead His people, to shoulder the onerous burden of governing the Land of Islam, that He might at least have spared His servant the pain and ignominy of piles.

The arrival in the audience hall of two guards, dragging a prisoner between them, stirred al-Rashid to further irritation. Today was such a vexing day. His arse was throbbing, a peach he had eaten for breakfast had a worm in it, and now he was going to have to order the execution of one of his best friends.

"Ah, Father of Locks. I am very disappointed in you."

He studied the man who knelt before him, robes spattered with blood, a secretive smile on his face despite his predicament. Abu Ali al-Hasan ibn Hani al-Hakami, known as Abu Nuwas, the Father of Locks, was still a handsome man, although he must be nearing fifty years of age. The belly that protruded above his belt was at odds with his rangy frame, but suggested years of good living rather than sloth or ill-health. His eyes were sapphire blue, though tinged with redness around their edges. The long hair that spilled from his turban was combed into tresses, like snakes curling over his shoulders. Al-Rashid shook his head in sadness.

"I am, as you know, a great admirer of your poetry, and take much pleasure in your company. I am most put out that I must have you killed."

7

"I share your chagrin, my prince."

Al-Rashid knew he should be angered by the poet's impertinence, but instead could not resist a smirk at the man's insouciance in the face of death. A twinge from his royal backside restored the Khalifah's sense of indignation.

"I cannot grant you your life, you must understand that. Your transgression is unforgivable. However, in recognition of our friendship, I will grant you one final boon. What do you wish for, Father of Locks? A jar of wine, perhaps, to ease the pain of your passing? A last meal? A virgin, or —"

The Khalifah's face expressed his distaste.

"— I suppose you would prefer a boy, for a final fleeting moment of ecstasy?"

Abu Nuwas bowed low.

"Your generosity surpasses measure to the very end, Commander of the Faithful. My request is a simple one. I would like someone to speak on my behalf."

Al-Rashid groaned. Now he would have to spend the rest of the afternoon listening to tedious legal arguments, instead of going hunting as he had planned. Really, he was a martyr to his own magnanimity.

"I warn you, Abu Ali, you must not hope for mercy. This will not be like the stories, where the ruler is moved by the condemned man's tale, and in the end pardons him, and rewards him with gold. You will die this day, I swear it on the life of my son."

"I would not dare dream of mercy, my prince; I know I cannot expect it, even from one as beneficent as Harun the Righteous. I wish only to give an account of myself, so that you might understand how your loyal servant came to be here, cast down before you, convicted of treason and murder."

"Oh, very well. I suppose you will want al-Shafi'i to plead your case? I believe he studied the Shariah under you. Or al-Waqidi?"

"As in all matters, my prince, your suggestions are impeccable. However, it is not the services of a jurist which I require. I ask instead for a storyteller. A man called Ismail al-Rawiya."

Despite himself, al-Rashid was intrigued.

"Masrur, do you know where to find this al-Rawiya?"

Masrur the Swordbearer, the Khalifah's bodyguard and executioner, stood at his master's side, as he always did. Al-Rashid was reassured by the giant eunuch's presence, the soft rumble of his voice and the sharpness of his blade.

"Yes, Commander of the Faithful. He was apprehended in the palace earlier today, and is in custody below."

"Then have him brought here. But I warn you, Father of Locks, if he is your accomplice in treachery, then you will both regret your choice."

Masrur signalled to a guard, who left the hall, returning moments later with a young man in tattered clothing. Short and slender, the youth's dark eyes stood in stark contrast to his pale skin.

"Are you the storyteller Ismail al-Rawiya?"

The young man bowed.

"That is indeed your servant's name, Commander of the Faithful."

"This man is sentenced to death, and wishes you to speak in his defence. Are you willing to stand with him?"

Al-Rashid saw the poet and the storyteller exchange a glance.

"If the Khalifah asks, I can do no other than obey."

"Good. Then speak, and quickly. What do you have to say on his behalf?"

"My prince, I have a story to tell you."

"A story?"

Al-Rashid's tone was testy, but secretly he was pleased. He liked stories much better than lawyers' speeches.

"Indeed, my prince, a story. It is a tale of adventure, of love, and deception, of destiny, daring, and death. It is a tale of kings, and warriors, and of beautiful princesses; but also of poets, pirates, and priests. It is a story to entertain and instruct, to stir the blood, to inflame the senses, to dizzy the mind and rouse the soul. It is one tale but also many, a tale of past, present and perhaps future too. It —"

"Yes, yes, very good. Get on with it then."
"My prince, I present, for your delight and edification..."

The Tale of the Wali's Gold

They came in the hour before dawn.

From the black silence of the desert night they came, in the breathless hour when even scorpions and vipers are still; when the darkness is so deep that beyond the firelight the world might have ended, and a man alone in the desert be the last man on earth, but not yet know it; in the hour when Azrail, the Angel of Death, loves to visit the sick and the old, and carry away their souls to judgement; that was when the Banu Jahm struck.

They were only a hundred paces from the caravan when the alarm was raised. The guard was a heavy man, and the suck and rattle of his breath as he leaned on his spear might have drowned out their approach, even if he had not been dozing, dreaming of houri lips where he stood. Nobody else was awake: the captain and the merchant, the camel-drivers and the boy all lay in the tent, stirring in shallow sleep. No moon illumined the camp, only a single torch shoved in the ground. Its feeble light wavered and was haunted by shadows.

The Banu Jahm had come this far by stealth, their camels' hooves shuffling across the sand. Now they charged, shattering the silence with terrible screams and yells. The guard jerked awake, his member still hard despite the terror, and saw only distorted shapes emerging from the gloom. Although his sticky eyes were open, he could not quite escape his dream, and thought a horde of ghuls came howling at him.

Now, to his horror, one of the shapes peeled away from the pack and headed directly towards him. The guard's spear wavered in his shaking hands. By the time he could make out that the shadow approaching him was not a monster, but a handsome youth riding a camel, the point of a lance was already at his throat.

"Put that down, friend. Is this really how you want to die?"

The guard slowly crouched down, and laid his spear on the sand. Sa'id ibn Bishr al-Jahm jumped down from his camel, and clapped him on the shoulder.

"Sensible fellow. No need for anyone to get hurt, eh?"

Sai'id's tribesmen were appearing all around him now, dragging the captives from their tent. He felt pride at the sight. They were skilled, his cousins, each knowing their place, carrying out their tasks in silence, no need for talk. This would be a good raid, a clean raid, with no blood spilt and no repercussions. A cracked voice interrupted his thoughts.

"Eh, Sa'id! Have you overwhelmed the guards single-handed? What courage! I must write some verses in celebration."

Abu Bishr, Sa'id's grandfather, walked towards them leading his camel. Sa'id glanced down at the big man grovelling on the ground.

"A warrior can only fight the enemy in front of him. It is no slur on his honour if the enemy is a coward, or a fool. Who taught me that, grandfather? I cannot recall."

Abu Bishr cackled.

"I do not know, but he must be very wise, and no doubt brave and virile too."

The guard flinched as the old man poked at him with a sword, tarnished from years in the harsh desert. Sa'id doubted the blade was sharp enough to cut the man's flesh, or that his grandfather had the strength to do it if he meant to. The Shaikh had told Abu Bishr that he need not join the raid, that there would be no dishonour in a man of his age staying behind, but Abu Bishr had scoffed at the idea.

"What, cower in the tent like the women and children? No, nephew, when I am too old to mount a camel and hold a sword, you may leave me out in the desert to die."

The dim scene flickered, then sharpened as the Banu Jahm

---

lit torches. Sa'id looked around.

"Then it is true, that this fat clod is their only guard?"

Abu Bishr spat contemptuously.

"It is an insult to the Banu Jahm! They cross our territory, without paying for our protection. Then they do not even trouble to hire any decent blades. Just this... toad with a stick. They might as well have pissed in our well as they passed."

Sa'id smiled, but his eyes expressed uncertainty. He pulled the guard to his feet, and hauled him over to where the men of the caravan knelt, ringed by warriors of the Banu Jahm. As he did so, he noticed a lanky figure seated in the dirt, watching the raid with cool interest. Sa'id walked over cautiously. In the shifting glow of the torches he could make out a softly bearded face, the face of one a few years his junior, little more than a boy. The boy's eyes flamed, and for a moment Sa'id thought they were lit from within, not merely reflecting the fire.

"Am I yours, then?"

The boy got up as he spoke, and it seemed to Sa'id that he uncurled, rising from the ground like a cobra. At full height he stood a head taller than Sa'id, even though he swayed slightly. His features were sharp and angular as a gemstone, and the fierce eyes fixed on his captor. Sa'id shuddered, although he was not sure why. Reluctant to touch the boy, he prodded him with his spear, goading him toward the other captives.

"Wait there. My uncle the Shaikh is coming."

Abu Wahb al-Zubayr ibn Tahir al-Jahm, Shaikh of the Banu Jahm, was a big man. Over four cubits in height, and broad as a mountain bear, he looked ungainly atop his camel as he trotted around his prisoners. His beard was bushy, and his eyes were bright. Generous to his guests, ruthless to his foes, protective of his family, devoted to his camels, he was a true Badawi: quick to draw his sword at an insult, slow to forget a debt of honour, easily moved to tears by a sentimental song. And when his booming laugh burst out in the night, startling the owls, his kin knew that all was well at the camp.

To Sa'id, his uncle was a great man; the most important

in the world. He knew, of course, that they owed allegiance to the Commander of the Faithful, al-Mansur the Victorious. But the Khalifah was far away in Baghdad. Here, in the Empty Quarter, Abu Wahb bent his knee to no one. When he spoke, his voice compelled the attention of both friend and enemy.

"Who is leading this misguided adventure?

The captives looked at the ground or at each other. Most of them were local camel drivers, well known to the Banu Jahm. A rotund man with bushy eyebrows hissed at the long-nosed man next to him.

"You said there would be no trouble!"

The long-nosed man slowly got to his feet.

"I am captain of this caravan, which is under the protection of the Banu Dahhak. You will regret this discourtesy."

Sa'id shifted uneasily, and squinted at his uncle. He noticed other heads turn sharply. Nothing had been said before the raid about the Banu Dahhak. Abu Wahb, however, was defiant.

"The Banu Jahm are a free people of the desert. If you would pass through our lands then you must seek our protection, not that of the Banu Dahhak."

The rotund man scrambled to his feet, bursting with indignation.

"But you pay brotherhood tribute to Abu Musa al-Dahhak!"

It was not clear whether his annoyance was directed at his captors, or the captain who had led him into the ambush. Either way, he was silenced by a swordpoint at his breast. The Shaikh addressed him in a low voice.

"And who are you, that is so knowledgeable in the affairs of the Badawi?"

Sa'id wanted to give the man a warning, tell him that when his uncle spoke in this tone it was usually a precursor to violence. But it was not his place to speak. Besides, the man's belligerence had been punctured by the mere sight of a blade, and he dropped his head.

"I am a merchant of Najran — nobody of consequence. I

meant no disrespect. This man assured me —"

Abu Bishr stepped forward, and with his rusty sword carefully pushed the Shaikh's blade away from the merchant.

"If they have the protection of the Banu Dahhak, we should let them go on their way."

Abu Wahb bristled.

"And bring shame on our clan? We would be mocked throughout the Empty Quarter — the Banu Jahm, who captured a caravan, then let it go out of fear! Why should we fear the Banu Dahhak?"

"Why? Because they outnumber us fourfold, that is why. If it came to war they would exterminate us."

The Shaikh folded his arms and smiled.

"You will understand why I took the gamble, when you see the prize. Bring the cargo of the caravan."

The men exchanged glances. Then one shrugged, and went off to fetch a saddlebag. Abu Wahb grinned as he took it, and emptied it out in front of them.

"Behold —"

The satisfaction on his face turned to astonishment, then anger. Bemused, the Banu Jahm surveyed the nuggets of tin spilling onto the ground. Abu Wahb dropped the bag, and stormed over to the captives.

"Where is the gold?"

The merchant and the captain looked up at him, then at each other. The Shaikh's voice fell lower and softer.

"Where is the gold?"

"What gold?"

The merchant, fear in his eyes, seemed to speak despite himself. With a speed that belied his bulk Abu Wahb leapt upon him, beating him around the head until the men of the Banu Jahm hauled him off. The Shaikh yelled at the unfortunate merchant, screaming inches from his bloodied face.

"Where is the gold, sucker of your mother's rod? Do not lie to me, or I will bury you alive in the sand. I know, I know what you are doing! The black boy told me..."

Abu Bishr tried to calm him.

"Easy now, nephew. This man can tell you nothing if you kill him, and fear is the enemy of truth."

Abu Wahb stood upright, and his breathing slowed. His anger seemed to have abated, and Sa'id hoped that calm sense would prevail. Then another voice spoke.

"I know where the gold is."

It was the lanky boy. He lay languorously, propped up on one elbow, watching events unfold as though it was an entertainment laid on for his benefit. The Shaikh's head swung round towards him. His eyes narrowed.

"Then tell me. Before I cut off your balls and feed them to the lizards."

The boy turned away, shrugging one shoulder.

"Well, if you are going to talk to me like that, I think I shall not tell you after all."

Abu Wahb's bristling eyebrows clashed furiously like two bears wrestling. He seized the youth's robes and hauled him to his feet. The Shaikh's rage was so great that he could barely squeeze out the words.

"Tell. Me. Where."

Seemingly unconcerned, the boy examined the Shaikh's crimson face.

"I have hidden it. Do you want to know where?"

Abu Wahb's nod was little more than a twitch. It occurred to Sa'id that, by forcing the Shaikh to answer his question, the boy had subtly taken control of the situation.

"I have hidden it..."

The boy's voice fell to a whisper, and a hush descended as the camp strained to hear.

"...up your mother's hairy old hole."

For an instant the hush persisted. Then a vast bellow erupted from Abu Wahb, and he snatched a dagger from his belt. The youth, however, twisted from his grip, causing the Shaikh to fall to his knees, and danced away laughing. The Shaikh scrambled towards him on all fours, growling like an animal. This time his kinsmen would not have intervened, had the captain of the caravan not jumped to his feet.

"He is the honoured guest of the Banu Dahhak! If you kill him they will not rest until your whole clan lies dead."

The men looked to Abu Bishr, who nodded. Quickly they restrained the Shaikh, while Sa'id pinned the boy's hands behind his back. Abu Bishr turned to the captain.

"Who is he?"

The captain stared venomously at the smirking youth.

"His name is al-Hasan ibn Hani, of the Hakami tribe. He is a city boy from Basrah, who has been travelling with the Banu Dahhak. Learning the poetry of the desert, or some such nonsense. When I came to seek their protection for our caravan, he asked to accompany us. I wish I had refused, but they told me he had powerful friends."

He spat the words distastefully, as though they were sour milk.

"For all I care, you can skin him alive and use his hide for leather. But for your own sakes you had best not harm him."

Abu Bishr put his arm around the Shaikh's shoulders, and drew him back. Sa'id released the hands of the boy, al-Hasan, who bowed in mocking gratitude. A cousin spoke up.

"Dawn is here. If the Banu Dahhak come upon us while we stand here chatting, then none of us will live to see noon. Let us take these men back to the camp, and sort it out there."

It was true; the eastern horizon was growing pale, and Sa'id thought he could see dark figures moving against it. Abu Wahb nodded his assent, and the warriors of the Banu Jahm prepared to leave. The camel drivers and the guard were released, deprived of their cargo but with sufficient food and water to take them back to civilisation. They were sullen, but made no trouble; the captain's tribe would recompense them for their loss, as was the custom. The captain himself though, along with the merchant and the boy al-

Hasan, were set on camels with their hands bound, and led away at swordpoint.

Sa'id was pensive as he mounted his own beast and followed his clan south. He was thinking about his uncle's words to the merchant.

"I know what you are doing! The black boy told me..."

Sa'id could see it now, when he closed his eyes: that day in Hajr, a month or two before. He and the Shaikh had gone to the town to trade for carpets. A storyteller was performing in the market, and Sa'id had drifted over to listen. While the man span implausible tales of princes and jinni, Sa'id let his eyes wander around. He was surprised to see his uncle in conversation with a small black boy in ragged clothes. He was still more surprised to see some coppers change hands. The Banu Jahm wanted for little, but they rarely had much coin, and certainly not enough to give away casually to strangers.

Sa'id would not usually have challenged his uncle, but the journey back to the camp was long, and his curiosity was great. On the third night, as they sat staring into the fire, he could bear no more.

"Uncle, why did you give money to that boy?"

"What boy? You mean that black boy? It was nothing — he was a beggar — God put charity into my heart."

Sa'id had seen his uncle every day since the day of his birth. However he had never before seen the expression that contorted his face when Abu Wahb answered him, an expression that spoke of fear and anger and shame. It was only when he lay awake at night, pondering the strange events of their trip, that he understood. For the first time in his life, he had seen his uncle tell a lie.

"What do you think of this business, Sa'id ibn Bishr?"

Sa'id had not noticed his grandfather fall in beside him as they rode. He stirred himself from his recollections, and considered the question put to him. It was not for a young man like Sa'id to judge the decisions of his elders. On the other hand, his grandfather had addressed him directly, and not to answer would be disrespectful.

"I think the whole thing stinks. The caravan is too small, and

18

travelling at the wrong time of year. They are neither carrying enough merchandise to make a profit, nor taking sufficient precautions to protect themselves. Fear grips my testicles like a cold hand."

Abu Bishr nodded slowly, his jowly head bobbing like that of his camel.

"My descendants will prosper under your guidance, some day; if God the Protector keeps us safe that long."

Sa'id accepted the compliment in silence. He knew that he had only told his grandfather half a truth, but could not bring himself to voice his innermost thoughts: that what frightened him most was not the suspicious nature of the caravan, nor any such rational concern. Rather it was the glittering eyes of the tall boy, al-Hasan ibn Hani, that chilled his blood, inducing a primitive, mindless terror as though he had seen a snake slithering through an oasis.

The sun was high by the time they returned to the camp of the Banu Jahm. Children ran out in excitement at their arrival, and wives offered silent prayers when they saw their husbands were unhurt. Sa'id was unmarried, and had no dependents to fuss over him. Once he had managed to evade his mother's solicitous attentions he was able to skirt the uproar, and take shelter in the shade of a tent wall.

From there he surveyed the confusion as the prisoners dismounted. Free men were not normally taken captive in raids, and nobody was certain whether they should be treated as guests or slaves. In the end the hostages were shown to the men's area of the tent where they were served camel's milk and bread. Outside the warriors of the Banu Jahm gathered around their Shaikh; but it was Abu Bishr who spoke first.

"You should not have put the family in danger, nephew. You may be head of this clan, but you have no right to keep secrets from us. Each man should share his knowledge, so that together we can decide on what is best for us all. Were you aware that the caravan had the protection of the Banu Dahhak, when you proposed that we raid it?"

Abu Wahb stood before his uncle like a child being rebuked,

shamed but still petulant.

"Why did you hold me back from killing that boy, that al-Hasan ibn Hani al-Hakami? He must die for what he said. We cannot allow such an insult to pass! The family would never recover from the dishonour."

Abu Bishr gazed at him sadly.

"Nephew, there is not a man here who would not risk his life to avenge an insult to your mother. But if we slay the guest of the Banu Dahhak —"

The Shaikh snarled.

"There was a time when the Banu Dahhak would shit themselves if they heard the Banu Jahm were riding by."

"Indeed, there was such a time. But that bright day is over. The sun set on that day when first we found the sores on our camels' mouths. The shadows lengthened when our animals sickened and died in scores. In the confusion of its twilight we conceived the calamitous notion of raiding the Banu Dahhak to replace our lost beasts. Dusk fell with the spear that pierced my son's heart, on that ill-fated venture. And when our kinsmen left to work in the cities like slaves, because there was no longer enough food for us all, the darkness was complete."

"But this gold could restore our fortunes!"

Abu Bishr sighed.

"Yes, nephew, the gold. Tell us all about the gold, for which we have put the whole clan in peril."

The Shaikh was defiant, but there was a hint of uncertainty in his voice.

"There was a boy... in the city of Hajr. He described the caravan — told me its route — knew everything about it. He said it was carrying tax money, embezzled by the Wali of Basrah."

"And you believed him?"

"But he was right about so many things..."

"And why would the Wali not send a regiment of men to guard his gold?"

Sa'id thought that, in recounting the story, even his uncle

was beginning to realise how implausible it sounded.

"He said that any movement of troops would draw the attention of the Khalifah's spies. That a small caravan, under the protection of the Badawi, would be of no interest to the Barid."

Nobody spoke. It seemed to Sa'id, though, that his uncle's leadership of the Banu Jahm hung in the balance. For the first time in his life, he spoke unbidden at a family council.

"The camels need pasture."

Everyone turned and looked at him. Then his grandfather smiled.

"Your words are wise, Sa'id ibn Bishr. Let us not risk the little wealth we have, arguing about a treasure that may not even exist. We will take our camels to pasture, and think about this matter before we discuss it further."

It was Sa'id's honour to be responsible for the she-camels with young. On the day of the raid he had decided to take them north-west, where sweet nasi grass sprouted from a long dune. It took some time to marshal his charges, and most of the men had gone by the time he drove his herd away from the camp.

Playful winds whipped up tiny storms in the sand, bringing freshness to the late spring morning. Sa'id enjoyed the contented lowing of the mothers and the clean desert air, and though he was usually alert, it was some time before he noticed the tracks that ran along their path. He had no difficulty recognising the hooves of his uncle's riding camel, al-Afzal. The Shaikh, his authority under greater threat than ever before, must have set out for the emptiness to contemplate his position.

Sa'id wanted to respect his uncle's need for solitude, but the camels had to eat if they were to produce milk for both their young and the Banu Jahm, and the Shaikh's path led inexorably toward the pasture. By the time he had arrived at the green outcrops of nasi, Sa'id could see the bulky figure of Abu Wahb below him on a rocky plain.

The Shaikh sat immobile on his camel, staring out to the hazy horizon. Sa'id wondered if he should call to him, but thought better of it. He was about to turn away, when he saw another figure approaching. It was the young man al-Hasan. He strolled toward the Shaikh as if he were promenading in a cool garden of Basrah, not deep in the inimical wasteland of the Empty Quarter. Sa'id noticed that he trailed a cloak behind him, seemingly casually, but with the effect that his tracks were obscured.

Without being wholly sure why, Sa'id slid from his camel and crept into earshot, just as al-Hasan greeted the Shaikh like an old friend.

"Peace be upon you, brother! What luck that I should stumble across you here."

The Shaikh's head turned slowly, as if it took great effort. His voice was so low Sa'id could barely hear it.

"If I kill you here, no man would ever know."

Al-Hasan seemed undeterred by this reception.

"Kill me? Now why would you want to do such an unpleasant thing?"

With astonishing lightness the bear-like Shaikh leapt from his saddle. He was shaking so violently that Sa'id could clearly see his tremors.

"For the sake of my kinsmen I will not harm you for now. But you cannot hide behind those sons of dogs, the Banu Dahhak, for ever. Some day I will hunt you down, like the filthy vermin that you are, even if you flee to the ends of the earth. And may God sear my soul for all eternity if I do not avenge the insult to my family."

The young man's face expressed mild dismay.

"Oh dear. I was so hoping we would be friends."

The Shaikh emitted a strangled noise of fury and frustration.

"You — you should crawl back to your cesspit, street rat. You do not belong here. You do not belong in the Empty Quarter, where the fierce sun and hot sands and dry winds scour a man's soul. You bring the filth, disease and insanity of the city into our pure lands. You are not welcome."

Even at this distance Sa'id could feel the scorch of the young man's eyes.

"Is this the famous hospitality of the Badawi? Oh, you wanderers of the wastelands! You think yourselves better than other men, while you live out here, in a place so parched and cruel you may as well be in hell already."

Abu Wahb had recovered his dignity.

"I could come and live in Basrah any day I choose, boy. But if you were alone in the desert, you would not survive to say your prayers at sunset."

"Perhaps that is so. Perhaps you would survive the city, although I think you underestimate its dangers. There are enough of your kind there now that you could find shelter, and kin. But it would be a mean life, and a miserable one. You would be nobody, mighty Shaikh, another termite clambering the mound. So rather than grovel to civilisation, you choose to lord it over the void."

The young man gestured across the Empty Quarter. A gust moaned, as though the spirits were unquiet at his call. Sa'id saw his uncle shiver, but stand his ground.

"You adorn yourselves in gold, you city dwellers, and gorge yourselves on forbidden pleasures. But God sees all, and will punish you for your sins."

Conviction was draining from the Shaikh's voice. The young man al-Hasan, in contrast, sang like a mu'addhin.

"Yes, Badawi, God sees into our hearts. What does He find, I wonder, when He looks into yours? The noble strivings of a warrior of the desert? Or is it something different, something darker?"

It seemed to Sa'id that his uncle swayed to the rhythm of the young man's voice.

"Does He see your revulsion when you come to your wives? Does He see you grimace at their mounds of flesh, their hairy darknesses, the smell under their arms and between their legs? Does he know what you think of, to make your manhood stand so that you can do your duty as a husband?

"The Persian sickness is in your soul, Abu Wahb al-Zubayr ibn Tahir al-Jahm. You have no secrets from me. And you did not catch the sickness in a city or a slum. It was in you from childhood,

23

wasn't it? All your life you admired the hard faces, the strong arms of men, the long legs of your friends as you ran together.

"And now you see only him, don't you, mighty Shaikh? When you cough and spit your seed on your heavy wives, the only face in your eyes is his, that young, admiring, idealistic face; the beautiful face of your nephew, Sa'id."

Abu Wahb, Shaikh of the Banu Jahm, fell slowly to his knees, and a great sob burst from his ursine head. Al-Hasan put out his hands and cradled the Shaikh's face.

"But I have the cure for the sickness, the only remedy for the pain that wracks your body and soul..."

Sa'id ibn Bishr al-Jahm turned away as their lips met, and walked thoughtfully back to his camel. The pasture here, he decided, was not so good after all. He would take his herd elsewhere.

The grassy erg was some miles away, and it was late by the time Sa'id returned to the camp that evening. The men were already gathered around the fire, with their prisoners sitting amongst them. The captain was in defiant mood, although the merchant sat meekly beside him hanging his battered head.

"How long will you keep us here? This goes against all reason and tradition. Surely you do not still believe in the Wali's gold?"

Abu Wahb stared at him, but said nothing. Sa'id noticed al-Hasan lounging nearby, smirking at the conversation. The young man winked at him, but Sa'id ignored the provocation. He had news to share.

"A rider is coming."

The captain smiled.

"Now we will have an end to this nonsense. The Banu Dahhak have sent to see what has happened to the caravan under their protection."

Even Sa'id's sharp eyes could not make out the rider at that distance, but as the figure approached the camp it became clear that the captain was right. Ibn Musa al-Dahhak dismounted from his camel and swaggered over towards the assembled men. The Shaikh went to greet him.

"You are welcome in my tent, son of my friend. Come and be refreshed, take milk with us."

Abu Wahb made to rub noses with his guest, but ibn Musa stepped away, avoiding him. The men of the Banu Jahm gasped at this open discourtesy.

"I have not come to enjoy your meagre hospitality, Abu Wahb. I would not take your food, and leave your scrawny offspring to starve. I have merely come to ensure the return of our friends and their possessions, which you have so rudely snatched."

Sa'id saw that his uncle was fighting to keep control of himself.

"They were in the territory of the Banu Jahm, and had not asked for our protection. They were ours to take, by the laws of the desert."

Ibn Musa laughed harshly.

"The Banu Jahm have no territory. You live on the lands of the Banu Dahhak, under our sway and on our sufferance. Either these men and their cargo leave with me, or we will drive your kin from the Empty Quarter for ever."

A thin hissing sound escaped the Shaikh. Abu Bishr took a step towards him, and Sa'id knew that if his grandfather had to intervene, then Abu Wahb's leadership of the family would be at an end. Fortunately Abu Wahb seemed to understand this too. He spoke proudly, but calmly.

"As a gift of brotherhood and friendship, from one free clan of the Badawi to another, I give these men and their possessions into your care."

It was only when he exhaled that Sa'id realised he had been holding his breath. From the soft sighs around him he guessed he was not the only one. The Shaikh's next words, though, caused him to draw air in sharply once more.

"All except the boy from Basrah. He is mine."

"What madness is this, nephew?"

Abu Bishr stormed forward, the men of the Banu Jahm in

close attendance. The Shaikh backed away from them, suddenly reaching down to yank al-Hasan to his feet and pulling a long knife from his belt.

"The boy knows the key to the riddle of the Wali's gold! He will stay with me until I get it out of him — whatever it takes. And I will kill any man who tries to take him from me."

Sa'id wondered whether his uncle still believed in the gold, or whether it was merely a cover for his own, darker secret. He looked into the Shaikh's face, but this time saw none of the contortions of untruth. It occurred to Sa'id that the man's desires must have fused into one, melting together in the furnace of his insanity: the gold. The boy. And Sa'id himself.

"Put the knife down, nephew. Nobody here seeks to do you harm. We are your kin."

From childhood Abu Bishr had taken second place. His younger brother Isa, quick, confident, and handsome, had acceded to the leadership of their family with such natural ease that Abu Bishr could not recall the matter ever being discussed. By the time Isa died, Abu Bishr had been deemed too old for the Shaikhdom, but was proud to defer to his son, and then his nephew after him. Abu Bishr had taken comfort from the fact that it was his grandson, if God willed, who was destined to succeed next. But now the old man stood at the head of the Banu Jahm, and his voice was calm and strong.

"Put the knife down."

Abu Bishr walked fearlessly towards his nephew, arms outstretched in peaceful supplication. Abu Wahb, however, did not lower his blade, even when the point pricked his uncle's skin, and a scarlet drop glistened in the low sun.

"Drop the knife, or I will put an arrow in your eye."

Sa'id was as shocked as anyone else to see that it was his hunting bow drawn in trembling hands, and his own voice echoing around the camp. Abu Wahb turned slowly to him, as though waking from a dream.

"But, nephew..."

A look of confusion crossed his face, and the knife wavered at the old man's throat. Then the boy al-Hasan gently peeled the Shaikh's fingers from his collar, and rose to his full height. Slowly, teasingly, he planted a lingering kiss on Abu Wahb's cheek. His eyes, though, were fixed on Sa'id.

Later, Sa'id could not recall releasing the bowstring. It seemed that al-Hasan blew lightly in his direction, and that the puff of air gave wing to the arrow, which leapt from its constraints, soaring like a spirit. In reality Sa'id's shaking must have become so violent that the string slipped from his fingers.

It was fortunate that his tremors diverted the missile from his target. Sa'id could hit a running hare from fifty paces, so for him to miss his uncle at such close range evinced how little his hands were under his own control. Abu Wahb let the knife fall from his fingers, fat tears rolling down his cheeks. Abu Bishr and Sa'id leaped towards him, the former to restrain him, and the latter to comfort him. Such was their relief that it was only the thud of a falling body that drew their attention to the arrow's actual resting place. It protruded from the throat of ibn Musa al-Dahhak, who lay on his back staring glassy-eyed at the desert sky.

II

"Ibn Musa al-Dahhak is dead."

The captain looked up from the body, his voice full of malicious satisfaction.

"Now you're going to hell. When they learn that you have killed their Shaikh's first-born son the Banu Dahhak will slaughter every last one of you, and defecate on your corpses."

The Banu Jahm stood around in silent consternation. Their Shaikh was sitting on the ground, rocking in the evening breeze. Abu Bishr gently prised the bow from his grandson's hands, and held them between his own to still their shaking. His voice was cold as he addressed the captain.

"Go. Your companions as well. Go to the Banu Dahhak, and carry the body of their kinsman with you. Whatever blood price they demand of us, we will pay it."

"And our cargo?"

The old man spat on the ground.

"That cursed metal has brought nothing but disaster to this family. Take it away, and may its ill luck go with you."

Sa'id watched this exchange as though he were not involved, but standing several paces away. He saw, rather than felt, the protective warmth with which his grandfather grasped his hands. He even imagined that he stared into his own grief-stricken eyes, and marvelled at the youth and vulnerability of the face before him. Then reason returned, sucking him back into his body.

The captain was struggling with the Dahhaki's cadaver. Reluctantly, as though fearing a trick, the merchant rose to help him.

"I will not go."

The boy al-Hasan crouched defiantly beside Abu Wahb, the Shaikh's helpless head drooping onto his shoulder. He fixed them with his glittering eyes as he spoke, as though daring them to contradict him.

"I am a free man, and serve neither the Banu Dahhak nor the Banu Jahm. Your chief has offered me hospitality, and I will not leave unless he commands it."

Everyone looked to Abu Bishr, but the old man seemed suddenly weary from the exercise of unaccustomed authority, and said nothing. Sa'id wanted to scream, to demand that they chase the boy away as if he were a rabid dog, stamp on him as if he were a scorpion. But his voice would not obey him, and he doubted that his family would either. The men of the Banu Jahm drifted off, taking comfort in familiar chores, as the merchant and the captain led away their camels, and their cargo of tin.

That night Abu Wahb did not lie with any of his wives. He spent the hours of darkness beyond the firelight, with the boy al-Hasan, but his moans and gasps could be heard throughout the camp. Sa'id did not know whether they were sounds of passion or pain, or, most likely, both; nobody went to investigate. Sometimes a hush would briefly fall, and his family would dare to hope he had fallen asleep. Each time, however, the cries would begin again, until a harsh dawn lightened the sky.

The prospect of a day alone with the camels was welcome to Sa'id, and he wasted no time in driving his herd from the camp. He was more glad, however, when his grandfather caught up with him after a few miles. They exchanged no greetings, but rode together, warmed by the ascending sun and each other's company.

Good grazing was becoming hard to find. The family would have to move north, the next day or the day after. When at last they came upon some vegetation, and the beasts were busy feeding, Sa'id finally spoke.

"How will we pay?"

Abu Bishr thought for a long time before replying.

"You mean the blood price? I can only hope that it is money, or livestock, that the Banu Dahhak demand. Tell me, my son; for I am an old man, my eyes burnt out by the remorseless glare of sun on sand. Do you see anything there, to the east?"

"Yes, grandfather. I see men riding."

"That is what I thought. How many men, do you think?"

"I cannot yet tell. Three, or more, on swift camels. If the blood price is more than we can afford, it will mean the end for this family, as free people of the desert. We will have to flee to the city, and sell our soul for a daily wage."

"You speak truly, my son. Perhaps, after all, it would be better to pay in blood. We have more of it to spare. Those men, to the east: are they coming towards us, would you say?"

"I believe they are, grandfather. There are four of them, and I see the glint of metal. Should we drive the herd back to the camp?"

"Can we outrun them?"

Sa'id wrinkled his brow, gauging the distance and speed of the approaching riders.

"No. We cannot."

"And we cannot let them take the foals and their mothers, or the family will indeed be ruined. Perhaps you should ride for help, while I guard the animals."

Sa'id merely shook his head, and drew the bow from his back.

The warriors of the Banu Dahhak separated as they approached, circling around Sa'id and his grandfather. They uttered no war cries; the sound of their attack was the muted thudding of camels' hooves and the jingle of tack.

The horn of the bow felt wrong in Sa'id's hands, now that he had killed a man with it. However he choked down his revulsion and pulled back the string. His first missile sang true, but he was relieved to see that it had only lodged in the Dahhaki's shoulder. The man was hurt, but not dangerously.

Then they were too close. Sa'id dropped his bow and jerked the long knife free from his belt. Abu Bishr hefted his rusty sword.

The Dahhakis were carrying lances, and charged, points

raised. The fastest could not control his mount, and veered wide, either he or the camel betraying inexperience. Another bore down on Abu Bishr, but the old man brushed the thrust aside with practised ease.

The third, however, drove his weapon into Sa'id's camel, causing it to scream in pain, and keel over. Sa'id rolled off quickly enough that his leg was not crushed, but the knife span out of his grasp. As he scrambled away he saw two of the warriors looming over him. One had left his lance in Sa'id's camel, but the other was still armed, and now poised to strike.

A terrible yell, drowning out the wounded animal, made the Dahhaki warrior pause, and look round. Then Abu Bishr al-Jahm crashed into him, his old cracked voice roaring and the rusty sword swinging. As Sa'id had suspected, the blade was too blunt to cut through the Dahhaki's flesh, but the impact of the metal clanging into his head was sufficient to leave him dazed. Sa'id took advantage of the distraction to dive for his knife.

He turned to see his grandfather surrounded. The warriors had unsheathed their own polished swords, and battered again and again at the old man's desperate defence. Sa'id staggered towards them, trying to draw their attention. But the mounted men were immersed in a narrow, desperate world of blows and grunts and the threat of imminent death. Sa'id may as well have been miles away.

While Sa'id watched, one of the blows broke through his grandfather's guard. Dark blood erupted into the bright sunlight. Abu Bishr fought on, but the wound had clearly weakened him. A second blade bit. He still roared, and the air was full of his war cry and the clash of metal. A third cut came, and a fourth, and then he did not fight back any more. A fifth and a sixth and a seventh silenced him.

The only sounds that survived were the screaming of the injured camel, and the shouts of Sa'id. The men of the Banu Dahhak turned to look at him. Sa'id held his knife proudly. If he was to die he would die like a warrior. However his enemies spurred their mounts, and rode away.

Sa'id could not understand why they had let him live. Perhaps they wished to tend to their kinsman, whom Sa'id had shot. Perhaps they felt they had done enough to avenge ibn Musa. Whatever their reason, he had duties to attend to. He put his knife across his camel's throat, ending its pain.

They buried Abu Bishr al-Jahm later that day. The men dug a hole while the women washed the body and wept. Sa'id led them in the prayer, stumbling over the words, then the old man was quietly interred.

After the ceremony, still standing around the grave, the men of the Banu Jahm debated their response.

"They have taken a life for a life. It is just. We should head north, let things calm down for a while."

"And not take vengeance for Abu Bishr? What sort of men would that make us?"

"If we kill another of the Banu Dahhak, they will kill another one of us, and where does that end? They are many more than we are."

"We could ask the Wali to enforce a peace..."

"Men of the desert do not go running to the cities to solve their problems. We should expel Abu Wahb. This whole mess is his fault."

The former Shaikh of the Banu Jahm had not participated in his uncle's funeral. He sat some distance away, with the boy al-Hasan wrapped around him and whispering in his ear.

"He is still our kin. Shaitan has possessed him. He is sick with love."

"Whether we fight or flee, this family is finished."

At this gloomy assessment the men fell quiet. Then they looked to Sa'id, who gazed at the horizon before speaking.

"There is one way we might save the family. But the risk is great."

One or two of the men smiled.

"We may regret what has passed, but we cannot go backwards. So we must go forwards, boldly and without hesitation.

We will raid the camp of the Banu Dahhak. Hit them so hard that they cannot hit back; so that they would not dare, even if they have the strength. We may yet turn this tribulation into a new beginning for our kin."

Now all the men were grinning, despite the sombre setting. The Banu Jahm had a new Shaikh.

***

They attacked in the hour before dawn. This time, however, the Banu Jahm had not come to steal, to surprise and disarm, but to kill.

The Banu Dahhak, fearing reprisals, had posted guards. An arrow from Sa'id's bow accounted for one of them, but the missile pierced his gut, and the noise of his slow dying roused his kinsmen. They emerged from their tents waving swords and spears. Sa'id ibn Bishr, Shaikh of the Banu Jahm, spurred his mount and led his clan into battle.

Around him men were yelling war cries, bellowing the names of their camels or their sisters. Sa'id tried to stay calm, to remain in control of his situation, in case he was needed to issue orders. As they came upon the Banu Dahhak a warrior stepped out in front of him. The warrior's turban was partly unwrapped, and dangled down by his side. Sa'id lifted his spear, and that was all it took to end the Dahhaki's life, the momentum of Sa'id's charge being sufficient to drive the point through the man's body.

The impact, however, nearly pushed Sa'id from his saddle, and his camel staggered. The young Shaikh climbed down from his beast, pulling a long sword from his belt. The weapon had belonged to Abu Wahb, and had been presented to Sa'id by one of his uncle's wives the previous evening. Sa'id had been reluctant to connive in this public humiliation, but Abu Wahb himself had seemed indifferent, preoccupied only with the boy al-Hasan.

Sa'id had considered driving the boy from the camp as his first act as Shaikh. However he knew that this would be tantamount to a death sentence for one raised in the city, that the boy could never survive alone in the Empty Quarter, and he could not find it in his heart to condemn him. He was also concerned that Abu Wahb would go too, and Sa'id had not lost hope that his uncle would return to his senses.

He was surprised, though, when both the former Shaikh and his incubus mounted camels to join them on the raid. Al-Hasan had even offered him a swig from his water bottle, and Sa'id warily accepted the gesture of friendship, although the water tasted bitter. The Banu Jahm would need every blade they could muster.

In the camp of the Banu Dahhak, the darkness was broken only by flickering torches and mazed by swirling dust and clamour. Sa'id quickly realised that any attempt to direct the battle would be futile. The Banu Jahm were outnumbered two to one; chaos was their ally. He lurched between the tents, looking for someone to kill.

When a man ran at him he could not tell whether it was kinsman or enemy, and his hesitation nearly allowed the Dahhaki to run him through. Sa'id barely parried a vicious lunge, and the man pressed his advantage. Forced backwards, Sa'id could make no attack of his own, but only bat away his opponent's blows; and concentrating on the slashing metal, he failed to see the tent rope behind him. He felt a tug at the back of his legs, then was sprawling on the ground, winded and weaponless.

The Dahhaki cackled as he raised his sword to strike. The expression of cruel mockery was frozen on his face by the blade that hacked into his neck, half severing his head, so that it hung quizzically to one side for a moment before he crumpled to the ground. A hand reached down to help Sa'id up.

"This is fun, isn't it?"

Sa'id was astonished to see that his rescuer was al-Hasan. The boy retrieved his sword from the mutilated corpse and wiped it on the Dahhaki's robes as calmly as if he were washing after a meal. Abu Wahb lumbered behind him, eyes darting around in confusion. Sa'id opened his mouth to speak, but could find no words appropriate to the situation. Al-Hasan pointed across the open desert to where a bowed figure stumbled over the sand.

"Over there."

The boy started in the direction he had indicated, followed by Abu Wahb. Sa'id tried to move, but found that his legs were suddenly heavy. Al-Hasan took his hand and dragged him along.

The fleeing figure turned to look at them. It was an old man, grey-bearded and fat. He increased his pace when he saw his pursuers, but tripped on his robe and fell. Al-Hasan gave orders to Abu Wahb as though he were a slave.

"Get him."

The former Shaikh of the Banu Jahm bounded forward like an eager dog. He fell upon the old man and grappled him to the ground. Al-Hasan loped up behind him and bound the captive's hands with a length of rope. Sa'id, his weariness now overwhelming, struggled towards them. As he approached al-Hasan grabbed the old man's beard, forcing his face upwards.

"Behold, the face of the traitor Amr ibn Shaddad, accomplice of the rebel known as Muhammad of the Pure Soul."

Abu Wahb looked from one to the other with a dazed expression, like a man waking from a long slumber. Sa'id, his head pounding, could stand no longer and dropped to his knees. Al-Hasan addressed him as he pulled a cloth bag over his prisoner's head.

"Ibn Shaddad has been a fugitive for ten years, hiding in the Empty Quarter under the shelter of the Banu Dahhak. Now he will be brought to justice, thanks to you and your clan. Perhaps God will be grateful to you, and welcome you into Paradise."

Sa'id's sight was dimming, and he remembered the bitter water al-Hasan had given him earlier.

"And perhaps you will survive; you did not take much of the poison. I would like to think that you will live. You have a beautiful soul, and had we met under other circumstances, I could have shown you such delights... But I am sure you understand that neither my desires, nor your family, are of any importance compared to the will of al-Mansur the Victorious, Commander of the Faithful."

Al-Hasan walked away, dragging the hooded rebel after him. And Sa'id ibn Bishr al-Jahm fell to the earth, and entered the blackness.

III

The Khalifah blinked, as though surprised to find himself in the audience chamber of his palace, and not in the deserts of the Empty Quarter. He shifted on his cushion, aware of his piles for the first time since the commencement of the story.

"An intriguing tale, but I fail to see the relevance. So this miscreant captured a Shi'ite rebel when he was still a young man, during my grandfather's reign. That hardly excuses his recent outrages. What was he doing there, anyway? Who had sent him?"

Ismail the storyteller placed his hand on his chest, in a gesture of respect.

"The Commander of the Faithful asks the most astute questions. The story goes on to explain all these things, but it needs a new teller. At this point, the Father of Locks himself must take up the tale."

Abu Nuwas seemed surprised.

"Me, Ismail? Are you sure that's a good idea?"

"It is a debt long owed to me, Father of Locks, and it is not within my power to tell in any case. I have spent many years collecting tales of your adventures, but the truth of how you came to join the Barid remains a secret."

"Well, somebody needs to tell me a story, otherwise we might as well just get on with the execution."

"The Commander of the Faithful is correct, as ever, to remind me that I have no time for vacillation. If a man promises something, it is just possible that one day, despite his best efforts, he might have to keep his promise. Once, long ago, we sat together in the wilderness, Ismail and I; and I told him that this was a story for another day. Well, today certainly is another day.

"I shall recount the events which led to my encounter with the Banu Jahm, and those which came after. It is a tale I shall call..."

The Education of a Postman

Once, in the city of Basrah, there was a poet. In fact there were many poets; the busy seaport on the Shatt al-Arab was lousy with poets, as it was with sailors, shysters, spivs and conjurers, hawkers and quacks and itinerants. But there was one poet who was cleverer and more talented and more beautiful than all the rest. And he is the one of whom I speak.

The poet's heart had been broken. He was eighteen years old at the time, and so his heart had been broken more terribly and violently than any heart had been broken before. It had been smashed and beaten and ground into pebbles, then into sand, then into fine, fine dust.

He had many friends who were willing to drink with him, to help him numb his pain; and many more who were willing to soothe him in other ways. Despair had its own fascination, and there were those who had once refused him, before he had decided to fall in love, but were now willing to lie with him, simply to feel close to his grief.

At times it seemed to the poet that his friends were enjoying the whole thing a little too much. If he was honest with himself, in a way he was enjoying it too. But though he took perverse pleasure in his pain, it did not lessen the pain, only mingled with it, sharpening the sensation.

The pain was drawn from the loss of his love, but not from that alone. The rejection had fathered a greater sense of loss, an understanding that, young as he was, each day died with possibilities and choices that would never come again. He hurt himself in his pain, with drink and fighting and violent sex, damaged his body to ape the pain in his soul. After all the physical pain could be controlled; most of the time.

Perhaps, too, he still believed that if he made the pain inside visible, that someone would come and save him, take him in strong arms and make everything well. His lover had rejected him, however, and his friends were slick and not to be trusted. His father had died before his birth, and he had long surpassed his mother in confidence and capability. And when he looked for God, he found only words and stories.

Then, one day, he was drinking at a seedy bath house, when he felt eyes upon him. The poet would swear later that he truly felt the eyes before he saw them, that they settled around him desirously and jealously. He craned around to seek out the source of the stare, but instead of the old lecher he expected, it was a boy, of around his own age. The boy was Persian, elegant, almost as handsome as the poet himself. He had a black beard, lush and defined, where the poet was still sparse around the chin. Beside him sat an older man, fierce and foreign.

The Persian boy acknowledged his attention with arched eyebrows, then looked away. The poet turned back to his conversation, but he was distracted now, waiting for the Persian to interrupt him, to call on him, to want him. However nobody came, and when he looked around, the Persian boy had gone.

The poet got to his feet, and pushed past his friend Abu'l Ishaq, who had taken too much wine, and was talking too loudly, as usual.

"So I farted and said to him, 'That's what I owe you, and a tip as well!' — hey, Abu Ali, watch where you're going! Where are you going? Did you hear what I said? I said to him, 'That's what I owe you, and a tip as well'. Did you hear that?"

Although Abu'l Ishaq was much older than the poet, having attained the venerable age of twenty-five, he still sought the younger man's approval, with a slightly desperate ingratiation which went beyond dignity. The poet sighed.

"A remark so witty, I might almost have made it myself.

Last night. At the house of ibn al-Ahnaf. Ah, my crazy friend, we just never know what madness you will come out with next. Instead of Abu'l Ishaq, we should call you Abu'l-Atahiyya, the Father of Madness."

Everyone laughed, and began teasing him, calling him Father of Madness. Abu'l Ishaq blushed, but looked secretly pleased. It was far better than his other nickname. Coming from a poor background, and not earning enough from his verse to live on, he had to make money working on a market stall, and was known as al-Jarrar, the Jug Seller.

The poet left his laughing friends, and wandered away. The drink and the heat had risen to his head, and he struggled to think clearly. Wine was not the only illicit pleasure available at the bath house. From dark corners the sound of grunts and rhythmic slaps echoed in the stone chambers. The poet avoided these corners. He knew, or perhaps just hoped, that the Persian boy was not so easily satisfied.

He found him in the robing room. The Persian was deep in conversation with a stocky young man, while the fierce foreigner helped him into a magnificent coat of blue and gold. When the poet approached, the foreigner leapt at him, hurling him against a wall and knocking the breath from his chest. The Persian, though, called him off.

"No, Ilig, he may come. Thank you, Yaqub, that will be all."

The stocky man Yaqub bowed and left, while Ilig the foreigner glowered at the poet. The Persian made a gracious gesture of welcome.

"Peace be upon you, friend."

"What do you want from me?"

The Persian smiled at this gruff greeting.

"Friend, I believe it is you who has been looking for me."

The poet said nothing, but waited. Finally the Persian spoke again.

"You are Abu Ali al-Hasan ibn Hani al-Hakami, hafiz and poet."

"Then if you know who I am, you know that you can have me. There is no need for games. One as beautiful as you, I would allow to do anything you wished to me. However depraved and dangerous."

The Persian nodded gravely.

"Not here. Come with me."

He walked out of the hammam and onto the cold street. Abu Ali asked no questions, but followed calmly. Without knowing why, he believed he was about to die, and felt more peaceful than he had for months. He also believed that before death, he would experience an ecstasy such as few would ever know.

They soon arrived at a postern set in a high wall. Ilig knocked, and the gate swung open to admit them. The Persian led the way through a maze of corridors, which twisted so that Abu Ali could not be sure that he could have found his way out again. Finally they arrived at a dark doorway.

"In here."

Abu Ali stepped obediently through, and the door slammed behind him, leaving him in chilly blackness. He moved to take a step forward, then something in the movement of the air caused him to pause. Lowering his foot slowly, he found that there was no solid ground beneath it. Abu Ali withdrew his step, and stood still, listening to his quickened breath.

A sliver of light appeared, some fifty cubits in front of him. It widened into the shape of an opening door, then two figures emerged, one carrying a torch. They did not approach him directly, but by a curving path, pausing from time to time to create more light, so that slowly the shape of their surroundings became apparent.

It was a circular chamber, with a wide hole at its centre. The two figures walked round its perimeter, lighting torches that hung on the walls. Abu Ali could see now that they were the Persian boy and his bodyguard Ilig. He leaned over the hole and peered down. The drop was a little more than his height, not so much that he would have been seriously injured had he rashly walked into it. The round floor at its base, though, was a mystery.

The floor had been painted with a peculiar arrangement of lines and circles in differing colours. To his right was a design like a round blue bottle with a short neck, itself dotted with small discs and bordered with variegated squares. The left hand side was dominated by a long line, which bifurcated towards the edge before meeting again at the end. This too was marked irregularly with blocks and dots.

As visibility improved with each torch that was lit, Abu Ali saw that there was writing on the floor, that each shape was neatly labelled. He focused on the circle at the very centre of the room, which had the largest lettering, and was able to make out the words: al-Madinat al-Salaam, the City of Peace. Baghdad.

"Is it not wonderful? The whole world, before us!"

The Persian boy had joined him, while Ilig continued his round of the torches. He swept a hand across the scene.

"To the west, the White Middle Sea, with all its islands, ports and peoples. To the east, the Silk Road, both the northern and southern routes, stretching all the way to China. And at the centre of it all the holy cities, the Black Lands between the rivers, and the Khalifah's new capital, the City of Peace. Is it not wonderful?"

"It is a map."

The boy laughed at Abu Ali's disappointment.

"What did you expect, poet?"

Abu Ali tried not to think about what he had expected, and instead struggled to understand what the elegant boy wanted from him.

"But — such charts are for sailors, and merchants. What interest has it for us?"

"Because, my friend, such charts have another use. One must be able to see the whole world, in a single glance — if one wishes to be its master."

The room was bright now. The Persian put his hands on the poet's shoulders and turned him so they stood face to face.

"My name is Ja'far ibn Yahya ibn Khalid al-Barmaki. My grandfather serves at the court of the Khalifah, as does my father.

And so too, some day, shall I.

"We live, my friend, in the most powerful empire in the history of mankind, an empire which dwarfs those of Darius, of Xerxes, of al-Iskander the Great; a realm mightier even than that of the Romans at their zenith. If you need proof that the Land of Islam is blessed, its rulers favoured by God, you need only look at the map in front of you, and see how he has put strength in the swords of his people. One can be a humble servant of this empire, and still enjoy greater power and wealth than all those rulers of old in their pomp.

"Across this vast land, along every road and between every city, my father is building waystations, stocked with horses and provender, so that a messenger can ride all day and always have a fresh steed under him. This may seem like humble work, the drudgery of the petty official; but only to those who lack vision. For those messengers can be more than mere bearers, no wiser than the horses that carry them. They can listen, and watch. They can ask questions, and seek answers. And if the situation demands it, they can act.

"Thus might a man sit at the centre of the earth, like a spider in her web, and feel every vibration, be aware of every movement. He can trap, and kill, without leaving his palace. In this way a man might truly be master of the world.

"And think what possibilities this offers to a young man of courage and learning, such as you! In the past, if you wanted to see the marvels of distant lands, you would have to travel for many years, and know that, more likely than not, you would never return to tell the tale of your adventures. Now, as a postman, an agent of the Barid, you can cross the entire Land of Islam in a matter of weeks.

"That, my friend, is what I want from you. To travel on my behalf, and carry out the will of the Commander of the Faithful. And this, below us, is what I am offering you: the thrones of Aksum, the wild steppes of the Khazars, the ruins of Old Rome, the mysterious island of Serendib. I am offering you the whole world."

"No."

Ja'far al-Barmaki seemed at first not to understand, as

though he had never heard the word before. His grand gesture still hung across the map, and the smile was fixed on his face, but his eyes were puzzled.

"What?"

"I said no. I do not want the world, nor to be master of it. I am a poet. A cup of wine; a beautiful body to give and take pleasure with; and the time to write, and think, and talk with my friends. That is all I desire."

A black cloud of fury crossed Ja'far's handsome face, then he controlled himself.

"Very well. I will not ask you again. However, I tell you now, Abu Ali al-Hasan ibn Hani al-Hakami, that the day will come when you will beg to serve me. And when that happens, if I choose to take you, you will be mine until I decide to release you. Now go."

The poet turned and fled, leaving behind the round chamber with the whole world in it. Terror and exhilaration guided him through the labyrinth and out onto the street.

Abu Ali's peculiar encounter with Ja'far al-Barmaki broke the fever of despair that had wracked his soul. He returned to his former ways with renewed appetite, enjoying the clashes and encounters, the ruthlessness and sycophancy. He waited until sundown before drinking wine, and wrote every day.

The Persian boy was far from his thoughts when, a month later, Abu Ali teetered home from a night at a monastery. His body sang for another boy, a tawny-eyed youth in silk robes as soft as his skin. The boy had sought out the poet, sat at his feet and listened to his words. Then, later, he had followed Abu Ali into a discreet garden, where he had lain down for the poet to taste each exquisite part of him.

Abu Ali still thrilled with the ecstasy of the evening as he walked, and scarcely noticed the thud of boots behind him. It was only when the steps quickened their pace that he turned, to see two thugs of the Wali's guard breaking into a run. The poet tried to outpace them, but the wine in his blood betrayed him. The ground seemed to tilt under his feet, and he crashed to the ground. The guards' heavy clubs fell onto his body, battering him into oblivion.

His next conscious sensation was a pitiless weight of rock pressing into his bruised back. As the room settled he understood that he was lying on a stone slab, and it was only the weight of his body that held him down. He struggled to open his eyes, but the light was too harsh.

"Take your time. You'll live long enough that you can spare a few moments now."

The voice was female, brisk, but not unsympathetic. Abu Ali rasped an incoherent response.

"Oh dear. I might have known you would be impatient. Very well then, here —"

A strong arm hauled him upright, and he felt a thick liquid dripping into his mouth. Then a stinging salve was applied to his eyes. He was laid back down, but began to feel his senses return. He blinked until he could make out a low ceiling, a plain room lit by low lamps. Beside him knelt a woman. Her hands were peasant shovels and her skin was loose with age, but her eyes were sharp.

"Who are you?"

"If I were in your condition, I wouldn't waste my breath asking silly questions like that. You can call me Rabi'a, if it makes you feel better."

"Who do you work for?"

She raised her eyebrows.

"Me? I work for God. Who do you work for?"

"I don't believe in God."

The old woman laughed, but not unkindly.

"Well, now, I knew you were vain, and reckless, and muddled, but I'd got the idea you weren't stupid. Not believe in God? You might as well say you don't believe in air, or water, or love. Whatever it is you think you don't believe in, it's certainly not God."

"I'm not sure I believe in love either."

Rabi'a tutted as she poured more of the liquid into his mouth.

"Nonsense, child. I've never seen anybody so thirsty for love. You don't believe in yourself, that's the problem."

45

"Myself? Now that's the only thing I do believe in."

"Oh, no, you don't. You believe in Abu Ali al-Hasan ibn Hani al-Hakami, poet and libertine. You don't even know where to start looking for yourself. Do you have the courage to relinquish your pride, your desires, to let go of everything that is Abu Ali al-Hasan ibn al-Hakami, and plummet into the unknown, trusting that God will catch you?"

The poet unexpectedly found that he was afraid.

"I have studied the Holy Quran, and the Hadith, and have never encountered these ideas. Is this heresy, or apostasy?"

"It is neither, my child. This is the secret knowledge of the Pure Ones, passed down from teacher to pupil since the time of the Prophet, peace and blessings be upon him. You will not find it in any book; and I fear that it may be an understanding you are too clever to acquire."

"And if you are so good, and this is the true way to God, why do you keep it secret?"

Rabi'a laughed.

"God protect you, child, it's not me who makes it a secret. The truth is in plain sight, but shines too bright for you to look at. Still, you are well enough for theological debate, and that's an improvement, isn't it?"

Abu Ali noticed that he was indeed feeling better, although the numbness of his skin suggested to him that the damage was masked rather than healed. He sat up laboriously, and it was only when he was upright that he saw that Rabi'a had gone. There was no time to ponder the means of her exit before a door swung open, and the guards entered the room.

They frogmarched him from the room, but with less violence than they had used in arresting him. Shuffling down long corridors Abu Ali was reminded of the house of Ja'far al-Barmaki, but instead of the Persian boy he was escorted into the presence of a fat Arab in costly robes, who sat in state at the end of a hall. Henchmen and petitioners stood around, in roughly equal numbers. The Arab ignored the poet as he was hurled to the ground in front of him. Only after draining a silver goblet did he turn his head, and address him in rolling tones.

"Do you know who I am?"

Servility did not come easily to Abu Ali, but he understood the gravity of his situation. He pressed his forehead to the ground, and did not raise it when he replied.

"Of course, my lord. You are al-Haytham ibn Mu'awiyah, Wali of Basrah."

The Wali looked away again, as though that were the end of the matter. After a while the silence became unbearable, and Abu Ali dared to speak again.

"Might I ask how I have displeased you, my lord?"

"I know who you are, Abu Ali ibn Hani al-Hakami."

"I am flattered to be worthy of your notice, my lord."

"It is not your verse, al-Hakami, that has brought you to my notice. It is your egregious flouting of every law God gave us through his Prophet, peace be upon him. It is your disorderliness, your profanity, your depravity that has drawn you to my attention."

At this Abu Ali really did feel flattered, but decided it would be imprudent to say so. It was true that most of his activities were technically illegal, one way or another. Crimes with no victims were rarely prosecuted, however, unless for reasons of piety or politics; and ibn Mu'awiyah was not reputed to be a pious man. The poet wondered on whose foot he had inadvertently trodden.

"If I have transgressed, my lord, I hope you will guide me to the path of repentance."

"It is important for a man to know those around him. He should know who are his allies and who are his enemies, who is the predator, who is the prey."

Abu Ali hesitated. He could not tell where the Wali was leading him, and the uncertainty bred fear.

"Your wisdom is justly celebrated, ibn Mu'awiyah."

"For example, do you know who it was that you violated last night? Do you know the name of the naïve young man, who came in search of learning and found only lechery?"

47

The words fell like a sword on Abu Ali's choking throat. He found that he was indeed struggling to bring to mind the boy's name.

"Hisham... he was called Hisham..."

"His name is Hisham ibn Walid ibn Mu'awiyah. He is my nephew."

Abu Ali closed his eyes, and wondered how close he was to death. After a while he guessed that he was expected to respond.

"What is the price?"

The whispered question hung in the air. When the Wali spoke, the bombast had vanished from his voice, which now sounded small in the great hall.

"I don't know... yet. Take him away."

As the guards led him out of the hall, Abu Ali noticed a stocky young man leaning against the wall. The man was smiling, though whether through sympathy or malice the poet could not tell. He was busy trying to place the man's face, sensing a slim hope. Only when halfway out the door did Abu Ali remember.

"Yaqub! Tell the Barmakid I beg to serve him!"

At the last moment he had recalled seeing the man Yaqub at the bath house, in the company of Ja'far al-Barmaki. Whether his shout was even heard, though, he could not tell.

IV

Back in his cell Abu Ali wondered whether he was going to die, or whether he would find himself wishing he had. He pondered, also, what he should do were these the final moments of his life. He had considered this question before, but only in the abstract, and in his imagination his choices had not been so severely restricted.

For some reason he felt that he should pray. Rationally, though, he knew that an All-Knowing God, if such a being existed, was unlikely to be fooled by a late, desperate fit of devotion. He made an idle attempt at pleasuring himself with his hand, but found that he was not in the mood. Instead, he found himself recalling happy days from his childhood, his mother carrying a tray of drinks into a sunlit garden where singing girls giggled and gibed.

So it was that when the guards came for him once more Abu Ali was lying on the stone slab, eyes closed, beaming beatifically. He thought they might kill him quickly, before he had time to panic, become difficult. He had heard that was how it was done, unless there was to be an audience. The guards, however, were armed only with truncheons, and jerked him to his feet.

I will not vex you with the poet's speculations on that walk, for you will know already that it was not a man with a sharp blade that awaited him behind the final door, but rather the startling brightness of an afternoon street. And on that street stood a stocky, smiling man with his arms folded.

"Come with me."

Abu Ali did not argue, but followed Yaqub meekly to the palace of Ja'far al-Barmaki. He expected the Persian to mock and gloat, but instead he was met with courtesy. There was no need for

Ja'far to assert his authority; it was unquestioned.

"You will go to the desert. There is a man I want you to find. His name is Amr ibn Shaddad."

He paused as if expecting a reaction, then saw the blank face of the poet. Ja'far frowned.

"You remember, I suppose, the rebellion of Muhammad of the Pure Soul?"

Once again Abu Ali thought back to his childhood. He remembered excited talk, a thrill of fear, and a harsh winter when he was not permitted to leave the house, his mother sending out slaves for provisions.

"I was only seven years old..."

Ja'far impaled him with a cold stare, then sighed.

"I suppose, too, your life, and your family, were not in danger, as mine were. Muhammad of the Pure Soul was the great-great-great-grandson of his namesake the Prophet, may peace be upon him. Sadly, he was seduced by evil men into rebelling against the Khalifah. His uprising nearly succeeded, too. The rebels seized control of the holy cities of Makkah and Madinah, as well as here in Basrah, before they were finally subdued."

"Everybody wore white..."

"Yes, I am sure they did. White is the colour of Muhammad's family, the Alids. Supporters of the Abbasids, the family of the Khalifah al-Mansur, wear black. By donning white clothing, the good citizens of Basrah were showing their loyalty to the rebel cause.

"These rebels, these Shi'ites, are the greatest threat of our time, a cabal of radicals and heretics more dangerous to the Land of Islam than the Romans or the Chinese. To combat their secret treachery, we need a secret army, warriors of the shadows. That is why it will be one of the primary duties of my agents, my Barid, to uncover and confound Shi'ite conspiracies wherever they take root.

"Amr ibn Shaddad was one of the leaders of this uprising, one of the men who corrupted the Pure Soul to treason and rebellion. When Muhammad was defeated and killed, ibn Shaddad managed to escape. Now the Khalifah has learned that he is hiding in the Empty

Quarter, protected by a tribe of the Badawi called the Banu Dahhak. You are to infiltrate them, and apprehend or kill the traitor."

Abu Ali considered the pretty youth in front of him, no older than himself, who was calmly issuing orders for a man's death. He found his thoughts frightening, and decided instead to address the practicalities.

"Why does the Khalifah not simply send his troops to seize ibn Shaddad?"

Ja'far was unimpressed.

"How many men do you think it would take to defeat a Badawi clan on their own territory? The devils of the desert attack swiftly, and disappear again before they can be overwhelmed. They know the tracks, the tricks, the quicksands and wells. Any force short of a regiment would be cut to slivers.

"Then, have you considered the cost of equipping such an expedition? Camels, baggage, water, weapons: our Khalifah, in his wisdom, is careful with his money. And even if their approach did not alert the traitor, causing him to seek a new hiding place, there are the political risks of openly attacking the Badawi tribes. They are loyal, in their way, but wild and unpredictable, and addicted to revenge.

"No, we will take him by stealth, by subterfuge. It will be discreet, and quiet, and cheap. And when we present the rebel's head to al-Mansur, he will be grateful to us, and understand the true value of his Barid, his postmen."

Abu Ali doubted his name would ever be mentioned when the rewards were being handed out, but he knew he had no choice. Whether Ja'far had set him up, or simply taken advantage of the inevitable consequences of his reckless promiscuity, was unimportant. He was the Barmakid's plaything now. One last question came to his lips.

"How does the Khalifah know where ibn Shaddad is hiding?"

Ja'far al-Barmaki looked at the poet in surprise.

"He has a magic mirror that shows him his enemy. Didn't

you know? Now get ready. We are going to Baghdad."

***

As a Basrah boy, Abu Ali assumed without question that he lived in the cultural capital of the world. Madinah had its scholars of religion, Dimashq its historians, but poets, philosophers, magicians and musicians were all drawn to the lively, cosmopolitan port. Baghdad, by comparison, was seen as a callow newcomer, brash and unsophisticated. He imagined it full of ambitious politicians, and fat old warriors bragging of their victories.

The city to which Ja'far al-Barmaki brought him, however, was a far more seductive place. It was true that there was no shortage of ambitious politicians and fat old warriors, but they had money to spend, and needed tradesmen, whores and artists on whom to spend it. The people who poured into the city to serve them came from all over the Land of Islam, and from beyond. And in the bubbling fusion of ideas, beliefs and languages that took place on the rapidly developing streets, a new alloy was forming, hard and bright.

The heart of the metropolis was the City of Peace, an exclusive district of mansions and palaces, bounded by concentric circular walls two miles round. The City of Peace had been the creation of the Khalifah al-Mansur, a new capital for a new dynasty. At its centre he built his palace, known as the Gilded Gate, with a vast green dome that loomed over the streets.

However, a foreign ambassador had pointed out how easily an assassin could slip in among the market traders, and al-Mansur had ordered the suqs moved outside the circular walls. Since then, the city had burst from its confinement, and in the decade since its founding had sprawled outward, ramshackle suburbs springing up around a tangle of canals and alleys. This wider conurbation was known by the old Persian name for the place: Baghdad.

Abu Ali tried to maintain a supercilious sneer, but it was hard not to be swept away by Baghdad's energy and optimism, so invigorating after the stuffy cliques of Basrah. He was kept too busy, though, to spend much time exploring the new city. His apprenticeship as a postman had begun.

He spent some weeks with Yaqub, who was known as al-Mithaq. From him Abu Ali learned about weapons, and how to kill without them. Then he was introduced to the Khalifah's astrologer, ibn Hayyan. In seeking the lost lore of the stars, Ibn Hayyan had delved deep into occult texts of the ancients, and he knew more than any man alive about the means by which information could be transmitted covertly. He taught Abu Ali how to conceal his messages, either by hiding them, so that enemies could not see them, or by masking them, so that his foes would not know what they were looking at.

Ibn Hayyan also revealed to him the secret principle that underlay astrology: "As above, so below." Each star and planet had a corresponding earthly substance, and these too had their uses. He showed Abu Ali wonders such as water that could eat metal, and an ink that could be read in the dark. He explained to him the applications of pastes and potions and poisons, the substances that madden, stupefy, sicken and slay.

For his final lessons, Abu Ali returned to Basrah, and to a former tutor. Khalaf al-Amar had once schooled him in poetry, and now undertook to coach him in the lore of the desert. Abu Ali was surprised at first to find Khalaf in the pay of Ja'far, but the shifty old fraud had always had an eye to any chance of gold. Their lessons consisted mostly of wandering around the fringes of the wastelands west of Basrah, never straying too far from civilisation, but going deep enough for Khalaf to offer baffling, unreliable advice.

"When the hawk is high, a north wind is nigh! Under stones at dawn, a dew will form! Always shake your shoes out first!"

Abu Ali prayed that he would never depend on Khalaf's lessons for his survival. However, he did at least learn how to saddle, ride and care for a camel. He did not see Ja'far al-Barmaki again before his departure; it was Yaqub al-Mithaq who came to inspect his progress, and gruffly proclaimed him ready.

In the small town of Jubail, Khalaf introduced his protege

to a man of the Banu Dahhak, who agreed to take him to his tribe. It was not unusual for young poets to travel and study with the Badawi. For all that the city dwellers sneered at the nomads' backward ways, they also prized the archaic and arcane vocabulary which the Badawi preserved, and would sift their conversation for new words as if panning mud for gold.

Abu Ali was greeted by the Banu Dahhak with the traditional hospitality of the desert, but there was also wariness in their welcome. His attention was soon drawn to a certain Uncle Anas, who avoided his gaze and his company. Uncle Anas stopped joining his clan for meals, but whenever Abu Ali tried to get closer to him, he was detained by a smiling but persistent Dahhaki, who was very keen to show him the spoor of a fox, or some other such item of interest. As the days wore on, the smiles wore thin, and so did his welcome.

When a camel-train captain arrived at the camp, seeking the tribe's protection for his caravan, Abu Ali had already resolved to depart with it, when one of the drivers pressed a small scroll into his hand. The scroll, when he had deciphered its hidden message, bore instructions from Ja'far. There was a new plan.

The caravan was a decoy, poorly guarded and with a worthless cargo. Ja'far intended it to be captured by a local clan who had fallen on hard times, and would be desperate for a chance to restore their fortunes. Once among them, Abu Ali was to provoke them to war, by any means necessary; the only way to crack open a Badawi tribe, Ja'far reasoned, was by using another tribe. Abu Ali looked at the final words of the unsigned note.

"Seduce them. Poison them. Mock their manhood. Whatever it takes to get to the traitor."

I will not trouble to retell what has been so eloquently told already. However, I promised the end as well as the beginning, so I must relate what took place after, as the Banu Jahm and the Banu Dahhak tore each other to pieces in dim light, and the boy Abu Ali al-Hasan ibn Hani al-Hakami fled through the desert with his prisoner.

He rode his camel hard, heading north and east, racing to

reach civilisation before their provisions ran out. Had the Badawi come to understand how they had been fooled, and pursued them, he would undoubtedly have been caught and killed. His luck held, though, and a sandstorm behind them erased their tracks.

For the first few days ibn Shaddad spoke not a word. Abu Ali kept him bound and hooded most of the time, in case he attempted to escape. One night, however, as they sat to eat, the boy noticed his prisoner gazing at him.

"What are you staring at, traitor?"

"I am wondering how you came to choose the Abbasid faction."

"Choose? There is no choice. I serve the Commander of the Faithful, the Khalifah al-Mansur."

"There are those who believe that he is a false Khalifah, a usurper. They would claim that only a blood descendant of the Prophet, an Alid, can be the Prophet's Successor."

"I have heard about these Shi'ites. They are heretics and seditionists."

"They would say that it is you who are a heretic. There are two sides to every coin. Black or white, Abbasid or Alid, Sunna or Shi'a; how do you choose your friends, and your enemies? Is it an exercise of judgement, or an accident of birth? Do you steer your own course, or simply run before the prevailing winds? Is it money that sways your judgement, or fear, or lust to be close to power? Does it matter to you who might be the true heir to the Apostle of God?"

Abu Ali scowled. It was true that such questions were of little interest to him.

"The Khalifate is not tied to a bloodline. We are not like the barbarians of the west, where the eldest son inherits power, irrespective of whether he is an infant, an incompetent or an idiot. It is the way of the Arabs for the senior men of the clan to gather and choose a leader from among their number. That is how it was on the death of the Prophet, peace be upon him, and that is how it should be in the Ummah, the Family of Islam.

55

"The Abbasid family are the descendants of the Prophet's uncle, Abbas ibn Abd al-Muttalib. They are of the Qurayshi tribe, and of the Banu Hashim. They are elders of the Ummah. And al-Mansur is a strong and diligent leader, who has restored peace and prosperity to Islam."

Ibn Shaddad leaned towards him.

"You have learned your lessons well. Are those truly your words, boy, or loaned to you by another? That is all I am asking you. Have you chosen which side you are on? Or has your destiny chosen you?"

Abu Ali stared at him disdainfully.

"Whatever side I am on, traitor, you can be certain that it is not yours."

After that night ibn Shaddad fell silent once more, and remained so for the remainder of their trek back to Basrah.

They were gritty and sore by the time they rode up to the city walls, and were relieved to see civilisation. Abu Ali was dreaming of the soft red wine and plump white buttocks which awaited him within, and was irritated when they were made to wait at the gates. Ibn Shaddad raised his head and looked around, clearly hoping for a belated rescue. At last the guard returned, gesturing for them to dismount from their camels.

"You are to come with me."

Abu Ali told himself they were being taken to Ja'far al-Barmaki to receive their reward, but fear was bristling the back of his neck. As they trudged behind the guard, the slow, grim recognition dawned that they were approaching the Wali's palace. In a matter of minutes he found himself once more in the great hall, prostrating himself in front of the glowering al-Haytham ibn Mu'awiyah, and awaiting the Wali's judgment.

"So, al-Hakami, you have earned your pardon."

Abu Ali was so surprised that he took the risk of looking up.

"I am glad of it, my lord."

Ibn Mu'awiyah smiled, a grin as mirthful as a skull's.

"I had thought you disrespectful, recalcitrant. However I

discover that you are, after all, tractable. You have faithfully obeyed my directions, carried out my plan. And as a result, the traitor Amr ibn Shaddad is mine to present to the Khalifah."

"But —"

The Wali's eyes narrowed in warning, and Abu Ali stopped himself. Whatever power Ja'far al-Barmaki had exerted to free him before, there was no certainty that he would use it again. For all the poet knew, this was indeed the price of his pardon.

"Your foresight and perspicacity was my guide through all dangers, my lord."

Ibn Mu'awiyah nodded.

"I am pleased to hear it."

He rose from his mat.

"And as for you, traitor, your death is imminent; only the manner of it is of your choosing."

Abu Ali heard a muttering beside him, and realised the old man was praying. The spark of hope ignited at the gate had been quickly extinguished.

"You will be beaten until you disclose the whereabouts of every Shi'ite who fought alongside you, or until you die from the blows. Is there anything you wish to say?"

"There is no god but God. Muhammad is the Prophet of God. There is no god but God. Muhammad is the Prophet of God..."

Ibn Shaddad's muttered prayers grew louder as the guards surrounded him, carrying wooden staves the thickness of their wrists. When the Wali's hand dropped, so did the staves. The prayers were punctuated by grunts and gasps, and the watching petitioners flinched and gagged at the flying gobs of blood.

Abu Ali, meanwhile, backed slowly away, sickened by the brutality and heedless of whether he had been dismissed. When he was sure that nobody was trying to stop him, he turned and fled the palace.

Abu Ali al-Hasan ibn Hani al-Hakami, poet and postman, did not report to Ja'far straight away. First of all he returned to his mother's home. Pushing aside her questions and embraces he slept, until trying to sleep was more exhausting than waking. Then he put on once more the sand-battered garb he had worn in the Empty Quarter, only changing his heavy Badawi headdress for a turban, and set out onto the streets of Basrah. He could, of course, have bathed and been given fresh clothes before he left the house. However, the opportunity to make a striking entrance was too good to waste.

"Abu Ali! By God the Protector! You are back!"

If he staggered slightly as he entered the hammam, then let us say that it was from emotion at seeing his friends once more, and not in any pretence of thirst or starvation. He did not have to explain his lengthy absence. Word of his appearance before the Wali had spread through the city, and was quickly transmitted to those who had not heard it.

"So you were working for ibn Mu'awiyah all along? You sly fox, Abu Ali. Tell us all about it."

Abu Ali decided it would be wiser not to make any mention of Ja'far al-Barmaki, nor, for that matter, of Abu Wahb or the Banu Jahm. Instead he concocted a tale of solitary courage, in which he ventured alone into the Empty Quarter and snatched the traitor away by stealth. His friends listened, wondered and mocked, perhaps doubting his veracity, but nonetheless enjoying his performance. Among them was Abu'l-Ishaq, and the poet was amused to discover that his offhand comment had stuck fast; the erstwhile Jug Seller was now universally known as Abu'l-Atahiyya.

The Father of Madness was watching Abu Ali speak with a mixture of jealousy and pride, desperately trying to make his own mark on the moment. At last he saw his opportunity.

"I like your hair, Abu Ali. Is that the new style?"

In the harsh air of the desert Abu Ali's hair had clumped and matted into long tendrils, which now escaped from his hastily tied turban and sprawled around his shoulders. He smiled and stroked a tress.

"How good of you to notice, my friend. It took simply hours to get it looking this way. I do believe everybody will be wearing it like this by autumn."

Abu'l-Atahiyya was bouncing with excitement that the younger man had played along with his joke.

"Then, instead of Abu Ali, we should call you Abu Nuwas: the Father of Locks."

Abu Ali winced slightly. It was, he thought, a dull monicker compared to the one he had coined, lacking the subtle edge of irony. However, it was already being passed around the room, repeated amid laughter and raillery. In an instant it had become part of the legend, a secret sign of admission to a circle which would widen out from that bath house on that evening, eventually becoming so broad that his real friends would tire of it, and revert to calling him Abu Ali.

He fell back into his old life easily, with only a tinge of apprehension at the prospect of a call from Ja'far al-Barmaki. However the days went by and the summons did not come. What came instead was news that ibn Shaddad was to be crucified in the suq.

Abu Ali could not understand why the Wali had not handed his prisoner over to the Khalifah, for the reward and the kudos that capturing a wanted man would bring. Out of curiosity he went to see the execution, and then he understood. Ibn Shaddad was too broken to be of any use, his mouth shattered, his bloodied eyes expressing no awareness of his passing. It was said that he had named no names, given no information, and the Wali had been unable to restrain his men so that the traitor could be saved for the subtler questioning of the Khalifah's guard.

Still no message came from the Barmakid, and the reality of the strange events blurred for Abu Ali, who told his improved version so often that he began to believe it himself. He decided that if he was going to be the Father of Locks, he needed to find a better way of styling his hair. Eventually he settled on a combination of oil and vigorous combing which produced a pleasingly serpentine effect.

He found, too, that his new identity infused his poetry. Now that he had spent time in the desert, and experienced the Badawi lifestyle, he had no desire to churn out the traditional platitudes about

camels and abandoned campsites. He dashed off a parody mocking
the conventions of the form:

> "The loser stops at the deserted camp, weeps for those
>   who have fled;
> I do the same at the drinking den, when my friends have
>   gone on ahead.
> May God never soothe those who cry over rocks,
>   Nor console those by tent pegs besotted.
> You sing of the lands the Asad tribe once wandered —
>   Well, who the hell, anyway, are the Asad,
> And the Qays, and the Tamim, that you drone on about?
>   These Arabs are nothing, in the eyes of God!
> Forget all that crap, drink some wine instead
>   A golden body with a sparkling head
> Poured by the hand of a slender beauty
>   Who flirts like a willow the wind has molested..."

He had intended it as a joke, but the poem caught on, and was quoted,
circulated and imitated all around the city of Basrah. Emboldened,
Abu Ali began to write in his own voice, the mocking, provocative
tone he used with his friends, rather than trying to sound like a Badawi
from the time before the Prophet. He chose subjects that reflected
his own experience: wine, friendship, sex, the preoccupations of a
sophisticated city dweller, not those of a desert nomad.

In the end the summons from Ja'far never came. Instead it
was Abu Ali who sought out the Barmakid, banging at the door of his
palace late one evening. Ilig the Khazar admitted him silently, and
led him to the map room, where the Persian boy was waiting.

"Peace be upon you, Abu Ali. Or should I call you Abu
Nuwas? Your poetry is much improved, since you returned from the
desert."

"I thank you, ibn Yahya. But I did not come here for praise."

"Indeed. Then may I ask what you have come here for?"

"To ask whether you have need of my services, and lay

them at your disposal."

Ja'far raised his eyebrows.

"I see. And what has brought on this effusion of servility?"

"I hear that al-Haytham ibn Mu'awiyah has been dismissed as Wali of Basrah."

"And now that you recognise I did not exaggerate my influence, you view me with a new respect?"

"Now, my lord, I understand that the vengeance of Ja'far ibn Yahya al-Barmaki is a thing to be feared."

"Oh, that was not my vengeance. That was the decision of our wise Khalifah. Properly handled, ibn Shaddad could have identified other Shi'ite subversives. Due to ibn Mu'awiyah's clumsy brutality, that chance was squandered. It was foolish, and Al-Mansur has no patience with fools. No, my vengeance is being enacted this very night."

At that moment the door opened, and a woman entered. Ja'far greeted her solemnly.

"Is it done?"

The woman bowed her head once in confirmation. Ja'far turned to Abu Ali.

"We have you to thank for the means of my revenge. I was as intrigued as I was impressed by the rapidity and totality of your dominion over Abu Wahb. Clearly there was something at work beside your undoubted charm, and the hashish paste ibn Hayyan taught you to use.

"It took lengthy inquiries among the less savoury fringes of your acquaintance, but at last your secret was revealed. There is an insect that lives on the northern shores of the White Middle Sea, a small green beetle, undistinguished in appearance. When crushed and applied to the human skin, it raises blisters; and when consumed, it causes erections which last for hours, although they are as painful as they are pleasurable.

"This is the notorious cantharis, the aphrodisiac which the Roman Empress Livia, wife of Augustus, used to provoke sexual indiscretions in her rivals and enemies. Having found a supply, your friends have been taking it to enhance and extend their perverted copulations. You, however, displaying the ruthless opportunism which wholly justifies my decision to employ you as an agent, realised its potential as a weapon. And now that I control the supply, I have taken your excellent idea to its conclusion.

"I gave our friend the Wali a gift, as a token of my respect: a singing girl, as artful as she is beautiful. Using cantharis, she took him to heights of ecstasy which none of his wives or concubines could achieve. But cantharis is a poison as well as an aphrodisiac. It was only necessary to increase the dose very slightly, to make it fatal."

The woman stared down at the map as Ja'far went on.

"Tonight, ibn Mu'awiyah began to experience discomfort during their coupling. First he felt a burning sensation in his gorge. He tried to speak, but the girl pushed him down, signalling silence. She straddled him as his spasms intensified. His mouth began to froth, his cries turning to terror, his guts bubbling and dissolving. Still she pinned him down, riding him, this time, to a different kind of climax. Her tears fell on his face, moistening his dry lips, although she had nothing but hatred for him. And at last al-Haytham ibn Mu'awiyah groaned and lay still.

"And that, my friend, was the vengeance of Ja'far ibn Yahya al-Barmaki."

V

"Master, I beg your forgiveness for interrupting, but the Wazir and the Chamberlain are both at the door, insisting that they must be admitted."

Harun al-Rashid groaned in frustration, and rapped Masrur on the head with his staff. It was, he was uncomfortably aware, as effective as beating an elephant with a fly swatter.

"In the name of God the Gentle, is it not enough that I have led the prayers today, and endured the stench of the common people? Am I to be permitted no respite from the burdens of duty?"

The Swordbearer knelt submissively, and said nothing. Al-Rashid sighed.

"Oh, very well. Let them be admitted."

He watched the two men approach. It was almost comic to see them, the tall Persian and the short, fat Arab, walking as fast as dignity would allow, jostling each other slightly. The long legs of Ja'far al-Barmaki gave him a slight lead by the time they reached the Khalifah.

"My prince, I must speak to you on a matter of the greatest urgency —"

"Commander of the Faithful, I beg you, dismiss these men and let me talk to you in private —"

Al-Rashid waved them to silence and they subsided before him. In his heart he much preferred the Wazir, who was witty and elegant, where the Chamberlain was fussy and prosaic. However their rivalry maintained a balance of power at court, and the Khalifah enjoyed seeing them compete for his favour.

"Peace be upon you, my two wisest counsellors. Ja'far,

this rascally rake has been claiming that he is an agent of yours, a member of your Barid. Can such a thing possibly be true?"

"He has been of service to me, and to the Land of Islam, on occasion, in certain delicate matters. It is for that reason that I hastened here, when I heard about his offences. Commander of the Faithful, I implore you, let me relieve you from this dreary business. I will take the poet into my custody, and ensure that he is dealt with appropriately. Your sons are waiting to take you hunting —"

Ibn Rabi the Chamberlain could not contain himself.

"My prince, do not listen to him. The execution should not be delayed a moment longer, and then I must speak to you alone —"

"Enough! By God, Chamberlain, do you dare to tell me what must and must not be? And you, Ja'far- are you suggesting that I am fit only for frivolity, that I do not have the patience to hear, or the wisdom to judge?"

As a rule Harun al-Rashid did not see why, having appointed ministers, he should do their jobs for them, any more than he would wash his own clothes or groom his own horses. He generally left them to get on with things, preferring to spend his time hunting and drinking. At times, though, and without warning, he would demand detailed reports, insist on making important decisions, and stubbornly refuse to follow their advice on any issue. This approach, he considered, kept them on their toes, reminded them who was really in charge. He surveyed the chastened officials with satisfaction.

"Get out of my sight, both of you. I intend to deal with this matter myself. If I have need of your advice, I shall summon you."

For a moment he thought ibn Rabi was going to argue, and felt a glimmer of curiosity as to what might incite the sycophantic Chamberlain to risk his neck with such uncharacteristic presumption. However, the ministers reluctantly withdrew, and al-Rashid turned back to Abu Nuwas.

"My Wazir suggests that you have carried out other such tasks for him. I suppose you intend next to recount for me one of these exploits?"

The Khalifah was pleased with himself for this deduction,

which he considered rather clever. Abu Nuwas bowed.

"If it is your will, my prince. The tale which I must tell is not one which gives me pleasure, but sometimes we must walk a painful path before we arrive at the truth. With your permission, Commander of the Faithful, I shall relate for you..."

The Tale of the Disputation of the Khazars

It was a filthy morning, when I first met Yitzhak ha-Sangari. Irascible grey clouds spat slugs of rain, as they had done all month, turning the roads into quagmires. I trudged up to the synagogue with my calves coated in muck, as if I wore stockings made of slime and horseshit, but that was the look that season, in Atil-Khazaran; everybody was wearing it. So pervasive was the dirt, that even the Muslims of the city gave up washing, only cleansing themselves ritually before prayer.

In fact it was a filthy year, the year that the Khalifah al-Mahdi passed away, and his son Musa al-Hadi succeeded to the throne. Many of the warriors came back from the summer raids without hands or feet, their extremities not lopped off in battle, but gnawed off by the cold. Ja'far al-Barmaki found himself out of favour with the new regime, his political ambitions stifled. I have always believed it was malice that caused him to send me north, malice and boredom, as a man kicks his slave when his patron has scolded him.

And there was no filthier place to be, on that filthy day in that filthy year, than Atil-Khazaran, capital of the Khaganate of the Khazars. They are nomads, the Khazars, by tradition and by inclination, and no amount of wealth and empire has brought them to an appreciation of the refinements of urban living. Atil is not so much a city as an overgrown trading camp, a noisy huddle of yurts that has taken root on the coast of the Qazvin sea and run wild. Its streets are unpaved, and churned to mud by the horses which act as the nomads' transport and which are also their currency, their tools, their livestock and their companions.

There are few solid buildings in Atil. Their construction is not forbidden as such, but is nearly impossible in a land with no architects, no masons or brickmakers, not even quarries for the raw materials. The synagogue had started out as a particularly large felt tent, then over time had acquired a kind of shell, of ill-assorted timber and stone, which gave it a veneer of permanence. Of course it could not accommodate all the Jews of Atil, who numbered in their thousands, but it served as a centre for important ceremonies, and a meeting place for the elders in times of trouble.

I pushed aside a door of oxhide stretched over a wooden frame, and ducked into the yurt. The orange glow of the fire hindered rather than helped my attempts to pierce the darkness within. I pulled the crud-caked boots from my feet, then, without thinking, the leather riding cap from my head.

"There is no need to remove your footwear — this is not a masjid — although I am grateful for the sake of our carpets. However I would prefer you to leave your hat on."

"Rabbi ha-Sangari?"

He was a small man, both in stature and in girth. He had the long nose of his people, and dark hair which fell in locks not unlike my own. His eyes examined me busily, though his mien was not unfriendly.

"You are welcome to our temple, Abu Ali al-Hakami."

My sight had cleared, now, and I took in my surroundings. The fire sat at the centre of the circular tent, so that the smoke could rise through the wooden lattice above. On the other side of the hearth was a wooden platform with a bookstand, and a plain chest where the holy scriptures were kept.

Ha-Sangari led me across the synagogue floor, which was strewn with grubby but dry carpets. A few men sat around in two and threes, deep in muttered discussions. I had expected to meet the rabbi privately, but the fact that we were not alone paradoxically made me feel safer, less conspicuous. We seated ourselves away from the other men, and away from the walls that might have hidden an eavesdropper. Nonetheless I spoke cautiously.

"Tell me about the shaman."

"His name is Papatzys. Much more than that, I cannot tell you. I do not know why the Romans are so interested in him, but their agents have been going around the city offering gold for information about him."

"This shaman, he is a priest of some kind?"

"Of some kind. He is a go-between, an intermediary who can cross the boundary between this world and that of the spirits. In order to be initiated, the shaman must die, travel to the spirit realm, then return to his body. Once he has made this journey, he can come and go as he pleases, seeking in the other world succour and guidance for his people. It is to the shaman, rather than the physician, that we look to for healing at times of sickness."

"We? You mean the Jews?"

"No, I mean we Khazars."

"But you are not a Khazar. You are a Jew."

"A Jew, and a Khazar. Anybody can be a Khazar. You do not have to be a hairy horseman herding on the plains, or to worship the sky god. You just need to live in Khazar lands, and under Khazar law, and pay a tithe of your trade. It's the secret of our success. I was born here, therefore I am a Khazar."

"But you are what they call a Black Khazar, are you not?"

Ha-Sangari smiled ruefully, as though I had exposed an embarrassing family secret, a mad grandmother or an uncle who should not be left alone with children.

"I see that you have not come to our lands entirely unprepared. Yes, I, like the great majority of my compatriots, am a Black Khazar. The White Khazars, with their pale skin and red hair, are a small elite within our nation, who only marry from within their own ranks."

"Then your society is not as equitable as you like to imply. You are permitted to pay taxes, but could never aspire to high office. And surely, as a Jew, you cannot put your health in the hands of these fraudulent shamans? Is your God not a jealous God, who will punish your children to the third and fourth generation if you worship false idols?"

The rabbi shrugged.

"The sky god Tengri is the creator, the supreme deity. In the language of the Khazars his name is used to refer to the God of the Jews and the Muslims. Perhaps he is the one true God, only seen from a different perspective. Perhaps, what they call spirits, I would describe as the Malakhim, the Cherubim and Seraphim and other messengers of God."

It seemed to me that ha-Sangari was an odd choice to represent the Jewish faith at the disputation. I doubted that the rabbis of Jerusalem would look kindly on his unorthodox indulgence of the local pagan deities.

What really surprised me, though, was that the Jews had chosen a mere local teacher as their spokesman at the disputation. To speak for the true faith of Islam, the Khalifah had nominated Abu Yusuf, Baghdad's foremost authority on holy scripture. It was as a reluctant member of Abu Yusuf's entourage that I had come to Atil-Khazaran. The Christians, too, had sent a famous scholar from New Rome to argue for their creed: one Brother Theodore, from the monastery of Stoudios.

The Jews, however, were scattered through the world, with no land to call their own, and no Khalifah or Emperor to elect their representative. The bek must have delivered his summons to the most prominent local rabbi, who, in the absence of any central authority, simply decided to answer it himself.

"So the Romans are looking for a shaman. What does this have to do with me?"

"I hear that you, too, are looking for somebody."

"Your sources are good, rabbi. I seek a Roman agent, a man known as al-Sifr."

"Al-Sifr: the Void? A curious name. What does he look like, this al-Sifr?"

"That, rabbi, is the problem. Al-Sifr is a spy, an assassin, saboteur and subversive. It is said that he was once a performer in ritual storytelling, the *theatron*, and that he can take on the guise of anyone that suits his purpose: old or young, man or woman. We do not know his real name or appearance, and so we call him al-Sifr: the

69

Void, the Nothing."

"So you are hunting for a man, but have no name or description, and cannot even be sure that he is a man at all? I admire your optimism, but do not envy you your task. Well, perhaps you will discover him by his deeds. Whatever the Romans are up to, it seems likely that he is behind it. Find the shaman Papatzys, and you may find al-Sifr."

I took my leave of ha-Sangari, and set off back to our camp. It is not always easy to find your way, in a city without permanent structures. Of course most of the tents had been in place years, or, like the synagogue, decades; but all the dwellings were portable, at least in theory. It was not unknown for significant landmarks to disappear overnight. I found myself relying on tricks I had learned in the desert, simply to navigate through the streets. Mud sucked at my feet, and my legs were weary by the time I got back.

"Peace be upon you, Father of Locks. I suppose I would regret it, if I were to ask you where you have been?"

Abu Yusuf the Qadi was an unpredictable man. At times he was so deep in his learning that he seemed to speak from a great distance away. On occasion, however, he could be sharp as a needle. I said nothing in response, but gestured with my eyebrows. Sighing, the qadi sent away the slaves and attendants, so that the three of us were left in the yurt: Abu Yusuf, myself, and Ilig the Khazar.

I had been surprised when Ja'far al-Barmaki ordered his bodyguard to travel with us. Ostensibly he was with us as guide and interpreter, but he rarely spoke, and in truth there was little need for him to do so. The disparate peoples of the khaganate used Arabic as their common tongue, not the Khazar language, just as they used dinars and dirhams minted in Baghdad as their currency.

The real reason Ja'far had ordered him to accompany us, I suspected, was so that he could keep an eye on me. Ilig himself seemed to resent being away from his master, and his surliness suggested he blamed me for it. I tried to ignore him and addressed Abu Yusuf, as we settled on a carpet near to the hearth at the centre of the yurt.

"This morning I received a messenger from Yitzhak ha-Sangari, the Jewish speaker at the disputation. He said he had some information that might be of interest to me..."

I told him about my meeting with the rabbi, and about the shaman Papatzys. The qadi listened to me intently, then sat back with eyebrows raised.

"I see. And if the rabbi has this valuable intelligence about a Roman plot, why has he divulged it to you, instead of taking it to the bek himself, and gaining favour for the Jewish cause?"

I was dumbfounded. The scholar had seen the angle, where the spy had seen only opportunity. I gaped foolishly, and Abu Yusuf shook his head.

"No, Abu Ali. I agreed to have you join my party, in place of a more learned man, because Ja'far al-Barmaki wished it. However I will not permit you to get involved in this kind of sordid intrigue. You will not jeopardise our entire mission, and the souls of millions, for the sake of the Barmakid's politicking."

I began to protest, but he silenced me with a gesture.

"That is my final word on the matter. We will convert these people to the true faith because it is true, and we will demonstrate it to be so, and because God will help us. If the Romans resort to such duplicity, they will be punished for it in the end. And if we do not prevail, then it is because God does not will it to be so. It is not for us to question his judgement."

He stood up.

"Come. We must prepare for the disputation."

We spent the rest of the day in the communal yurt, poring over the qadi's speech, checking each scriptural reference and debating the resonance of every word. Even though there were a dozen scholars, scribes and students gathered around, Abu Yusuf made a point of consulting me often. I suspected that he was making sure I had not crept away to find the shaman. I had to wait until after the night-time prayer, when everyone had bedded down and the yurt was filled with snoring, grunts and farts, before I could slip out.

I was hopping around on the track outside, trying to pull my boots on, when a voice disturbed me, causing me to tumble over in the mud.

"If you are going to sneak around at night, you had better be coming to visit me."

I was pleased to see that it was Abu Lu'lu'ah; but then, I was generally pleased to see Abu Lu'lu'ah. In repose his oval face resembled a pearl, so bright and smooth and shapely it was. When he smiled, however, the pearl warmed, and his eyes danced with wit and fun.

He was a young scholar, who had been studying under Abu Yusuf in Baghdad, and had shown such promise that he had been selected to accompany him to the land of the Khazars. I cannot imagine what the strict qadi would have done, had he seen what I was teaching his pupil on the long journey north. Although, in my defence, Abu Lu'lu'ah taught me a few things, when we were able to escape camp together and meet up beyond the firelight.

I picked myself up and strolled over to him, trying to appear nonchalant despite dripping with mud. I raised a hand to stroke that lustrous face, but he pulled away from me.

"I don't think your new friend would be very pleased if he saw you doing that."

"What new friend?"

"The one you are skulking off to see. Maybe I should wake the qadi, and tell him of your desertion."

I grew serious.

"My love, you know who I am and what I am. I have to venture out tonight, to defend the honour of the Ummah."

"Perhaps. But your outing does not have the approval of Abu Yusuf, or you would not have been rolling around in the mud like that."

"Ah, your cleverness is as infuriating as it is beguiling. Can I buy your silence with a kiss?"

"That coin is somewhat devalued by the filth smearing your face. You know what I want, Father of Locks."

"Now? Here? This is neither the time nor the place —"

Abu Lu'lu'ah folded his arms and gave a petulant little toss of the head.

"Then I am sure the qadi will be very interested to hear about your nocturnal wanderings."

I sighed.

"Very well. As it happens, I have something new, something that might please you."

Lowering my voice, so that he had to put his ear to my lips to hear, I recited:

> "O you oathbreaker, you covenant killer,
>> O you king of cruelty, of coldness bitter,
> O you, proud as Qarun, like Urqub in false promises,
>> You whose name I will not speak, nor whose
>> secrets utter.
> O you fragrant as incense, smoother than cream,
>> O you who are sweeter than candy and sugar,
> O you with a heart hard as diamonds — no, harder,
>> O you like the stars — no, even remoter —
> You who, if a drink, would be beer sweet as honey,
>> O you who, if balm, would be musky grey amber.
> And you who could only be a rose, if a flower.
>> No! By gambling and wine, by saffron and
>> lavender,
> Jamil did not suffer as I've had to suffer,
>> Nor did Qays who loved Lubna, nor Amr, Da'd's
>> lover,
> Will I ever get my hands on your wayward tiller?"

Abu Lu'lu'ah said nothing when I had finished. Instead he seized my head with both hands and kissed me passionately, pressing his cheek against mine so that the mud daubed his face too. He whispered in my ear.

"Nothing that I ever do will be as worthwhile, as magnificent, as being your muse."

"Hush. You are young, and brilliant. You will accomplish things that neither of us can yet even imagine. Now, have I bought your silence?"

"That, and more. You will lay your hand on my tiller tonight, I promise you."

I reached inside his coat, and through his thin linen pants I could feel his zabb, throbbing with pride. He tried to push me away, without conviction.

"No... not like this. Later."

"There might be no 'later'. I could be dead before the dawn."

It was true, I suppose, but the flare of shock and desire that lit his eyes was my real purpose in saying it. He stepped closer to me, pushing his hand under my waistband, and I shivered as he brushed my quivering member.

I would have preferred to prolong the pleasure, but the risk of being discovered heightened our excitement to an almost unbearable degree, as well as making haste advisable. I stroked and pulled in the way I wanted him to touch me, and our breathing grew hot and quick together. My legs shook, and my spine shuddered in mounting convulsions. Then, for a few seconds, we were no longer standing in a quaggy field in the pissing rain, but soaring to the stars, pulsing with ecstasy, our gross nature briefly transcended.

Once our lust was spent, we stood forehead to forehead, arms around each other's waists, laughing in delirious relief at the madness of it all. At last Abu Lu'lu'ah stepped away, and recomposed his clothing.

"I suppose I could bring myself not to tell the qadi, after all."

"Then I can go?"

"Wait, just a moment, while I get my boots."

"What?"

"I am coming with you."

I stared at him, horrified, and gripped his hands.

"You crazy boy, you have no idea what you are suggesting. Unknown perils threaten on every side. You are a scholar, not a warrior —"

"Have I not learned much about subterfuge and deceit? For you and I to pursue our love under the nose of the qadi has required cunning and care. The unspoken signals, the casual lie, the evasion of watching eyes: I am now practised in such things. Besides, are two together not safer than one?"

He kissed me again, and something gave way within me. After all, Atil-Khazaran was rough, but it was not enemy territory.

"All right. Be quick."

I was glad of his company as we made our way through Atil, not so much because I thought we were safer together, than because I had someone with whom to share the thrill of exploring a new city at night. For the traders and nomads who visited there, Atil represented a brief respite from long months in the saddle, an extravagant contrast to the emptiness of the steppes. In any city worthy of the name, each man can find the object of his desire, however obscure or outrageous, and despite the lateness of the hour, many were out seeking it.

We did not need to blunder far in darkness before we found a reveller willing to light our torches from his own. Then, we simply followed the sound of laughter and music, tightly holding each other's hand.

I had no real plan for how we were to foil the Roman plot, or find al-Sifr or the shaman Papatzys. We stopped at a variety of inns, brothels and other dives in search of information. All were packed with roisterers, drinking, boasting and singing. The music came mostly from long-necked string instruments called dombras, similar to our tunburs, augmented by the twang of the mouth harp and the coo of clay flutes. The nomads danced side by side in lines, turning and waving their arms in woozy unison, and laughing uproariously when one fell over or got the sequence wrong.

It is one of the few benefits of travelling beyond the Land of Islam to be able to purchase a drink without the need for discretion, and enjoy it free from the lurking fear that the shurta might kick down the door at any moment and arrest everybody. When I asked for wine, though, the serving boy laughed at me. The nomads, it seemed, preferred fermented horse milk, which they called *kymyz*.

Reluctantly, I ordered two cups, but as soon as I took a mouthful I immediately spat it out again, with a grimace that made Abu Lu'lu'ah laugh.

"It tastes like vomit."

"Surely it can't be that bad."

"That was not a figure of speech. It literally tastes like vomit. Try it, if you don't believe me. Ah, don't spray it all over my clothes! I warned you."

We had to buy a drink at each establishment we visited, so we choked down a fair quantity of kymyz, so much in fact that it began to seem almost palatable. It was not very strong, but Abu Lu'lu'ah was unused to intoxicants, and became giddy with drink and excitement. We also handed over a lot of silver coins, following rumours and whispers which led nowhere except to more kymyz.

Then, at last, we talked to a spice merchant, who knew a blacksmith, who told us where to find a horse trader, whose name was Chat. Chat sat on a stool in a crowded yurt which was rank with the odour of men, horses and milk, and stared sourly at the inane grin on Abu Lu'lu'ah's face.

"So, you want to know about the Romans?"

Chat was a stout man with an oddly thin face, which made his head look like an almond stuck on the top of a pear. He had a huge, misshapen nose, and his hair and beard were dyed with henna.

"I can show you where their camp is. But it will cost you."

I sipped my kymyz, and tried not to pull a face.

"How do you know where the Romans are?"

"Sold them some horses. Hung around a bit, and heard them talking. I suppose they thought I wouldn't understand them, but my mother was from Kerch, and I speak some Greek. I can take you to their camp, for ten dirhams."

He held out a gloved hand, but I hammered my fist on the table.

"No. I need some proof first, that you really have dealt with the Romans. You might be a swindler, plotting to take our money, then lose us in a back alley somewhere. Tell me what they were talking about."

Chat grunted.

"That information costs extra. Twenty dirhams."

"Fifteen. Five now, the rest when we've seen the Roman camp."

He nodded, and I handed over the silver. He examined the coins carefully and concealed them somewhere within his tunic, before he spoke.

"They were talking about the shaman. The one who tends to the khagan's son."

"Papatzys?"

I could not keep the excitement from my voice. This confirmed the rabbi's story. Chat seemed startled by my enthusiasm, and answered warily.

"Yes. That was the name they used. I think they have abducted him. They are holding him in a yurt at their camp."

I glanced at Abu Lu'lu'ah. I should send him back, if things were going to get dangerous. However in his milk-sotted state he might never find his way home, and certainly could not keep our expedition secret if he did.

"Take us there now."

"Very well. Where are your horses?"

"We do not have horses. We are on foot."

"On foot?"

If I had told Chat we had been carried there through the air on the wings of a peri, he could not have looked on us with greater contempt and disbelief. He insisted on going to fetch horses for us, even though we were only travelling to the other side of the city, and for a few moments we were left alone.

"Are you all right?"

Abu Lu'lu'ah smiled as though he were about to make a joke, then saw my face, and composed himself.

"Yes. Yes, I am all right. Why have the Romans kidnapped this shaman?"

"I don't know. However, I think I can guess. Chat said that

Papatzys tends the son of the khagan. If the boy is ill, and Tuzniq is relying on the shaman to heal his heir, then whoever holds the shaman holds the destiny of the Khazars in his hands."

"I'm sorry, I didn't understand a word you just said. Who or what is Tuzniq?"

"Tuzniq? He is the khagan."

"What is a khagan?"

I nearly spilled my kymyz in amazement.

"You do not know of the khagan? Has Abu Yusuf told you nothing about this land, and its customs?"

"I have no need to know about the Khazars. My object of study is the Quran, and the Hadith."

"How can one so acute also be so obtuse? You continue to astound me. The khagan is the sovereign of this land, ruler of all the Khazars. The word means Khan of Khans."

"But I thought it was the bek who ruled over the Khazars? That is the title of the one who convened the disputation."

"The bek is only a minister, like the wazir. The khagan is the priest-king, sent by the sky god Tengri to watch over his people. However in recent generations the khagans have become increasingly reclusive. Once, the khagan used to ride at the head of his troops. The present khan of khans, this Tuzniq, has never even left the fortress of Khazaran.

"Now the bek carries out most of the functions of government; he commands the army, makes the laws and appoints the judges and governors. Nonetheless he acts in the name of the priest-king, the khagan Tuzniq. And the khagan has only one child, a son. The boy is his heir, the future ruler of the Khazars. If the khagan's son is sick —"

But Abu Lu'lu'ah had stopped listening. He was staring at the door through which Chat had left. Suddenly he giggled.

"Why does the horse trader dye his beard like that? It makes him look ridiculous."

"I suppose he wants to look more like a White Khazar. He has the blue eyes and pale skin; perhaps, with red hair, he can pass for one, in poor light."

At that moment Chat returned with the horses. We rode west to the edge of the city, where the yurts were more sparse and temporary, little huddles clustered around the main road to Tanais. Here Chat stopped his horse.

"Over there."

He was pointing to a circle of yurts, set back slightly from the road.

"That is the Roman camp. The shaman is held in one of those tents, but I can't say which one."

Having received his coin, he rode off. I drew my sword, and a look of fear and arousal crossed Abu Lu'lu'ah's face. He had never seen me armed before. I climbed down from my horse.

"Right. You wait here, and I'll go and have a look —"

"No."

Abu Lu'lu'ah was also dismounting.

"I'm not sitting around in safety while you risk your life. If you got hurt, I could never forgive myself. And if you died, I would not want to live without you. We go together."

He seized my hand, and I gazed in despair at his ardent, fearless eyes. Then I had an idea.

"You must mind the horses. If we are pursued, we will need to get away quickly."

He nodded.

"You speak, I suspect, more from love than from strategy, but your argument makes sense. Very well, I will stay."

I crept toward the yurts. My heart seemed to beat so loud that I was sure it would give me away. The night was entering its final watch, and the darkness of the suburbs was smothering. I glanced back at Abu Lu'lu'ah. His torch glowed like a firefly, tiny and distant.

At last I reached the camp, and slunk between two tents. From around the corner, I could hear a voice.

"The shaman cannot hold out for much longer. Soon, he must divulge the secret —"

It was only the slightest of sounds behind me that alerted me to my danger. My hand flew to my mouth in an involuntary gesture of surprise, and it was only this that saved my life. The bowstring that looped around my neck caught my wrist as it drew tight, so that my windpipe was protected from being crushed.

The assassin behind me pulled harder, squashing my hand against my chin and dragging me down. At the same time another man ran around the corner and tried to grab my legs. I kicked out, and caught him square in the face with a mud-crusted boot. He staggered back, spitting teeth from a bloody mouth.

My sword hand was pinned to my throat, so with my left hand I scrabbled in my sleeve and found a tiny knife which I kept there for peeling fruit. I brought it up to my chin and from the inside hacked at the bowstring until the silk fibre snapped. The strangler fell backwards, and I landed on top of him. He thrashed at me with his fists, but I managed to turn over and jab the knife repeatedly into his face and chest.

At last he lay still and I rolled off his body, just in time to dodge the sword that swooped down on me. The bloody-mouthed man had returned, but succeeded only in jamming his weapon in his partner's breastbone. While he struggled to wrench it free, I launched myself at him, knocking him to the ground, where I pinned his shoulders down with my knees.

I poked the knife into his throat so that he could feel its point. In the darkness he could not have known how small it was, and he froze, fear in his eyes.

"Where is the shaman?"

"I don't know —"

I smashed my fist into his face, breaking his nose, but he had already given away a crucial piece of information. I had addressed him in Greek, and by thoughtlessly responding in the same tongue he had revealed that he was not a Khazar brigand, but a Roman agent.

"Tell me where he is, or I'll carve my name on your face."

The Roman whimpered. Perhaps he was not an agent at all, but simply a scribe who had been recruited to assist in my murder.

"I don't know, I swear! He is in Khazaran somewhere."

"In Khazaran? Then you have not taken him?"

"No! It is to be tomorrow..."

The horse trader Chat had betrayed us. Approaching footsteps reminded me of the danger that surrounded me, so I jammed the knife into the Roman's gullet and left him choking on his own blood.

I scurried back to where I had left Abu Lu'lu'ah and the horses. I was halfway there before I realised what was wrong: the light from the torch had gone out. Abandoning caution, I drew my sword and sprinted across the rough ground.

The horses were still there, grazing idly. At first, though, I could not see Abu Lu'lu'ah. When he blundered toward me from behind his mount I nearly ran him through, but then I heard his plaintive voice.

"Oh, Abu Ali, I'm frightened! Hold me..."

He threw himself at me and clung to me.

"What's the matter, my love?"

"He was here..."

My midriff was growing warm. I put my hand on my stomach, and it felt wet.

"Who was here? What has he done to you?"

"I feel tired. I need to sit down."

He slumped to his knees. I put an arm around his shoulders to steady him.

"Let me see —"

"I am frightened, Abu Ali. I don't want to die."

I looked down at his belly, at the sodden, ragged blackness slowly pulsing there.

"You're not going to die. Don't be afraid, my love. Was it al-Sifr?"

"I'm thirsty. I want a drink."

"Yes, of course, in a moment. But you must concentrate, listen to what I'm saying. What does he look like?"

"In the name of God, Abu Ali, I beg you. Please get me a drink."

I looked around. There were yurts a few hundred paces away, but I had no idea which might contain our enemies.

"I have nothing to give you. We need to get away from here. Can you stand?"

"It doesn't matter now. It's too late anyway."

"Nonsense. Come on, I'll help you up —"

My hands were slick with blood, and as soon as I tried to haul him upright I could see that it was hopeless. He must have been stabbed twenty or more times. I sank down beside him.

"I'm sorry. Oh my love, I'm so sorry."

His next words were whispered so weakly I could not hear them, so I put my ear to his mouth.

"What did you say, my love? I am here. I am listening to you."

"It was worth it. To be with you."

I found that I could not talk, but then Abu Lu'lu'ah spoke quite clearly.

"He said you would find me."

"Who did?"

"He said if you lived, you would find me. Either way he won."

I howled like a wolf, no longer caring whether our enemies heard us. If every Roman in the world had descended on me then I would have fought them all. Abu Lu'lu'ah uttered a harsh groan, as though he was joining in my cry; but it was only the sound of his soul leaving his body. I held him and wept for a while; then, aching and floundering, I hoisted his slippery corpse onto the horse's back, and rode back to the camp.

VI

There was a valley, just beyond the outskirts of Atil, where a ridge curved round to form a bowl in the earth. As we approached it, shortly before noon the next day, there were already thousands of people gathering on its slopes. The rain had eased, but a thin drizzle persisted. Those who could afford it had slaves holding canopies over their heads; the common people crouched under sheets and boards. Many of the White Khazars remained seated on their horses, peering superciliously across the crowds, ignoring the spatter on their faces.

Despite the weather there was a cheerful mood in the valley. Vendors hawked snacks, and there was laughter and snatches of songs in a score of tongues. The bek's men, however, met us at the edge of the city, and whisked us past the festivities. Any merrymakers that impeded our progress were roughly shoved aside with spears and fists.

We were taken to the bottom of the valley, where a crude platform had been erected. Our arrival caused a ripple of interest in the onlookers, who now surrounded us on three sides. They edged forward, and the tone of their hubbub shifted, from a low murmur of anticipation to a high buzz of excitement.

A wooden staircase at the rear of the platform led us to uncomfortable exposure at its top. The Romans were already there, trying to look stoic in the damp wind. It was not hard to guess which was Theodore of Stoudios, a long-limbed, wild-eyed holy man to whom the others deferred. I studied his entourage carefully, hoping to spot al-Sifr; but there was no way of knowing, among the anonymous bearded students, which might be him.

Abu Yusuf saw what I was doing, and scowled at me. He had

not raised his voice to me when I arrived at dawn with the blood-drenched body of Abu Lu'lu'ah, but could not conceal his rage at the young life wasted. It was only because of my obvious grief that he spared me the castigation I so richly deserved. In cold tones he had informed me that I was forbidden from seeking revenge, looking for the shaman Papatzys or indulging in any further politicking. I was to stay with the scholars and behave myself.

I had not seen the Rabbi ha-Sangari, and assumed that he was yet to arrive. Then I noticed him standing in quiet isolation at the other end of the platform. He came over to us, but did not acknowledge me. Instead he greeted Abu Yusuf.

"Peace, qadi. Let us pray that God will guide the bek, so that he chooses for the best."

"And peace be upon you also, rabbi. Are you alone?"

Ha-Sangari looked round at the qadi's attendants, his scribes and students and servants, at Ilig and me, at a similar score of men on the Roman side.

"Yes. The Jews of Atil are traders and artisans, not scholars. Whom should I have brought with me? Only one man is allowed to speak for each faith."

They wished each other blessings, and the rabbi took his leave. I watched him stop to greet the Christian priest, Brother Theodore. A few words drifted across, and I realised that ha-Sangari was speaking in Greek.

The bek almost came upon me unawares, so quiet was his approach. There were no fanfares, no drums or trumpets. All such symbols of kingship belonged to the khagan; the bek was simply the man who got things done. The first we knew of his arrival was when soldiers appeared on the platform, swiftly and silently taking up positions all around us. I knew enough of military matters to recognise that their disposition was tactical, not ceremonial.

There was no mistaking Bhulan himself, however, when he ascended the steps. Although dressed in simple clothing, he was richly robed in sureness and authority. His jet-black moustache drooped like his pot belly, and his words carried across the valley, while his voice remained calm.

"You know me. I have served the Khazar people, and my lord the khagan, all my life. I have sought to obey the law of man and the law of god. I have tried to do what was right."

Barely a whisper troubled the hordes on the hillside, as they strained to hear Bhulan speak.

"One night, as I slept, an angel came to me. In his presence my body was cold as glass and my limbs froze to my mattress. I heard him, not with my ears, but with my heart and stomach and liver. 'Your intentions are pleasing to God,' he said. 'But your actions are not.'

"The angel's words filled me with terror. I redoubled my efforts, made sacrifices to Tengri every day. Yet the angel came to me again, and again I heard: 'Your intentions are pleasing to God; but your actions are not.'

"At last I understood. The world is changing. Mankind is waking from the darkness, our vision clearing. Where once there seemed to be many gods, there is now revealed to be but one, creator of all that is, lord of all lands and peoples. The old religions, the beliefs of our ancestors, are dying.

"Yet even among those who worship the one true God, there is no agreement on how He should be worshipped. The angel's meaning was unequivocal. It is not enough that I am virtuous in my soul, I must also be righteous in my customs: how I dress, what I eat, when and in what form I pray.

"And so I have invited here today the wisest men from the three great creeds, the followers of Musa, of Isa ibn Maryam, and of Muhammad. Each will speak in turn, explaining why it is their laws which are the pure, uncorrupted will of God. I swear now, before you all, that whichever makes the best argument, to their authority I will submit myself, and it is their teachings that I shall follow every day that remains, of the life that God has given me.

"I make this decision for myself alone. I continue to serve the khagan, and every Khazar is free to worship in their own way, as they have always been. However, for me, I cannot ignore the messenger

God sent to me, and condemn my soul to damnation."

Bhulan sat, in a wide chair that had appeared unobtrusively behind him. The spectators seemed to breathe out collectively, and a froth of muttered discussions arose.

The substance of his speech was no surprise. It was over a year since the messengers had left Atil, bearing his request for scholars to speak at the disputation. The story of the angelic vision, and his intention to convert, were well known throughout the khaganate. Everyone understood, however, that the event was a performance. The bek's decision to hold a public debate, rather than take religious instruction as a private individual, carried its own significance.

That was why they had come, after all. The khagan might deliberate in secret, but everything the bek did resounded across the lands of the Khazars. Now they pounced on his words and pulled them apart for meaning, like birds scrapping over seeds.

While they chattered, servants brought forward a large bronze candlestick. It had three branches, each of which bore a single, slender candle. Once they had placed it at the centre of the platform and withdrawn, Bhulan rose again.

"I welcome and thank my guests, who have come to expound their beliefs. In order that none may gain an unfair advantage, each will speak for as long as it takes one candle to burn, and not a moment more."

This was unexpected. I looked at the shocked faces of our party as they realised Abu Yusuf would have to cut down his prepared oration to a fraction of its length, with no time to rewrite it. When I looked across to the Roman side I saw similar consternation; only the rabbi remained serene. Bhulan himself held a taper to the first candle, and it sprang alight.

"Qadi, perhaps you would honour us by speaking first?"

The scribes began passing notes, trying to assess whether this was a mark of favour, or a subtle slight. Certainly it gave the Christians longer to adapt to the new restrictions. Abu Yusuf, however, was unperturbed.

"Mighty bek, I am grateful to you. Your hospitality, and that of the Khazar people, is renowned throughout the civilised world. However I must tell you that this debate is unnecessary; that the question you ask has no meaning."

Abu Yusuf gave the crowd a moment to absorb what he had said. For a holy man, he had excellent timing.

"You ask whether you should follow the religion of Musa, to whom God gave the commandments on tablets of stone. Or that of Isa ibn Maryam, born of a virgin. Or of Muhammad, peace be upon him, the last of the Prophets. Yet this is no choice at all, for just as there is only one God, so there is only one true faith, now, and throughout all time.

"God has sent prophets to all the nations of the earth, guiding them to righteousness and away from the darkness. Musa was such a prophet, as were Nuh, and Ishaq, and Lut, Ilias and al-Yasa and Zakariyya. And so was Isa ibn Maryam.

"Every nation has had its prophets, not all of them now remembered, but one nation was favoured above all others. To the children of Isra'il, God sent messengers again and again, generation after generation, warning them of their errors and reminding them of the truth. At best the Jews would submit for a while, before returning to sin. At worst they killed the prophets, or drove them away. They even sought to have Isa ibn Maryam crucified by the Romans, but when the traitor Yahuda al-Skarioti came with soldiers, God took Isa bodily up into heaven. He gave Yahuda the likeness of Isa, so that he died in the place of the man he had betrayed, and even Maryam umm Isa failed to realise that the man on the cross was not her son.

"The sin of the children of Isra'il was the greater because they were given the true faith, but refused to submit. And so God cursed the Jews. If you seek evidence that their ways are corrupted, that they are a condemned people, you need only consider their history. They were enslaved by the Egyptians, massacred by the Assyrians, and exiled by the Babylonians. Twice their temple has been destroyed, and after the second time it was never rebuilt. Now they wander the earth, with no kingdom of their own, and everywhere they are alien, despised.

"The Christians, too, have received God's word, but perverted it. They say that Isa ibn Maryam is the Son of God, and worship him as part of a trinity of deities, along with the angel Jibril, whom they call the Holy Spirit. They will tell you that this is not polytheism, that the three are one. They tell you this, and expect you to believe it in the face of all the evidence, in the same way that a man might tell you his ass is in fact an eagle. However, if the animal brays, and plods, and cannot fly, then you will judge as any wise man would.

"Likewise they will tell you that they are not idolaters, then get on their knees and pray to pictures, of prophets and saints and holy men, images that they worship as gods. Worst of all, however, they deny the revelation of Muhammad, peace be upon him, even though his coming is foretold in their own holy book. For does it not say, in the Injil of Yahya, that Isa spoke of a Witness, who would come after him, and teach his followers all things?

"I mean no disrespect to Isa ibn Maryam, peace be upon him. He was a Messenger of God, and one of the most important of the prophets. In the last days he will come again, to defeat the false Messiah, al-Masih al-Dajjal. Yet he was a prophet, and no more than that, and as such one of many sent by God.

"The Hadith tell us that God has blessed mankind with one hundred and twenty four thousand prophets, and of those three hundred and fifteen were Messengers, who brought books of God's law. Although there were differences in their teachings, they were all true prophets; each described the will of God in that time and place.

"However, there are to be no more. The age of the prophets is over. When every nation dwelt in isolation, barely speaking even to their neighbours, then every nation needed a revelation of her own. Now, when diplomats and traders travel the whole world, carrying goods and ideas from east to west, from north to south, God has delivered his final testament, his message for all peoples and all time.

"Muhammad, peace be upon him, came to perfect and complete the law of God. The Quran, dictated to him by the angel Jibril, has existed throughout eternity, and will guide humanity until the end of the world. It replaces all previous holy books, even those that were true revelations in their day, like the Tawrat and the Injil. In the same way Muhammad is the Seal of the Prophets, the last and greatest of their line.

"So, mighty bek, you will see that you can follow the teachings of Musa, and of Isa, and of Muhammad as well; for they are one and the same. There is only one God, and all that the angel requires of you is submission to His will."

The candle flickered out just as Abu Yusuf uttered his final words. He nodded a brief bow to his listeners and stepped back. The bek rose once more as servants hurried to light the second candle.

"My thanks, qadi. Your learning and wisdom are rightly renowned. Next, I ask the spokesman for Christianity to make his case."

Theodore of Stoudios hurried forward, keen to make the most of his allotted time. For the first time I observed how young he was. Instead of a senior churchman, all of whom were busy at home scheming for their own personal advancement, the Romans had nominated an ambitious junior on his way to a glittering career in politics. He cleared his throat.

"Mighty bek, you have heard the qadi speak. He is indeed a man of learning, his erudition only outweighed by his eloquence. However, his arguments against Christianity are based on a fundamental error. And when that error is exposed, it shatters not only the qadi's argument, but the whole foundation of Islam.

"The qadi has called us polytheists, suggesting that we worship three gods, not one. In this he fails to understand the doctrine of the Trinity. Christians worship one God, eternal, omnipotent and indivisible. God is of one substance, one essence, yet He also is three persons, Father, Son and Holy Spirit. The Father is not the Son, and the Son is not the Holy Spirit; yet the Father is God, and the Son is God, and so too is the Holy Spirit. Such is the subtle miracle of the Trinity.

"A man of learning such as the qadi would surely know this. Yet he chooses to dishonour his hosts by deceiving you, and slandering us with false accusations. Why would this man, this good and godly man, do such a foul thing? In the answer to that question, you will find the reason why you must reject his religion.

"The qadi must say that we believe in three Gods, because the Quran says that we do. And the qadi considers the Quran to be perfect and complete, the unadulterated word of God. Therefore if the Quran's description of Christian doctrine does not accord with what we in fact profess, then he must accept what is written in the Quran. It does not matter to him how many times we tell him that the Three are One, he cannot listen or admit his error, without admitting that his own beliefs are mistaken.

"And his falsehoods do not end there. The qadi identifies the Holy Spirit with the angel Jibril, which we do not; then by extension implies that we worship the angel as a God, which we do not. But in doing so he evades the question of how the Quran really describes the Trinity. The fifth Sura talks of Christians regarding Isa and his mother as two gods beside God. It is clear that the author of this book imagines Maryam to be the third person of the Trinity. You must decide for yourself whether such a book is the work of God himself, of a spirit sent by Him, or of a fallible man.

"Their message, then, is demonstrably flawed. But what of their messenger? Evidently, he was a great warrior and leader. He united the tribes of Arabia, and founded an empire that has conquered half the world. But was he a man of God? I will tell you a story, and let you judge. It is the tale of the Banu Qurayza.

"The Banu Qurayza were a Jewish tribe of Madinah. They were allies of Muhammad, but betrayed him at the Battle of the Trench. Their treachery is not in doubt, although they never actually left their camp during the battle, let alone took up arms against Muslims. However the punishment they received, simply for negotiating with the enemy, was terrible.

"Muhammad and his companions besieged their stronghold, and the Banu Qurayza surrendered. They agreed that their fate would be decided by a chief of a related tribe, the Banu Aws. They did not know, though, that the man chosen, Sa'd ibn Mu'adh, had fought at Muhammad's side during the battle and sustained a wound, of which he would later die. From his deathbed Sa'd pronounced sentence: the men of the Banu Qurayza were to be killed, and the women and children sold into slavery.

"Muhammad approved of the decision, saying that it was like the judgement of God. So the Muslims dug a deep trench in the marketplace, near to where the prisoners were held. Then the Jews were led out, a few at a time, and beheaded, and their bodies thrown into the trench.

"The prophet executed some of the prisoners in person, and his cousin Ali also helped with the task. Most of the killing however was carried out by the Banu Aws, so that they would not be able to deny their responsibility later. All day long the slaughter went on, and the corpses piled up in the trench. Adolescent boys had their private parts examined; those who had grown hair were decapitated, those who had not were sold as slaves. By evening some seven hundred men lay dead, and the Banu Qurayza were no more. Muhammad picked out one of their women for himself, and took a fifth of their wealth as his share of the booty.

"This story is not a source of shame for Muslims, but is celebrated in the thirty-third sura of the Quran. It is taken by their lawyers as a model of how to deal with allies who break their word. Mighty bek, you will know that Christian kings and emperors have on occasion perpetrated such massacres, sometimes even in the name of Christ. However Christ himself practised only humility and gentleness. He healed the sick, fed the poor and raised the dead. Who will you choose, mighty bek, to lead you to salvation: the man who gave his own life, so that all mankind might live for ever? Or the man who killed untold numbers of others, many in cold blood, while enjoying ever greater wealth, power and carnal pleasure?"

It seemed that Theodore had more to say, but at that moment the second candle guttered and died. This was a signal for a shocked babble to break out among the spectators massed around the valley. One of the scribes behind me could not contain his indignation, and was complaining loud enough for the bek to hear.

"This is a travesty! Must we listen to his lies, and have no chance of rebuttal? He has completely misrepresented the meaning of the Holy Quran. This was no defence of Christianity, simply an outrageous attack on Islam! He didn't even mention Judaism! This disputation is a sham. Nobody who truly sought God would do so by means of such a facile game..."

As his rant continued I became aware that the servants were struggling to light the third candle. A raw wind had whipped up and was swirling around the valley, frustrating all efforts to ignite the wick. Slowly the excitement in the crowd was replaced by amusement, the servants' efforts met by ironic cheers and groans.

Bhulan realised that his ritual was becoming an object of ridicule. He came forward smiling calmly.

"It seems that God wishes me to meditate on what we have heard, before we go any further. We will assemble again tomorrow, when the rabbi will speak — and I will make my decision."

His departure, though unhurried, was as efficient and rapid as his arrival. The onlookers, too, began to drift away. The scribe who had been complaining glared furiously at Theodore, but Abu Yusuf made a calming gesture.

"Enough. Whatever the outcome of this debate, it is God's will. Do not demean yourself by matching insult with insult."

We filed slowly down the steps. At the bottom, Ilig seized my shoulder.

"Take me to your friend the rabbi."

"But — Abu Yusuf said — "

Ilig moved so that his face was uncomfortably close to mine.

"Who would you rather answer to? The qadi, or me?"

"Abu Lu'lu'ah is dead."

"And do you not want to avenge him?"

I could not look into his blue eyes, and dropped my gaze.

"Good. The qadi may resign himself to the will of God. My purpose is to execute the will of Ja'far al-Barmaki."

This struck me as an unusually eloquent phrase for the taciturn Khazar. I wondered whether his heavy accent masked a fluency in Arabic which he preferred to conceal. We slipped away from our party in the confusion as we left the valley, and hurried after ha-Sangari.

We caught up with him a couple of streets further north. He turned as we approached, gazing at me sympathetically.

"I am sorry about your friend."

"How do you know about that?"

The rabbi was unperturbed by Ilig's aggression.

"A weeping man leading a horse with a bloody corpse slung across it will excite comment, even in a wild town like Atil. What happened?"

I was embarrassed to admit to him how easily I had been fooled.

"The Romans paid off a local to lead me into a trap, on the pretext that they had already kidnapped the shaman. I interrogated one of the assassins, though, and he told me that the abduction is planned for tonight. The shaman is still in Khazaran."

"In Khazaran? Now that might present a problem..."

VII

He led us to the shore, by a shred of black beach. Atil-Khazaran is sited where the Atil river flows into the Qazvin Sea. It is a flat, monotonous land of reeds and marshes, but the water is fresh, unlike the salty stretches to the south. A short distance away a pontoon bridge formed a slender link to the island of Khazaran.

"Impressive, is it not?"

I studied the triangular walls of the khagan's enclosure, constructed of baked brick to the height of two men. I supposed they were impressive enough if you had spent your life in a land of tents; but for one who had seen the City of Peace, or the gargantuan fortifications of Merv in Khorasan, they elicited little awe. I feigned interest.

"Why three walls?"

Ha-Sangari laughed.

"Do you not know the story we tell, of the origin of the Khazars?"

I shrugged. He was clearly going to tell me anyway.

"We say that the father of the Turkic people was a man called Togarmah. He was the last of his tribe, a clan so feared by their enemies that they were all murdered in a foul act of treachery. All, that is, except the boy Togarmah, a mere infant, who was mutilated and thrown into a swamp.

"There he was found by a she-wolf, who rescued him, licked his wounds and fed him with her own milk. When he came to maturity he fell in love with the wolf. They mated, and she bore him ten sons, born in a cave, and they were named Uygur, Tiros, and Avar, Oguz, Bisal and Tarna, Kozar, Sanar, Bulgar and Savir.

94

Kozar was the seventh son, a flame haired strutting horseman, most beloved of the sky god. He himself fathered twin boys, called Gog and Magog.

"Gog and Magog were giants, fearsome cannibals with pointed fangs like their grandmother the wolf. They and their kin terrorised the lands between the seas, until the day a warrior appeared, wearing golden armour and followed by an army of millions. The warrior was al-Iskander the Great, on his journey of conquest to the ends of the earth.

"Al-Iskander realised he could never defeat the cannibal clan, even with his countless legions, so instead he ordered his men to pile up stones across the lands between the seas. So numerous were they, and so diligent in following his orders, that they constructed an entire mountain range, that today we call the Caucasus. And so the sons of Gog and Magog were trapped between three walls, the sea of Kazvim, the Black Sea and the mountains."

A long, uncomfortable silence followed, until he added:

"Or perhaps it is just the shape of the island."

I tried to bring him back to the matter at hand.

"You said there might be a problem, if the shaman is in Khazaran?"

The rabbi's face grew serious.

"You must understand the nature of this place. Atil-Khazaran is not a single settlement, but a marriage of two cities. Atil is the husband, a hustling, fleshy merchant, dealing with the outside world and bringing home the provisions. Khazaran sits on her island, behind her walls, secretive and intense, laying down the rules. It is a fortress, a palace and a sacred precinct. It is also forbidden ground to all but pure bred White Khazars. The punishment for trespassing is death."

"I see. That may, indeed, be a problem. I cannot cross the water, then scale a sheer wall, while remaining undetected. Do you know of a White Khazar who could be bribed or persuaded to help me gain entrance to Khazaran?"

"Sadly, no. They are a haughty people, and do not much

fraternise with anyone outside their own kin."

"Then I do not see what we can do."

"You could ask me."

The rabbi and I turned in surprise to Ilig. I stared at his red hair and fair complexion, and wondered why it had not occurred to me before that he might be a White Khazar. Vague memories stirred, of tales that he had had to flee his homeland in disgrace. However, he insisted he could get me in, and I could not afford to argue. The qadi's question came back to me though, and I needed an answer.

"Tell me, rabbi: if your information is good, why would you come to me? Why not use the intelligence to the advantage of the Jewish faith?"

Ha-Sangari's head dropped, as if he were a little ashamed.

"I have no chance of winning the disputation, even if I were the cleverest man alive, even if I saved the bek's life. The khaganate bumps against both the Land of Islam and the Roman Empire, like a boat navigating between two dangerous rocks. Our very prosperity makes us vulnerable; we command the northern Silk Road, and have a monopoly on the trade of furs from the Rus. The bek will have to accept the protection of one of the great powers, Christianity or Islam, or risk being torn apart by them as they compete for our wealth. This is the true purpose of the disputation: so that Bhulan can decide with whom he will throw in his lot.

"A man must look after his kin, to the extent of his capability. The bek must protect the interests of all the Khazars; I must consider the Jews of this land. Under Christian rule my people are insulted to their faces and slandered behind their backs, their word not accepted against a Christian's in a court of law. In the Land of Islam we are respected as People of the Book, and can practise our ways unmolested.

"If we must submit to one side or the other, then I would rather it were yours, Abu Ali al-Hakami. Whether you foil the plot, or simply inform the bek, it can only further the cause of Islam.

"Besides, I am a simple scholar. These games of mighty empires are not for me. You, on the other hand, are a master of secret machinations. It is better that you handle it."

So it was that, as night fell, I found myself bumping along the pontoon bridge, sealed inside an oil jar strapped to the side of a packhorse. Ilig had tried to persuade me that he should go alone, just kill the Roman spy, but I had refused to submit. Since Ja'far had not told us who took orders from whom, he backed down at last, and we had concocted a scheme to get me inside.

It had seemed a simple plan. I in a jar on one side, a jar actually containing oil on the other for balance, and Ilig leading us through the gates of Khazaran. As you can see, though, I am long of body and limb, and while the jar was large enough to contain me, I had to contort myself painfully in order to fit. My situation was worsened by the fact that, although the jar had been emptied, it had not been cleaned out. Every time I found a position in which the discomfort was bearable, a lurch or bounce would cause me to slide around in the slippery oil, bruising my elbows and knees and straining muscles for balance. As a crowning insult, it was not the gentle pressings of olives that the jar had contained, but pungent simsim oil that filled my nostrils and soaked into my clothing.

A violent jerk suggested we had halted. I guessed we had arrived at the gates. It occurred to me suddenly that our ruse was as thin as the lid of the jar, that if the guards bothered to inspect its contents I would be discovered immediately. They did not, of course. They had no reason to suspect anything. I was desperately curious to know what passed between Ilig and the guards, but even if I had been able to hear them through a thumb's breadth of clay, I could not have understood the weird, singsong Khazar language.

The jar tipped again, mashing my nose against its side, and as I drew in the reek of simsim the gates opened to admit us to the forbidden city. I had expected that Ilig would lead the horse around the nearest corner, then release me. Instead the jog of the jar continued relentlessly, until I began to lose any sense of how long I had been inside. I tried to push the lid open, but was appalled to discover it had been sealed in some way.

The air had become stale, and the stench of simsim choked

me. Since that night I have never been able to stomach simsim seed, be it in cakes, sauces or pastes. I began to question whether this was all some bizarre prank by Ilig, to keep me out of trouble until the disputation was over. When I felt the jar released from the horse's side, to drop to the ground with a shuddering jolt, I feared treachery of a worse kind. Instead the lid came open, mercifully allowing clean air into my simsim-stinking nightmare.

"Thank God the Liberator! I thought —"

"Hush. I cannot stay here."

"You cannot stay? But you are a White Khazar!"

"The guards were suspicious. Since they did not know me, they questioned me on my tribe, my parentage. I could not tell them the truth, of course, and they mistrusted my answers. I persuaded them that I had to deliver the oil, but if I do not return quickly, they will raise the alarm. You are on your own, Abu Ali."

He walked away, the horse clopping behind him, before I could get out of the jar to argue with him. In fact, my efforts to free myself nearly led to disaster. My muscles had frozen in my confinement, and attempting to move my limbs resulted only in searing pain. As I struggled to stand, the jar tipped slowly, then toppled over with a resounding crash.

The noise seemed so loud that I was certain it would attract attention. However, there was no reaction, and at last I managed to slither out of my oily womb and spill out onto the mud. Rubbing my agonised legs, I looked around at the sacred fortress of Khazaran.

My first reaction was to wonder why the Khazars went to such trouble to protect so undistinguished a place; in the moonlight it appeared no more than another huddled mess of yurts separated by mud tracks, just like Atil. I did not have long to consider it though, as voices and the sound of hoofs intruded on my thoughts.

I scrambled to the shelter of a large yurt that stood nearby, and cringed from a flare of torches at the end of the street. Three Khazars approached on horseback, laughing and shouting. I pressed myself against the yurt wall, hoping that they would pass by. However the fallen oil jar attracted their attention, and they stopped.

I did not need to understand their language to guess the meaning of their conversation. One began to dismount. At any moment the torchlight would fall on me, revealing me to the nomads. As quietly as I could, I slid open the yurt door, and slipped inside.

I found myself in a small, cluttered tent. Its wooden furnishings were painted with elaborate patterns in bright colours, reds and yellows and purples. On the walls hung blankets stitched with peculiar figures, one-legged men with hooves instead of hands and antlers on their heads.

At first I thought the yurt was empty. Then I heard a thin, high voice.

"Are you a spirit?"

A young man reclined on a bed, draped with so many sheets that at first glance in the candlelight I had not seen the human shape beneath them. He had the pale skin, blue eyes and red hair of the White Khazars, but he was hollow-cheeked and sickly in appearance.

"I asked you a question, and you must answer me. Are you a spirit?"

The man sat up. He wore an embroidered green tunic, and around his neck was a slender scarf of knotted silk. The scarf resembled a noose, and suddenly I realised that the man in front of me, the man whose vacant eyes gazed placidly at the intruder in his tent, was Tuzniq, khagan of the Khazars. The ceremonial cord around his neck was the signifier of his kingship, not a crown but a relic of the days when the khagan ruled for a fixed term of years before being hanged as a sacrifice to the sky god.

Tuzniq looked away from me and sighed.

"I used to commune with the spirits. These days they stand dumb before me. They used to come to me and show me such wonderful things, sing such funny songs..."

Now I understood why the bek had taken over so many of the khagan's traditional powers; it was obvious that Tuzniq was feeble-minded, little better than a drooling idiot. A thought occurred to me.

"Your son, khagan — does he commune with spirits also?"

Sadness glimmered in the vacant eyes.

"My boy. My poor boy. The spirits are not kind to him. He screams and thrashes when they come to him. Papatzys says he must banish the spirits. He says we must drink only from the healing cup."

He pointed to a heavy goblet of dull grey metal which stood on a chest nearby. I picked it up and examined it. Around its exterior danced one-legged deer men similar to those on the wall hanging, while its inner surface was carved with concentric rings. The faces of the deer-men were flat and featureless, and I realised that they had been worn smooth by generations of handling. It was empty, but smelt vaguely of lemon juice, which I guessed was used to clean it.

I turned to the khagan.

"The spirits command you to sleep. You must not tell anybody that I have been here, or your son will be tormented for a hundred days."

Fear tightened the khagan's jaw, and he climbed obediently back into bed, pulling the blankets over his head. I poked my head out of the yurt. The street was empty, so I slunk away silently. It seemed odd to me that the ruler of a kingdom one thousand miles across slept without a guard at his door, but by now nothing surprised me about the Khazars. It must have been unthinkable to them that anybody could gain access to the holy sanctuary of Khazaran.

I prowled on through the fortress, my mind racing. If the khagan's son was showing signs that he had inherited his father's imbecility, it would explain why everybody was so interested in Papatzys. Unless the shaman could cure the boy, the disease would pass to a second generation, and the bek's hold on power would become irreversible. In that context Bhulan's decision to give up the religion of his people, the religion in which the khagan was worshipped as a living god, began to seem less like piety and more like hard-nosed politics.

I had no idea how I was going to find the shaman's yurt. When I came across it, however, there was no mistaking it. Although it was of the same construction and dimensions as the others, it was surrounded by ritual emblems: a carved totem resembling an eagle, a ring of stones around blackened earth, elaborate fetishes of intricately woven twigs hanging from the roof.

I crouched by the door, and listened. A voice was pleading in Arabic.

"No, it is not true, I swear it! Please, I beg you, let me go..."

Drawing my sword, I shoved aside the door panel and burst into the yurt. Inside were two men. It was easy to identify the man kneeling on the ground as the shaman Papatzys. He was heavily built, his red hair hanging to his waist in knotted clumps. A drum was strapped to his back, a round frame with skin stretched across it. In his hand he held a baton decorated with feathers. The other man, I knew as the horse trader Chat, but I understood now that he was more familiar to me by another name.

"Al-Sifr."

The Roman snickered.

"Is that what you call me? Well, I've been called worse."

Looking at him again, I could hardly believe that I had been fooled. His false nose, his crudely dyed hair and beard seemed childishly obvious. And because of my stupidity, I had led Abu Lu'lu'ah into the trap that had cost him his life.

At that thought, I hefted my sword, and set my jaw.

"You shall pay for what you did to my friend, Roman."

"Was he only your friend? I had hoped he was so much more to you than that."

I lunged for him, but he had provoked me to draw the stroke, and knocked it aside with ease, hacking at my face so that I had to pull back. The sharp steel flashed past my eyes. I was off balance, staggering backwards, and he advanced, stabbing and swinging with every step.

Then the shaman Papatzys decided to take a hand. He must have viewed me as his rescuer, because he chose to smash his drum over al-Sifr's head. The goatskin split, and the frame landed on the Roman's shoulders like a horse's collar. The blow could not have been very painful, but the unexpected attack disconcerted him. I lashed out with a muddy boot, and al-Sifr's sword spun from his hand.

He stared at me contemptuously, and I drew back my blade to chop his head from his shoulders, that hateful, ludicrous head with its fake nose knocked askew by the drum. At that moment Khazar warriors poured in through the door, armed with spears and armoured in fur and leather jerkins. I swung my sword anyway, but a Khazar grabbed my hand and plucked the weapon from my grasp. Once the warriors were all in place, and the yurt was secured, their leader strutted in like the cock who has just crowed. It was Bhulan, the bek.

"Peace be upon you. I would hate to have to raise a blade to my guests, so I am sure you will not mind telling me: what you are doing in Khazaran?"

This was too much. I was probably dead anyway, and past caring.

"I might ask the same of you. You are no more a White Khazar than I am."

Bhulan did not flinch. He did, however, switch to speaking in Greek, presumably because most of his men would be fluent in Arabic.

"Things change. I am sure the people will understand. Such an invasion, striking at the very heart of our empire — the threat had to be countered. I took responsibility, rose to the challenge. The khagan will pass a decree giving me authority to enter Khazaran, for a temporary but indefinite period. In a year's time nobody will remember it was ever any other way.

"In many ways you have done me a favour. I am grateful to you, and to the rabbi who alerted me to your machinations. Nonetheless, you still deserve death. How would you, Muslim, treat a Khazar who invaded the Kaaba in Makkah, waving his sword around? Or you, Christian, how would you respond if I defiled your holy places in Jerusalem?"

"Mighty bek, you should be grateful to me for more than just opening the door to Khazaran for you. This Roman here, as false in his countenance as he is in his conduct, planned to kidnap the shaman, and hold the future of your nation to ransom. I came here tonight only to stop him."

Al-Sifr bowed.

"On the contrary, mighty bek, my sole purpose here was to protect the future of your nation. The shaman Papatzys is poisoning the son of the khagan, causing the very illness he claims to be healing. The rabbi told me —"

He stopped. It must have just sunk in, as it had with me, what Bhulan said about the rabbi; and like me, he was just coming to understand how ha-Sangari had stuffed the Christian goose with the Muslim pheasant and served us both up on a platter to the bek. Bhulan meanwhile was interrogating the shaman, in much the same tone one might use to a wayward child.

"Now, Papatzys, is this true? Are you giving the khagan's son bad medicine?"

The shaman babbled and grovelled.

"No, mighty bek, I swear it! It is nothing but spring water, and a few herbs..."

A guard brought over a grey metal healing cup similar to the one I had seen in the khagan's yurt.

"Then you will not mind drinking it, will you?"

Bhulan smiled menacingly as he passed it to the shaman, but Papatzys seized it in grateful hands and gulped it down, thin dribbles of water trickling through his beard. When he had finished he offered the cup to the Roman with a triumphant flourish.

"See! It is only water..."

Al-Sifr's only response was to spit on the ground, so I took the goblet instead, staring into the dregs as though I could see my future within. That future looked to be as meagre as the dribbles of water at the discoloured bottom of the cup, but now the bek was talking about mercy. There was something about the value he placed on the friendship of the Emperor and the Khalifah, some warnings about the penalty for future misbehaviour, a guard to watch over us until we left their territory. I wasn't really listening.

I was thinking about something ibn Hayyan, the Wazir's

astrologer, had told me once. He said that lead, when it became rotten, made rotten any water that touched it. That water, in turn, would rot the brain, particularly in children, if consumed over a long period. Ibn Hayyan said that it was why old Rome had fallen to the barbarians: their lead piping, of which they were so proud, had turned them into imbeciles.

And I thought about a heavy cup of dull grey metal, polished by the centuries, corroded by lemon juice. I thought about a king who communed with spirits, and a boy who screamed every night when the shadows came.

I stared at the bek, who was describing a glorious future of peace and prosperity for all of our nations. I wondered whether I should tell him that it was the healing cups that were destroying the khagans. Then it occurred to me that he might change his mind about mercy, if this was something he preferred not to know about. Meekly I allowed myself to be escorted back to my yurt.

***

The following morning was dark and low, but the rain held off, and the candle took light at the first attempt. The crowds on the hillside seemed to hold their breath, for fear of extinguishing it, as the rabbi ha-Sangari stepped forward.

"Mighty bek, you have heard the arguments of the qadi and the priest. Like me, you will have been dazzled by the brilliance of their intellects, awed by the depth of their learning. With great skill they have set out their cases to be considered the heirs of the faith of Ibrahim and Musa. You may be asking yourself why you should bother to listen to a poor threadbare rabbi from down the road.

"However, you might also ask yourself why a man would seek the heir, when the owner himself stands before you. We Jews are the guardians of the true faith, the Chosen People. To us it was given to understand that the Creator was One, when every other nation worshipped many gods. All knowledge of the divine begins with us.

"Our holy book chronicles the whole history of the world, since the Creation. It provides myriad proofs that God favours the Jewish people: he blessed us with prophets and miracles, led us from slavery, fed and guided us in the desert, gave us the Law. The truth of this history is not disputed by Christians and Muslims, and why should it be? How could it not be accurate, when it is the history of our people, of our fathers and grandfathers? Would somebody not have protested, when lies or errors were introduced? The Injil is full of inconsistencies, as are the Hadith. Even the Quran contradicts itself, so that scholars must puzzle over the order of the verses, and determine which abrogates which other. Only the Tanakh is clear, harmonious, irrefutable.

"If you doubt God's care for the Jews, consider the fact that he gave us Palestine for our home. The sons of Japheth occupy the frozen north, the children of Ham the blazing south; but to the descendants of Shem was apportioned the temperate centre of the earth. Our land is holy, a place of pilgrimage, to both Muslims and Christians.

"You might ask why it should be so, why God would not watch over all men equally. Yet that is not how He has ordered His creation. Everything has its place in the divine order. Plants are superior to inanimate objects because they are infused with the breath of life. Animals are superior to plants, man is over the animals, and the prophets and patriarchs highest of all. You may as well ask why God has not given animals the power of reasoning, so that their souls too can survive the death of their bodies.

"You must understand, mighty bek: if you adopt our faith, it will not make you one of us. The blood of Ibrahim and Ishaq does not run in your veins. However, it will make your actions pleasing to God, and bring you closer to him.

"Both the Christians and the Muslims will have you believe that God will forgive all your sins, if you speak but a single word of repentance. How can He be a just God if that is so? How can a man come to God, except through right deeds, right prayer, and meticulous observance of the rituals prescribed by Him? Circumcision, resting on Shabbat, eating only what is lawful: these are the practices that bring a man into harmony with the divine order. The good man is like a righteous prince, who nourishes his organs, disciplines his senses, masters his desires, and finally marshals all his faculties in order to attain the highest degree of union with the Lord.

"All of this should be self-evident, and the father of religions should be held in the highest respect, as the elder takes precedence over the younger in any well-regulated society. Yet we are, as the qadi pointed out, few, scattered, and of low status everywhere, exiled from our homeland and with no place where we are sovereign. The qadi and the priest will offer this as evidence that we have been rejected by God. On the contrary, it is the final proof that we are the Chosen People.

"The father who punishes his children does not do so because he hates them, or no longer cares for them. He does so because he hopes to guide them to righteousness. The heart, as the seat of the soul, is affected by every sickness that afflicts the body, such as sadness, anxiety, wrath, envy, enmity, love, hate, and fear, and in its fine sensibility the heart continues to suffer when lower organs such as the limbs sleep peacefully. In the same way the children of Isra'il could not hope to avoid the wrath of God, when mankind is so disobedient.

"Both Christianity and Islam, when they were new, endured slander and persecution, and now take pride in the adversity they bore. We Jews must atone for our sins, and our burden is greater in proportion to the reward that is promised to us. And so we bear it gladly, knowing that one day we will return to Palestine, to be reunited with God."

The flame of the candle winked out, and a thin wisp of smoke ascended to the grey skies. The bek got to his feet. Somewhere on the brow of the hill a baby cried, its wailing clear in the hushed valley. Bhulan turned to Abu Yusuf.

"Qadi, if I tell you that I cannot accept Islam, which of the other faiths would you advise me to adopt?"

There was an involuntary cry of disappointment from one of

the scribes, but Abu Yusuf was impassive.

"Then I would tell you to listen to the rabbi."

"And you, priest, if I say that I cannot be a Christian, what would be your counsel?"

Theodore spoke sadly, as if knowingly walking into a trap but unable to help himself.

"I cannot ask you to damn yourself by following a false prophet. I must urge you to convert to Judaism."

"Then my decision is clear."

The bek spread his arms wide, encompassing the whole valley.

"Khazars, you have listened to these wise sages, and the subtle arguments they have adduced in defence of their beliefs. It is obvious that, for all their cleverness, they cannot all three be correct. The Muslims and the Jews do not accept that Isa ibn Maryam was the Son of God; the Jews and the Christians do not consider Muhammad to have been the Messenger of God. However all agree that God spoke to the children of Isra'il, and sent prophets to guide them. So I choose Judaism. I will be circumcised, and follow the law of Musa. I will ask the rabbi to be my instructor in the path of righteousness. And I pray to God that He will help me lead you to peace and prosperity."

The valley rippled and rumbled as if a great storm had been unleashed, and perhaps it had. On the other hand, perhaps it had been averted. The bek did not stay to watch. He left with his usual unfussy swiftness, guards manoeuvring silently to cover his exit. Yitzhak ha-Sangari came over to me.

"I am sad to hear that you will be leaving us. I understand, though, that the bek is keen for you to be on your way."

"Call yourself a holy man, rabbi? You have proved yourself more devious than a brace of spies."

"Oh, I am no saint, just a simple teacher. I was only making sure the game was played by its rules."

"Game? A young man, brilliant and beautiful, died playing your game."

"Yes, and for that I am truly sorry. However it was you who brought him into the game, ibn Hani al-Hakami, not I. And the bek's decision may yet save the lives of thousands more young men, and old men, and women and children."

"What do you mean?"

"Do you think the Roman Emperor would tolerate an expansion of Muslim influence across the Black Sea? He would feel surrounded, sense that the balance of power is tipping irreversibly against him. And if Christianity had triumphed, how would your Khalifah have viewed a new enemy on his northern border?

"The result would have been war, either way; and not the polite formality of a war you go through every summer, to sate your hotheads and blood your youths. When Christianity and Islam fight in earnest, there will be no quarter, no truces, no single combat, no prisoners. It will be the kind of war where cities are burned, women raped, and children butchered. It will be the kind of war where even the winners lose.

"Perhaps our bek will find a way to steer between the rocks after all. He is no fool, as you have seen. By choosing Judaism he declares his neutrality, and that of all the Khazars. And so we shall live free and independent; at least for now. That is why I won the disputation."

The rabbi smiled.

"And, of course, because I am so marvellously clever."

VIII

"So you were bested by your enemy?"

"On this occasion, Commander of the Faithful. However, this was only the first of our encounters. There was the time in Aksum, City of Thrones and Pillars, when we contested for the Ark of the Covenant —"

"Is that another immoral story? Does it have men — *doing it* with other men? I really don't wish to hear any more of that sort of thing."

Ismail stepped forward.

"My prince, in his eagerness to please you, the Father of Locks forgets that he has engaged me to speak on his behalf. Allow me to take up the tale, and I shall regale you with such wonders, that you will be transported with delight."

"Well, mind that you do. I seem to recall that I was promised beautiful princesses."

"Indeed, my prince, and that is the very story which was springing to my lips. With your permission, Commander of the Faithful, I shall recount to you..."

The Tale of the Palace in the Sky

The third most exciting thing to happen in the life of Princess Citta was when she found the dead body. That is to say, of the three most exciting things that had ever happened to her, it was the last in sequence, not in precedence. She did not rank them, as if they were horsemen in a tournament. Each had been beautiful in its own way. Each was a sweet, sharp storm, which had made her belly tingle with the realisation that this slow life in the palace in the sky would not go on forever. Gods, too, must die in the end, and their heavens crumble away.

The dead body was not beautiful in itself, like a painting or a prayer. It was the corpse of a man, an enormous stinking hairy one. It was obvious that in life he had not been clean and handsome, as were her father and brothers and cousins and even her servants, and death had done him no favours. An unshaven growth hung from his hollow cheeks, and his cracked lips sagged open.

No, it was not the cadaver itself that was beautiful, but the incongruity of its appearance in her flower garden, the odd juxtaposition of disordered limbs sprawling across neat beds, the scattered petals of crushed orchids. The lifeless hand trailing in the lotus pond. It was startling and evocative, like a poem.

The man wore farmer's clothes, but did not have the bent frame that characterised the few peasants whom the princess had encountered, in the palace in the sky. In fact, as she examined him from a careful distance, she began to wonder whether he was human at all. Certainly he was not of the Lion People. Perhaps he was a naga, a snake spirit who had crawled up from the seventh underworld to die on earth, in human form. Manichandra once told her a story about a naga who approached the Awakened One and asked to join his followers, but was told that a spirit could not achieve enlightenment until he was reborn as a man. This, apparently, was to remind her to be grateful for her humanity.

She knew she should tell Ayah about the corpse. She certainly would tell Ayah, very soon. Then Ayah would scream for help and rush her away, and Citta would have to spend the day in the house, and by the time she was permitted to enter the garden again there would be no trace that the man had ever been there. But first she would tell Nimali.

The arrival of Nimali had been the first most exciting thing to happen to Citta. Before it everything was a jumble of images, the chants of the monks, running in the stubble fields, the moth that landed on her hand, her mother's smiling face. Then there were the strange, sad farewells, the rough riding blanket, the stench of horses.

Her real memories began where that journey ended. Suddenly it was evening, and the long shadows sloped across the royal road. The Lion Rock itself crouched ominously on the horizon, awaiting her.

With its flat top and nearly vertical sides, the Rock looked nothing like a mountain, and more like the footstool of a giant asura. In the low sun, Citta stepped into the cold and dark cast by the rock half an hour before she reached its foot. There was little talk as she and her attendants struggled up the carved staircase, icy slivers of gravel nipping at her toes. It seemed that the climb would go on forever, but at last they came to the Lion itself, the talons on its paws bigger than her entire body. As darkness fell, Princess Citta stepped into the Lion's mouth, and onward to the palace in the sky.

The dawn was bright, in the palace in the sky, the warmth of the sun tempered only by a perfumed breeze that tingled the skin. Yet the chill did not leave her flesh from the night she arrived at the Rock, and her sight was clouded. She missed her mother, and did not understand why they had to part. Despite the kindness shown to her by the maids and the gardeners and the monks, she paled and sickened.

Citta was lying on her couch when Nimali entered, although it was mid-afternoon. The princess had a headache, and could not stand the light on her skin. A girl walked in, defying Citta's order that she be left alone, a tall, skinny girl a year or two older than her.

"Hullo, Citta. Do you remember me?"

"Nimali?"

They had been playmates, before Citta could remember, in the old days. Their mothers had been friends, and the two girls had been left to run around with each other while the women gossiped. Nimali had enjoyed bossing the younger girl around, and Citta was awestruck by her elder's knowledge and sophistication. Now, Nimali's sudden appearance in the palace in the sky left the princess speechless.

"They've sent me to live here, with you. I think I'm meant to cheer you up, or something. What's the matter with you, anyway?"

Citta looked down at her young body shrouded in blankets and gloom, and found she couldn't remember what the matter had been, to begin with.

"Come on, let's go outside. The bearer that brought my baggage was chatting up one of the maids. Let's see if we can catch them kissing."

Six summers had passed since then, and she had barely spent an hour of it that was not spent in the company of Nimali. The princess saw herself reflected in her friend, saw how she appeared in the eyes of others: spoilt, moody, ungrateful. Yet the bitter truth was sweetened by the love that Nimali felt for her, and Citta was inspired to try to be the person that love deserved: calm, kindly, and clear-headed.

Now, however, there was no doubt that she must tell Nimali about the dead man, before she told Ayah. For all the invented romances, breathless laughter and breaches of minor rules that enlivened their days, life was mostly dull in the palace in the sky. Any excitement, however small, was treasured, each aspect of it discussed and debated. If Citta did not share this extraordinary gift, this harbinger of mortality, with her friend, she would never be forgiven.

She found Nimali bathing in the pool, still sulking over the row they had had earlier.

"Here comes the princess. I hope you're ready to apologise, Ummadha Citta. I am not a servant, for you to abuse whenever you —"

"Never mind that, Nimali. I have to show you something."

Nimali lay back so that the water covered her ears, and her hair floated in a fan spreading out from her head.

"I can't hear you."

Citta looked around at the servants, at Ayah dabbling her feet. She gave her friend the secret sign that meant "I need to talk to you in private."

"I am sorry, Nimali. I didn't mean to hurt you. Please, just come and see. Please...?"

Nimali examined Citta through narrowed eyes. Slowly she stood up, water streaming down her long body, and climbed up the steps and out of the pool. Citta grabbed her hand and dragged her to the flower garden.

"Why all the mystery, Citta? I'm still dripping wet. I don't understand what — oh."

They held hands and stared at the corpse.

"Who is it? I don't recognise him. How did he get here?"

"I don't know."

Suddenly Citta gave a little shriek.

"His foot! It was in the pond before. Now it's on the grass."

"Could somebody else have found him?"

"And moved his foot, then just left him here? No, he must be... alive."

They edged forward, hands clasped tightly together. Now they could see the faint shifting of the man's chest, and hear the thin whistle of his breathing. Nimali released her friend's grip and crept closer.

"Careful! He might —"

"What might he do? He is unconscious, and close to death."

She scooped up water in a cupped palm, and trickled it onto

the man's mouth. His lips twitched. Then his eyes opened.

That was when they decided not to tell anybody about him. The pact was unspoken but immediate, and afterwards it seemed that there had never been any choice. All that happened was that Nimali said:

"We will have to move him. He will be found here."

It was hopeless, of course. Two young women, unaccustomed to physical labour, had no chance of lifting the dead weight of a fully grown adult male. However the prolonged grappling seemed to rouse the man, and finally he groaned, rolled over and pulled himself onto his hands and knees.

"Where can we put him?"

"The south terrace. In the mango grove."

The journey to the mango grove was agonising. The man dragged himself across the gardens with Citta hovering nervously over him, guiding him with pats as if he were a mule. Meanwhile Nimali danced around, checking that they were unobserved. A young groundsman obstructed their path, sweeping gloomily, and a blushing Nimali had to flirt with him to lure him away. Citta was left to escort the man alone down the final stairs to the south terrace.

The terrace lay at the very edge of the palace in the sky. Beyond the mango grove was a bone-shattering drop to the city below. However, it was the most secluded place on the rock, being at the opposite extremity to the Lion Gate, and gave a godlike perspective over the lands to the south, reducing the canals, and fields, and the great iron mines at Alokalavava, to slug trails and anthills.

Consequently it had always been a favoured haunt of the girls, and it was not unusual for them to order the servants to keep away. Sometimes during the dry season they would sleep there, lying on thick rugs in the gazebo and watching sparks of distant torches creep along invisible roads. It was there that they practised kissing one night, laughing each other into euphoric exhaustion. Their guardians did not worry about them being alone there, for what harm could come to them in the gardens of the palace in the sky?

The man tumbled down the last few steps to the terrace, and crawled under the shelter of the gazebo. Citta pulled over a cushion, and found an apple left over from their last picnic. The man stared at her, his green eyes glittering in the darkness. He did not speak, although he still wheezed noisily. She held out the apple to him.

"Here. Do you speak Sinhala?"

He made a slight movement of his head that might have been a nod.

"Take it. It's not poisoned."

He passed a rough tongue over his lips and gasped out a single word.

"Water."

Citta shuddered at the suggestion of command, at the idea that a scruffy foreigner could issue orders to a royal princess descended from a lion. However she decided that the urgency of the situation warranted indulgence, and went outside to where a rivulet trickled down an artificial waterfall into a stone basin. There were no cups, so she filled a discarded coconut shell with water, and took it back to him. He tried to grasp the shell, but his hands were shaking too badly. Citta held it to his mouth, awkwardly conscious of his bitter odour and the intensity of his gaze.

"What do you think you are doing, you filthy harlot?"

The princess screamed and dropped the shell. She turned to see the laughing face of Nimali, her arms loaded with fruit and pillows.

"You — you witch! I'll have you flogged!"

"Oh, you will have to pardon me, princess. If you could have seen your own face you would pardon me, because it was the funniest thing since Ayah farted during meditation. But what would Thandivarman say if he saw you there, on your knees giving succour to another man?"

Citta started at the mention of Thandivarman, who was the second most exciting thing that had happened to her. It had all started with her father the king coming to visit, and that was a significant event in itself. Her father sometimes forgot to bring her a gift, but he always brought masculine certainty, a noisy, lively entourage that set the whole household buzzing, and a sense of occasion.

On this visit he did not summon Citta to the upper palace for three days. By the time the herald finally came to call her she was trembling, wondering what she had done to make her father angry. When she entered the throne room, however, he smiled warmly on her. She knelt before him, but he raised her up and kissed her on the forehead.

"Ummadha Citta, can it really be two years since I saw you last? You have grown into a beautiful woman. It is the sad burden of a king, that he must neglect his own kin to care for his subjects.

"You have always been my favourite daughter, and now I bring wonderful news. You are to be married."

Citta's betrothed was called Thandivarman. He was a prince of the Pallava, son of the famous king Nandivarman, who had restored his dynasty's fortunes and reigned over his empire for half a century.

"But — then he is not of the Lion People? Does he even speak our language?"

"Love needs no language, daughter. You will soon learn Tamil, when you go to live with him on the mainland."

"I have to leave the Island?"

The full meaning of her father's words shattered Citta's universe like lightning striking a tree. She had never given much thought to the world beyond the Island, and certainly never intended to visit it. For the past seven years she had not even set foot outside the city walls that surrounded the Lion Rock.

After some weeks of howling and sulking, however, she came to peace with the idea. In part this was because the monk Manichandra explained to her that all things were transient and that change was an inevitable attribute of existence; in part because her father said Nimali could go with her to her new home, and Ayah too. He also promised that the ceremony would take place on the Rock, although it would have to be in the Shaiva form. Citta talked to Manichandra about this.

"But if I worship the gods of the brahmins, it will distract me from the Noble Path."

"No, child, there is no harm in it. Deities are beings like any other, and worthy of our compassion. They live so long that they believe they are immortal, and dwell in such bliss that they can never achieve enlightenment. So make your sacrifice to the fire god, and hope that he has the good fortune to be born human in his next life."

Thandivarman himself was still across the sea, in his father's kingdom. The day of the wedding would be the first time that bride and groom would meet. Instead Citta had been presented with a portrait of him, painted on a wooden panel. She had seen enough paintings of her father to know that the image would be ideal rather than accurate. In truth it imparted little information that she could trust, other then that he was a man, with brown skin, black hair and a long moustache, and even those things she doubted occasionally.

Somehow, though, the fact that she knew so little about her prospective husband made him seem more alluring. Into the emptiness created by Thandivarman's absence Citta poured her wishes and longings and fantasies, so that he grew day by day, taller and stronger and more handsome. In her dreams he resembled a deva when he came to her, his arms enfolding her, his body crushing hers, and she would wake trembling and flushed.

Now, however, Nimali's reference to Thandivarman filled her with shame. She contemplated the strange man lying in her sanctuary, and he no longer seemed like a sublime symbol of impermanence. Instead he engendered the same horror she would feel on finding a snake in her bed.

"Oh, Nimali, what have we done? We must tell Ayah immediately."

Nimali stroked her friend's face.

"And if we tell her, what would happen? They would hack off his head and throw his body on the dung heap. Caring for him is an act of compassion, and will earn us great merit."

The princess bit her lip. Nimali was right; only their silence protected the man from summary execution. She dredged up some anger against the thuggish guards who she knew would commit such brutality against a fellow human without hesitation or compunction. Anger helped fuel her defiance.

Citta had always been rebellious, despite, or perhaps because of, her tranquil upbringing and profoundly spiritual bent. She had been delighted to learn that she was named after a distant ancestor, who was still remembered a thousand years later for an act of disobedience that changed the destiny of the kingdom. The first Ummadha Citta spent her childhood confined to a room in a tower, as a consequence of a horoscope that predicted her son would kill his nine uncles and seize the throne. Despite this precaution, however, she fell pregnant when she was sixteen. Her brothers were prepared to kill the child as soon as it was born if it was a boy, but with the connivance of her maid and her mother the queen Ummadha Citta swapped the baby for a girl child. The boy was smuggled to the southern kingdom of Ruhuna, from where he would one day return to fulfil the prophecy.

Citta remained unclear as to how her ancestor had managed to conceive, and who the boy's father was. A maid had begun to tell her that part of the story once, but Ayah had caught them and sent the maid away, never to be seen again in the palace in the sky. Nonetheless the princess liked to imagine that she was not only descended from the first Ummadha Citta, but perhaps was the same irrepressible soul reborn.

Encouraged by these thoughts, she helped Nimali settle the man on the pillows. Once he was made comfortable, Nimali addressed him loudly and slowly as if he were deaf.

"What... is... your... name?"

The man muttered something.

"Did you say Hashan? What are you doing here, Hashan? Where have you come from?"

He did not reply, but slumped on the pillows, eyes closed.

"Are you hurt? Where is your injury?"

Hashan gestured, haltingly but unmistakably, towards his groin. The girls looked at each other, and Nimali shrugged.

"It is an act of compassion."

They found the wound as soon as they began to unwrap his sarong. At the top of his thigh, a vile black patch of dried blood glued the fabric to his skin. Citta gasped, but Nimali was pragmatic.

"It will have to come off. Are you ready, Hashan?"

She ripped the cloth away suddenly. The man jammed his hand in his mouth to stifle his agonised roar. Citta examined the ragged, discoloured wound, which was now oozing blood again. Compared to its sickly horror, his genitals seemed unthreatening, a shrunken member lying meekly dormant on sagging balls.

"What do we do?"

Citta suspected Nimali knew little more about treating injuries than she did, but the older girl's confidence was compelling. She found clean cloths, soaked one in water and bathed the wound, then bound it with the others. Hashan's eyes showed his pain, but he remained silent. When she was finished, Nimali sat back and viewed her handiwork.

"Well, we'd better get you some clothes."

They returned after the evening puja, bringing more food and a fresh sarong. The man was sleeping, so they draped it over his loins, and left him in peace. The next morning they found him sitting up.

"Thank you for saving my life. Could I have some wine?"

His voice was still thick, and his accent heavy, but the words were clear. Citta was taken aback.

"Wine? But wine stupefies the consciousness and leads to reckless acts."

"Yes. Can I have some please?"

"We are followers of the Noble Eightfold Path. There is no wine on the Lion Rock."

Hashan was crestfallen.

"I suppose that means there is no meat either?"

Citta's shocked face answered his question, and he accepted a breakfast of water, bread and fruit without complaint. As he ate Citta noticed something.

"Why do you keep staring at our breasts?"

Hashan seemed embarrassed by the question, and mumbled his response.

"In my country... it is the custom for women to cover their bodies. A man will only see a woman's naked breasts at a time of... intimacy."

The girls looked down at their bodies in surprise.

"What, bind our breasts like peasant women labouring in the fields? It is a privilege of our rank to decorate ourselves and adorn our bosoms with jewels. If we are to hide our youth and beauty away, we may as well cover our faces!"

"Actually, in my country... no, never mind."

Citta decided that, if the man was able to talk now, that he owed them an explanation.

"Tell us how you sustained your injury."

"I was set upon by thieves, while travelling to Polonnaruwa. I am a merchant from the city of Basrah, who came to the Island on business. At the port of Gokanna, I met a man who promised to sell me cinnamon if I journeyed inland to the capital. It was a trick, though; the bandits were lying in wait for me on the road.

"I killed one of them, but his last action before death was to pierce my thigh with his sword. Bleeding, I crept away and hid under a bush. In the darkness the bandits could not find me, although they took my horse and all my belongings. After they left I tried to reach the nearest village, but the loss of blood from my wound sapped my strength, and I fell into oblivion."

Citta listened to his story open-mouthed in wonder. Nimali, however, was not satisfied.

"Then how did you end up on the Lion Rock?"

"I don't know. Perhaps a deva picked me up and placed me here, so that you could find me and save me."

When Hashan smiled, Citta realised that she had not considered him truly human before. She had thought of him as some kind of animal that she had found hurt, and wished to nurse to health. In an instant everything became real. Her voice was cold, but from fear rather than antipathy.

"You follow the path of Muhammad. You do not believe in devas."

He seemed to catch her mood, and grew serious.

"I am not so sure. They say that the first dwellers on the Island were spirits. Men used to trade with them, before the Lion People came and drove them away. One cannot walk this land without feeling the — forgive me, I do not know the words in your language. It is hard for me. In my own land I am considered a fair poet."

"You speak very well, and I understand exactly what you mean. The presences all around you that cannot be seen. Some say the Island is a gateway to other worlds."

"I can believe it. Besides, Muslims recognise the existence of powerful but invisible spirits. We call them Jinni."

Nimali interrupted testily.

"This is very uplifting, but we need to go back to the palace and do our chores. Otherwise someone will come looking for us."

An awkward silence followed, in which Citta would not meet her eyes. Finally Nimali stamped her foot.

"All right then, princess. I will go and do your chores for you, so that you may sit with your naga. I shall console myself with the knowledge of the merit I will earn by my skilful actions."

Left alone with the man, Citta was shaken by an unfamiliar sensation of freedom. In that moment she understood what the monk had said about gods, and how they could never achieve enlightenment. Her tranquil existence on the Rock had protected her from harm, but also had denied her the full breadth of experience that led to wisdom.

Hashan asked if he could wash himself. It was too dangerous for him to go out in the open, so Citta helped him over to the stone basin. He had bound the sarong around his loins, but his hairiness seemed somehow obscene, implying a bestiality at odds with his sensitive soul. All the men she knew were perfumed and shaven, face and body, except perhaps for an oiled moustache. The Moor

Hashan had heavy tresses hanging from his scalp, a thick beard and dark curly fur on his chest.

He glanced across at her as he scrubbed his face.

"Might I know the name of the one who has saved my life?"

Citta tilted back her chin.

"You would not be able to speak my full name, nor remember it. You should call me Princess Ummadha Citta."

"A princess, and yet you have chores?"

Citta blushed.

"My teachers say that it is not beneficial to my spiritual development to be spared all menial tasks. They tell the story about the novice who goes to see the wise old master, and says,

"'Master, how do I attain Nirvana?'

"The master replies,

"'Have you eaten your rice?'

"'No, master.'

"'Then eat your rice.'

"The novice returns an hour later.

"'Master, I have eaten my rice. Please tell me what I must do to achieve enlightenment.'

"The master answers,

"'Now wash your bowl.'"

Hashan's baffled smile revealed that he did not understand the story, and Citta felt abashed. It had seemed so profound, so loaded with meaning, when Manichandra had related it to her, but from her own young lips it sounded empty, banal. The man sensed her embarrassment, and changed the subject.

"You are a woman of courage, princess Ummadha Citta, as well as learning. You take a grave risk in protecting me."

"I am not so courageous. What punishment can they impose on me? They will not beat a princess of the royal blood. At worst they will give me more chores, which, since they tell me it is beneficial for my karma, is a blessing, not a burden."

She was not entirely sure why she did not mention her forthcoming marriage, and the potentially catastrophic consequences of any scandal.

"It is you who are in danger, follower of Muhammad. If the guards find you they will surely kill you."

"They would murder an innocent merchant, the victim of an unfortunate misadventure? Are they, then, not followers of the Eightfold Path?"

"There is no king of any nation, no matter what his creed, who would hesitate to slaughter an intruder apprehended in his private palace. Even if a deva put the intruder there."

"I understand. Rulers who place principles above pragmatism seldom rule for long."

"It is not like that. My father — the king must sometimes sacrifice his own hopes for awakening, in order to care for his people. It is not enough simply to do what appears to be right. Through awareness and wisdom, we can better understand the consequences of our actions, and make choices that best promote the welfare of all beings. We call these skilful actions, deeds which are not only virtuous but also wise."

"Perhaps, then, the skilful choice for you now is to help me get better, so that I can sneak away, and nobody need come to any harm?"

"Liar!"

They were relieved to see it was Nimali who interrupted them, but this time she was not playing a trick. Her face was stiff with fury.

"Well, *merchant*, are you going to cover your lies with more lies? Or will you confess the truth? Either you tell the princess who you really are, or else I will."

Hashan met her gaze with cool eyes, but said nothing. Nimali turned to Citta.

"You had better return to the palace quickly. A company of guards has arrived, and everyone is in uproar. Apparently they are looking for a foreign spy. They caught him on the road two nights ago, but he escaped — despite being wounded in the leg."

Citta looked at the Moor, whose face showed no emotion.

Then she ran from the gazebo. Nimali spat, and followed her.

Ayah was waiting for them by the door to the lower palace.

"Oh, girls, such a relief to see you! Where have you been? What have you been doing?"

Her voice was worn and familiar, like an old blanket, a voice in which the same tone expressed complaint and affection. It occurred to Citta that she cared more for the old woman than she did for her real mother. It would certainly be very wrong to put at risk not only Ayah, but everybody else at the palace, for the sake of a barbarous stranger.

"We were making a shrine on the south terrace. We like to meditate there, it's very peaceful."

Ayah did not miss Nimali's sharp glance at Citta, but jumped to the wrong conclusion.

"Well, perhaps you can cultivate your loving-kindness when you are there. I heard about the row you two had. You are so lucky to be young and intelligent and healthy, to have time to study and meditate. Why waste your time nurturing the poison of hatred, just to use it on your best friend?"

Citta kissed her on the brow.

"Ayah, you are so wise, I am sure that in your next life you will be born an arahant. Now what is there to eat?"

Nimali tossed her head as she followed them inside but said nothing. The turmoil within the palace was in marked contrast to the usual serene calm. Servants scurried and gossiped, while soldiers stood around in officious groups, striving to combine surly deference with mistrustful menace.

"What is happening, Ayah?"

The old woman gripped her arm.

"Such a worry! An assassin, they say — at the very heart of the island. Your father is on his way. And so is your husband. Thandivarman is making the crossing from the mainland, and will be here in a matter of weeks. Before two moons have turned you will be a married woman."

Citta was more shocked at the prospect of the imminent

arrival of her betrothed, than she was by the possibility that she had been harbouring a dangerous foreign agent. She had made such an idol of the Pallava prince, idealised him to such an extent that it now occurred to her the reality could only be a disappointment. Once he arrived, his glorious potential would collapse into a dull mundanity that she would have to live with for the rest of this life.

They were restricted to their quarters for the day, while the soldiers searched for the spy. Citta sat meditating, avoiding the need to lie to Ayah or face Nimali's recriminations, half hoping and half fearing to hear of Hashan's capture. She tried to focus her mind on her breathing, calmly to observe its ebb and flow. Unbidden to her mind, however, came images of the Moor dragged from his hiding place, thrown to his knees, the swords piercing his flesh. Melancholy odour of incense touched her senses. She wondered whether Nimali would betray her.

When Ayah came in, the princess made her wait for long minutes before she rose from her cushion. She had spent the time deciding that she would pretend to faint when the old woman spoke, to conceal her reaction to her words. However her tidings brought relief.

"They have found nothing. Nobody truly believed any threat could penetrate the palace. They have posted extra guards on the Lion Gate, but most of the soldiers have gone to search elsewhere."

Citta wondered whether she should faint anyway, just go limp and crash down, take a rest from the constant torment of having to decide what was the right thing to do, enjoy the sympathy and mothering and the reassurance that people around her loved her. She swayed, but the lure of the south terrace kept her upright.

Of course Ayah was still concerned about her going out alone, especially in the twilight. Citta insisted that she needed to calm herself, after the day's excitement, and that a stroll in the gardens would be soothing.

"Besides, if there was any danger, the soldiers would have found it, wouldn't they?"

Citta was far from calm as she walked down the steps to the

terrace. Her heart fluttered and her hands shook. The gazebo was empty though. Perhaps Hashan had somehow escaped from the Rock.

"Thank you for not giving me away."

He stepped from the shadows, and again she was startled by his maleness, his bulk and the rough hair on his chest.

"How did you evade them?"

"They are stupid, and lazy, and did not expect to find anything."

She remembered he had lied to her, and forced herself to an anger she did not truly feel.

"Who are you? Is it true that you are a spy, and not a merchant?"

"Yes."

Although he towered over her, he hung his head diffidently, like a child who had been caught misbehaving.

"Why are you here?"

He raised his head and looked directly into her eyes.

"I have come to stop you marrying Prince Thandivarman."

IX

Citta was choked by fury, confusion and a crazy surge of hope.

"You are risking your life to prevent my wedding? Why do you care? What is it to you, or to your masters?"

Hashan sat down, crossing his legs.

"You are a princess, Ummadha Citta, the daughter of a king. Your forthcoming marriage has nothing to do with love, and a great deal to do with politics."

"What do you mean?"

"What territory does your father rule, Citta?"

"The Island. He is King of the Island."

"In name at least. In reality, however, his authority diminishes the further you travel from the capital. Ruhuna in the south, the Tamils in the north, even my people — the Moors, as you call them — will all defy him in an instant, if they think they can get away with it. When he came to the throne he had to reconquer much of his territory, which had seceded from the kingdom.

"And his rebellious subjects are the least of his problems. The Tamil nations on the mainland, the Pallava, Pandya and Chola kingdoms, eye this land greedily from across the sea. It is only their constant wars with each other that prevent them from invading and annexing his realm."

She wanted to deny it, to insist that the Lion People feared nobody, but she had heard enough gossip about affairs of state to know that he was telling the truth.

"The Pallava are our friends, and allies."

"It would be a foolish king who did not take shelter under the wing of one of the mainland powers, and your father is not a foolish

127

man. He supports the Pallava in their conflict with the Pandyas, and in return he is given their protection."

"Then my marriage to Thandivarman will strengthen the alliance, and make my people safe."

Hashan smiled.

"You have a natural grasp of statecraft, princess. Unfortunately, like your father, you do not see far enough ahead, and place too much trust in your Tamil friends.

"A son born from your union with Thandivarman will be the heir to the kingdom of Pallava. But he will also have Sinhala royal blood flowing in his veins. Do you not imagine that he will consider the Island rightly his? It would not be hard to find an excuse to intervene in the affairs of the kingdom; an uprising, a rival claimant, such things are frequent occurrences. He would come as peacemaker, as arbiter, but he would come with an army. As for the rest of it — well, the usual way would be to have the king assassinated, put the blame on the Pandya, and assume control as an emergency measure. The details aren't important.

"With a Tamil king would come their language, their religion. The brahmins would drive out the bhikkhus, and the Lion People would follow the Noble Eightfold Path no longer. Your son, princess, will destroy your nation, and its way of life will be forgotten in the dust of history; if, that is, you marry the Pallava prince."

Citta pulled herself to her full height.

"So you have come to save the Lion People, as an act of pure altruism?"

"No, princess. I would not insult you by expecting you to believe that. My masters have a stake in maintaining the balance between Pallava and Pandya, and promoting a resurgence of the Chola. Do not ask me what that stake is. They do not discuss such matters with me. It is unlikely to be anything obvious; the man who sent me here has a taste for the convoluted and indirect.

"It is his interests that I am pursuing here, but it so happens that those interests coincide with yours. If you care for the future of your people, then you will tell your father that you refuse to wed

Thandivarman. Otherwise, I may have to kill your prince."

Citta shivered, although the fear was mixed with a thrill of excitement.

"You admit that you would murder another human being, just to further your sordid political machinations?"

"Princess, the real world, beyond the gardens and pools of the palace in the sky, is a vicious place. Whoever is not the predator, is the prey. If you want to save Thandivarman, then do not marry him."

The princess was conscious of the weakness of his argument. How could he claim to know with such certainty what would happen in the future? However his words cracked the shell of her destiny, and something was flooding in, something that might be light and air, or might instead be disease. Hashan spoke urgently.

"Citta, when your father comes he will have a man with him, a foreigner, whom you have never seen before. It is he who has persuaded your father to this calamitous path. I cannot tell you what he will look like, but when you see him you will know who he is. And then you will know that I am telling you the truth."

Citta shook, trying to shake the fear from her spine.

"Enough. I will not sink to your depths of brutality. You may stay here until you are well enough to escape. However if you try to interfere with the affairs of my family or my kingdom, I will hand you over to the guards and you can meet the fate you have chosen for yourself."

That night Nimali crept into Citta's room and snuggled beside her. The older girl clung to her friend anxiously.

"What are you doing, Ummadha Citta? Do you even know?"

"I am practising what I have been taught. I am doing what is right."

"You cannot truly imagine that our elders would be pleased with your actions, or you would not keep it secret from them. That man is dangerous. If a snake came near your baby, you would not hesitate to crush its head."

"Then will you tell them, Nimali?"

Neither of them spoke again till the morning.

***

The strangest of circumstances can come to seem normal, once they have set into a routine. Citta brought food to the south terrace morning and evening, almost every day. Hashan would remain concealed until he was sure it was her, then emerge noiselessly, never from the same place twice. She found his sudden presence frightening at first, but made it a matter of pride not to let the fear show. After a week or two she grew accustomed to it, and entertained herself by guessing where he might be hiding.

In time her fascination overcame her fear, and she would sit and watch him eat.

"How many men have you killed?"

He glanced up from his meal.

"I don't know."

The shock made her voice shriek embarrassingly.

"Is it so many that you have lost count?"

"No, princess. I do not know because it is not always convenient or prudent to stop and check whether your enemy is dead or merely wounded. Why do you ask? Is there a number which is acceptable? What difference does it make, if the answer is seven, or seventeen, or seventy?"

"Is it seven, then?"

"No. How would you have me count it? Shall I only number men whom I have slain with my bare hands, or include those whose murder I have arranged? What about those whom I let die, though I could have saved them?"

"You are mocking me."

"No, it is you who are mocking me, princess. How many men has your father killed?"

She sipped her water, and he chewed his bread.

"What is it like, to kill someone?"

"You seem unduly interested in the subject, Ummadha Citta.

Do you harbour murderous impulses which at times you struggle to contain? Directed, perhaps, at those you most love?"

She stared into her cup, and he went on.

"Besides, the question has no answer. You might as well ask what it is like to talk to someone. Every death is unique. The enemy whose spleen you pierce as he charges you waving his sword; the beloved uncle whom you gently smother when he begs you to put an end to his pain; the man you murder at night because you have sold your soul, and you strangle him for silence, so that you have to watch his eyes plead and puzzle and pop and finally fix on infinity: these are not experiences that have much in common."

She should have felt horror, when he spoke in this way. Instead she knew a profound pity, compassion for the suffering which was the inevitable consequence of his wrongdoing, arising from it as night arose from day, and sadness at the damage that must have been done to him, that caused his evil to arise in turn.

"You said once you were a poet in your own land. Was that, too, a lie?"

"No, that was true; and I hope will be true again some day."

"Will you recite to me one of your poems?"

"Poetry cannot survive the journey from one language to another. It is not a cargo to be traded between lands; it is a kiss that lives only in the moment of creation, but which you hope to remember forever. I cannot give you my verse, here where my tongue is meaningless. I can sing to you sounds that will carry no sense, or mouth to you words that have no magic. Neither will be my poem."

"Then do both, and I shall imagine that they are one."

He thought for a moment, then recited:

"La tabki Layla wa la tutrub ila Hindi
        Washrub ghal al wirdi min hamraa' kalwirdi..."

His language was soft and melodic, rich in husky breaths pronounced deep in the throat. Although she did not understand the words, the poem sang and danced for her, light and effervescent. When he had finished, she clapped.

"That was beautiful. What does it mean?"

"I cannot convey the sense fully, but it means something like this:

"Don't cry for Layla —"

"Who is Layla?"

"Are you jealous, Princess? There is no need. There was a real Layla once, but she is long dead. Now she is more of an idea. Her name is used in our verse to represent any unattainable woman. If I may continue?

"Don't cry for Layla, don't rejoice over Hind —"

"Who is Hind?"

"This isn't going to work. Wait, let me try it this way:

"Don't waste your breath on hoary old poetry,
      Pledge your rose rather with wine bright and rosy.
Drink from a cup which, when poured down the throat,
      Paints cheek and eye all alike red as ruby.
The wine is carnelian, the glass like pearl,
When you're served by a girl whose fingers are dainty;
She dispenses delirium, in glasses and glances,
      Eyes and then wine, till you are drunk doubly.
My friends have one drug, two intoxicate me
      And I am the only one blessed with such bounty..."

He looked to her for applause, but Citta was frowning.

"Why would you write poetry about wine?"

"Because it is what interests me. Because it is a delight to the senses, and a comfort to the soul. What should I be writing about? What do your people write about?"

"About the emptiness of all material things, and the quest for enlightenment."

"That sounds like fun."

Citta was peeved by his mockery.

"Would you like to hear a poem in my language?"

"I would like that very much, princess."

She got to her feet, and proclaimed shyly:

"Flower-snared, sotted with desire, a bee
bites the stalk and hums, seduced by pleasure,
trapped in misery.
Full moon kisses petals of the night-blooming lily, but she
has no mercy. We are different, we can fly; we are free."

Hashan was silent for a moment. Then:

"I owe you an apology, princess. That was very good. Who wrote it?"

Citta sat down again, biting her lip.

"Actually, I did."

The Moor bowed, seeming genuinely impressed.

"Then I have underestimated you. But surely you do not believe, as your poem suggests, that pleasure and beauty are snares to trap us?"

"Desire and repulsion alike are illusions, born of ignorance."

"And if we rid ourselves of them, we are free to fly away, unlike your bee?"

"The Awakened One Tathagata taught us that eight things are necessary to achieve enlightenment: right understanding and right intentions; right speech, right action and right living; right effort, right awareness and right concentration. By practising these things, we aim to escape the cycle of existence."

"But I like existence. I plan to go on existing for as long as possible. Why would I not want to live?"

Citta was taken aback by this argument.

"Because of the Four Noble Truths: that suffering is an inescapable part of life, that the origin of suffering is attachment, that suffering can be ended, and the Eightfold Path is the way to end it."

"I can handle a little suffering. Suffering passes in the end. It is the concept of a universe without me in it that I find unthinkable."

"Is it not a tenet of your religion that you will suffer for eternity after your death, if you have displeased your god in life?"

"It is. I am pinning my hopes on a last minute repentance."

"But why would you take the risk? You might be cut down before you can be forgiven, particularly as you court danger so assiduously. Why would you not want to do what is right? How can you knowingly choose to do wrong, by drinking and killing and philandering?"

"Because wrongness is the salt that gives life flavour. Too much of it will spoil the feast, I grant you, but without it how would you know you were alive at all?"

Citta tried another tack.

"But if you were to achieve enlightenment; if, in an instant, you perceived and comprehended the whole universe, saw the future and past, were conscious of the oneness of all things; why, then, would you want to carry on existing after that?"

"After that? I think I'd probably need a drink."

He grinned.

"Do you think, next time, you can bring me a knife? I would like to be able to cut my bread."

The more she talked to Hashan, the more Citta realised how bored she was with the company of Ayah, of the servants, even of Nimali. The palace gossip which would once have fascinated her sounded to her now utterly trivial: the row between the cook and the gardener, the maid who had fallen pregnant, the theft of a silken canopy which was to have been used at her wedding, all seemed bland and unsatisfying. To one who subsisted only on milk, fruit and grains, the Moor brought the rich savour of meat, the sensation of tearing flesh with her teeth; at least in her imagination. As the weeks drifted by she spent more and more time on the south terrace, listening to his tales of adventure and romance.

The servants were glad to keep away, since it gave them less work to do, and Citta kept the gazebo clean, so that on their occasional foray to the terrace they did not have to linger long. Ayah commented on the amount of food she took there, but asked only if Citta was fattening herself up for her husband, with an attempt at a suggestive leer which was so out of character in the old woman that the girls imitated it for days afterwards. Nimali was often short-tempered and resentful, but she held her peace, and took supplies to Hashan when Citta could not.

The deception was so simple that it was easy to pretend it could go on forever, despite the growing number of messengers that came and went through the Lion Gate. However the day of the king's arrival dawned at last, as every day will in the end, no matter how longed for or dreaded. Citta waited in her quarters listening to the thud of drums and the trumpeting of elephants in the city below, and pictured Hashan on the south terrace hiding in the bushes, wondering what the noise portended.

This time she did not have to wait to be summoned. Her father must have barely settled himself in the throne room before she was escorted into his presence.

"My precious daughter. This is your husband, Prince Thandivarman."

The man who stood beside him was short, his head little higher than her father's although the king was seated. Remarkably he resembled his portrait, being smooth and fragrant, with a long moustache. Citta bowed, and he addressed her, incomprehensible words in his own language. Another voice spoke at the same time.

"I am overjoyed to meet you, Princess Ummadha Citta. I have heard tell of your beauty, but all the poets of all the nations singing at once could not do it justice."

Citta wondered who the portly official was, who dared to talk over a royal prince. Then she realised that the man was translating Thandivarman's words. He appeared to have the ability to listen and speak at the same time, as he did not wait for his master to finish before he began interpreting.

Unsure how to respond, she bowed again, and again, while the official burbled about how the Pallava rejoiced that she was to be their queen, the skies and the seas themselves frolicked at the prospect of their union, and the earth trembled in anticipation of the mighty line of kings and warriors that would spring from her loins. The prince, it was suggested, wished he could hasten the turning of the sky, so that two sunsets would pass in a flash, and the day of their wedding would be upon them. Then Thandivarman bowed, and she bowed again, and she was ushered from the room, and the audience was over.

It was only when she was outside that Citta understood what she had been told. Two sunsets; she was to be married the day after tomorrow.

Later that evening, after dispatching Nimali to tend to Hashan, Citta crept through the corridors of the palace. As she approached the guards outside her father's private chambers though, she stood upright and announced herself.

"Princess Ummadha Citta, to see the king."

Never before had she dared to present herself in this way. Always she had waited to be summoned, and to do otherwise seemed an inversion of the natural order, like a river running uphill. One of the guards went to seek instructions, while the other stared six inches above her head. In time the first guard returned, and silently gestured her through the open door.

Her father sat on a stool wearing only a sarong. He seemed smaller, older without his regalia. His head was bowed and his shoulders stooped, as though the weight of his responsibility was crushing him. He gave her a thin smile.

"What is it, child?"

There was a woman with him, in his room. Citta halted in the doorway, thinking for a moment that she had interrupted her father's lovemaking. The woman, though, was tall and heavy, with thick brows and a long face. Her skin was dark, and streaked as though dirty. She covered her chest in the Tamil manner, but Citta could see that her breasts were low and sagging.

"Father, I am not sure I want to marry Prince Thandivarman."

Citta thought for a moment he was about to strike her, and flinched. However he mastered himself, and took a deep breath.

"Why not?"

"I fear that some day my sons will contend with my brothers and their children for supremacy over the Island."

The king's laughter was so brutal and bitter that a guard stuck his head into the room to check all was well.

"Oh, Ummadha Citta! I thought you would say you do not love him, or some such girlish nonsense! But no, your concern is for your people. That is why you are my favourite; if only your brothers had your perspicacity and sense of duty."

Citta was slightly shamed by this praise, which she did not feel she deserved. She was relieved when her father went on.

"Believe me, child, I have considered that possibility. I have lain awake at nights pondering it, ever since King Nandivarman proposed the union.

"However no man can predict the future. Anyone who pretends to is a charlatan, whether they observe the skies, examine entrails or claim that God is talking to them. It may come to pass that you have no sons, although I do not wish that fate on you. It may be that the Pandyas finally defeat the Pallavas, and the situation on the mainland changes. It may be that another, presently unknown force will come and blow us all away."

Citta fancied she saw him glance at the woman, who stood, arms folded, in the shadows.

"Besides, if my sons and my grandsons cannot defend their kingdom, then they do not deserve to be kings. Your marriage will strengthen our position, for now. Let those to whom the future belongs worry about the future."

"Thank you, father."

She ran from the palace into the gathering gloom. On the way down to the south terrace, she passed the bathing pool, and was astonished to see a red cloth lying on the path. It was the sarong which they had brought for the Moor to wear. As she bent to pick it up, there was a slosh from the water beside her.

Hashan emerged from the pool, rising slowly into view. Threads and ribbons of water streamed from his long, tangled locks and crawled down his hairy body. He was healthy now, his skin golden and his muscles swelling. As he stepped out she could see that he was naked, his cock hanging and swinging with each step.

"What are you doing? My father is in the palace! If they found you here —"

In response he stretched, thrusting his chest and groin slightly forward.

"I have to bathe occasionally, or they will track me down by my scent."

She grabbed the sarong and shoved it at him.

"You must leave by tomorrow. On the day of the wedding there will be nowhere to hide. Is your wound healed?"

"I am not sure. What do you think?"

He took her hand and placed it on his thigh, pulling her closer to him. In response his member twitched and lengthened. It lolled to one side, stretching and shaking, before raising its head like a snake bewitching its prey.

Citta snatched her hand away. Hashan chuckled. He lazily pulled the sarong around his waist, but his member stuck out like a tentpole, lifting the fabric out from him. It looked so ridiculous that Citta laughed, her fear falling away.

"Come on then, ape man. If you want me you'll have to catch me."

She ran to the south terrace, heedless of risk. Hashan puffed behind her. He was strong and long legged, but she knew the ground, and he stumbled and cursed in the dark. Once under the sheltering safety of the gazebo she collapsed on the ground giggling. He fell next to her, his member hard and shockingly long against her thigh, but she pushed him away.

"No. In two days I am to be married, and there is nothing you can do to stop it. You can leave before then, or you can hurl yourself to your death on the sharp spears of my father's guards, as you choose."

He shrugged. A mad thought possessed her.

"So you like danger, ape man? Then come with me."

She jumped to her feet, and raced back to the herb garden. There she found the handcart which she had noticed earlier, left behind by a careless groundsman, next to a pile of cuttings to which he had obviously intended to return. Hashan stood behind her, puzzled. She pointed to the cart.

"Get in there."

"Why?"

"I want to sprinkle some salt on my life, while I still can."

Reluctantly he clambered into the cart. She piled the branches on top of him until he was covered, ignoring his complaints.

"Shut up. Your life might depend on your silence."

Once he was concealed, she lifted the cart's handles, and pushed it clumsily along the path. The man was heavy, but the cart well balanced, and she managed to struggle along to the Lion Gate, where the guards eyed her approach curiously. She gave them a rueful grin.

"I have been guilty of pride, and Sri Manichandra has prescribed gardening work as a corrective."

The guards looked dubious, but she was after all a princess. They stood aside to let her pass, and watched as the cart bumped down the steps.

The Lion Gate guarded the final ascent to the palace in the sky. When Citta had first encountered its fearsome gaze, she had been a child, no taller than one of its paws. She had walked into its mouth in terror, expecting the stone jaws to crush down, devouring her hungrily. Of course it was no more than carved rock, but she felt that in some way the Lion had indeed consumed her. Although she had often come and gone through the gate since then, part of her seemed to remain in the palace, and her forays to the world below were brief and reluctant.

Now Citta felt that she was smuggling that part of her back out of the Lion's maw. She ignored the pain in her hands and arms, concentrating on manoeuvring the cart down the steep walkway. Once the path had curved round the edge of the rock so that she was out of sight of the guards, she stopped, and pulled away the branches.

"Get out."

Hashan clambered from the cart, groaning and rubbing his bruised limbs.

"What are we doing here?"

"I wanted to show you this."

She indicated the wall which ran alongside the path. It was coated with a ceramic glaze, that shone even in the darkness. Their faces glowed reflected in its sheen, staring back at them like ghosts.

"It is known as the Mirror Wall. It has stood here for three centuries, pristine and perfect."

"Very impressive, but surely you did not bring me here to admire the brickwork."

He pressed her against the wall and moved to kiss her, but she put her hand over his mouth.

"Give me your knife."

He took out the sharp little knife she had given him, but there was a glint of fear in his eyes. He glanced down at his groin, as if he suspected she would castrate him. Instead she turned toward the wall.

"Tell me if you see anyone coming."

And with the knife Princess Ummadha Citta, daughter of a king, began scratching symbols into the shiny surface of the Mirror Wall. Hashan peered over in interest.

"What are you writing?"

"Can't you read?"

"Not in your language. I have learned to speak it, but do not know your script."

"It is my poem. About the bee."

Her hand shook slightly, but she etched the four lines of verse neatly onto the wall, then stood back to contemplate her handiwork.

"Aren't you going to sign it?"

She looked askance at him.

"I'm sure my father would be very impressed to learn that I have damaged one of our national treasures. No, it's enough that my work will endure for centuries. I don't need my name to be attached to it."

"Very nice. So what now, Ummadha Citta?"

"Now? I return to the palace. And you go home."

Hashan's jaw fell.

"You didn't think I was going to wheel you back up the path, did you?"

"Was he there? The man I told you about — was he with your father?"

Citta could not meet his eyes.

"There was a woman..."

"That is him. Sometimes he passes himself off as female. But you knew, didn't you? As I said you would. You knew when you saw him."

"Who is he?"

"He is an agent, from a distant empire. It is he who has convinced your father to marry you to the Pallava prince. He is my enemy."

It took a moment before Citta remembered what the word meant.

"Your... enemy?"

"He killed the one I loved."

The expression on his face was so terrible that she almost believed him. However, she had already made her decision.

"No, Hashan the Moor. I saved you, tended you, nursed you because I was trying to do the right thing. Now I understand the skilful course. My path is clear, and I will not be swayed by your cunning tongue.

"I've got you past the Lion Gate. I'm sure you're resourceful enough to escape from here. I'll let you have the knife, but you are not to hurt anybody with it."

"And how will you stop me?"

"You will respect my wishes, Hashan the Moor, or whatever

your real name is, because I saved your life. And out of friendship. And because it is the right thing to do."

Hashan bowed.

"Princess, if anybody comes at me with a weapon, seeking to take my life, then I will do what I have to do to survive. But I swear to you, I will not use this knife to harm any unsuspecting victim."

"Good enough."

Citta stood on tiptoe and kissed him on the cheek.

"Goodbye, and good luck."

She turned and ran back to the Lion Gate. The guards ducked and lowered their weapons at her approach, and she danced past them, feeling more free than she had at any other time since first arriving at the palace in the sky. That night she could not sleep, her head exploding with liberation. She had to stroke herself between the legs, thinking of life and death, of poetry and destruction, and most of all of Hashan's ugly, outrageous member, until everything shuddered to an overwhelming culmination.

The next morning she followed Ayah and Nimali to the herb garden, but a retainer stood in her way.

"Your father wants to see you, my lady."

Citta gagged in terror, but tried to hide her reaction. She trailed behind the servant on the path up to the palace, gazing at the flowers as if it was the last time she would see them. She could not even imagine what might be the punishment for defacing the Mirror Wall. Such a thing was without precedent.

Instead, however, the king met her at the door. Thandivarman stood beside him.

"Peace, daughter. Your husband would like to walk with you, in the grounds of the palace. I said you would be pleased to accompany him."

The princess bobbed and wavered, until Thandivarman stepped forward to take her arm. He steered her gently but firmly back toward the gardens. Courteously, he waited until she had steadied herself before he spoke.

"Your father tells me you are worried, about our marriage."

142

Citta had not even noticed the interpreter jogging along beside them, until his sonorous tones chimed in, drowning out Thandivarman's voice. She said nothing, hoping that her betrothed could not feel the tension in her muscles.

"It is natural, that you feel concern. I, too, have asked myself whether it is right that I should ally myself with a woman of a different faith, a different tongue."

It came as a shock to Citta to discover that Thandivarman might feel reluctant to marry her. She was pretty, and clever, and accomplished, with a slender waist and full, firm breasts. Why was he not madly in love with her? The two voices chimed on, muddying and clashing.

"However I have reassured myself by considering my duty. Those of us born to be leaders and warriors have privileges, but we also have responsibilities. It is the burden of our caste that we may not marry according to our whim, but must consider the needs of our nation."

"I do not believe in caste. The Awakened One taught that it is not birth that makes one a priest or a pariah, it is how one behaves."

The interpreter, who seemed to hear only his master, only noticed she had interrupted when the prince stopped talking, and had to ask her to repeat herself before translating uncertainly into Tamil. Thandivarman looked at her properly for the first time.

"With your gentle heart it is natural that you would have concern for all men, no matter what their status. However I too care for my people, which is why I sacrifice myself to maintain order and stability. It is not compassionate to ask a herdsman to be a warrior, or a carpenter to be a scholar. It is cruel."

Citta pictured Hashan listening secretly nearby, sneering at the prince's words. Thandivarman was warming to his theme.

"The Creator does not make all animals alike. The elephant is not the same as the mouse, the eagle unlike the eel. Each has their place; the eagle can no more live in the water than the eel in the air. And every beast only mates with its own kind.

"That, in the end, is what unites you and me. Whatever our

differences of language or belief, we come from the same class, and that is what is important. However repugnant this union might be to us, we must obey our elders, and trust that we will come to admire each other in time. What is the matter, princess? Are you unwell?"

Citta spent the rest of the day in her room, complaining of a headache. Ayah brought her food at sunset, but the princess did not acknowledge her. Later that evening, Nimali crept through the door.

"Citta? How are you feeling?"

The princess turned over.

"I suppose they have sent you to see what is wrong? Is that it, Nimali? Are you their spy?"

"You would know all about spies, wouldn't you, Ummadha Citta? No, I have come to see how you are, because I am your friend."

"I have not been a good friend to you recently, Nimali. I have neglected you."

Nimali lay down beside her.

"I understand, Citta. These are strange times — with your marriage looming, and..."

"Nimali, I cannot marry Thandivarman."

Nimali stroked her hair.

"I guessed that might be it. You do not love him?"

"He does not love me! He did not even bother to pretend. Why does he not love me, Nimali? What is the matter with me?"

"You are the sweetest darling on earth, and he is an idiot if he does not love you. Perhaps —"

"Don't you dare say we may come to love each other in time! I do not intend to take that chance. Besides —"

Citta hesitated.

"Nimali, can you keep a secret? I think I am in love with someone else. With Hashan the Moor."

She had expected her friend to be shocked, perhaps scared, by this revelation. What she had not anticipated was the cold fury that seized Nimali's face.

"You – you — *princess*! You always have to have everything, don't you? You always have to be the first, the loudest, the cleverest, the sickest, the most important, the centre of the world. Thanks to you I was dragged away from my family and brought to live in this — this prison disguised as a paradise, just because you were feeling sorry for yourself. Now the handsome prince is not enough for you, you must have the glamorous stranger too.

"Well, just for once this story is not about you. If you were not so busy admiring yourself, you might have noticed that it is not you that Hashan wants; it is me. We have been in love for weeks. And I am carrying his child."

Citta struck Nimali across the face. The act was done before the question of what to do had even formed. It was not a heavy blow, but her nails drew blood, three beads dotting her friend's cheek. Nimali grinned, a hard malicious smile of triumph.

Nobody tried to stop Citta leaving the palace, although she was sobbing. It seemed even the new guards were aware of her reputation for moodiness and nocturnal wandering. She flew through the gardens, avoiding the pool, and jumped down the last few steps to the south terrace.

"Where are you, you bastard?"

A faint breath told her he stood behind her. She spun round, and beat at his hairy chest.

"How could you? Here? This was *our* place..."

"Now, princess, attachment is the cause of suffering, is it not?"

He seized her wrists and tried to kiss her. She backed away, but he did not let go, walking with her until she was trapped against the rock wall of the terrace. He pressed his bearded mouth against her lips.

Citta allowed her body to go limp, and he released her wrists. With one hand he stroked her cheek. The other grabbed her breast, squeezing it as if it were fruit he was testing for ripeness. Her knees gave, and she put her arms around the back of his neck, hanging off him to keep herself upright.

He released her breast and reached down. She could feel him tugging at her loincloth, tearing the expensive fabric until loosened,

unwound and fell away from her. He must also have removed his
sarong, as his member was poking impatiently at her belly.

She had imagined he would lay her down and hold her when
he entered her. Instead he turned her round and pushed her onto her
hands and knees. One huge hand covered her mouth, the other he
used to position her body so that he could force himself into her
portal. Citta thought she felt something tear as he shoved. It hurt.

Afterwards, he asked her only one thing.

"You said this was our place. Did you mean yours and mine?
Or yours and hers?"

She fled back to the palace, stopping halfway to arrange her
loincloth so that the damage to the fabric was not visible. The guards
stared straight ahead as she approached, however, and noticed
nothing.

Princess Citta's wedding day dawned dull and cloudy. She
had been spared the lengthy rituals that usually preceded a Shaiva
ceremony, but Thandivarman would not consider them to be truly
married unless they took the vows and made the sacrifice. Women
came from the prince's household to prepare her. They swathed her
in the long dress customary on the mainland, which felt strange
and heavy to Citta, but concealed the bruises on her breasts, black
marks of fingers spreading like spider legs. They painted her hands
with henna, intricate patterns of swirls and dots, leaving only a small
circle undecorated in the centre of her right palm.

Citta endured these attentions with listless indifference. She
did not know what was going to happen to her, and did not care.
Thandivarman would know immediately she was not a virgin, that
much was certain. Hashan had left enough evidence on her body of
his trespass. Perhaps her husband would kill her on their wedding
night. She had no experience to guide her as to what happened in
these circumstances. Perhaps there would be a war.

As evening fell Ayah came to her room.

"It's time, sweetheart. Are you ready?"

Nimali was with her, but the girls did not look at each other.
The rage was spent; there was only emptiness. Side by side they

walked out of the palace and into the gardens.

A small stage had been erected, with a canopy over it. Her father stood there, by an elaborately carved chair, beside which was a sheet of cloth of gold held up by two servants. Citta trudged through the guests who surrounded the stage, both Lion People and Tamils, all in their finest apparel. She noticed the long-faced woman, whom Hashan had told her was really his enemy, standing at the front of the crowd.

When Citta arrived on the stage her father indicated that she should sit in the chair, then took her right hand and passed it underneath the cloth. Another hand seized hers, causing her to jump. Her father was intoning verses in Sanskrit, stumbling over the unfamiliar words.

As he finished the cloth was pulled away, revealing Thandivarman holding her hand. He wore a white turban on his head, and a garland of flowers around his neck. He was smiling, but did not turn to look at her. Beside him was an old man, whom she guessed must be a Brahmin.

Now the old man stepped in front of them, and separated their hands. He placed a coin on the unpainted circle in the middle of her palm. Then he took a corner of her dress, and the end of Thandivarman's pancha, and tied them together.

At the centre of the stage was a copper bowl on a stand. The Brahmin took a flaming torch from an attendant and touched it to the bowl. Flames leapt up.

Citta got to her feet. Her brother poured rice into her palm, and she allowed some of it to trickle into Thandivarman's hand cupped beneath hers. They threw the rice into the bowl, a gift for Agni, the fire god, while Citta spoke the carefully memorised Sanskrit words. It was a prayer to Yama, lord of death, asking that he spare her husband and allow him a long and healthy life.

Now they began to walk around the fire, four slow circles for the four goals of a good life. The first represented righteousness, the second material wealth, the third sensual enjoyment. For the fourth, spiritual liberation, Citta took over the lead.

There were seven more steps to be taken around the fire, then the ritual would be complete. At each step the Brahmin would recite a prayer; and after the seventh step they would be married.

"May the Lord, Great Vishnu, follow your steps. May he grant you plentiful food. May he grant you health and vigour. May he impel you to perform the rituals required by the Vedas, throughout your lives. May he grant you happiness. May your cattle and other livestock fatten and proliferate..."

Citta barely raised her eyes from the ground as she walked, so it was not until the fifth step that she noticed a figure at the rear of the wedding guests. She could see him clearly, as he was a head taller than any of the Lion People, or the Tamils who had come with Thandivarman. His hair was long and tangled, and his beard unshaven. Hashan the Moor had come to her wedding.

"May he make all the seasons of the year profitable to you..."

She had stumbled into the sixth step without thought, driven mainly by shock at his appearance and Thandivarman's insistent tug. The next time her foot hit the ground she would be married. Hashan smiled and beckoned to her. Princess Ummadha Citta turned and ran.

Thandivarman released her hand in surprise, but something tugged at her ankle, and she fell to the ground. She had forgotten that she was tied to him. Desperately, she began to wriggle out of her dress. Ayah and Nimali rushed over to her. The men hovered nervously, fearsome warriors reduced to ineffectual uncertainty.

"I think she's having some kind of fit..."

Freed from the heavy fabric of the dress, Citta staggered to her feet. Ayah tried to restrain her, but she writhed away from the old woman's grip, sprang from the stage and darted away, dodging between startled guards and guests.

These unexpected events commanded everybody's attention, and so far Hashan had gone unnoticed. It was only when she burst out of the circle and flung herself at him that they saw him. A woman shrieked. Hashan grinned.

"Come with me, and live."

"They'll kill us both."

Despite her words she was already racing off. The Moor bounded after her. The guests were milling in confusion, impeding the guards, who had been concentrated around the stage, and were now trying to mount a pursuit. A spear flew past Citta, and she heard a cry of "No!"

Hashan had caught up with her, and without any discussion they headed for the south terrace. The guards and the wedding guests thundered after them. Citta noticed the glint of metal in Hashan's hand. It was the knife she had given him.

"No. If you use that, I stay here."

He laughed, and hurled it away. Hand in hand they leapt onto the terrace. Behind them was a pack of furious warriors. Ahead lay a sheer drop, the lands of the Lion People sprawling below.

"Well, this is it. Do we jump to our deaths, or wait for the steel?"

Hashan flung his arms round her, and span her around as if in a crazy dance. She did not resist. If she was about to die, she wanted to be kissed. He did not kiss her, however, and was looking elsewhere. His attention was focused on a belt, consisting of long strips of cloth tied at their ends, which he was winding round them both. Each spin bound their torsos more strongly together.

She swung her head away from him, and saw the guards descending the steps. They would be on them in an instant. She shook Hashan urgently, and he stopped their dance, instead lurching towards the precipice. Holding her tightly, he hurled himself into the air.

At first they dropped heavily. Then they stopped with a jerk, as if a giant asura had grabbed the end of the cloth rope, which trailed away above them. Citta nearly slipped, but the belt and Hashan's arms gripped her tightly. She looked up, and saw that a silken canopy, like that under which she was to have been married, had opened out above her.

They still fell, but the canopy slowed them, just enough. It also carried them away from the Lion Rock, drifting over the city wall before the ground rushed up and slammed into them.

Citta landed on top of Hashan, and gave thanks that it was not his huge body crushing hers. She got up first.

"Are you all right?"

He groaned, and heaved himself upright.

"I'll have to be."

"So what now? They will have horses, and elephants, and hunting dogs. We still have to travel one hundred miles to the coast, with the entire country pursuing us. Then find a ship to carry us —"

"Hush. Follow me. I have everything under control."

X

"Well, what happened? Did they get away?"

"The Commander of the Faithful favours us with a fine jest. If they had been caught, your servant would not be standing here before you today."

"Yes, yes, of course. I knew that. And what of the princess?"

Abu Nuwas shrugged.

"I brought her safely to Baghdad, where she made a good marriage to an officer in the Shurtah."

The Khalifah fidgeted on his cushions. His backside was troubling him again.

"This is all very diverting, but I fail to see what it has to do with your current crimes."

"All will become clear, Commander of the Faithful. The next story —"

Masrur broke in.

"Master, Prince al-Ma'mun and Prince al-Amin are without. They humbly inquire whether you will be joining them on the hunt this afternoon."

"Good, good. Have them brought before me."

Al-Rashid puffed with pride to see his sons enter the chamber: strong, handsome boys on the cusp of manhood. He could see himself in each of them, although in contrasting ways, as though he was viewing himself in a mirror from different angles. Al-Ma'mun, the older, was pale, with his great-grandfather's commanding, angry presence, while the younger al-Amin was dark, slender, and serene. Al-Ma'mun bowed.

"Commander of the Faithful, we come to learn your will. If it no longer pleases you to ride out today, we shall dismiss the servants and go about our business."

"I have not yet decided. The poet Abu Ali ibn Hani al-Hakami, known as the Father of Locks, has been condemned to death, for the crimes of murder and treason. He has requested that this storyteller speak on his behalf, and together they have beguiled me with tales, but as yet offered neither excuse nor explanation. What do you say, my sons? Should I hear them out, or make an end of it and go hunting? What is your counsel?"

Al-Rashid observed the tension in his sons' faces. Although he had already made his wishes known as far as the succession was concerned, it was not too late for him to change his mind, and every such question was a test which might determine their destiny. Al-Ma'mun was first to venture an opinion.

"Father, your people have missed you, while you have been away on pilgrimage. There is much to be done in Baghdad: petitions to be heard, appointments to be determined, disputes to be settled. My counsel is that you do neither, but instead spend the afternoon at your diwan."

The Khalifah smiled indulgently.

"My son, your diligence does you credit. However, you must learn that pleasure is a duty for a ruler of men. A prince who thinks only of his responsibilities finds his mood souring, his spirit darkening. In time, the great weight of care will crush him, bring him to madness and tyranny. You must find the time to hunt, to be with your women, to listen to songs and stories, for the good of your people."

Al-Ma'mun's pale face turned whiter still. Al-Amin fussed with his robes, teasing the red silk with delicate fingers, before speaking.

"If their yarns entertain you, Commander of the Faithful, then by all means let them speak. However, should they be wasting your time, simply delaying the execution for as long as possible, then they both deserve to be punished. Let the storyteller share the poet's fate, if his testimony proves to be unconvincing."

Harun al-Rashid clapped his hands.

"Excellent! Such wisdom, such acumen. I see that I was right to name you as first in line. Storyteller, if your tale's end does not satisfy me, then your end will follow promptly after."

Out of the corner of his eye he noticed the shock on the face of Abu Nuwas. The poet, so nonchalant until now, mouthed a horrified, silent apology to the storyteller, who simply nodded. For a moment al-Rashid regretted his pronouncement, but he knew that he could not appear weak and indecisive in front of his sons. The storyteller bowed.

"If I fail to please you, Commander of the Faithful, then my life is worthless in any case; so I shall dally no longer, but proceed with my tale. It takes place in the city of Rome: not New Rome in the east, capital of Christendom, but in the ancient city of that name, which lies in the west, in al-Italiya. And the name of this story is..."

The Tale of the Elephant and the Dragon

Fucking the Pope had not been nearly as much fun as Hervor had expected. For one thing, there was an air of desperate gratitude about the old priest that both repelled Hervor and made her feel guilty. Pope Leo was clearly no virgin, but neither was he accustomed to beautiful women propositioning him. She had only to place temptation in his way, and he seized it eagerly. And when they were finally alone together, he spurted all over her before even entering her, and it took all night to coax him back to action.

She would not normally have accepted such a commission. She was a warrior, not a courtesan. However, there was something about the sacrilege which appealed to her. Hervor had been raised in Christian lands, she attended mass and even took communion, but it always seemed to her to be a foreign religion, alien and effeminate. In her soul she still favoured the gods of her people, one-eyed Odinn, fierce Thorr and the trickster Loki.

Besides, it had been a difficult time for her. She had just come to the end of a torrid romance with the pirate Rurik. After swearing eternal love to her, he had succumbed to the grumbling of his crew, who objected to having a woman on board and complained that she was making him soft. He had abandoned her in a flophouse in Neapolis, sneaking out at dawn and sailing away, leaving her heartbroken and penniless. When the message came from Paschalis, inviting her to Old Rome, it offered not only a chance to make some money, but in some obscure way to avenge herself on Rurik, by defiling the memory of the passion they had shared.

She had fulfilled her side of the bargain, using the letter Paschalis gave her to secure an audience with the Pope. Once Leo set eyes on her, she had little difficulty in persuading him to smuggle her into his private quarters. If Paschalis had managed to capture the Pope as planned, she would be on her way to Paderborn now, bags laden with gold. However the inbred buffoon had botched the arrest, and in consequence she now languished in a cell in the Mausoleum of Hadrianus.

As she sat through the long, tedious days she tried to occupy herself with fantasies of revenge on Paschalis, but she could not muster any real hatred. In truth she blamed her own stupidity more than she blamed the Roman. She was no silly maiden but a mature woman of twenty-six years, and should have known better that to get involved in such an ill-considered venture. Instead, her reveries dwelt on Rurik, on his hot, mocking eyes and lean body. Unexpectedly, she also found herself thinking about the first person to have broken her heart, a pale, slight boy she had met one summer, in the faraway city of Baghdad.

It was not the first time she had been imprisoned, and certainly not the worst she had been treated. The cell was bare but dry, with a crude bed on which to sleep, and she was not beaten or molested. Previously though she had always been able to rely on the intervention of the King of the Franks to liberate her. On the rare occasion that his word was not enough to open the door, force had soon followed. Now, however, she had acted without his sanction, fled from his service. When a familiar figure entered her cell, therefore, hope and dread battled in her breast.

"Hervor, my dear, whatever have you got yourself entangled in now?"

Angilbert was a sleek man, growing portly with advancing years but still handsome. He wore the robes of an abbot, but his costly belt and oiled moustache spoke of worldliness and wealth. He sat on the bed beside her, and the guard locked the door from outside.

"Can you get me out of here?"

Angilbert patted her hand.

"Well, now, my dear, I don't know about that. We'll have to see. King Karlo was very upset when he heard that the Pope had had his eyes put out and his tongue cut off."

"Then he must have been very surprised when the Pope walked into his palace to tell him about it in person."

"Yes, well, the Holy Father explained that. It seems that God intervened, miraculously restoring his sight and speech, demonstrating irrefutably that Leo is the rightful Vicar of Christ."

"Divine providence is truly a wondrous thing."

"Indeed. But you must understand, we cannot have armed men bursting into a church and kidnapping the Bishop of Rome in the middle of mass. It simply won't do."

"Even if he is guilty of fornication?"

"Ah, now we come to the crux of the matter. Paschalis and his accomplices were motivated by jealousy and arrogance. They cannot accept that a low-born cleric such as Leo might rise to the office of Pope. They believe that the post should be reserved for members of a handful of patrician dynasties; their own family, of course, being one. They have concocted these charges purely to discredit him."

"But I —"

"The Pope is not guilty of fornication."

Angilbert's tone was bright and hard as steel, and Hervor dropped her head. He stood up.

"You understand how these things work, Hervor, better than anyone. If you had been some common trollop you would already be lying on the dungheap with your throat cut. However, I like you, and you have served us well in the past. You should never have run away —"

Hervor's eyes blazed.

"I am a free woman, Father Abbot, a shieldmaiden of the Rus. I am not your slave, and I am not bound to you or your master by any oath of allegiance. I go where I please."

"So you do, and I would not have it any other way. Consorting with pirates, though, and conspiring against the Pope: these are not the actions of a woman who wishes to remain free."

"What do you know about Rurik? Have you been spying on

me?"

Angilbert laughed.

"I need no spies to tell me about you and Rurik. A beautiful golden-haired woman who wields a sword like a man, sailing with a notorious privateer? You are the talk of the western Mediterranean. However, your question is curiously apposite to my purpose in visiting you."

He sat down again, and Hervor tried to concentrate. When Angilbert became prolix, it usually meant that the serious business was about to begin.

"Are you familiar with the Satires of Decimus Junius Juvenalis?"

Hervor looked blankly at him.

"No, of course, the appeal of the literary arts has always been lost on you. What was it you said to me once? 'I have no appetite for poetry, give me a fight, a feast and a fuck any time.' So charmingly and succinctly expressed, it has stayed with me to this day..."

"Get on with it."

"As you wish. The Sixth Satire poses a very interesting question: *'Quis custodiet ipsos custodes?* — Who will watch the watchers themselves?' Our friend Juvenalis was concerned about the fidelity of his mistress, and the risks inherent in asking his friends to keep an eye on her. We, however, might consider another interpretation of the question: who will spy on the spies?

"It is a problem that must be considered by any ruler of consequence. Every state must have its secret servants, its agents of intelligence and discreet violence, just as a body has its private functions which are necessary but are not to be discussed or displayed. Yet this vital organ of government also brings with it dangers. For when the left hand does not know what the right hand is doing, how can it be certain that the right hand is not plotting to do it harm?

"Have you ever stood between two mirrors, so that each reflects the other, and looked upon your image, echoing within itself into infinity? Such is the world of the spymaster. One must have agents within the enemy's agents, agents to report on one's own agents, agents among one's agents whom the enemy believes to be secretly working for him, but are in fact working for you. At times the layers of deception threaten one's sanity, and it is no longer clear which is reflection and which is reality.

"But such ruminations need not concern you. Ever pragmatic, I can see you are waiting for the part where I release you from this cell. Well then, I have a task for you. When it is complete, you may go where you will, and do as you like. There are two conditions, however. The first is that you do not attempt to cross me. Bear in mind, that just as I will set you to spy upon a spy, so I will also be spying on you. I have spared your life once; do not assume that I will do so again."

"And the second?"

"You did not fornicate with the Pope."

"You mean —"

"I am not asking for your silence on the matter. I am informing you that, whatever you think you remember happening, you did not fornicate with the Pope. Are you experiencing any difficulties with your memory in this regard?"

"No, I clearly recollect not fucking the Pope. I remember not doing it as though it were not yesterday."

"Good. Now then, to your task. An old friend of ours has arrived in the city. Do you recall our visit to Baghdad, some eleven years ago?"

"You mean when my father was killed?"

"Yes, that was unfortunate. You may remember then a certain long-haired poet?"

"The one they called Abu Nuwas."

"Indeed. He is in Rome, accompanying the embassy of the King of the Persians."

"Do you want me to kill him?"

"No, no. Not yet at least. I simply want to know what he is up to. I hope, Hervor, you do not harbour any primitive Northern urges to avenge your father?"

"My father fell in battle, in the war that he had chosen to fight. He is at peace."

"I am pleased to hear it. There is another spy in the city, too, from the court of the Empress Irene in New Rome. Unfortunately I do not know who he is. If you happen to discover his identity, feel free to indulge your murderous inclinations."

"Did I hear you correctly? I may kill Irene's spy, but not the Arab? Has King Karlo converted to Islam, then? Do we no longer owe allegiance to the Empress as the head of Christendom?"

"The King of the Franks acknowledges the supremacy of the Emperor of the Romans — as long as she does not presume to interfere in his affairs. There are those, of course, who argue that a woman cannot occupy the throne, and therefore the office of Emperor is currently vacant. These questions are not relevant to us, however.

"In the world of the mirror, left becomes right and right left. In the world of the spymaster, one's friends are a greater threat than one's foes. Enemies can be relied upon, they are dependable in their antagonism, but allies are uncertain and treacherous. The presence of Abu Nuwas in Rome is intriguing, but that of Irene's agent is intolerable."

"I understand, and accept your gracious offer, Father Abbot. How do I find this Abu Nuwas?"

"You might try going to see the elephant..."

***

Abu'l-Abbas was thirty years old. He stood nearly eight cubits tall at the shoulder, and weighed around a thousand pounds. His skin was white, which was unusual for his kind, and hung in wrinkled flaps from his enormous frame. He contemplated Hervor with a sad yellow eye, and flicked his trunk in idle indifference.

Elephants had once been a common attraction in old Rome, in the days when the city was the heart of an empire. Now they were rarely seen, and when Abu'l-Abbas first lumbered off the ship onto the harbour at Portus he had caused considerable consternation.

Officials scuttled around, frantically seeking a place where the beast could safely be accommodated. At last someone recalled that the old Flavian amphitheatre contained pens specifically designed to hold elephants, and so Abu'l-Abbas had entered Rome at the head of an impromptu procession of loafers, gawkers and shrieking children, and plodded ponderously and very publicly through the streets to his new home.

After this ostentatious arrival, everybody in the city wanted to see the elephant, from the haughtiest nobleman to the foulest beggar. Hervor had to elbow her way through the crowds to get near it. The pen had long been in use as a warehouse, so the merchant whose stock had been unceremoniously removed to make way for Abu'l Abbas was trying to recoup his losses by charging for access to the beast. Hervor had forked over a gold solidus, and found herself in a draughty stone vault that reeked of straw, shit, and an unknown odour that could only be elephant.

The beast himself stood patiently at the centre of the pen. Beside him a bent old man, presumably his keeper, was tapping him gently with a long pole and muttering into his flapping ears. There were other Romans around; those curious and wealthy enough to have paid to get close to him walked slowly around him, in a circle the bounds of which were precisely delineated by the equilibrium of fascination and fear.

The animal looked dolorous and sick, starved of sunlight. Hervor was not given to sentimentality, but her recent imprisonment engendered a pang of compassion. A teasing voice intruded on her thoughts.

"An interesting choice of gift, is it not? I think I would rather have had gold. It does not smell quite so bad."

She turned to see who had spoken. Beside her was a tall, dark man with a beard and turban. He was older than when she had first met him, a little heavier and more lined, but it was unmistakably the poet Abu Nuwas. She wondered whether he recognised her, and kept her response carefully neutral in tone.

"They say it is a great honour, that the elephant is a symbol of royalty, and that by this gift the King of the Persians recognises Karlo as a monarch of equal standing."

Abu Nuwas stroked his beard.

"One might say that. One might also say that it suggests the King of the Franks is an ignorant barbarian, easily pleased by flashy baubles of no real value."

He grinned at her shocked expression.

"White elephants such as this are known to be sickly, useless for war or transport. In any case, the Righteous One would never consider your Karlo as an equal. Our ruler is no mere king. In our language we call him Khalifah, which means Successor to the Prophet. He leads us in spiritual matters as well as temporal; something like your Pope and Emperor combined in a single person. But then you know that, don't you, shieldmaiden?"

Abu Nuwas seemed very pleased with himself. Hervor resolved not to give him the satisfaction of showing surprise.

"I was young when I visited your country, little more than a child, and did not learn to speak its language. The finer points of its political structure escaped me at the time. How is Ismail?"

The poet's smile faded.

"I have not seen him for a while. He left Baghdad suddenly, without saying goodbye. Would you like to meet Abu'l Abbas?"

Hervor noted how quickly he had changed the subject, but did not pursue it.

"Is it safe to approach him?"

"Unless you intend to poke him with a stick or blow a trumpet in his ear, then yes. He is a gentle soul, and accustomed to being handled."

They walked over to the animal. The handler greeted them in Arabic, but Abu Nuwas waved a finger.

"In Latin, if you please, Ziri! We cannot have my friend here thinking we are keeping secrets from her."

The old man coughed and squinted. He seemed to embody the rule that keepers came to resemble their beasts, for his nose was long and his ears drooped from the side of his bald head.

"Very pretty, Abu Ali, but not your usual type, eh? Eh?"

"Ziri, may I present an old friend of mine. This is..."

She realised, to her annoyance, that he did not remember her name.

"Hervor. My name is Hervor."

Then she added, with a touch of defiance:

"Hervor, Gorm's daughter."

Abu Nuwas did not react to the mention of the man he had killed. Instead he took her hand.

"Don't be afraid."

He pressed her palm against the elephant's flank. Its skin was warm, rough, but not unpleasant, like wrinkled leather. She watched Abu Nuwas stroke the elephant with absent-minded familiarity.

"Did you travel with it from Egypt?"

"No, I only joined the embassy at Tunis. However Abu'l-Abbas seems to have taken a liking to me on the voyage."

Hervor jumped as something touched her neck. It was the elephant's trunk, which it now draped affectionately around her shoulders. The keeper Ziri sidled up to her.

"Do you know, miss, about the elephant and the dragon?"

She shook her head, a little nervously.

"The dragon sits in the branches of a tree, along the road which the elephants follow to their feeding grounds. When an elephant passes by, the dragon drops from the tree and wraps the elephant in its coils, strangling it and sucking its blood. When the elephant dies, it crashes to the ground, crushing the dragon beneath it; and the dragon too is killed."

Hervor shivered, puzzled by this strange tale. Ziri stared at her as if expecting some response. She shook off the fear, and spoke calmly.

"That must be why you see so few dragons these days."

Ziri laughed, a wheezing, sputtering noise.

"So few dragons... that's very good. I like you, Hervor Gorm's daughter."

Abu Nuwas gently removed the trunk from her shoulders.

"Come, shieldmaiden. Shall we walk?"

They pushed their way through the throngs outside the pen, and strolled slowly around the amphitheatre. In the galleries below the seats, where gladiators, wild beasts and prisoners once waited to face their deaths, there were now workshops, storerooms and cheap apartments, the kind where sleeping space and cooking space were separated by a rough curtain, and everything else took place outside. Children ran and skipped and begged, and Hervor placed a protective hand over her purse.

Abu Nuwas steered her down one of the tunnels that opened out onto the arena. Here, a small church and cemetery radiated a sombre calm. The winter sun was shining, and after three months in a windowless cell Hervor was glad to see it.

"Strange to think how many must have died on this very spot... and now it is a graveyard. This circle must be a well, a pit where darkness seeps into the world."

Hervor shivered at the poet's grim words.

"Take me away from here."

The banks of seats that ringed the arena had become common ground, a place for workmen to eat a meal or drunkards to sleep away the afternoon. Abu Nuwas clambered up some tumbled blocks, and hauled Hervor up behind him. They found a spot away from other people, and sheltered from the brisk wind.

"So, shieldmaiden, what are we doing then?"

It was a dangerously vague question. Almost any response she made would give him information. Hervor stared at him unflinchingly and waited for more. After a while, he obliged.

"All right then. Let me tell you what I believe we are doing, and let us see if we can share any articles of faith."

He scratched at his chin.

"You are Angilbert's agent, that much is given, but why has he sent you? Not to kill me, or you would not have come so brazenly. To watch over me, then. To find out what business I have in old Rome."

He leaned forward, peering at her face as though there

really were words written there.

"Your pallor, the hunger in your eyes... you have been ill. No, in prison. An argument with your masters, perhaps?"

Hervor tried not to move a muscle, but could not prevent a twitch of her left eye. Abu Nuwas sat back.

"I see I am right. Then you are here because that is the price of your freedom, to spy on me and find out what I am doing here. Well, I shall endeavour to remain interesting enough to be kept alive.

"And we need not be enemies, you and I. I speak, you understand, not as Abu Ali ibn Hani of the Hakami tribe to Hervor Gorm's daughter, of the Rus. I speak as the Land of Islam, if that is not too presumptuous, to you, the Kingdom of the Franks and the Lombards. Inasmuch as we represent our employers, there is no reason why we should fight. We have no common borders or disputed territories to contest; our interests do not conflict.

"We do, however, share a common foe. You know what I mean, shieldmaiden. Why should King Karlo, warrior, conqueror, and leader of men, have to bend his knee to the Emperor of the Romans? Particularly when that Emperor is a Greek woman who appoints her eunuchs and secretaries to run the army and the church?

"Your enemy is our enemy. So we need not be enemies, you and I; unless, that is, we have personal matters to settle. I might mention, at this point, that it was entirely business, between your father and me. He was trying to kill me, and I got there first. I say this only so that you know the truth. You must do whatever you think is right. Do we have personal matters to settle, shieldmaiden?"

Hervor found she could not talk, and shook her head.

"I must hazard my life on whether I believe you or not... but I find that I do. I am glad. Vengeance is a painful hunger, and leaves only sorrow behind when it is sated. I thank God the Compassionate that you have been spared it.

"Your masters sent you to learn why I have come to Rome. I shall save you the trouble of doing whatever it was you were going to do to find out. I will tell you what I am here for, as a gesture of friendship, and so that your masters understand that I am not acting against the interests of the King of Europe. You may inform your employers that I have something to sell. Ask them what they would be prepared to pay, for an original, sealed copy of the Donation of Constantinus."

Abu Nuwas waited expectantly for a response, but Hervor's face was blank. He sighed.

"You have no idea what that means, have you? I suppose you have never heard of Pope Sylvester, the Dragon, and the blood of three thousand children? Then I shall tell you. It is a tale that takes place five hundred years ago, when Christians were as few in number and as scattered as the Jews, and the emperors of Rome still worshipped the pagan gods..."

***

It was a time of discord and division, of conspiracy and civil war. An empire cannot thrive with two rulers, any more than a man can live with two heads. Yet the Emperor Diocletianus, who had fought so hard to reunite the Roman provinces, found them unmanageable, bloated and fractious. So he appointed a second Emperor, an Augustus, to assist him; then, as his health failed, divided their powers once more, so that four men, the Tetrarchs, shared sovereignty.

When Diocletianus, at the age of sixty, relinquished his burden and retired to Dalmatia to potter around his vegetable gardens, the outcome was inevitable. The Tetrarchs mobilised their legions and contended with each other for supremacy. For twenty years war raged across the Empire, bringing slaughter, sickness and famine wherever it passed. Finally a victor emerged: Constantinus, who had been proclaimed emperor in the city of Eboracum, in the chilly northern province of Britannia Secunda, and now entered Rome in triumph as undisputed sovereign.

Constantinus, though, was not to enjoy his victory. For no sooner had he taken up residence in the imperial palace than a hideous rash appeared across his handsome face. Despite the best efforts of both physicians and priests, who sacrificed daily to the god Asclepius on his behalf, the rash worsened, spreading across his whole body, his skin flaking and rotting. In time he could no longer bear to be seen in public, and spent his days secluded in his chamber.

His ministers offered an extravagant reward to anyone who could cure the emperor of his disease. There came an Arab to his court, a learned man, who examined Constantinus, then asked to speak to the ministers in private.

"This is not a natural malady, and therefore it requires an unnatural cure. There is one recourse which we might try; but only if you are certain that every other possibility has been exhausted, for it is a terrible and cruel thing that you must do."

Despite the Arab's ominous words, they insisted that he tell them his remedy. The Arab answered reluctantly.

"Then you must fashion a vessel of pure silver, large enough to immerse a man completely. Fill it with the blood of children and babies, each no more than seven years of age. When the emperor bathes in the blood, his disease will be cured, and the blemishes fall from his skin."

The ministers were shocked at this suggestion, but decided that they needed to put it to Constantinus. The emperor looked up at them, his blotched face weary.

"Is it truly the only way?"

They talked late into the night. At first they all agreed that it could not be countenanced, that it would be an abomination. Then the conversation turned to the recent civil war, and the stability that Constantinus had brought to the empire. If he sickened and died, further upheaval was inevitable. How many would perish then? How many children would starve, or be orphaned, or otherwise suffer?

In the end it came down to numbers. Three thousand children, they decided, was a price worth paying. They were to be drawn from every part of the empire, like tax, so that the grief would be spread thin. While the emperor's smiths melted down silver to make the bath, messengers boarded ships with the decree written on a strip of leather, from which the grim instructions could only be read if wrapped around a cylinder of a precisely measured girth.

The secret could not be kept for long, though. When shiploads of screaming children began to arrive at Ostia, understanding spread like a plague, the knowledge of the awful choice that faced the empire.

There was no protest, no outrage or insurrection. The necessity for the sacrifice was understood. Throughout all ages youth is the coinage in which war extracts its price. The Romans sought to make a bargain with the gods, offering to pay a heavy price now in order to avoid a much greater one at a later time.

No, there was no anger at the emperor's decree. Instead the mothers gathered at the walls of the palace, near the cells where their children were held. They wept, and prayed, and called to the infants, cries of love and reassurance. It scarcely mattered whether it was their own issue with whom they communed; it mattered only that the little ones were comforted.

All that night Constantinus listened to the shouts and sobs from outside in the darkness. He heard women's voices catch as they offered consolation, made promises that they knew to be false.

"Hush, my child. All will be well. All will be well..."

In the morning the emperor summoned his ministers.

"This has gone far enough. Who are we, to balance one life against another as though souls were merchandise that we can weigh and measure? Who is to say that my life is worth one of these children's, let alone three thousand? It seems to me now that one cannot trade misery for misery. No act of cruelty prevents or ameliorates another; rather, each evil deed only augments the world's store of evil.

"Send the children home; I will place my life in the hands of the gods. He who would be master, must always be servant to pity."

It was as though the whole empire breathed out at once. The gates of the prison were opened, and the people rushed to embrace the infants. And that night, the Emperor Constantinus slept peacefully for the first time in months.

He was awakened in the noiseless hour before dawn by a

presence in his bedchamber. Two men stood there, pleasing to look upon but indistinct. One was bulky and bearded, a common artisan. The other had a scholar's sparseness, and was dressed in priestly robes. Words rumbled through the emperor's being.

"Constantinus, because you have shown mercy, mercy will be shown to you. Twice you will be healed, first in your soul, then in your body. Do not be afraid, because your sickness will not worsen while your servants seek out Sylvester, leader of the Christian church in Rome, and bring him back to the city. You will need no other physician than him."

Constantinus tried to get up, but found that his limbs would not obey his commands. He tried to speak to the men, desperate to prevent or delay their leaving.

"I thank you, my lords, but please, I need to know... when I send to Sylvester, who shall I say recommended me to him? What are your names, and what is your social class?"

"We are Petrus and Paulus, who died here in Rome for our faith. Now we call on Sylvester to baptise you, so that the Empire of Rome might become the Kingdom of the Lord."

They disappeared, and Constantinus jerked awake. At that moment the first glimmers of dawnlight trickled into his chamber. He summoned his attendants, and by noon men were riding through the city in search of Bishop Sylvester.

Sylvester was a gentle and pious man, who had held to his faith throughout the persecutions ordered by Diocletianus. When he saw the soldiers approaching he assumed that they were coming to arrest him. His companions urged him to hide or flee, but instead he calmly knelt and prayed. A centurion dismounted before him.

"The Emperor needs you. Come with me."

In Rome, Sylvester was astounded to be escorted, not to a prison cell, but to the imperial palace and the chamber of Constantinus himself. The emperor told him of his disease, the dreadful remedy that had been prescribed, and of his vision. Sylvester grasped his hands in joy.

"Praise the Lord God who has bestowed such blessings

upon you!"

Words bubbled out of Sylvester, inspired and irresistible. He talked about the Fall of Man in the Garden of Eden, how God had sent his only son to die for men's sins, and of the resurrection and judgement that was to come. Constantinus listened with his head bowed, and when Sylvester had finished there were tears in his eyes.

"Father — *Pappas* — I am ready to accept Jesus Christ as my Lord and Saviour. Will you baptise me?"

Sylvester ordered them to bring the silver vessel, that had been forged for the emperor's bath of blood. They filled it with pure water, and Constantinus immersed himself therein. At once a dazzling light streamed down from the heavens. Scales fell from the emperor's body like those of a fish, and his skin was left whole and flawless.

The people rejoiced at their ruler's recovery, but Constantinus' mother, Empress Helena, was troubled by his conversion.

"My son, I am glad that you have forsaken the worship of false idols. However, I do not understand why you have fallen in with this cult, and venerate a mere carpenter, an executed criminal. Surely the faith of the Jews is the true faith of the One God?"

So Constantinus ordered the twelve wisest and most learned of the Jews of Rome to attend on him, and debate with Sylvester and his priests in the Forum. Two pagans were appointed to judge the disputation. The rabbis argued cunningly, but Sylvester answered every point, using reason and his knowledge of scripture to refute their case. The pagans announced that Christianity had triumphed, but the leader of the Jews, a man called Zambry, would not accept their judgement.

"I marvel that you who are considered sagacious have been so easily swayed by mere words. Very well then, let us leave words and turn to deeds."

He clapped his hands, and at once a fierce bull appeared in the Forum. The people were astounded, and the women screamed in fright. Zambry however walked coolly up to the bull and whispered in its ear. The beast dropped dead on the spot. Sylvester was unperturbed.

"It is no great matter to kill a bull. Any butcher can do as much. Let him bring it back to life though, and I will believe that his power comes from God, not from evil sorcery."

Zambry scowled.

"No man can restore life once it has departed the body. If you can resurrect this animal in the name of Jesus of Galileia, then I and all my followers will embrace Christianity."

Sylvester breathed a silent prayer, then knelt by the bull.

"You devil that has killed this poor creature, I command you to depart; and you, bull, arise and leave this place."

The bull snorted, kicked and struggled to its feet, then walked from the Forum as meekly as a lamb. All those present were baptised that very day, including Zambry and the other rabbis. The Empress Helena, too, converted, and went on pilgrimage to Jerusalem, where she was miraculously to discover the True Cross.

However Satan would not relinquish his grip on the empire willingly. He caused a dragon to appear in a cave near the city, which killed hundreds with its noxious breath. The priests of the pagan gods complained to the emperor.

"Since you have embraced this upstart religion, it has brought only disaster on your people."

Constantinus begged Sylvester to deliver Rome from the dragon, so the bishop set out for the cave accompanied by two priests. It was not difficult to locate the monster's lair, for the land before it was blasted by its foul vapours. No vegetation grew there, and the rotting corpses of animals lay scattered around.

Undeterred by the appalling stench, Sylvester and the priests entered the cave bearing lanterns. One hundred and fifty steps they took into the bowels of the earth, and then the vile worm reared up before them, black eyes glittering in its crested head. Sylvester however was unafraid, as Saint Petrus had appeared to him in a dream and told him how to defeat the monster. He called out in a forceful voice.

"Our Lord Jesus Christ, that was born of a Virgin, died on

the cross and rose again, will come on the last day to judge the living and the dead. I bind you, demon, to remain in this place until that day."

And he sewed shut the mouth of the dragon with thread, and sealed it with the sign of the cross. Having subdued the worm, he returned to the surface, along the way discovering two of the pagan priests, who had followed him to see what he would do, and had passed out from inhaling the dragon's breath. He brought them back to the city where they recovered and converted to Christianity, as did thousands of others, in gratitude for their liberation from the dragon.

Constantinus too wanted to show his gratitude. He called Bishop Sylvester before him, in the presence of a great multitude.

"Father, you have saved the city from two deaths: the death of the body, caused by the poisonous breath of the dragon, and the death of the soul, to which we were doomed by our idolatry and impiety. In the same way you have twice healed me, cleansing my spirit with the word of God, and purging me of the disease that disfigured my skin.

"In all this, I am mindful that you have been guided by Saint Petrus, your predecessor in office as Bishop of Rome. You have taught me that Christ gave the fisherman Simon the name of Petrus, meaning 'rock', and said to him, 'On this rock I will build my church.' Further, the Lord told him, 'I give to you the keys to the kingdom of heaven. What you bind on earth shall be bound in heaven, and what you loose on earth shall be loosed in heaven.'

"I therefore decree that the office of Bishop of Rome shall be exalted and revered throughout Christendom, having authority over the other four Patriarchs and all other churches of God. Furthermore, I give to you and your successors in perpetuity dominion over the city of Rome itself, the towns and provinces of Italia, and all the lands of the west, from Britannia to Sicilia. In token of this I bestow upon you the Lateran Palace, finest of all my residences, and confer upon you the right to wear the tiara, the royal diadem.

"I shall depart these shores and take myself to the east of the empire. There I will build a new capital for myself, on the site of the ancient city of Byzantium. I will make this New Rome my home and the seat of my power, so that none may deny your authority, both spiritual and secular.

"This is my imperial decree, which I declare to be binding on the Senate, the people and all my successors until the end of time. If any should oppose my will, let him be cast from the church of God, and burn in hell with Satan and his minions for all eternity. May God bless you and preserve you for many years, holy father, *Pappas et Pontifex*."

XI

"Is all that true?"

"Whatever do you mean?"

"An emperor of Rome, ordering human sacrifice, the slaughter of children, on a massive scale? And his people tolerating it? Even Caligula never attempted such an atrocity. Frankly, I found the dragon more plausible."

"It is a pity, young lady, that destiny drove you apart from my friend Ismail. You and he share a grimly prosaic obsession with literal truth. On what grounds do you challenge my veracity?"

"Well, for one thing, in your story Constantinus referred to the four Patriarchs. They are the bishops of Jerusalem, Antioch, Alexandria, and...?"

"New Rome, of course."

"Which he then announces his intention of going to found. How can the city have had a bishop, when it didn't exist yet?"

Abu Nuwas frowned impatiently.

"A mere detail. What is important is not whether it really happened or not, but whether people believe it did. And consider the implications for your masters. When the Emperor failed to protect Rome from Lombard aggression, the Pope turned to the King of the Franks for help. Your Karlo conquered the invaders and made himself their king. Since then he has been the Pope's most important ally.

"If the Bishop of Rome is the supreme authority in the western lands, then Karlo owes allegiance only to him, and not to the Emperor. The King of the Franks and the Lombards would no longer be a vassal of Irene, but her equal. Now, if we could produce an original document, sealed by Constantinus himself, proving that the Donation was a genuine imperial decree, what price might they put on such a thing?"

Hervor cocked her head to one side, and studied him. Then she nodded.

"So where is this precious document?"

"I don't know. But I have a friend who does."

An early dusk was settling as they approached the house of the scholar Vadomar. The poet's friend, he explained as they strolled the arrow-straight streets of Old Rome, was an Allamanus from the icy Alpes mountains. Vadomar had come to the city in search of knowledge, and trained as a priest purely so that he could learn to read and write. Nominally he was still in holy orders, but the church had made it clear to him he could not look to them for employment, after the unfortunate incident with the son of the advocate.

Now Vadomar lived like a mole, burrowing amid libraries and manuscripts, sniffing out juicy worms of erudition. There were not many who had need of his services, and fewer still who could afford them. However there were always matters of inheritance, of precedence and precedent, that required evidence from historical sources. And there were some very rich men with very specific interests, who provided the remainder of his income.

Abu Nuwas had encountered him in Alexandria. The Great Library had long ago burned down, its contents scattered across the globe, but many of the scrolls had not travelled far. Rare codices still turned up, in marketplaces or in the hands of dealers and fences. He and Vadomar had competed for possession of one such document, but had found their mutual love of the abstruse and arcane outweighed their rivalry. They had maintained a correspondence as valued as it was sparse, lengthy letters which arrived every year or two, entrusted to merchants and ambassadors who made the dangerous journey across the Mediterranean Sea. When Vadomar found a clue to the whereabouts of the Donation of Constantinus, he thought first of his friend in Baghdad.

This, at least, was the story Abu Nuwas told Hervor on the

way to the unfashionable Trans Tiberim district, where the scholar lived in modest quarters. Some of the old "islands", the apartment blocks built in the days of Rome's glory, still survived there, hulking edifices that towered three or even four storeys high. Vadomar dwelt in one such block on an upper floor, sacrificing comfort for anonymity and cheap rent.

The shops on the ground floor were pulling down their shutters by the time they arrived at the island. Abu Nuwas led the way to a side door which opened onto a staircase. The wooden steps smelt of urine, and the walls were scratched and smeared with offensive messages and crude drawings of genitalia. On the second storey they passed a huddle of surly youths who were gambling with knucklebones. The youths ignored their polite requests to move aside and continued their game, as if daring the strangers to push past. Hervor stepped through them carefully, one hand holding her mantle so that it did not brush the youths, the other gripping the short sword concealed by her side.

At last they came to Vadomar's floor. Even from the head of the stairs Hervor could see that the door to his apartment was open. Abu Nuwas clapped her on the shoulder.

"See, my friend is expecting us!"

The concern on his face, though, was apparent, and he waited, listening, on the landing before stepping into the apartment.

"Vadomar? It is I, Abu Ali. Are you here?"

The room which they entered was full of manuscripts, both vellum and papyrus. Some were rolled into scrolls, others bound in books, or scattered as loose documents. They were stacked on shelves, spread over the broad table that dominated the room, even strewn across the floor. Of Vadomar, however, or any other human presence, there was no sign.

Abu Nuwas picked up one of the books from the table and flicked through it distractedly.

"Something is very wrong. Vadomar would never leave his precious manuscripts exposed to thieves in this way."

"You'd better come here. I think I've found your friend."

He followed Hervor's voice into the next room. There, between a narrow bed and a chest, she indicated something on the floor. It was a body, dressed in the Roman style in long tunic and sandals. Where its head should have been, however, was a messy pulp of bone, flesh and gore. The cranium had been shattered into tiny pieces, and most of its contents squeezed out through horrible gashes, so that the skin sagged like an empty bag.

Abu Nuwas knelt to examine the corpse with trembling hands.

"Oh, Vadomar. What have they done to you?"

He turned the body onto its back, and the remnants of a face could just be discerned on the mashed, limp skull.

"Is it him?"

"I believe so."

Pulling the dead man's cloak over the shattered head, Abu Nuwas got to his feet.

"He cannot have been killed here. Such a savage beating would have left brains and blood all over the place, and his screams would surely have attracted interest, even in this unneighbourly neighbourhood."

"Then why take the risk of hauling the body back to the victim's home, and dragging it up three flights of stairs?"

"Perhaps as a warning. Perhaps for us to see. But who knew we were coming?"

Hervor frowned.

"Angilbert mentioned a spy from the court of the Emperor..."

She was shocked by the snarl of cold hatred that erupted from Abu Nuwas.

"Al-Sifr. It must be. The combination of cruelty and provocation is typical of the man."

He noticed her puzzled expression.

"Al-Sifr is an old adversary of mine, an agent of the Roman Empire. His name means Void, Emptiness — in your language, Nihil. If the Donation exists, the Empress would certainly want to suppress it. And Nihil would relish the chance to murder my friend, then taunt me with his bloody handiwork. He must somehow have learned of Vadomar's discovery."

"Or maybe your friend was playing a dangerous game, seeking more than one buyer for his document to drive up the price. It doesn't matter now, anyway. Without Vadomar, we have no chance of finding the Donation."

"No. Vadomar was a scholar. He understood the fragility of knowledge, how easily it can be lost if it is not duplicated. He would have left a record somewhere, some sign to point our way."

"Then Nihil would have taken it."

Abu Nuwas shook his head.

"My friend was not so crude as to leave it in plain sight. It will be concealed somehow, perhaps within another text."

Hervor indicated the profusion of manuscripts in the other room.

"Are you saying we must go through all those documents, looking for hidden secrets, but not knowing what form they take?"

"If need be. Can you read?"

The shieldmaiden bridled at his question, but swallowed her anger.

"Yes, I can read. Latin, at least."

The grey light from the window was fading fast. Abu Nuwas found candles in the chest, and lit one for himself and one for Hervor from an oil lamp which illuminated the landing. By the flickering light he began to sort through the manuscripts. Those written in Latin he passed to Hervor for scrutiny; those in Greek, Arabic or other, unknown, scripts, he examined himself.

Despite her indignation Hervor's literacy was functional rather than scholarly, and she struggled to make sense of the complex works of philosophy, history and poetry that composed the majority of Vadomar's collection. After the first couple of documents she began scanning through the pages, looking for key words like "Constantinus" that might indicate a reference to the Donation. She found nothing though, and as the candle burned down her eyes ached and her head pounded.

"This is a waste of time."

Abu Nuwas looked up at her distractedly.

"What? No. I know Vadomar, and the key will be here somewhere."

"Perhaps, but this is like searching for a truffle in a dungheap. Look at this:

> 'Garlic.
> Sausages.
> Wine.
> Almonds.
> Lentils.
> Soup.
> Lemons.'

"Either it's the worst poem I've ever read, or it's your friend's shopping list."

She was startled to see Abu Nuwas leap to his feet.

"Give that to me."

He snatched the list from her hand, and studied it fiercely. Then he began to laugh.

"Vadomar, you cunning old devil. Look, don't you see? '*Allium, Botuli, Uinum, Amygdalae, Lenticulae, Ius...*' The initial letters spell out Abu Ali! This has to be it, the message he left for me."

"Then what about the lemons, '*Citri*'? What does the extra 'C' indicate?"

"I don't know. There must be more, somewhere."

He studied the document intently in the candlelight, turning it over and examining both sides.

"This is paper, not papyrus or vellum. That in itself should have given us a hint. Paper is still rare in this part of the world, and would not be used for such casual jottings. Yet I can see no other letters or markings."

"Well, be careful. You're going to singe it, holding it so

close to the flame."

The kiss which he planted on her mouth was so enthusiastic
that she was left rubbing bruised lips. Abu Nuwas was dancing, an
unexpected and clumsy little jig.

"Of course! Lemons... paper... fire... it is so obvious!"

"Is it? Not to me."

"Come here. Watch this."

He held the paper over the candle flame.

"I shall look very foolish if this doesn't work."

As Abu Nuwas waved the candle around, delicate, rust-
brown lines began to appear below the shopping list. He drew in
breath sharply, and concentrated the flame on that area of the paper.
Slowly, the lines formed into letters.

"Such a simple trick. Has Angilbert taught you nothing?
Words written in lemon juice are invisible to the naked eye, but
reveal themselves when heat is applied."

"What does it say?"

Together they stared at the inscription.

EXPLICEVLTIMACCABALARESPICE

"Oh dear. I had hoped for something less opaque. That was the
problem with Vadomar. He was always a bit *too* clever."

Hervor shifted nervously.

"Father of Locks — you asked me just now whether
Angilbert taught me anything. One thing he did teach me was never
to become so caught up in my own affairs that I forgot about my
foes. He taught me always to put myself in my enemy's place, and
ask what I would do if I were him."

"I see. And what would you do, if you were Nihil?"

"I would let you find the secret, then come and kill you and
take it from you."

In the silence that followed, they could hear a scratching
and shuffling from outside; perhaps rats, perhaps a group of armed
men trying to keep quiet.

"Very well. We will interpret this elsewhere. Let us go."

He shoved the paper into the capacious sleeve of his coat, and they headed for the door. There were no armed men waiting for them there, but when they descended to the landing below their candles picked out shapes huddled in the shadows. The youths they had passed previously were waiting for them in the darkness, leaning against the walls in such a way as to block the corridor. The young men's arms were folded, their knucklebones forgotten, and they clutched vicious little knives in their hands. Abu Nuwas stepped forward, with a confidence that Hervor could not help considering misplaced.

"Good evening, gentlemen. If you would be so kind as to allow us to pass..."

"I don't recall you asking for permission to go up the stairs. But now you want permission to go down them. Do you recall them asking permission to go up, Libo?"

The speaker appeared to be their leader, an ugly, heavy-set young man who resembled a cross between a baboon and an alaunt. Libo, who was taller and thinner than his friend, shook his bony head.

"They cross our territory without paying tribute, and they don't even ask permission."

Abu Nuwas sighed.

"How much then, gentlemen? How much tribute, to cross your territory?"

"The other man gave us ten solidi to make sure you never leave the island. So you'll have to come up with twenty, if you want to live."

Hervor gasped. It was an enormous sum. Abu Nuwas, however, was diverted by another issue.

"What man?"

"The other man. The old man with the sack. I reckoned you must know him. He knows you all right. Now, have you got the money or not?"

"Not on my person. If you allow us to go and get it, we

could bring it back for you..."

The leader of the youths snarled.

"Do you think we are stupid? If you can't give us the money right now, you die."

Although the young men stepped forward, brandishing their knives before them, they did not attack; and when Hervor pulled out her sword, they wavered visibly. There were five of them, but in the narrow confines of the corridor they could not use their numerical advantage to flank her. She noticed that they held their weapons awkwardly, and guessed that for all their bravado they were unused to fighting anybody who actually fought back. It might be possible to escape without a brawl after all.

Then Abu Nuwas's arm jerked upward. Libo staggered back, a feathered dart sticking from his face. The youths yelled and hurled themselves at Abu Nuwas, who threw his candle at them and swung a heavy stick from beneath his cloak.

Hervor dropped to her haunches and watched the young men sway back from the poet's swipe. They took a pace back, stamping and gesticulating, yelling curses and threats, seeking to summon up the courage to attack. The screams of Libo, as he stumbled around clutching his bleeding face, provoked prudent caution rather than a thirst to avenge their injured comrade. With only the flame from her taper illuminating them the youths seemed to be performing an obscene dance, a spastic caper of agony and cowardly violence. In a flash she realised why Abu Nuwas had thrown his candle, and she sent her own after it.

The landing was plunged into blackness, and without a word spoken she and Abu Nuwas charged forward. From her crouching position her shoulder crashed into a young man's groin, propelling him back so that he collided with his comrade. Beside her there was a crash as someone fell to the ground, but their rush had not forced a way through. She leapt back before the youth recovered enough to use his knife.

There was quiet in the dark, except for heavy breathing and Libo's whimpers. In the wall between the antagonists a door swung open to reveal a worried face hovering over an oil lamp. The door quickly shut again. Hervor listened for the breaths, trying to judge the youths' positions and condition. She estimated four still standing, winded but unhurt. The chance of surprise was gone, and their enemies though wary were not in retreat.

A snap and rustle behind the youths, and a faint glow, suggested that someone was approaching. Hervor hunkered down, offering as small a target as possible, while she waited to see how the newcomer might tip the balance.

The newcomer, however, was not human. It was only when she saw orange tendrils scale and writhe behind the youths, flicking long shadows down the corridor that she understood. One of the candles had fallen in a heap of rubbish, where its flame had swiftly sprouted in the fertile detritus. The fire wound itself up the dry rotted beams of the old building, flourishing on centuries of poverty and neglect.

The youths looked anxiously behind them, then scarpered, dragging the unfortunate Libo behind them. Hervor and Abu Nuwas moved to go after them, but a flurry of sharply thrown stones forced them back. Beside them the door flew open, and a woman appeared with a baby in her arms. She looked at Abu Nuwas beseechingly.

"Please, master? May we go?"

Abu Nuwas scowled.

"We are not monsters. Get out."

The woman ducked past the growing conflagration, followed by a man with a small child holding one hand and a bag in the other. He appeared only mildly shamefaced at having sent his wife into jeopardy first. As the man disappeared down the corridor, a roof beam dropped down behind him, bringing with it a deluge of bricks and shattered masonry. The exit was blocked.

Abu Nuwas spoke with eerie calm.

"The skeleton of the building is collapsing. We could be buried within it any moment. Go through that apartment and climb from the window down to the courtyard. I'll join you in a moment."

"Where are you going?"

"To Vadomar's room, to save his manuscripts."

"Are you mad? You'll be killed."

"The prize is worth the hazard."

Hervor knew she should take him at his word, save herself and abandon him to the idiotic fate he had chosen. However she found herself reluctant to leave him. She wished she had at least memorised the enigmatic message found beneath Vadomar's shopping list.

"Come on. Don't you want to find the Donation of Constantinus?"

Abu Nuwas looked toward the upper floor wistfully.

"But... the wisdom lost to mankind..."

Suddenly she understood what she needed to do. She gripped him by the arm.

"If the knowledge in those documents is true, it will be discovered again. If the words they contain are inspired, they will have been copied elsewhere. But if you die, what beautiful creations will never be brought into existence at all?"

He seemed startled, then nodded solemnly. She hoped that the tears in his eyes had been brought on by the thickening smoke, not by his pomposity. However there was no more time for posturing. She pulled him after her into the apartment.

The room was larger than Vadomar's but empty of any possessions except a low table and a couple of stools. It seemed that the man had been carrying not just the family's valuables but everything portable they owned. This impression was reinforced as Hervor burst into a second room which contained only a wide straw bed on which all four must have slept. Fortunately though the room also featured a window onto the courtyard, its shutters hanging open.

Hervor dashed to thrust her head through the casement, but so did Abu Nuwas. There was an awkward moment when they were jammed together in the narrow frame, chest against chest. Then Abu Nuwas recollected himself, and grinned.

"Forgive me. Women first."

He scraped back out of the frame, and Hervor swung a leg over the sill. As she did so there was a groan like the death rattle of a giant, and the earth seemed to tilt. A choking huff of dust belched out of the window. The roof of the island was crumbling, and the walls falling inward.

Hervor scrambled through the casement, and slithered down the external wall. It was sufficiently aslant to offer safe, if abrasive, passage to the ground, where a few confused residents of the island milled around and stared at her suspiciously. She ignored them and looked back to the window. Abu Nuwas was struggling to ease his lanky frame through the narrow gap, and the buckling of the wall was now rapid enough to be visible. He seemed to climb out of the building as if shedding a garment, pushing it past his hips and down to his ankles.

By the time he popped his feet over the ledge he was able to stand on the wall and run along it. Haste was necessary though, as holes gulfed suddenly in the brickwork near his feet, and debris from the disintegrating ceiling tumbled after him like scree in a landslide. Ten huge strides carried him from top to bottom, and he hurled himself onto the packed earth of the courtyard just as the island finally expired, the five hundred year old edifice subsiding in a gruff detonation of heat, grit and flying rock.

Hervor pulled the poet to his feet.

"We'd better get out of here."

Occupants of nearby buildings had gathered in scores, to help or to gawp or in the hope of looting the rubble. Abu Nuwas and Hervor scurried between them, seeking to escape unnoticed. On seeing the grime that caked them some onlookers stepped forward with concern and questions, only to back off at the strange, strained faces of the dark man and the golden haired woman. They were several blocks away before they slowed enough for Hervor to catch her breath and speak.

"Well done, Father of Locks. We have obtained a single line of gibberish, and all we had to do to obtain it was to maim a few locals, destroy a block of flats and be observed fleeing the scene by the entire neighbourhood. The only blessing is that Vadomar's body will be crushed beneath the rubble, and we will not be held responsible for his murder. Perhaps that was Nihil's intention after all."

She regretted her jibes when she saw his face. Now that the crisis had passed, the loss of his friend had impacted on Abu Nuwas. He sighed.

"Poor Vadomar. Still, he was always going to get his head battered in one day. Scholarship is a surprisingly dangerous business; at least, it is the way Vadomar went about it. I believed though that he was smart enough to stay one step ahead."

"We too must stay one step ahead. The penalty for arson is death, and we are not safe from arrest yet. That is to say, you are not. If I were imprisoned, Angilbert would have me released within hours. Nobody in Rome would dare refuse the friend of King Karlo."

"A friend of King Karlo? Is Angilbert intimate with the King of the Franks, then?"

"You might say that. He's fucking Karlo's daughter."

Hervor was secretly pleased at the shocked expression on his face.

"Really? And I can only assume, since you have not mentioned any contract of marriage, that they are not wedded to each other. Where I come from, such conduct would result in the stoning to death of both parties. If the man was lucky, that is; the Khalifah might choose to have the fornicator's skin removed from his living body, inch by screaming inch. Does your King not know then?"

"Everybody knows. Bertha has borne him two children."

"And is Angilbert not a man of the church, too? You are strange people, you Franks."

"Things are different, in the north. Ceremonial is less important. They say that Karlo's mother was never married to his father, strictly speaking."

"You mean the king is a —"

"Don't say it. Things are not that different in the north. Anyway, I am not a Frank. I am Rus."

"My dear, I am sure you will understand that I say this with the greatest respect, but to be absolutely candid with you, you

Christians are all the same to me."

"Where are we going anyway? You need to lie low. When word spreads that a tall Arab has been disturbing the peace, it will not be long before they come looking for you. You cannot return to your quarters."

"There is one place we can be safe, until morning at least."

Abu'l Abbas did not seem put out to share his bedchamber with them, but knelt down stoically while his keeper scrubbed his back with water from a pail. Ziri had produced a candle for them, so that they could examine the paper. Abu Nuwas sat himself on the ground, heedless of the dust and dung. Hervor peered over his shoulder, gagging slightly at the pungent stench of the elephant, but trying to concentrate on Vadomar's enigmatic scrawl:

EXPLICEVLTIMACCABALARESPICE

"Now then, let us see what Vadomar was trying to tell us. 'Unfold, furthermost *ccabala*, look back!' It is Latin, at least, but what is 'ccabala'?"

"Perhaps he was trying to write 'horse', '*caballa*', but wrote 'C' twice and 'L' once, by mistake?"

"'Unfold, furthermost horse?' It makes no sense. Besides, Vadomar was a scholar. He would have rather cut off his own hand than misspell such a simple word."

Abu Nuwas stared at the inscription, as though it could be made to give up its secrets by the intensity of his gaze alone, and spoke quietly, as much to himself as to Hervor.

"There is another meaning of the word 'cabala', and one that seems more in harmony with Vadomar's character. The Cabala is the secret lore of the Jews, passed down from master to pupil since the time of Abraham. It describes how God created the cosmos through the Ten Numbers and twenty-two letters of the Hebrew alphabet. The Numbers are set out in an arrangement called the Tree of Life, with the letters representing paths connecting them. Adepts of the Cabala are reputed to be great magicians, able to summon and bind angels and demons."

"'Unfold, outermost lore...' It suggests the solution of a mystery. But why must it look back? And what does the other 'C' represent?"

"Yes, that is where my theory runs into difficulties. I might almost be tempted to consider it an error, given that Vadomar would not have been able to see what he was writing. However it was a stray letter 'C' that revealed the means by which the message was hidden. This one, too, must have significance. Where has it come from, this vagrant character, this orphaned letter? Where does it belong?"

"It sits at the exact centre of the phrase, not on the fringes; more like a king, than an outcast. Perhaps it is not a letter, but the number one hundred?"

"I have considered that. But the Cabala is singular, both by tradition and as written here. One cannot have a hundred Cabalae, and there is nothing else for the numeral to attach itself too. "

"You spoke of the importance of numbers to this Cabala. Does one hundred have meaning?"

"There are only ten Numbers making up the Tree of Life. In Hebrew numerals, one hundred is represented by the letter Qoph, the Monkey. In the system of Pythagoras, on the other hand..."

He trailed off, staring at the wall. Hervor nudged him.

"Who is Pythagoras?"

"Bugger Pythagoras!"

Hervor was taken aback by this outburst, but when Abu Nuwas turned to her, his eyes were shining.

"Pythagoras believed that one could reveal a man's destiny by rearranging the letters of his name, to form new words. Do you see what Vadomar has done? He has had us spiralling into ever more profound complexities, chasing after occult knowledge, when the answer was present before us all the time.

"*Explice* here means not 'unfold', but 'rearrange'. If we reorder the letters of VLTIMACCABALARESPICE, we will find the hiding place of the Donation. The 'C' is simply the stone left over after the mosaic has been completed, the stray thread which reveals the weaver's art."

He jumped to his feet.

"Forgive me, my friend, but I have need of you."

For a moment Hervor was puzzled as to whom he was addressing. Then she saw that Abu Nuwas was scooping up muck from the ground and using it to daub letters on the elephant's flank. He did not apply them in the order in which they appeared on the paper, but dotted them at random around the beast's hide. When he had finished, he stepped back and admired his work.

"There. Now what can you see?"

"I can see a dirty elephant."

"Words, girl, what words can you see?"

Hervor squinted.

"*Caeli*, the skies... *clamat*, he cries..."

"You are telling stories. That is how we got lost before. We are not looking for narrative, but for a place, or perhaps a person."

Hervor folded her arms.

"Then find it yourself, and stop shouting at me. I am a warrior, not a scholar. This sort of puzzle gives me a headache. And this is your quest, not mine. I know what you are doing, anyway. You are using me to help clarify your own thoughts, just as you are using this poor animal..."

She gestured at the elephant, and found that there was a name on its hide. The letters straggled unevenly and in some places were reversed, but she could see it as clearly as if it had been written there deliberately.

"Priscilla."

"What did you say?"

"Priscilla. There is your name."

Abu Nuwas looked back at the elephant, and gasped. He seized the pail of water which Ziri had been using and smudged the letters of the name, one by one. Then he studied what remained.

"*Caeca*... Blind Priscilla? No, the remainder makes no sense. A place more likely than a person, I think. *Meta*... a Greek influence? *Cata... catacumba*..."

He faced Hervor triumphantly.

"*Catacumbae Priscillae*. The Catacombs of Priscilla. Should that turn out to be the burial place of Pope Sylvester, then I think we can be confident that we are on the trail of the Donation."

XII

They agreed to wait until the following evening before seeking to penetrate the catacombs. They needed rest, and Abu Nuwas could not risk going out in daylight in case he was arrested as a saboteur. Hervor left him engaged in an animated if somewhat one-sided conversation with the elephant, and wandered out of the amphitheatre into the night.

Angilbert was waiting for her by the Colossus. He stood at its left foot, head level with the statue's enormous toe, watching her approach as if he had known the route she would take. Hervor groaned wearily.

"God damn you to hell, Father Abbott. Could you not let me sleep first, and eat, before you come to harry me?"

"And a good evening to you, Hervor Gorm's daughter. You should be flattered that the King's minister himself is guiding you on your mission, instead of some seedy local agent. I don't do this for everybody, you know. It is only because of our personal friendship, and because I happen to be in Rome..."

"And because you are curious about this Abu Nuwas, I am sure. Why are you in Rome anyway?"

"I have come with the King, of course."

"King Karlo is in Rome?"

"You did not know?"

"I have spent the last few months in prison."

"My apologies. I assumed that, since you were so deeply involved in the scandal, you would be aware of the furore it has created. Instead you must be the only person in Rome who does not know what is happening. Walk with me, and I will tell you."

They strolled around the square. A chill winter wind blew, and Hervor wrapped her shawl more tightly around her.

"When your friend Paschalis learned that the Pope had escaped to the court of King Karlo, he sent emissaries to the King himself, arguing that Leo was not fit to hold office. The King was placed in the awkward position of having to decide between their claims. On the one hand, to discredit a Pope would damage the church. On the other hand, Paschalis and his family were important people, and could not just be ignored."

"What jurisdiction does the King of the Franks and the Lombards have over a Bishop of Rome anyway?"

"A good question, and one that troubled the King himself. He consulted my colleague Alcuin, a learned scholar from the north of Britannia, at the edge of the civilised world. Alcuin told him that there were three men in the world who surpassed all others in eminence: the Pope, the Emperor of the Romans, and the King of the Franks. Since the other two had both been deposed and mutilated (even if Leo has since been miraculously restored), that left Karlo in charge."

"A very convenient answer."

"Take a look at the Colossus, Hervor. Whom does it represent?"

Hervor had to crane her neck to survey the giant statue from head to foot. It was the figure of a man, eighty cubits in height. Virile and confident, he bestrode the square, one hand raised in an ambiguous but masterful gesture. Spikes of silver radiated from his bronze head, giving him a jagged halo.

"It's Christus, Light of the World."

"Yes, that is what they say now. But this statue was erected by the Emperor Nero, who was the last of the family of Julius Caesar to reign in Old Rome. It is a portrait of a persecutor of Christians, a demented tyrant who killed his own mother and burned down the city so that he could rebuild it to his own taste."

"That would explain it. The Son of God doesn't usually look so, well... inbred."

"Precisely. After Nero's death the halo was added, and the Colossus became the God of the Invincible Sun. A century later, the Emperor Commodus had the statue's head replaced with a likeness of his own, and a lion placed at its feet, and declared the Colossus to be himself as the God Hercules. That head did not long outlive its model though, and the old one was restored."

"What does this have to do with the King of the Franks?"

"Patience, girl, I am coming to it. There is a saying in these parts, that while the Colossus endures, Rome will endure. However it does not matter whether the Colossus represents a Caesar, or a sun god, or a northern king wearing trousers and a moustache. You can change the head, or the name, or the accoutrements. It matters only that Rome has a Colossus to look up at and admire.

"Historians will tell you that Rome was conquered by barbarians, by the Goths and the Vandals. What they forget is that those barbarians immediately put on togas and began to learn Latin. Rome absorbed them, as it absorbs all invaders. Every empire which aspires to hegemony in the west declares itself the heir of Rome. They like to believe that they are not simply greedy warmongers, but that through the stoicism and courage of their men, the virtue of their women and the brilliance of their engineering, they are bringing civilisation to the world.

"So you will see the wisdom of Alcuin's judgement. There is a void at the heart of Rome, where its Colossus should be, and that is a dangerous thing for us all. With the church divided, and a woman occupying the imperial throne, who else can fill that void, other than the King of the Franks and the Lombards?"

Hervor made no response. In truth such high politics did not interest her, and she regretted having asked the question. Angilbert went on.

"Karlo sent a commission to investigate the allegations against the Pope. That is what led to your arrest and imprisonment. I believe that you were personally questioned by the head of the enquiry, Archbishop Arno."

"Yes. He is a pompous prick."

"As you say, Archbishop Arno is a wise and judicious man, who soon understood the complexity of the situation. Having reviewed all the evidence, the commission has concluded that it does not after all have the right to sit in judgement on the Pope. Leo is to swear an oath declaring his own innocence, and that will be sufficient to exonerate him of all charges."

"So the Pope is to add perjury to his sins of embezzlement and fornication, and then we will all pretend that nothing happened?"

"Be very careful, my dear. I thought we agreed that nothing is exactly what happened? And in order that everybody else is clear that nothing happened, the King himself has come to Rome to witness the taking of the oath. He will attend Mass in the basilica on the Holy Day of the Nativity, and receive communion from the hands of Pope Leo."

Suddenly Hervor felt sad and alone. The Nativity was celebrated on the same day that, for her people, marked the midwinter feast of Yul, sacred to the Mother Goddesses. It brought back memories of her own mother, and the cold but convivial homeland she had left as a child, never to see again. Hervor hated the Nativity and usually spent it getting outrageously drunk. Angilbert must have detected the change in her mood, because he became brisk and business-like.

"So then, have you discovered what our friend Abu Nuwas is doing in Rome?"

"He is seeking an original copy of the Donation of Constantinus, which he proposes to sell to you for money or diplomatic advantage."

Despite his smooth exterior Hervor could tell that Angilbert was intrigued.

"I see. Such a thing would indeed be of interest to us. Does he know where it is to be found?"

"His informant is dead, his head battered to mush. However he left a secret message, which Abu Nuwas believes reveals the location of the document. It is buried in the Catacombs of Priscilla."

Angilbert rubbed his chin.

"The remains of Pope Sylvester are said to be interred there. It is not impossible that a copy of the Donation might have been placed with them. Thank you, Hervor Gorm's daughter. You have done well."

"Then I can go? Am I free?"

"Free? But if you leave, who will accompany Abu Nuwas on his search for the Donation?"

Hervor stared at Angilbert, aghast.

"But I have told you where the document is to be found, if it exists at all. Why do you not send men to seize it, while the Arab sleeps?"

Angilbert placed a hand on her shoulder.

"My child, you are young. In time, you will come to learn that sometimes the quest is more important than the prize. No, that is incorrect; my apologies. I should have said, the quest is *always* more important than the prize. Ultimately, you will discover, the prize is an illusion; the quest is all there is."

She shook her head, baffled. Angilbert smiled at her.

"Go and rest, girl. You have work still to do. All will become clear in time."

***

At sunset the crowds were drifting away from the amphitheatre, and Hervor had to fight her way through against the tide. As she approached the elephant pen Ziri the keeper ran towards her waving his arms.

"No, no more visitors today! Abu'l Abbas is tired! You must — oh, it is you. Forgive me, my lady, I did not recognise you. My eyesight is not what it was."

He led her to the room at the rear of the pen. She peered through the door to see Abu Nuwas was washing his face with water from the elephant's bucket, and hailed her cheerily.

"Greetings! I am pleased that your masters have permitted you to accompany me."

"To be honest with you, I have no idea what my masters are plotting. However it seems that we are to work together, at least for the time being."

She had brought torches treated with brimstone and lime, which could not be extinguished by water, and flints in case they needed relighting. Abu Nuwas took with him a shovel which Ziri used to muck out the pen, his cudgel and a small mattock. Thus prepared, they set out for the catacomb.

Like most of the underground tunnels, the Catacombs of Priscilla were situated beyond the city walls, and it was nearing midnight by the time they arrived there. Hervor spent the journey in a state of edgy alertness. Bandits were common on the roads approaching Rome, and only the foolhardy travelled at night without an armed escort. They were fortunate, however, and arrived at the crypt without incident.

The entrance to the catacomb was a stone gateway built into the side of a hill. The frame boasted impressive columns and a carved arch, but the wooden doors had long ago rotted away, and the entry was blocked by planks crudely nailed across the gap. Abu Nuwas prised them off with the flat end of the mattock head, and the underground tomb exhaled its cold, dead air.

"Now then, if I have not reappeared by the time your torch is exhausted, then go and seek help. You should —"

"Don't insult me. I am not going to stand around here waiting for you. Either I come with you into the catacomb, or I turn around and walk back to the city. Which is it to be?"

Muttering under his breath, Abu Nuwas waved her into the entrance, and followed after her.

"The Holy Quran is right when it says that women should be obedient to men... this is the last time I leave the Land of Islam, I swear it, and the last time I go underground... when I die they can stick my body up a tree to rot, like the Magi do..."

His grumbles rang around the long, narrow stairway which led them downward, giving his words a crisp, cold echo, desiccated as a bone. At the bottom of the stair a chamber opened up to one side, while the tunnel continued directly ahead of them. The chamber was panelled and painted in the old Roman style. Its frescoes, faded and blotched with age, were an odd mixture of the pagan and the Christian. On one wall the companions of Daniel gazed piously to heaven, oblivious to the flames that surrounded them; on another, Hercules battled the Nemean lion. At the end of the chamber were niches where the bodies of wealthy Christians would once have lain.

Abu Nuwas held his nose.

"It stinks down here. Like rotten eggs."

"Perhaps it is the brimstone from the torches. In any case, what did you expect a charnel house to smell like?"

"There is no rotting flesh down here. The skeletons here were stripped bare centuries ago."

A chill draught caused Hervor to shiver.

"Should we search the chamber?"

"No, anything of value has long since been looted this close to the entrance. If we are to find the Donation, we must go deeper."

Beyond the chamber the tunnel separated into two branches. Abu Nuwas considered them.

"Left or right? Which path should we take?"

"Right."

Abu Nuwas raised the torch and studied Hervor's face, clearly surprised by the alacrity of her response. Then he turned and marched down the left hand passage.

A few moments later, he appeared back at the junction, where Hervor waited, tapping her foot.

"It was a dead end. How did you know?"

Hervor allowed herself a little grin of satisfaction.

"If you had observed the curve of the hill as we approached, you would have seen that the left tunnel could not run far, given the position of the entrance."

Abu Nuwas sniffed.

"Or possibly you just guessed correctly on an even bet, and now seek to make yourself look clever with spurious justifications."

Hervor glared at him, and set off down the right tunnel, with

Andrew Killeen

Abu Nuwas following. The passage down which they walked was lined with niches carved out of the rock. These had once been sealed, but the slabs had mostly been shattered by grave robbers. In some of the alcoves grim heaps of human bone could still be glimpsed.

"The scavengers have done a pretty thorough job. What makes you think there is anything left here to find?"

Abu Nuwas shrugged.

"To tell you the truth, I cannot be certain. But I trust Vadomar. He was rarely wrong about these things."

The tunnel now declined steeply. To their right small rooms had been cut into the wall, each with resting places for one or two skeletons; even in death the rich occupied a better class of accommodation. Hervor stepped into one, but Abu Nuwas pushed past her and continued along the passage.

"That is not the tomb of a Bishop of Rome."

The further they penetrated the catacomb, the worse the stench became. Hervor found that her eyes were watering and her throat growing sore, and remembered the tale of the dragon, who had killed men with his noxious breath. However she was ashamed to voice such childish fears to Abu Nuwas, who was striding rapidly along the tunnel, so that she had to hurry to avoid being left behind in the darkness.

The tunnel seemed endless, but at last they came to a junction where passages stretched away to left and right. Even by the deceptive light of the torches, they could see that the path ahead came to an end after only a few paces. Abu Nuwas turned back to Hervor.

"Erm... left or right?"

She was tempted to pretend to some arcane knowledge, but the foul air made her feel sick, and it did not seem like a time for playing games. She shook her head.

"I have no idea."

"Neither do I. In that case, we must consider — wait! What is that, on the ground there?"

At some distance down the right hand passage, his sharp

197

eyes had spotted a dark shape on the tunnel floor. As they approached, Hervor could see that it was the body of a man, lying face down. This was no ancient skeleton, but a fresh, fleshy corpse, fully clothed with cloak and hood. Abu Nuwas rolled the body over, and Hervor gasped.

"I know him. His name is Fortunatus. He is an agent in the service of the Pope."

"Well, he is not very fortunate any more."

Abu Nuwas looked up at her pale face, and frowned.

"I am sorry. That was thoughtless of me."

"Don't apologise. I hated him. He was a louse. Angilbert must have sent him to snatch the Donation ahead of us after all. Oh, don't give me that look. Of course I told Angilbert what we had discovered, what did you expect?"

Abu Nuwas said nothing, but searched the body thoroughly.

"If he did find the document, he no longer has it now. Perhaps he had a companion who abandoned him here."

"How did he die?"

Abu Nuwas pulled back the man's collar to reveal his neck.

"I don't know. There are no marks suggesting violence."

"So do we go on, knowing we may already be too late?"

The Arab's face was set.

"Yes, we go on. Until we are certain."

The presence of the corpse had decided them in favour of the right hand path. There were no niches in the walls here, only a rough bore carrying them ever deeper into the hill. Abu Nuwas began to cough, and Hervor felt an odd sense of relief that he was not immune to the effects of the malodorous miasma which made her head throb. At the end of the tunnel they were again faced with a choice of passageways.

"Right will take us back on ourselves. Left leads further down to a lower level. I think our choice is clear."

Hervor was suddenly aware of the great weight of earth above their heads, and of the fragility of their situation. She sucked air desperately, and stumbled against the walls, unsteady on her feet.

The tunnel twisted around and down, and even Abu Nuwas seemed to be losing confidence.

"How far do these catacombs stretch?"

"I don't know. Miles, I think."

He stopped, and Hervor bumped into him. She grabbed his arm.

"We must go back. I cannot breathe."

His own eyes streamed as though he were weeping, but his voice was steady.

"Such sour air is common in deep mines. You can return to the surface if you wish. I have not come this far to turn back now."

He walked away, and was soon out of sight. Hervor leaned against the wall, barely able to stand. The thought of going on made her nauseous, but she feared more to be left alone with the dead in the underworld. Then a shout made her jump.

"Here — quickly!"

She stumbled after Abu Nuwas, who was not far ahead. She found him standing in what could only be described as a small chapel, with murals on the walls and a stone altar at one end. Behind the altar was a recess, in which lay a complete human skeleton.

It was the mortal remains of Pope Sylvester. She knew this in part because of the inscription, which though worn with age could clearly be read: "SYLVESTERPPEPISCOPUSROMAE." More striking, however, was the fact that the recess had been painted with an image of a fearsome dragon, mouth open in a silent roar. The dragon's mouth seemed to be brighter than the surrounding paint, a lurid blood-red maw drawing her in toward a crushing death. Hervor stepped forward involuntarily, and was vaguely aware of Abu Nuwas talking.

"He sewed up the serpent's mouth with thread, and sealed it with the sign of the cross... Give me your knife."

Hervor did not realise he was speaking to her until he impatiently snatched the dagger from her belt. He plunged the blade into the dragon's mouth. Instead of the clang of metal clashing against rock, there was a ripping noise, and a terrible roar. Then the sky fell in.

The shieldmaiden dreamed that she was back home, in the land of the Rus. Her mother, who had died twenty years before, was pressing her to her breast, and Hervor revelled in the maternal embrace. Something was wrong, though, and Hervor could not breathe. Her mother became a serpent, crushing her in its scaly coils, suffocating her slowly. The serpent's tail beat against her face, and she drew in a huge gasp, to find that she was still in the catacomb, with Abu Nuwas slapping her face.

"Wake up, or you will never wake again. The sour air is choking us, and you passed out. We must get out of here as quickly as we can."

She staggered to her feet, and Abu Nuwas dragged her out of the chamber and up the tunnel. He was walking with difficulty, and Hervor wondered whether the toxic air had affected him more than he was admitting. It was only when they passed the body of Fortunatus that she thought to croak out the question.

"The Donation... did you get it?"

Despite the tears that streaked his cheeks, he flashed her a grin.

"Yes, I got it. Fortunatus must have perished without finding the hiding place. The document was in the mouth of the dragon. The cavity was concealed by a piece of fabric, painted to appear part of the fresco. It seems that a knowledge of unlikely old legends has its uses after all."

They wasted no more breath on talking. Despite their slow progress the return to the entrance seemed to pass much quicker than the descent, and the air became clearer as they neared the surface. By the time they reached the gateway she was able to stand unaided, and had begun to plot how she might obtain the Donation from Abu Nuwas. The Arab's eyes were wide, like one in the grip of a mania. As they ascended the final stair he began to babble excitedly.

"Poor Fortunatus... he must have been searching and searching, poking through the bones, while he slowly choked. When he felt the poison dimming his sight, he crawled away, gagging on the stench of failure. He could not flee fast enough, though, to escape the dragon's breath. Whereas I am just a little quicker, just a little smarter, and that is why I now possess the document. That is why — good evening, gentlemen."

They emerged from the catacomb to find half a dozen men standing around the gateway. It was obvious that they were waiting for Abu Nuwas and Hervor to appear; and obvious, too, that they were not doing so in order to congratulate them on their success. These were not bragging guttersnipes like the youths from the island, but hard, scarred men, with boiled leather tunics and polished dirks. Uttering no boasts or threats, they closed in implacably.

It occurred to Hervor that they could retreat back to the catacomb. Even if the men followed them, their numbers would count for nothing in the narrow corridor. In the next breath, however, she realised that she would rather be cut down where she stood than go back into the crypt. She drew her sword and prepared to fight.

She was exhausted, though, weakened by the poison. As the first attacker approached she swung her torch and lunged with the sword, but the man easily parried her attack. A gloved fist smashed into the side of her head, and for the second time that night she plunged into oblivion.

***

When Hervor was next aware of anything, she was aware only of pain. So overwhelming was the sensation that she thought for a moment she must have died and been condemned to the infernal punishment that her dissolute life had merited. Then she began to distinguish individual notes in the cacophony of agony that engulfed her senses. Loudest of these was the throb of her bruised temple pressing on cold stone. This, at least, suggested that she was still alive.

Her head pounded, and her mouth was dry. Her muscles ached, and when she moved to ease them by stretching her limbs, she found that her arms and legs were trussed so tightly she could not even wriggle. She tried to raise her head, but it was trapped between the stone floor and something flat and solid a few inches above her.

"Do I see movement? The girl is awake. Good; that will make things easier."

The voice seemed at once familiar and strange to her. Hervor blinked furiously in the hope of clearing her vision, and saw a pair of booted feet nearby. Beyond it were only dancing shadows.

"She can tell you nothing, because she knows nothing."

The second voice was that of Abu Nuwas, hoarse but defiant. The first speaker sniggered.

"Yes, I am sure that her ignorance is comprehensive. I did not imagine for a moment that you would have told her what you have done with the Donation. However, it will be easier if she is conscious because, for all your bombast, you are soft and sentimental. When you hear her screams you will beg me to make a swift end of her, and give me whatever I ask. I know you too well, *Pater Cincinnorum*, Father of Locks."

There was a third presence in the room, Hervor realised, but he said nothing, only betraying himself through the soft rumble of his breathing. It sounded almost as though he were snoring. Hervor struggled to speak through puffy lips.

"I am on your side, you fool! I serve the King too. Let me out of here!"

Her captor sniggered again.

"The stupidity of the girl is truly wondrous. Are all of your kind so dense? Does the cold northern air dull your intellect? I know you serve the King, you silly little whore. I, however, do not. I serve your master's master: Irene, Emperor of the Romans."

"You are the Emperor's spy? You are Nihil? But... how did you know where to find us? Who betrayed us?"

"You betrayed yourselves, girl. All I had to do was sit here and wait for you to come and tell me everything you had done, and everything you were going to do."

The booted feet walked towards her, then disappeared as their owner knelt down. A face loomed into view.

"Good evening, my lady."

"Ziri!"

The keeper was subtly transformed in appearance as he was in voice. He seemed younger, and a dangerous cruelty possessed his features.

"Yes, that has been my name, for the last few months at least. Ziri the keeper, a mere menial, fit only for shovelling shit. A nothing indeed, a man so inconsequential that you would discuss your great secrets in front of him as if he did not even exist. Now I will crush you to nothing; that is, my friend Abu'l Abbas will."

At last Hervor recognised her surroundings. She was in the pen at the amphitheatre, where the previous night she and Abu Nuwas had unravelled Vadomar's message right in front of their most dangerous enemy. And the object that hovered just above her head, ready to descend and flatten her skull just as it had Vadomar's, was the foot of the elephant, whose breath rumbled in the cold air.

"Let us both go, and I will give you the Donation."

Ziri's face vanished as he got back to his feet.

"You seek to bargain with me, Father of Locks? Your life is forfeit, whether I obtain the document or not. All that remains is for me to determine the manner of your death. A pleasure so long deferred should not be rushed at its consummation.

"As for the girl, she has seen my face, and cannot be allowed to live. No, your choice remains the same. Hand over the Donation, and Abu'l Abbas will stamp his foot, snuffing her out like a candle. Deny me, and he will press down slowly, so that she can feel her cranium crack and her brain squeezing out of her ears. Which is it to be?"

Despite her desperate predicament, all Hervor could think about was how Abu Nuwas had managed to hide the Donation during their hurried flight from the catacomb. He must have secreted it while she was unconscious. Or perhaps he had not actually found the document after all? She had not seen it herself. If he was lying, it had proved to be a dangerous, perhaps fatal, deception.

She craned her head round, looking for the Arab, and

saw a pair of naked, hairy feet. The legs above them were tied to a chair. She guessed that Ziri must have stripped him in search of the document. When Abu Nuwas spoke, he sounded defeated.

"My cudgel. If you unscrew the hilt, it is hollow inside. That is where I have hidden the Donation of Constantinus."

She saw Ziri's boots stomp over to a heap on the ground, then his hands rifling through it. From it he plucked the Arab's club, and raised it out of Hervor's sight.

"If you are lying to me, Father of Locks, both you and the girl will pay. I see, though, that the hilt does indeed unscrew, and it does appear to be hollow. And within it, we find — aah!"

Something dropped at Ziri's feet. At first Hervor thought it was a strip of leather, but then she noticed how it writhed and slithered, before Ziri crushed it under his boot. At the same moment Abu Nuwas lurched forward. His legs were still strapped to the chair, but as he and Ziri crashed to the ground she could see that the coils of rope around his arms were loosening, falling away, and even in the uncertain light she could make out the frayed ends flapping.

Abu Nuwas and Ziri grappled on the floor. Abu Nuwas, bigger and heavier, pinned Ziri down and battered the spy's face with his fists. The ropes still hampered him though, and Ziri wormed away. He crouched on all fours, dripping blood from his nose and cuts on his cheeks. Then he yelled up at the elephant.

"Abu'l Abbas, *sum baith*! *Sum baith*, you bastard!"

The elephant reared up on its hind legs, ready to strike the fatal blow. Hervor tried to roll out of the way, but knew it was hopeless. Abu'l Abbas looked down on her with its mournful yellow eyes, needing only to place its foot to end her life. Oddly, she found herself wondering where its penis was. Surely such a gargantuan beast would have a member of similar proportions? That was her final thought before the feet came down, and Hervor closed her eyes.

She felt the ground shake around her, but the impact did not come, and she cautiously opened her eyes again. Abu'l Abbas had planted his feet with meticulous precision on either side of her head, and now ambled toward its keeper, who was screaming at it.

"*Sum baith, sum baith*! Crush her, you dumb brute! What are you doing? I am your —"

A naked body landed across Hervor, blocking her view. It was Abu Nuwas, who had managed to free himself from the chair.

"Don't look. Trust me, you will sleep better in future years."

Hervor was going to protest that she was a warrior, a shieldmaiden of the Rus, that she had killed many men herself, and watched many more die. However, as she listened to Ziri's agonised shrieks and the crack of breaking bone, she decided that he might be right.

Abu Nuwas took a knife from the heap of his belongings and slashed Hervor's bonds. She rubbed and slapped her legs, trying to bring them back to life. While Abu Nuwas pulled on his clothes he gazed down at the remains of the snake which had been hidden in his cudgel.

"Farewell then, Azi. You were a vicious little bastard, but I was very fond of you."

He helped Hervor up.

"But how did you cut the ropes that bound you?"

"I should not reveal my secrets to you. We may not always be friends. However, since there is nobody else around to admire my cleverness, I shall advise you to toughen the calluses on your pretty hands. You can then conceal beneath the hard skin a piece of sharp blade with which to saw through any cords that restrain you; provided, of course, you can keep your enemy talking long enough."

"Very impressive. And where did you hide the Donation?"

Abu Nuwas smiled.

"I suppose it was worth a try, but while I may be vain, I am not stupid. The location of the document is not something I am willing to discuss with you, until we have agreed a price. Now, shall we go, before anyone arrives and starts asking awkward questions?"

Weary, bruised and poisoned, they had to help each other walk, and must have made a strange pair stumbling through the amphitheatre: the tall Arab, his long, matted hair falling around his face, and the young woman with golden hair, leaning against each other like a pair of drunkards. So dazed were they, that they almost walked into Angilbert as they crossed the square of the Colossus.

"Hervor, how good to see you looking so well. And my fellow scribbler Abu Nuwas, a pleasure to meet you again, after so many years. Felix, Clemens, would you assist my friends please?"

The Abbot's burly attendants took them politely but firmly by the elbow, both supporting and detaining them. Standing in front of them, Angilbert held out his hand.

"And now, if I could examine the Donation of Constantinus?"

"We don't have it."

Angilbert raised his eyebrows.

"Indeed? You do surprise me. I would have thought that, with your intelligence and Hervor's skill at fighting — forgive me, my dear, but it really is that way round — your success would be assured."

He looked pointedly at Hervor, who shrugged.

"He claims he took it from the catacomb, but I have not seen it, and the Emperor's spy could not find it despite stripping him to his skin. I think he must have slipped it into one of the alcoves where the bones are kept. There are hundreds of them down there, but you could send soldiers to search..."

Angilbert nodded, but his eyes were now fixed on Abu Nuwas.

"I could. I could send soldiers to search the catacomb. Or I could just lock up our friend here, and wait. After all, you have to defecate some time, don't you?"

Hervor stared in bafflement, but Abu Nuwas grinned guiltily.

"Now how did a man of the church like you work it out, when that depraved old devil al-Sifr could not? No, don't answer that, I don't want to know. There is no need to lock me up; I will hand over the Donation. May I then go home?"

"Of course. You have done a great service for the King, and besides, I would not deprive the world of so brilliant a poet. Please tell me, though, that the document was in some kind of container?"

"Yes, have no fear, it was in an ivory case. You will not have to get your hands dirty. As, indeed, you have managed to avoid doing throughout this whole adventure."

Comprehension was dawning on Hervor's face, along with disgust.

"You mean you hid the document up your —"

"I am afraid so. There is no need to look so appalled. It was a very small object really, and far from the worst thing that has been up there."

***

The basilica was packed for mass on the morning of the Feast of the Nativity. Hervor suspected that many of those attending were motivated less by piety than by curiosity to see how the King behaved toward the Pope. That was certainly why Hervor was there. Leo had sworn to his innocence in front of an assembly of bishops, and was thus held to be exonerated of all charges; but there were those who still hoped that he could be persuaded to step down and retire to a monastery somewhere. Every move, every expression on the face of the King would be analysed and discussed.

She was surprised to see Abu Nuwas standing at the rear of the church, clad in the long coat and loose trousers of his people. She walked over and greeted him.

"I did not expect to find you here."

"And why not? In my own country I often frequent monasteries and churches, and not just for the wine and pretty boys. I think sometimes that Christianity is more to my taste than Islam. I would consider converting, were it not a capital crime to desert the true faith."

"I meant that I did not expect to see you in public. Should you not be staying out of sight?"

"Not at all. The good Abbot was kind enough to smooth over any small difficulties relating to our escapades. I am once again an honoured member of the delegation from the King of the

Persians."

"You seem in very cheerful mood, considering you had to hand over the Donation for nothing."

"My most hated enemy is dead. That alone has made the journey worthwhile."

At that moment those members of the congregation who had crowded onto the pews rose to their feet as one. The choir began to chant the Introit, and Frankish soldiers marched through the doors of the basilica. Abu Nuwas leaned across to Hervor.

"Here comes the King."

In fact the King and the Pope entered simultaneously. This had clearly been planned, to spare them the embarrassment of deciding who took precedence. Hervor knew Pope Leo all too well, but despite her years in his service, she had never before stood in the presence of King Karlo. She therefore ignored the sleazy little man processing toward the altar in a cloud of incense and hypocrisy, and examined instead the warrior striding down the nave.

Karlo, King of the Franks and Lombards, would have stood out in any company. He was nearly five cubits tall, and his thick neck and barrel chest made him an imposing figure even without the regal assurance of his mien. To honour the occasion he wore a toga in the old Roman style, although it looked incongruous with his drooping moustache and long hair. Despite the unfamiliar clothing, however, he maintained his dignity as he made his way to the throne which had been placed for him in front of the altar.

Hervor found Mass profoundly dull, and as usual her mind wandered during the long ritual. She found herself drifting into a daydream in which she was being ravished by King Karlo. The King was nearly sixty years old, and far fleshier than the stringy youths that were her general preference. However the idea of being squeezed against that enormous chest was oddly appealing, and there was something reassuring, almost paternal, about his calm authority.

She was distracted from speculating about the King's royal member, which she had decided would be stubby but satisfyingly fat, by the rustle at the head of the church as communion was about to be administered. Karlo rose from his throne and walked forward to receive the sacrament first. Pope Leo, however, did not offer him the bread and wine. Instead, he gestured to an attendant, who ran forward with a glittering object on a cushion.

The Pope took the object in both hands and raised it in the air. It was a golden crown, encrusted with gemstones and surmounted by a cross. He lowered it slowly and set it on Karlo's head, then addressed the congregation.

"To Carolus, most pious Augustus, crowned by God, great and peacemaking Emperor, long life and victory! *Salus et victoria!*"

Uncertainly at first, then more clamorously, the congregation echoed him.

"*Salus et victoria! Salus et victoria!*"

Abu Nuwas whispered in Hervor's ear.

"Did what I think just happened really happen? Did the Pope just proclaim him Emperor and Augustus? That will stir up some interest in New Rome, when they hear of it."

As if to preclude any ambiguity, the Pope fell to the ground and kissed Karlo on the knees, in the traditional gesture of deference to the Emperor of the Romans. Leo then got back to his feet, stuck his thumb in a small silver pot and daubed something on Karlo's forehead. It was Hervor's turn to mutter to Abu Nuwas.

"What is he doing?"

"Anointing him with oil, I think. It was the practice of the Jews to have their kings and prophets anointed in that way, usually by the high priest of the Temple in Jerusalem. A cunning move, to legitimise the Pope's role in the accession. I wonder whether it was his idea, or the King's?"

Just then Karlo, having finally been given the bread and wine, returned to his chair. Instead of the pride or serenity that Hervor was expecting, though, his expression was one of pure fury. He stamped away from the altar, and the thud as he hurled his heavy body into his chair resounded around the basilica. Abu Nuwas gasped.

"In the name of God! He did not know... the King did not

know about the plan to crown him Emperor! And by the look of things, he is not best pleased about it either. He could not refuse the honour in public though, not without humiliating a man whom he has gone to much trouble to support. It will make diplomacy with Irene and New Rome very difficult, I would imagine."

"Then why —"

Hervor was interrupted by a young priest, who shushed her furiously. They fell silent, and watched the congregation file up for the sacrament. It was not until the end of Mass, when Leo had dismissed them and the King had marched out of the basilica, that they were able to resume their conversation.

"Why would Leo do such a thing? Why would he trick the King into accepting a title he did not seek? With different Emperors in the two Romes, is there not a risk that Christendom will split apart?"

"Why? Because Leo is the real victor here. As King of the Franks and Lombards, Karlo ruled by right of inheritance and conquest; as Emperor, he draws his authority from the Pope. The King may no longer be subject to Irene, but Leo has raised himself higher still by climbing onto Karlo's shoulders."

"Yes, who gave the Bishop of Rome the right to appoint the Emperor anyway?"

"We did. When we found the Donation."

"Ah. True. Convenient for Leo, wasn't it, that an original copy should show up, just when his position was so shaky?"

Abu Nuwas did not seem to be amused.

"I have been wondering about that. And about a few other things too. I suppose though we shall never know the truth."

His expression changed from chagrin to glee as he stared at a passing face in the departing congregation.

"Or maybe we will after all. Brother Catwulf! Brother Catwulf!"

With a wave and a cheery grin he greeted a saturnine man of around his own age, who was dressed in the robes of a clergyman. A momentary twinge of fear crossed the man's face as he saw Abu

Nuwas bearing down on him, but he rapidly composed himself and answered with urbane ease.

"Ah yes, you must be the emissary from the court of the Persian King. A pleasure to make your acquaintance."

"I am hurt, Brother Catwulf. Surely you have not forgotten me, and the jolly times we spent together in Baghdad?"

Catwulf's smile was implacable.

"You must pardon me. That was many years ago, and I met such a great number of fascinating people. And I am no longer a mere Brother. You should address me as Bishop Catwulf."

"Apologies, your excellency. Your advancement has been rapid indeed. What is your diocese?"

"I do not have a diocese. I am a titular bishop, engaged in special work for the Holy Father."

"Of course you are. I am familiar with the kind of work in which you are a specialist."

Catwulf paled slightly, and tried to change the subject.

"How fortunate you are, ambassador, to have been present at the coronation of an Emperor. What has happened today has changed the world forever. After half a millennium of dominance by the east, the west is rising again. You can tell your masters that you have witnessed history in the making."

"Indeed, it is a privilege to see history in the making. It is a greater privilege, though, to observe the hands of the craftsman as he makes it."

"What do you mean, ambassador?"

"I have been thinking about Fortunatus."

"I do not know the man of whom you speak."

"Really? He also serves the Pope, engaged in special work. Or rather I should say 'served', since poor Fortunatus is dead now."

"May God have mercy on his soul."

"Quite. I came upon his body in the catacombs where we found the Donation."

"Then he, too, was seeking the document."

"So it seemed, at the time. However something was not

right. His body was cold."

"Corpses usually are."

"Not straightaway. It must have lain there for at least half a day, to have cooled to that extent."

"I fail to see the problem. Obviously he had entered the catacomb that morning."

"However his body was also limp. It takes around three days for the stiffness of death to pass. So he must have been there some time. Yet we only discovered the location of the document the previous day. What was the Pope's man doing in the catacomb earlier in the week?"

Catwulf's jaw tightened, but he said nothing. Abu Nuwas pressed on.

"Then I thought about the document's hiding place. The paint on the dragon's mouth was not faded like the rest of the mural, but appeared fresh, almost new. And the cloth that covered it: what fabric could have survived for five hundred years?"

"I do not understand what you are asking me, ambassador."

"Does Angilbert know? That is what I am asking you. Does Angilbert know that the Donation is a fake, planted a few days ago for me to find? Did you cook it up between you, or is he just another piece in your game? Does Karlo know? Does the Pope know? I imagine they do not, for otherwise, what would be the point of this elaborate charade? A good story, to give the document credibility..."

Catwulf hissed at him.

"It is fortunate for you that you are under the Emperor's protection. However if you continue to ask impertinent questions, or impute dishonesty to the Holy Mother Church, then I cannot guarantee that you will leave Rome alive. Go home, poet. Keep your mouth shut and go back to Baghdad."

He stalked away. Hervor's mouth hung open, but Abu Nuwas seemed pleased.

"He called me 'poet'! So he did remember me after all."

They walked together out of the church. Hervor turned to her companion.

"Then the Donation was —"

"Do you know, I believe the good bishop's advice was sensible. There is nothing to be gained by poking this nest of vipers, and much to be lost. I just wanted to know the truth, that is all. Now that my suspicions have been confirmed, I am leaving Rome, and I suggest you do the same. This place reeks of corruption and death, and it is not a dragon that exudes the poison, but men greedy for power. Get out of here, Hervor Gorm's daughter, while you can still breathe."

Hervor felt a pang of loneliness at the prospect of his departure.

"But where can I go?"

"Well, there is one, who might take you away from here..."

Hervor sighed, and wondered how to explain that, however desperate she was, running away to a land where she would have to hide her face, with a libertine who drank too much and would drop her for the first pretty boy to flutter his eyelashes, was not the solution. Then she realised that he was indicating a figure standing in the crowds outside the church; a man in sailor's garb, with a lean frame and mocking eyes.

"Rurik! You stupid bastard, what are you doing here? They will behead you for piracy if anyone recognises you."

"I came to find you —"

"No, what am I saying? Beheading is all you deserve. I should denounce you myself. I should whip your arse with a knotted rope until your cheeks are in shreds. I should ram your foremast up your fundament. I should —"

"Yes, my angel, you should do all those things. Then, when your fury is sated, will you come to my ship?"

"And why would I want to do that?"

"Because I love you. Because now that I have realised what a fool I was to let you go, I will never make that mistake again. Because even the crew are missing you, illegitimate pox-ridden scum that they are. I cannot promise you comfort, or security, but I can offer a life of adventure, and freedom, and passion. So I will

ask you once more, and then never again: Hervor, will you sail away
with me?"

XIII

"And did she? Did she go with him?"

"I cannot say, Commander of the Faithful. The tale ends there."

"You cannot say? What does that mean? You are the storyteller, you can say anything you choose to say."

"Very well. She sailed with Rurik the pirate, but they were captured a few months later off the coast of al-Andalus and both were executed."

"No! That is not what happened!"

"Then what would the Commander of the Faithful like to have happened?"

Harun's forehead creased.

"Obviously she sailed with him, but they are alive and well to this day."

Ismail bowed deeply.

"Indeed, my prince, I find myself recalling now, that they discovered a great treasure buried on the shores of Ifriqiyah, and were able to give up their criminal ways. They dwell in comfort and security in Benevento, and have an infant child on whom they dote. A boy, I believe."

The Khalifah sat back.

"There now, that is better. If I decide to let you live, then mind that, in future, you finish your stories properly."

"And how is that, Commander of the Faithful? Please instruct your lowly servant as to how a tale should end."

"Why, every question must be answered, of course! Even a child knows that."

Ismail bowed once more.

"Your merest whim is as a sacred obligation to me, Commander of the Faithful. Every question will be answered."

"I am pleased to hear it. Really, it comes to something when a prince must teach his subjects their own trades. As for you, Father of Locks, your story is over. Your enemy is dead, and we have come to the end."

"So it would seem, my prince."

"Are you ready to die?"

"Our lives are yours, Commander of the Faithful, to give or take as you see fit. However, there is one final turn to the tale, if you wish to hear it. Then, my prince, all your questions will be answered, and my story will be complete."

"Father, how much longer will you allow these charlatans to spin their lies? It is not seemly —"

"Be silent, Abdallah al-Ma'mun. I said I would hear them out, and I will not break my word. Storyteller, speak swiftly and to the point. The shadows are lengthening, and your death draws ever nearer."

"As it does for us all, Commander of the Faithful. However, we also come close to the truth, which at times shines so bright as to blind, or burn. Let the children be shielded from its glare; I beseech you, send the young princes away."

Harun al-Rashid stared, dumbstruck at the ragged storyteller's audacity. In the end, though, he nodded. and the princes departed, al-Ma'mun in silent fury, al-Amin with lofty grace.

Ismail closed his eyes for a moment, then raised a hand.

"And now, with your indulgence, Commander of the Faithful, I shall relate the dark deeds of last night and this morning, the events which have led us to stand here before you, the sentence of death hanging over our heads. It is a tale never told before, and never to be told again. It is called...."

The Tale of The Tenth Element

I was not sure why I was running; but what was beyond doubt was that the men were running after me. I stopped for a moment when I reached the canal, gasping for breath and hoping that they had abandoned the pursuit, but almost immediately they both appeared at the end of the alley, loping toward me with the steady, tireless gait of wolves. Their booted feet thudded in unison, suggesting military training, although they wore the cheap clothes of labourers.

Perhaps it was this that had warned me, although they had approached with smiling faces. It was not unusual for people to wait around to speak to me after I had finished performing: to enthuse or pick faults, to offer me a tale of their own, or simply so they could say they had met the famous storyteller al-Rawiya. My years on the road, though, had given me an animal instinct for danger. I had noticed these two men striding toward me, their ragged clothes contrasting with well-fed faces and sturdy boots, their ingratiating expressions unable to conceal an habitual air of menace, and I turned and ran. I was alarmed, though unsurprised, when they took off after me.

The canal was too wide to jump. I considered swimming across, but the idea of struggling through the filthy water while my pursuers closed on me was unappealing. Instead I sprinted along the bank, heart racing as fast as my bare feet, seeking a means of escape.

There was nobody around. I ducked down a side street, and in the brief interval while I was out of their sight scrambled up the wall of a building, fingers and toes digging into cracks between the mud bricks. I hauled myself onto the rooftop and lay still, trying to quiet my noisy breath.

I could hear the men's rhythmic footsteps drumming below, but to my horror the beat slowed and stopped, directly beneath my hiding place. No whispered conversations reached my ears; they must be communicating with signals. Whoever they were, it was clear they were seasoned hunters. In the silence the call to noonday prayer pealed from the minarets, the words darting and spiralling around each other like playful skylarks. At last my pursuers began to move on, slowly at first but away from me, until they could no longer be heard.

I waited on the rooftop until I had counted one hundred breaths. Then I counted another hundred, just to be sure, before dropping lightly to the ground and walking back the way I had come, toward the canal.

They grabbed me as soon as I turned the corner. They must have circled round and simply waited for me to double back. One of the men hauled me into a recess where two ramshackle walls leaned drunkenly together. The other stood in front of me, hands on hips.

"What did you run away for? That wasn't very friendly. All we wanted to do was talk to you."

His reasonable words were contradicted by his cruel smile, and by the fact that his friend was pushing my right arm up behind my back as far as it would go, and then a little further. I could barely gasp the words.

"So talk."

The man put his face closer.

"Where is he?"

"Who?"

"You know who. Your friend, the poet. The Father of Locks. We went to his house but the door was broken in and the place was empty. Where is he hiding?"

"I don't know."

The man behind me twisted my wrist, and I could not help crying out. The other man lifted an object from his belt, a curved piece of metal blotched with black clots, ending in a vicious barb. It was a butcher's hook.

"We should introduce ourselves. You can call me Munkar, and my friend here is Nankir."

He was expecting some reaction, but the names meant nothing to me. Munkar snickered.

"I see you have not been properly schooled in the true faith, or you would show us angels more respect. Let me be your tutor, then. Let me teach you about the Torture of the Grave."

He put his hook to my face, and I felt the sharp point dig into my skin.

"When you die, storyteller, which might be sooner than you had hoped, your soul will not fly straight to the afterlife, but will stay buried in the earth until the Day of Judgement. It will listen to the fading footsteps of the last mourner leaving your funeral, if you are fortunate enough to have one. Then two angels will come. They have twelve blue eyes that flash like lightning, teeth that curve like the horns of a cow, and long black hair that hangs to their feet; and the names of these angels are Nankir and Munkar. They will sit your soul upright in your grave, and ask it three questions: 'Who is your Master? Who is your Prophet? What is your Religion?'

"Your soul cannot dissemble, as your body can. If you have lived by the Shari'ah, prayed and fasted at the proper times, then you will answer correctly: God, Muhammad, Islam. If you cannot answer, then... the angels begin your punishment. Shall I tell you, storyteller, the punishment for those who spread deceit?"

I held myself still, as the barb scratched down my cheek.

"The angel jabs a hook into the liar's mouth, and rips his face from front to back. Next he hooks his nose, and again gashes him front to back. Thirdly he sticks his hook into the liar's eyeball, and gouges round to the ear. Then he starts on the other side..."

Nankir cackled.

"Munkar is generous with his learning. You must enlighten us in return. Tell us where we can find the poet."

"I don't know where he is. I left Baghdad five years ago and haven't seen him since."

Munkar peered into my face.

"Do I believe you, storyteller? I think not. I think you are a deceiver, and need to be punished. Of course, the torture of the soul differs from that of the body in one important respect: in the grave your face will grow back each time, so that you can suffer until Judgement Day. I, on the other hand, will only be able to punish you once. When I have finished with you, there will not be anything left worth calling a face. So, I will give you one last chance to spare yourself. Where is the Father of Locks?"

"Is someone looking for me?"

A tall figure stepped from the shadows. Munkar drew a long knife, leaving the hook hanging from my mouth, and Nankir tightened his grip on my arm. Abu Nuwas bowed.

"Peace be upon you, brothers. And upon you too, Ismail; it has been too long. Is nobody going to wish me peace in return? The Holy Quran enjoins us, when offered a friendly greeting, to answer it with a better one. No? Then perhaps you could allow my friend to leave, if it's me you were looking for."

"Give us your sword, then we'll let the storyteller go."

"My sword?"

Abu Nuwas brought his right hand round from behind his back, and seemed surprised by the length of glittering steel in its grip.

"This? A mere toy, of no account. Release my friend, and you can have it."

Munkar shook his head. I felt Nankir's grip loosen slightly as the man reached for a hidden weapon, and I saw my opportunity. I span round so that my arm untwisted, and at the same time snatched the hook out of my mouth and jabbed it into Nankir's groin. Munkar's knife flashed past my ear, and I danced away.

Nankir was howling on his knees, blood dripping through his cotton breeches. Munkar stabbed at Abu Nuwas, but the parry knocked the knife from his hand, and Abu Nuwas kicked it into the river. The self-styled angel contemplated the swordpoint wavering in front of him, and fled. Abu Nuwas put his sword to the throat of the injured Nankir.

"Now, let us see what we can learn. Who sent you? What did you want with me?"

Nankir spat.

"See you in Jahannam, traitor."

Abu Nuwas pressed his swordpoint against the man's gullet, but I restrained him, to his great indignation.

"But he —"

"No. We are not butchers."

Abu Nuwas sighed, and contented himself with a kick to Nankir's injured groin, which left him screeching on the ground.

"Come on then. We'd better go, before Munkar comes back with help."

We ran until we had left the deserted warehouses of the docks and arrived at the markets of Karkh, where we took refuge in the anonymity of the crowds. Abu Nuwas led the way to an unremarkable green door on a side street. In answer to his knock a greasy man admitted us to a dingy courtyard, and brought us drinks. I refused the offered wine, and instead sipped at a cup of sheep's milk, while Abu Nuwas grinned at me.

"By God, I am glad to see you again, Ismail al-Rawiya."

"I wish I could say the same, but I would not imperil my immortal soul by telling lies."

"Such cruel words. Is this the thanks I get for saving your life?"

"My life would not have been at risk if it were not for you. Who were those men? They seemed rather more formidable than the usual debt collectors and outraged fathers that come looking for you."

"I don't know; but they are not the first. Three men battered down the door of my home last night, and tried to kill me in my bed. I fled to a lover's house, but he betrayed me to my foes, and I had to leap from a window to escape. I didn't know who else to turn to, so when I heard my old friend Ismail was back in Baghdad, I came looking for you. Unfortunately, it appears my enemies got to you first."

221

"Your enemies are determined, but they lack subtlety. If I wanted to kill you, Father of Locks, I would not send men with swords and knives. I would send a pretty boy with a cup of poisoned wine."

Abu Nuwas started, spilling his drink slightly. Then he smiled.

"My friend, there are some things for which it is worth risking your life. Besides, wine is a very poor means of administering poison. Most toxins stink, or taste repulsive, when present in enough quantity to do you harm."

"So what do you want from me? I have no home in which to hide you."

"I want you to come with me."

"Why? I would be little use as a bodyguard."

"I don't need a bodyguard. I need a friend. My enemies are everywhere, and I have no idea whom I can trust — except for you, Ismail."

"Your friendship brings me nothing but trouble, Father of Locks. I left Baghdad to get away from you. Whenever I go anywhere with you, I end up with a knife at my throat, or in a prison cell, or running for my life."

"But we always have fun, don't we?"

Abu Nuwas smiled, rather desperately. I looked at his eager face, more like that of a child hoping for a treat than a man facing death, and sighed.

"Begging does not become you. I don't suppose I have much choice in any case. I notice that our greasy host has disappeared; I suspect he will not be alone when he returns. So where are we going?"

The nervous smile on Abu Nuwas' face became a delighted beam.

"I knew you would not let me down. We are going, Ismail, to see the Wazir."

***

The palace of Ja'far ibn Yahya al-Barmaki, while built for pleasure, defends him from the intrusion of the impertinent as securely as any fortress. Guards stand at the door, and more fearsome still are the secretaries who govern access to his diwan. Few, indeed, are those who can drop in on the Wazir uninvited.

Abu Nuwas and I did not present ourselves for the scrutiny of the guards or the secretaries. We sidled round to a small, undistinguished door in a back alley where shops and boarding houses slouched up against the palace walls. The poet fumbled in his sleeve, and pulled out a tarnished key. He jiggled it in the lock for some time before turning to me sheepishly.

"They appear to have changed the lock. How embarrassing. I don't suppose you could...?"

I pushed him aside from the door roughly, and worked at the lock with two bent pins, until it clicked open.

"There. They watch who comes in this way, you know."

"Oh, don't worry about that little misunderstanding over the key. The Barmakid will be delighted by our visit."

We entered, and followed a short corridor to where it opened out into a hall lined with sleeping rugs. Ilig the Khazar was waiting for us. His northern accent was still heavy despite half a lifetime as Ja'far's bodyguard.

"The Wazir will see you, but he tells me to tell you he is very cross."

The attendants bowed as the Khazar passed, and the guards stepped aside. The secretaries tutted and pretended not to see him, but they did not bar our passage. At last we entered the diwan of Ja'far al-Barmaki.

The Wazir sat in a bright garden, where shrubs of sandalwood scented the air. A spring bubbled nearby. The spring always bubbled when the Wazir was in the garden, but only when the Wazir was in the garden. This was because the bubbles were produced by a slave, concealed from view in an adjacent room, frantically pumping air into a pipe that ran beneath the ground. No sign of this industry, however, disturbed the tranquillity of the afternoon.

Around the garden sat the petitioners, screened and shepherded by discreet rings of bureaucrats. To reach this far, they had pleaded and argued, leaned on tribal loyalties, and where necessary paid hefty bribes. They had invested heavily, in time, effort and money, just for the chance to be heard, each driven by his own cause, his burning desire for justice or his overpowering sense of self-worth. Now they stared angrily at the huge Khazar and two other interlopers trampling across the invisible lines that structured their world.

The Wazir dismissed the man in front of him with a curt wave as we bowed before him.

"Go — I will see that your business is taken care of. Abu Ali, peace be upon you. Such a joy to see you. And who is this with you? Can it be Ismail al-Rawiya? It is many years since I caught you in the tower of the House of Wisdom."

"It is, my lord."

"You should visit the House of Wisdom, now you are back in Baghdad. You will find it much altered. What brings you to my diwan, Abu Ali? You have not visited for some time."

"You changed the locks, my lord."

Ja'far smiled, with what appeared to be real affection, and spoke quietly.

"I am sure you understand, my friend. Your moon is on the wane, and the Khalifah does not favour you. However the heavens will turn again. The fashion for prayer and piety will grow old, and there will once more be a demand for good booze and dirty jokes. In the meantime I must keep a distance between us."

"I understand, my lord. I hear that you, too, have felt the Khalifah's indifference."

The warmth disappeared from Ja'far's handsome face.

"You should be careful where you put your ears, Abu Ali, or you may find that someone cuts them off. What boon do you seek?"

"Somebody is trying to kill me."

"I see. Who is this man?"

"I do not know."

Ja'far leaned back on his rug.

"Then what, Abu Ali ibn Hani al-Hakami, would you have me do? I cannot arrest every man you had ever offended, insulted or argued with — there are not enough policemen in all Baghdad."

"No, my lord."

"And I cannot offer you an armed guard. It would look, you must agree, rather odd."

"I could not ask such a thing, my lord."

"So your petition is...?"

The Wazir's patience was wearing fast. Abu Nuwas raised his hands awkwardly in supplication.

"You see all and hear all, my lord. Who comes and who goes, who lives and who dies, who attacks and who defends. If there is anything that could help me, any dark place in which I can delve to find my foe, then you can tell me. You are the All-Knowing, the Merciful One; save me, my lord."

Ja'far whispered.

"Be careful of your blasphemy, Father of Locks. Such words are dangerous in these times."

Abu Nuwas waited with his head bowed. Finally the Wazir leaned back and addressed the winter skies.

"My sources tell me that al-Sifr is in Baghdad. Yes, I too had believed him dead. If I had known he was still alive, I would have used every means at my disposal to hunt him down. And when I caught him, I would have ordered my men to cut him into pieces, and then burn the pieces, and then to bury the ashes, just to be sure that he could not come again to bring deceit and disaster to the Family of Islam.

"Now, however, it is too late. Somehow he has infiltrated the capital, and has disappeared into the crowd, lost among the suqs and alleys. In what guise he has come, and what he is plotting, I cannot tell you."

"Then how, my lord, are we to track him down? Even I have never seen his face undisguised."

"Go and see Yaqub al-Mithaq. He has retired from my service, but he fought al-Sifr at your side in the past. Perhaps he can help you."

With that, the Wazir turned away. Abu Nuwas and I hurriedly bowed as Ilig hustled us out, and moments later, we were back on the street. I had been pondering Ja'far's words, and found them troubling.

"You know, Father of Locks, I have been informing my audiences that al-Sifr was killed by an elephant three years ago. Have I been misleading them?"

"How flattering that you are still telling stories about me. I must confess that in my haste to flee that horrible place I neglected to ensure that he was truly dead."

"That was careless of you. Still, it seems to me that if the Wazir really wanted to help us, he would have given us more information. If he does not know what al-Sifr is doing, where he is or what he looks like, I wonder why he is so sure the Roman is in Baghdad at all."

"Ah, it was ever thus. Ja'far al-Barmaki tells as much as he wants to tell, and no more. If we had asked, he would only have told us that the Khalifah saw him in his magic mirror, or some such nonsense. However, while his advice may be equivocal, it is usually well-informed. I find it best to do as he says."

"Well, I have no better plan to suggest. Where does one find Yaqub al-Mithaq these days?"

Harbiya used to be a wild part of town, back when Baghdad and I were still young: a rough and riotous neighbourhood, the ex-soldiers who lived there having never quite shed the habits of barracks and camp. Now, most of the veterans have left the luxurious houses that were their earthly reward, and passed onto still finer dwellings in Paradise. Their sons, who grew up in wealth and comfort, are quieter in their ways, having driven the whores and gamblers from its streets, but no less independent of spirit.

We crossed the Tigris by the North Bridge, and arrived at a long building with a high roof. Its windows were unshuttered, and the chatter of women, the clack of wood and the slosh of water could be heard from within. Wide double doors stood open at one end. Abu Nuwas took off his shoes and we entered.

Shafts of light from the windows illuminated the industry inside. Skeins of wool and silk hung from the ceiling, or stretched the length of the workshop, veined like rainbows in bands of bright colour: crimsons, golds, greens and purples. At the end of each skein women sat, hunched and cackling, fingers threading and knotting faster than my eyes could follow. Half-finished carpets were stretched on frames, their elegant designs dissolving at their base into rivulets of yarn. In corners heavy hanks of thread were soaked in tubs of dye, or hauled out dripping and darkening.

"Abu Ali! I thought I told you — Ismail? Is that you?"

I felt arms round my waist, squeezing me so that I could barely breathe. I craned my head round, and found myself nose to nose with the grinning face of Yaqub al-Mithaq.

"Peace be upon you, Ismail al-Rawiya! It is good to see you after all these years. Follow me — you, there! Bring refreshments for my guests. Yes, Abu Ali, I suppose you had better come too."

He led us to a wooden platform, reached by a short flight of stairs like the pulpit in a masjid. From the top there was a clear view right to the other end of the workshop. The platform was covered in thick rugs, and I sank down, grateful for its comfort after our long walk. Al-Mithaq noticed my expression and laughed.

"Yes, it is one of the benefits of being in the carpet trade. I never sit or sleep on anything but the finest lamb's wool."

The former postman was now in late middle age, broad of girth and with grey hairs twinkling in his black beard. His eyes, though, were still sharp, and he contemplated us thoughtfully as we sipped on sweet, ice-cold sherbet.

"So, Ismail, where have you been? What brings you to my door?"

I opened my mouth to answer but Abu Nuwas interrupted.

"Al-Sifr is in Baghdad."

Yaqub al-Mithaq blanched for a moment, but scowled and

looked away.

"I was not speaking to you, Abu Ali al-Hakami. Besides, I have left all that behind. I am no longer a postman. Al-Sifr is nothing to me now. This —"

He waved a hand at the workshop.

"— this is my business now."

Abu Nuwas persisted.

"Surely you cannot be satisfied with this? With weaving, and women, and sitting on soft carpets while your backside expands? A man like you, who has seen the wonders of the earth?"

"Why not? I have had my fill of travel, and adventure. I am making good money. Tomorrow is Friday, and I have orders to complete before the end of the week. Why should I risk my life, to go chasing foreign spies?"

"Because if al-Sifr is here, nobody is safe."

Abu Nuwas spat out the words with startling vehemence.

"You have seen yourself what he is capable of. Your ease, your fortune, are only as secure as the society on which they rest. Al-Sifr has not come to the heart of Islam merely to kill me; he will be satisfied with nothing less than the complete destruction of our way of life. His plots, his conspiracies, are even now eating away at the foundations of everything you have built, like woodworm gnawing through the legs of this platform, unseen and unheard. By the time everything comes crashing down, it will be too late."

Al-Mithaq was silent now, chewing on stray hairs from his beard. Abu Nuwas sensed weakness, and closed in for the kill.

"Anything you can tell us, Yaqub. You still know virtually everyone in the Barid — you must have heard something."

"Ibn Idris came to see me last night. You remember ibn Idris al-Sughdi?"

Abu Nuwas nodded. Al-Mithaq was speaking quietly, with occasional nervous glances at the weavers, who toiled away obliviously below.

"He was frightened. He is a hard man, ibn Idris, as you know, but I have never seen him so scared. He said he needed a place to stay for the night. I asked him why he did not go the Wazir's palace, to the Barid quarters there, but he answered that it was not safe. There is a traitor in the Barmakid's household, and nobody there is to be trusted.

"I gave him the key to a storeroom I own nearby, which happened to be empty. But he never arrived there. Somewhere along the way, he disappeared."

Abu Nuwas leaned forward.

"What else did he say to you? You must tell us everything you know."

Al-Mithaq's eyes betrayed his reluctance, but the words came spilling from his mouth.

"He had been in the west, in Egypt, in the town of Hulwan. An informant told him of a Roman agent living there, a dark-skinned man like a Hindi, plump and beardless. The next day, the informant was found dead. His intestines had been pulled from his still living body, and stuffed down his throat.

"Ibn Idris traced the dark-skinned man, and followed him to a clandestine rendezvous. There, he heard the man addressed by a name that caused his hairs to stand erect in horror: al-Sifr."

A shriek from the women below caused me to jump, but they were only laughing at some piece of salacious gossip. Al-Mithaq continued.

"The next day al-Sifr left town. Ibn Idris could not wait for instructions from the Wazir, but set off in pursuit. He tracked al-Sifr as he travelled east, each step taking them closer to the City of Peace. At Kufa he managed to send word to Ja'far, but instead of help, a killer came in the night, and ibn Idris barely escaped with his life. He realised that his message must have been intercepted, that there must be a traitor close to the Wazir. So when he arrived in Baghdad, he came to me. He put his trust in me, and I sent him into danger."

"What has happened to him? You must have some idea."

"My informants say that he has been taken by the fityan of Abu Dujana. That is all I can tell you."

Yaqub al-Mithaq stared out at his workshop, but he was

not looking at the women, or the wool. He was gazing beyond, as if trying to see something in his past. Abu Nuwas stood up.

"Thank you, my friend."

He held out a hand. Al-Mithaq considered it for a moment, then grasped it with his own.

"Be careful, Abu Ali. Remember, al-Sifr strikes as swiftly as a snake. Crush his head, before he sinks his fangs. Do not stop to question or parley. And you, Ismail — do you have a weapon, lad? You should carry one. The city is a dangerous place at the best of times."

We left the workshop, and Abu Nuwas set off down the street with a determined gait. I scurried after him.

"Where are we going? Do you know this Abu Dujana, whose fityan took your friend?"

"I am oddly pleased to discover, Ismail, that your ignorance of the true faith has been little diminished by the years. Abu Dujana was a Companion of the Prophet, peace be upon him, and a ferocious warrior. When he tied a red band around his head, it meant he would fight until every last idolater was killed, or he himself was. At the battle of Uhud, the Prophet gave him his sword, favouring him over his son-in-law Ali, and Umar who was later Khalifah.

"That Abu Dujana, however, died a martyr nearly two centuries ago, may God be pleased with him. This one, this man of the fityan, is new to me.

"Captains of the fityan come and go; their business is fierce, and ruthless. They prefer to operate in secrecy. When their name starts to be bandied around by courtiers and storytellers it is usually a sign that they are losing their grip, and they rarely last long thereafter."

"So how are we going to find him, if you don't know who he is, or where he lives?"

"Simple. We'll just sniff around Harbiya and look for trouble."

XIV

Trouble, I reflected, was never hard for Abu Nuwas to find; and Harbiya was the right place to find it. We had not gone far before we encountered a pack of young men, swaggering in our direction. The young men's gait was imperious, long limbs swinging, confident that other men would step out of their way. They exchanged insults as they walked, and laughed, but their laughter was hard and bared their teeth.

Abu Nuwas pulled me to one side.

"See — around their turbans. Each of them wears a red band. That marks their allegiance to the fityan of Abu Dujana, or I will eat my shoe."

"What are you going to —"

"Peace, friends! I wish to talk with you."

He was already marching up to the young men and standing in their path. They gathered around him menacingly, but his fearlessness unsettled them.

"Be careful, son of a dog. We are no friends of yours."

"Are you sure? If you got to know me better I think we could be very good friends indeed."

Abu Nuwas smiled a viper's smile. One of the youths strutted up to him, and stared into the poet's face, his own a mere hand's breadth away.

"Are you the one they call the Father of Locks?"

He was young, not twenty years of age, and good looking, with curly hair and dark brown eyes. Abu Nuwas preened at the recognition.

"Why, yes, I am."

"What do you want, Father of Locks?"

"I would like to speak with Abu Dujana."

"Then you had better come with me."

The curly-haired youth set off down a side alley. Abu Nuwas started after him, and beckoned me to follow. I joined him reluctantly.

"Are you sure this is a good idea?"

"Don't worry, I'm absolutely certain that —"

As soon as we set foot in the alley, the youths fell upon us. Abu Nuwas was swift in his movements, and had his sword half out of his scabbard, before they overwhelmed him. They slammed me against the wall, a dagger at my throat.

"Are we going to kill them, ibn Ghassan?"

One of the younger thugs, his voice still breaking, addressed this question to the curly haired youth, and received a resonant slap in return.

"Use my name in front of outsiders again, and I'll kill you myself. No, this one is worth money. They say the Spider will pay gold for him, but we need to find out which part of him they require as proof, before we start cutting. As for this one, I don't know what he is. You, Father of Locks, give me one reason why I should not kill you immediately."

"Because it would be a terrible loss to the world of poetry?"

The curly haired youth, ibn Ghassan, snorted.

"Not good enough. And you —"

He turned to me, revealing a long, narrow blade in his right hand.

"Who are you, I wonder? A servant, or a lover? Or —"

A look passed over him like a cloud, a strange blend of fear and sadness. With a shaking hand he put the knife to my face.

"I am going to ask you one question. Think well before you speak, because if you answer wrongly, you will be dead before the last word falls from your lips. Give the right answer, and I will let you both live."

I nodded carefully.

"Then tell me this: what were the horse's wings made of?"

Finally I understood, and answered in a whisper.

"The wings of the horse were of gold and silver."

Ibn Ghassan lowered the knife, then dropped it to the ground. He flung his arms round my neck, and wept on my shoulder. His cronies were puzzled, and the boy he had slapped reached a hand out to him, but ibn Ghassan pushed it away, and they stood around listening to his sobs in embarrassment. At last he stepped back, wiping tears from his face.

"This man saved my life, when I was only a child. He is not to be harmed."

"Then what are we going to do with them?"

Ibn Ghassan rubbed his chin.

"We will take them to Abu Dujana. He will decide."

His companions prodded us through the alleys with a wary mix of belligerence and deference. Abu Nuwas was most put out that ibn Ghassan had not remembered him.

"'This man saved my life' indeed! It was I who found him, and carried him out of that dark cellar, though I get no thanks for it. Son of Ghassan... I should have realised. How is your father, Ghassan the porter? Is this the life he dreamed of for you? I believe he hoped you would be Wazir one day."

"There are many routes up the mountain, Father of Locks. But we don't all set out from the same place at its foot."

"And are you proud of what you have become, Ahmad ibn Ghassan? Was it for this that we saved your life?"

Ibn Ghassan shrugged.

"Since I am alive, and poor, I must live how I can. We are not so bad, in the fityan. We do not hurt anybody unless it is a business matter, and we only steal from those who can afford it. Would you condemn me, had I become a soldier, or a policeman?"

"If you had joined the army, or the shurtah, you would not now be working for the enemies of Islam. Ahmad, you said that the Spider would pay gold for me. Who is the Spider? Tell me that, at least."

"You saved my life, for which I am grateful, and I in turn

have spared yours. Do not ask me to speak words which will get us all killed."

He hustled us through high double doors, broad enough to admit a laden camel, into a large courtyard. The place looked like a merchant's house, the kind of building that was as much workplace as domicile. Ibn Ghassan went inside, leaving us in the custody of his men, who shifted awkwardly as we waited.

When ibn Ghassan reemerged, he was following another man. The newcomer was well dressed, in a long coat and jewelled turban, and just arriving at the prime of life. His face was disfigured by a birthmark across one cheek, and bore the lines of a life of struggle, but there was rigour in his bearing, and wisdom in his eyes. I walked over and kissed him on both cheeks.

"Peace be upon you, Mishal ibn Yunus al-Rafiq."

"And upon you, Ismail al-Rawiya. But I am called Abu Dujana these days. Real names are dangerous. Names reveal kinship, and if an enemy knows your kin it only gives them more ways to hurt you. Where have you been these many years, since we last fought side by side?"

"Oh, here and there. I see you have prospered in that time."

I indicated the fine clothes, but Abu Dujana shrugged.

"Is it prosperity, when a moment's carelessness could see it all snatched away from me? Do prosperous men sleep with one eye open, and a dagger in their hand? But this is no way to celebrate the reunion of old friends. Let us eat, and drink."

Servants came running with silver trays, bowls of fruit, milk puddings and saffron rice, and jars of ice-cold water. Without being asked Abu Dujana had wine brought for Abu Nuwas. I ate sparingly, wondering how Abu Nuwas was going to broach the subject of the kidnapped postman. It was Abu Dujana, though, who broke the silence.

"I know what you have come for, but you cannot have it. If the Wazir's man is your friend, then I am sorry; but some choices are not ours to make."

"What is he paying you? We will double it."

"What is who paying me, Father of Locks?"

An uncomfortable silence ensued. Abu Dujana laughed.

"You do not even know who your enemy is. From what I hear, Ja'far al-Barmaki tells you whom to fight, and you charge off obedient to his command.

"In fact, I have lost a substantial sum betting that you would be dead before now. I even considered helping things along, but I was so confident that you would bring your demise on yourself, through drink, or disease, or a cuckold's blade, or the executioner's sword, that it did not seem worth the trouble. Besides, if a man cheats on a wager, it is no longer sport, but merely business."

Abu Nuwas clenched his fist.

"Listen to me, Abu Dujana Mishal ibn Rafiq. This is no matter of petty thefts or feuds, but a great affair of state, compared to which the concerns of your fityan are like the games played by children. The man you have captured carries vital information about a dangerous foreign agent, a spy who threatens the security of the whole Land of Islam. It is your duty, to God and to his Khalifah, to hand him over to us."

Abu Dujana replied calmly.

"That's funny. The man who paid us to kidnap him said almost exactly the same thing. And you can take it from me, he is not somebody whom you cross, simply because you have had a better offer. No, there can be no bargaining, no negotiation. You may stay here as my honoured guests, or leave in peace, as you choose; but if you try to steal him from me, then you will know for sure who your enemy is; for it will be me."

Abu Nuwas smiled.

"So, you will not give us your prisoner, nor will you sell him to us. Therefore, by the laws of the fityan, I challenge you to a wager."

A hint of amusement crept into Abu Dujana's stern visage.

"What do you know of the laws of the fityan, poet?"

"No man of the fityan can refuse a wager, provided the challenger puts up a stake equal in value to the prize."

"I do not know which traitor has been blabbing our secrets, but your information is wrong in one vital respect: the law only applies to other members of the fityan. So unless you have taken the oath, I am under no obligation to accept your challenge."

Abu Nuwas smiled.

"Then I must inform you that, as a young man in Basrah, I was inducted into the fityan of al-Ashar by Rafi ibn Rafi."

"Prove it."

Abu Nuwas took a step towards the gang leader. His bodyguards moved to block his way, but Abu Dujana ordered them back with a gesture. Abu Nuwas whispered in his ear, and Abu Dujana's face darkened.

"Very well. You are a man of the fityan. But what stake can you offer, equal in value to my prisoner?"

"Name your price. What is the Wazir's man worth to you?"

"I have told you already, the one who commissioned me in this business is a serious man, powerful and unforgiving. No amount of gold is worth the risk of antagonising him."

"Is there nothing, then, that we have, which you desire?"

Abu Dujana stroked his chin.

"Perhaps there is something, after all. Wasil, bring me my necklace."

A servant bowed, and scampered off. He came back a little later, bearing a length of cord. From it hung a score of small objects, which appeared to be irregular scraps of brown leather. It was only when the servant held it in front of us that I recognised them as human ears.

"I have assembled this collection, partly for my own amusement, and partly to deter any who seek to obstruct me. This one, for example, belonged to ibn Sahl, who went around the suq bragging that he was not frightened of Abu Dujana. And this one to Abu Alqamah, who robbed innocent passers-by without asking my permission first. When I wear my necklace to business meetings, you would be amazed how swiftly problems get resolved."

Abu Nuwas was still smiling, but doubt had crept into his

eyes.

"You want to cut off our ears?"

"No, Father of Locks, I only want to cut off yours. Ismail al-Rawiya is my respected friend and comrade. You, on the other hand, are an insufferable braggart, whose appendage would be an ornament to my collection. One ear will suffice, though. I am not a greedy man. You may keep the other."

I glanced across at Abu Nuwas, whose lips moved silently; calculating, perhaps, or praying. Finally, he answered.

"Very well then. The bet is on. Since I laid down the challenge, you have the right to choose the game. What is it to be? Dice? Nard? Shatranj?"

"No. We shall play Fiyal."

Abu Nuwas' voice was shrill with astonishment.

"Fiyal? Surely, an issue of such gravity should not be settled by a children's game? We might as well throw a coin in the air, and guess which side it will land on! Let it be a game of skill, a game for men…"

"As you said, Father of Locks, since you named the prize, it is for me to decide on the contest. Fiyal it is. Wasil, my pebbles."

The servant brought seven small stones, of a smooth rotundity that only the sea could shape. I seized the opportunity to whisper to Abu Nuwas.

"A game of Fiyal? You are willing to risk mutilation, on the outcome of this infantile entertainment?"

"If we cannot find al-Sifr before he finds us, then a worse fate awaits me than merely losing an ear. In any case, there is more to Fiyal than luck. If you are skilled at reading faces, you have a better than even chance of guessing right."

While we were talking the gang leader crouched down with his back to us, his bodyguards standing over him to ensure his actions could not be seen. At last, he turned round and sat cross-legged.

"Now then, which one has more?"

He was pointing to two small mounds of dirt on the ground. He and Abu Nuwas locked eyes, and the game had begun.

I saw the poet's gaze flickering across his opponent's face, searching for clues. Abu Dujana meanwhile sought to keep his countenance steady. As the tension mounted, though, it was apparent that he kept glancing down to the right. There was an awkward moment when he seemed to notice me watching him, and after that he looked upward, staring fixedly at the darkening sky.

Then Abu Nuwas leapt forward, scrabbling in the dirt to Abu Dujana's right. One after the other he pulled pebbles out of the ground, until there were four in his hand. He sat back triumphantly.

"I knew you would not think me so stupid as to be fooled by your obvious hints. It followed that you wanted me to choose the left-hand pit; and therefore the one you were so crudely indicating must be the correct one after all. Now, if you would bring out the prisoner..."

Abu Dujana, however, had unearthed the other three pebbles, and now handed them to Abu Nuwas.

"Your turn. You must win two rounds in succession, to take the game."

"What? That is not how we played it when I was a child!"

"That may not be how you played it in Basrah. However, we are in Baghdad, and play by Baghdadi rules."

Abu Nuwas began to protest, but one of the bodyguards moved behind him and held a knife to his ear. Abu Dujana narrowed his eyes.

"I could simply take what I want. You know that, don't you?"

Abu Nuwas kept his voice steady.

"Yes, but then it would be no longer sport, merely business. Is that not so?"

He turned his back on Abu Dujana, and dug two small troughs in the earth with his fingers. In one he placed five pebbles, in the other two. Then he scraped the soil back over them, and faced his opponent.

"So, make your choice."

Whatever Abu Dujana saw, it happened so quickly that I did not spot it. Almost immediately he leaned forward and brushed away the soil to reveal five stones.

"How kind of you, to make the answer so obvious. Now, if you would return my pebbles to me, we can conclude this business."

"Certainly. And perhaps you would ask your baboon to remove his knife from my ear? It's terribly distracting."

"Is it? Good."

Abu Dujana busied himself under cover of his cloak, then revealed the two heaps of earth.

"Take your time, Father of Locks. It will make no difference in the end."

This time he did not so much as glance at either pit. Abu Nuwas studied his face carefully, but the gang leader only smiled.

"You call this a children's game, Father of Locks, and so it is. But the games we play as children teach us all the most important lessons we will ever learn: about hiding and hunting, leader and follower, predator and prey. This game for example, this Fiyal, is no mere matter of guesswork, or chance. It favours the man who understands men, who can discern truth from lies, who can distinguish an enemy from a friend.

"But there is more still, that Fiyal has to show us. The pebbles lie unseen within the earth like seeds of possibility, yet to flower into being. For the duration of the game, two realities coexist simultaneously: more and less, winning and losing, life and death. When they are exposed, uncertainty dissolves, and the world becomes clearer, but also diminished. Knowledge is control, but doubt is potential."

Abu Nuwas interrupted this homily by impatiently grubbing in the earth and extracting pebbles. One. Two.

Three.

He poked around frantically, but there were no more stones. Abu Dujana grinned like a crocodile, and raised an eyebrow to the thug behind Abu Nuwas, who hefted his knife.

"Stop!"

My intervention startled everybody to stillness.

"Show us the other pit."

Abu Dujana did not move, so I crouched down and rooted out the stones myself. There were only two.

"Open your hand, Mishal. Your left one."

Slowly, like a man who was not accustomed to obeying commands, Abu Dujana extended his palm. In it lay the two remaining pebbles. Abu Nuwas snarled.

"Don't tell me. Baghdadi rules?"

Abu Dujana placed the pebbles in the poet's hand.

"Baghdadi rules."

It was the turn of Abu Nuwas to bury the stones. Crouching over, his coat hanging loose, he shrouded his actions so thoroughly that even I had no idea how he had allocated them. As he sat back, though, Abu Nuwas seemed very pleased with himself.

"Shall I tell you what I did with them?"

Abu Dujana was irritated, his concentration broken.

"What? Is this a pretext for some crude jest?"

"No. I will tell you where the pebbles are. There are six in the left hand pit, and one in the right."

The gang leader's eyes widened, then narrowed again.

"Oh no, Father of Locks. You will not distract me with your drivel."

"Drivel? Far from it. What I tell you is simple fact: six there, one there. My mother taught me always to speak the truth. Does the Holy Quran not forbid ever knowingly concealing the truth?"

"Yes, but according to the Hadith it is permitted to lie in times of war."

"Are we at war, Abu Dujana? I thought we were playing a game."

Abu Dujana reached out a hand toward the right hand pit. Abu Nuwas waved a finger.

"Now, my friend, take your time. There is only one stone there, as I already told you. It is not too late to change your mind."

For a moment I thought Abu Dujana would lash out. The whiteness of his face made the birthmark appear fiercer, livid crimson on his cheek. Instead the gang boss began to scratch at the earth, frantically, as though trying to drown out Abu Nuwas' needling voice.

"Such a shame. Only one pebble. Yet you cannot now admit you are wrong, even though you know you are, even though you know I am not lying, even though in a few moments you will have to hand over your prisoner to me, with all the trouble that will bring to you and your interests. You cannot change your decision, because the tiny glimmer of uncertainty remains: is this all an elaborate bluff to distract you from your impulse, which was right all along, because you *must* be right, because if you cannot trust your hunches then you cannot trust anything, and you stand all alone in a cold, meaningless world?

"But of course that is all empty nonsense, because you have found there what I told you all along you would find there: one single stone."

Abu Dujana gave up his efforts to find anything else in the hole, and flung the pebble at Abu Nuwas. The poet ducked it effortlessly, and with a single movement scooped out the left hand pit and trickled the remaining pebbles onto the ground, all six of them.

An icy stillness descended on the courtyard. I could almost hear the tight muscles of Abu Dujana's men, straining to act. Abu Nuwas spoke quietly, so that they could not overhear.

"You may have the upper hand now, Abu Dujana Mishal ibn Yunus al-Rafiq. You should remember, though, that you are no more powerful than the rituals that sustain you. If you break your own rules, the cracks will begin to riddle your world, and before you know what is happening it will no longer be the cleverest and the cruellest who is in charge, but the strongest. Is that you, Abu Dujana? Are you the strongest?"

The gang boss did not look at the men around him, tough, dumb and brutal. He only barked out an order.

"Bring the prisoner."

Ibn Ghassan and another man went into the house. In the awkward silence that followed, the afternoon call to prayer could be heard floating through the sharp winter air. Then they returned, hauling between them a shape swathed in cloth. They dumped it on the ground in front of us.

"There. Take him and go."

Abu Nuwas got to his feet and walked over to the shape. He rolled it over, and the cloth fell away to reveal a pallid face fixed in a ghastly grimace.

"He's dead."

Abu Dujana stood up.

"The terms of our wager made no mention of the man's condition. I have kept my word; now get off my property."

He stalked off into the house, leaving Abu Nuwas and me to manhandle the body onto the street, watched by ibn Ghassan. The great double doors swung shut behind us.

Abu Nuwas leaned into ibn Idris with the practised precision of a man accustomed to supporting drunks. I ducked under the corpse's arm on the other side.

"Where are we taking him?"

"I don't know, but we need to get him away from here. People are beginning to stare."

"And point. We need to be a little less obtrusive."

"Indeed. Do you think you could move his legs? No, rhythmically, as if he is walking. Left, right, left, right. That's the way."

"I don't think it's working. Maybe you need to hold his head up too."

"That doesn't help. His tongue is sticking out and his skin is blue. In fact, those men are coming after us now. I think they want to discuss with us what we're doing carrying a dead body down the street. Can't you move it any faster?"

"It rather spoils the illusion if we do."

"They do not appear to be fooled in any case. Let us hasten."

"It's no use, they are gaining on us. Was this man a good friend of yours, Father of Locks? How would you feel about abandoning him?"

"I have just endured considerable danger to liberate him. However, I was rather counting on being able to ask him some questions, so his value to me is somewhat diminished. Besides, those men are very close, and look very angry, so it might be an idea if we say a swift farewell to ibn Idris, and then — run!"

The men of Harbiya abandoned the pursuit a few streets away, their sense of civic duty extending no further than the bounds of their own neighbourhood. We leaned against a wall, and I was first to catch my breath sufficiently to speak.

"I feel rather bad about poor ibn Idris. Does he not have loved ones, who would want to mourn for him?"

Abu Nuwas laughed harshly.

"He was a postman. They rarely stay still long enough to be loved. I'm sure his is not the first body to be dumped on the streets of Harbiya. Some rich veteran will probably arrange for a funeral as an act of charity. Of more concern to me is the fact that he cannot now help us find al-Sifr."

"Perhaps he can help us after all. I took the liberty of searching his clothes as we walked."

I held out, between finger and thumb, the pellet I had found concealed in the folds of his robe. Abu Nuwas snatched it from him, and shook it out, revealing it to be a scrap of silk.

"What's this? Some form of writing..."

He stared at me, trying not to look impressed.

"How did you find it?"

"You forget, before I became a storyteller, I earned a living from thieving. I could steal the shirt from your back without you noticing. What does it say?"

Abu Nuwas peered curiously at the marks inked onto the silk.

"I do not know. It is no script I have ever encountered. It is not Arabic, nor Greek, nor Latin, nor any language written using those alphabets. Nor, I think, is it Chinese or Tibetan, although it has something of the look of the latter."

I craned over his shoulder to see the strange characters.

"That character looks like an alif, and that one a ha'. Here, though, appears to be a Roman V, and there the same figure inverted. They are arranged in three lines, four groups on the first two lines, five on the third. Each group is a pair, except this one, where the alif character is written three times, and this figure, which stands alone."

Abu Nuwas raised his eyebrows.

"Very good, Ismail. So not a language, then. The patterns are too regular."

"Should we take it to the Wazir?"

"No. Do you not remember what Yaqub al-Mithaq said? There is a spy in the Barmakid's household. Nobody there is to be trusted. We do not need courtiers, anyway. We need the help of scholars, of learned men. We must go to the Bayt al-Hikmah: the House of Wisdom."

XV

As the Wazir had suggested, the House of Wisdom we encountered that evening was very different to the place into which I had crept as a trembling adolescent, half a lifetime before. Back then it had been a vault of mysteries where knowledge was hidden away, protected by locks and riddles. Now the Bayt al-Hikmah was dedicated to the dissemination of learning, through the copying and circulation of manuscripts. Even at that late hour, with the sunset call to prayer hushing the Round City, its doors were open, and inside the wide hall swarmed with scribes and students.

Abu Nuwas ignored the shelves and scrolls, and strode to an open door at the rear of the hall. I followed him through the door, and thence to a staircase which spiralled up into the tower. At the head of the stairs we emerged through a hole in the floor, into what had once been the Chamber of the Ancients.

When I had last seen the round room at the top of the tower, the entire wall had been faced with wooden compartments concealing Greek and Roman texts. Now the shelving had been stripped out, and the room was filled with artisans' workbenches covered in peculiar objects. There were beakers and bottles of all descriptions, scales and dishes, and a number of small braziers. Many of the bottles were made of glass, with necks and spouts that had been stretched and twisted to give them a bizarre, animal appearance. A fire burned in one of the braziers, and liquid boiled in a flask held over it by a metal tripod.

It seemed more like a place where food was prepared than one where philosophy might be studied. The odours that filled the room, though, were not appealing: rotten egg and urine, the stink of brimstone and the unmistakable whiff of flatulence. At the centre of this strange kitchen, its master cook greeted us cheerily.

"Abu Ali, you gorgeous devil! What manner of arcane depravity brings you to my diwan this fine evening?"

"Peace, ibn Hayyan. I have a puzzle that I think may intrigue you."

I realised that the man must be the Wazir's astrologer, who had long ago schooled Abu Nuwas in potions, poisons and hidden writing. I could not help though still thinking of him as a cook: a dapper old man skipping merrily between the bubbling pots, smiling with pleasure at his creations even though they are destined to delight another.

"A puzzle? How delicious. You never let me down, Abu Ali."

Abu Nuwas rolled out the silk onto a bench, and the astrologer scratched his beard.

"I have seen these markings before, in books from al-Hind. However it is not Sanskrit or Pali. We must consult an expert on these matters, and fortunately there is one close at hand. Boy!"

The sudden shout startled me. A slave jumped up from where he had been skulking unseen in a corner, scraping black residue from a brass plate.

"Boy, fetch me al-Majousi, immediately."

The slave ducked his head in acknowledgement, and ran down the stairs. Abu Nuwas cast an eye around the room.

"I see you are busy, ibn Hayyan."

"My friend, I work day and night, as you can see. Paper has become incredibly cheap since the new workshop opened, cheaper than parchment or papyrus, and more practical too. Now every rich man wants to have a library of his own. We cannot copy fast enough."

"And all this? How does this monstrous glassware help reveal the secrets of the stars?"

He picked up a container that looked like two bottles mating. Ibn Hayyan took it from his hands and placed it carefully back on the table.

"That is an apparatus of my own devising, which I call al-

246

anbiq, the cup. It is not for astrology though. I know as much as I need to know about the movements of heavenly bodies. It's hard enough to pick out the true knowledge of the ancients from the made-up rubbish as it is, and getting harder. Everything is becoming corrupted.

"No, this is al-khimiya, the study of the nature of matter. Astrology is dying; this is the philosophy of future generations."

Abu Nuwas wrinkled his nose.

"Then the future stinks."

"The future is glorious. Astrology is uncertain, obscure, and often only reveals its meaning after the event. What practical use is that to mankind? Al-khimiya, on the other hand, is reliable. When I heat this liquid I know that it will turn into a white powder, that the powder will have certain properties, that a given volume of liquid will yield a certain weight of powder. The process can be repeated until doomsday, and the results will always be the same.

"Besides, the astrologer can discover nothing new, only refine the knowledge of the past. Al-khimiya is a book waiting to be written. See, here — I am working on nothing less than a new classification of the elements.

"The ancients teach us that there are four basic constituents of matter: earth, air, fire and water. At first sight this accords with our observation, for certainly things are dry or moist, hot or cold, or so on. Yet the possible combinations are too few to account for the diversity of substances I examine here, and the variety of their behaviours.

"I believe that brimstone, the metal which burns, is an element, as is quicksilver, the liquid metal. It is the combination of elements that determines the nature of materials. My ultimate goal is to discover the formula, al-iksir, which will allow me to alter the balance of their inner structure; and in so doing, to change their very essence."

"So you could transmute one to another? Say, turn lead into gold?"

Ibn Hayyan leaned closer.

"My friend, that is a petty ambition. By unravelling the riddles of the universe, man approaches union with God the Creator. With al-iksir, I could bring inanimate matter to life."

There was silence in the chamber, apart from the pop and seethe of little fires. Then Abu Nuwas grinned.

"In that case, perhaps you could start with my zabb. The old man is increasingly torpid these days, barely bothering to raise his head. He would benefit from some reanimation."

Ibn Hayyan scowled.

"You may mock, Abu Ali. Through my study of al-khimiya, I have concocted a brew which dissolves gold. Can you imagine what one might do with this royal water? It is more use than your poetry, at any rate."

"I meant no offence, ibn Hayyan. Although I would argue that poetry has tremendous power to refine, purify and exalt. It can transform animal lust into sacred love, base sycophancy into high panegyric, and crude insult into sophisticated wit. As for al-khimiya:

"You may struggle and strive, until you grow old,
   But the only way you'll make gold, is from gold."

Ibn Hayyan's face purpled, and I wondered if Abu Nuwas had gone too far, but the astrologer released a barking laugh.

"Well, God alone knows which of us is right. And history will determine whose work is remembered in years to come, long after our deaths. But see, here is al-Majousi."

The newcomer was small and nervous. His gaze darted around the room, unable to look anybody in the eyes. Ibn Hayyan clapped him on the shoulder.

"Now, lad, this is my good friend Abu Ali ibn Hani al-Hakami, better known as the Father of Locks. You are to answer his questions, but not to disclose to anybody what you see and hear here, or I will have your tongue ripped out and fed to the crows, is that clear?"

Al-Majousi nodded, a brief, sharp movement.

"Good lad."

Abu Nuwas was eyeing al-Majousi suspiciously.

"You are called al-Majousi? The Magus? Are you from the east, then?"

"Yes, from Khwarezm."

"And do you tell fortunes and worship fire?"

Al-Majousi stared at the floor, but his tone was defiant.

"It pleases ibn Hayyan to call me al-Majousi, since he knows that I am descended from the priestly caste of the Magi. However my father converted to Islam, and I was raised in the true faith."

"Very good. Now —"

Al-Majousi, though, was not finished.

"And the Magi do not worship fire. That is a malicious slander, repeated by the ignorant. We were the first people to recognise that there is only one God. We give the name Zurvan to the dimensions of time and space from which the universe itself, and the rival forces of good and evil that war within it, must have emanated.

"We are an ancient people, guardians of occult lore that has otherwise been lost to humanity. The Jews learned monotheism from us, during their exile in Babylon. The stars guided us to acknowledge the prophet Isa ibn Maryam, when he was still a child. You will show respect to my ancestors."

Abu Nuwas was taken aback by the little scholar's vehemence.

"My apologies, friend. I meant no disrespect. Now, if you would be so kind, please tell us what this says."

Al-Majousi glanced at the silk.

"Those are not words, they are numbers."

"Numbers? In what tongue?"

"In no tongue and every tongue. The system was invented in al-Hind, but it is a pure language of number, for the use of all mankind. Here, let me show you —"

Al-Majousi pulled over a scroll covered with arcane markings, turned it over, and scratched on the reverse with a reed pen.

"This line is one. Add a dash at its head, to make two, and

extend the dash for three. This is four, like a Greek epsilon. Five is a small ring like a ha', and six is a dash with a long tail. Seven is an arrow pointing down, and eight the same pointing up. Then for nine draw a circle with a tail."

Abu Nuwas frowned.

"I fail to see how this is superior to the abjad. At least that uses familiar characters. What are the symbols for ten, and twenty, and one hundred?"

Al-Majousi looked directly at him for the first time.

"But that is the wonder of it! No such symbols are needed. Depending on its place, this line can be one, or ten, or one hundred, or one million. Look, the first number written here: a two, followed by a nine. Coming in the second place, the nine represents nine tens, so your number is ninety-two."

"Then here, a two to the left of a six, that is twenty-six?"

"You see, it is so simple, a child could understand it!"

Abu Nuwas turned to me.

"You did well to find the silk, Ismail. This may be the clue that we need, if we are to thwart al-Sifr."

Al-Majousi's reaction to his words was striking. The nervous little man paled and choked.

"I must go... important business... I am sure you can work it out for yourselves now..."

Abu Nuwas grabbed him by his sleeve.

"Wait! What do you know about al-Sifr?"

"Take your hands off me!"

Reluctantly Abu Nuwas released him. Al-Majousi straightened his coat.

"By what authority do you seek to hold me against my will? I warn you, my cousin is a captain in the Khalifah's guard, and if he hears that you have mistreated me, he will have you thrown into the Matbaq.

"Now, I have explained the Hindi numerals to you. Unless you have any further questions, I will take my leave."

And he scurried down the stairs. Ibn Hayyan appeared about

to call him back, but Abu Nuwas shook his head.

"No. Let him go. As he said, we can work it out for ourselves now. Ismail, do you have the paper where he wrote the numerals?"

He spread out the paper next to the silk, and we huddled round the workbench. Abu Nuwas called out the numbers, while I wrote them down in abjad. I noticed that ibn Hayyan was making his own copy as we talked.

"Ninety-two and twenty-six we already know. Then four and ten makes fourteen, and five and ten makes fifteen. It's hard to make out some of these numbers, there are ink spots on the silk. Now the second line: Eighty-nine... seventy-four... ninety-five... twenty-nine. Here, on the third line, there's sixty-two, then there are three ones, so that must be one hundred... and eleven. Have you written that down, one hundred and eleven? Then seven, forty-nine, ninety-eight."

They stared at the numbers. Abu Nuwas muttered, half to himself.

"There is no obvious pattern to the numbers. For them to contain information, we must assume that they can be converted to words, or ideas. They do not form Arabic words when written in abjad."

Ibn Hayyan nodded.

"In secret communications of this kind, there must always be some consistent element, a single key that will unlock the whole puzzle. A system in which each element has its own separate solution has no value, it is a message empty of meaning. The question is, to what do the numbers correspond?"

"Perhaps there is a second part to the puzzle: a document, or a book, that lists the numbers and the words they denote..."

Abu Nuwas glanced oddly at me, then gathered up both paper and silk and bundled them into his sleeve.

"Well, I am sure its meaning will become clear in time. However, we have pressing business to attend to, and must defer this intriguing riddle for another day. Come, Ismail."

"One moment, Abu Ali."

Ibn Hayyan rooted under a table and pulled out a sealed

bottle. Abu Nuwas smirked.

"What is this? Magic potion which turns water into wine?"

"No, fool, it is simply wine. It is, however, the finest red wine from Lebanon. It is a gift for the Khalifah, which I would like you to present to him in person next time you are fortunate enough to be in his company. However, you must swear to me that you will not drink it yourself, but will give it to the Righteous One unopened."

"My friend, I cannot believe what you are suggesting! Is my name so besmirched that you think I would steal —"

"I am serious, Abu Ali. Swear it."

The smile disappeared from the poet's face.

"Very well then. In the name of God the Witness, I swear that I will not open this bottle, but will deliver it to the Khalifah at the earliest opportunity."

"Good. May God steer your steps."

On the street, I could not conceal my incredulity.

"What was all that about? What business could be more pressing than somebody trying to kill us?"

Abu Nuwas unleashed a self-satisfied grin.

"Do not concern yourself, Ismail. I believe I have found the key to the mystery. However, I deemed it prudent not to blurt out my insight in the astrologer's workshop, in front of his slaves and apprentices. There are traitors everywhere. Besides, Ibn Hayyan prides himself on his mastery of such secret languages. I shall let him sweat a little longer before I reveal the solution."

"Well, are you going to tell me, or am I too under suspicion?"

He showed me the paper on which the numbers were written.

"You provided me with the answer yourself, when you suggested there must be a book with the numbers and their corresponding meanings. Of which book will every educated man have a copy?"

"I suppose... the Quran?"

"Exactly. Then consider the first number on each line. The ninety-second Sura is known as The Night. On the second line, Sura eighty-nine: The Dawn. And here at the third, sixty-two. The Friday

Prayers."

"Tomorrow is Friday."

"Night. Dawn. Friday Prayers. If the numbers represent suras of the Quran, then the first number of each line is a time of day. What if each line is a set of instructions, for tonight, and then tomorrow?"

"Instructions? From whom, and to whom?"

"Ibn Idris. Al-Sifr. Who knows? The message was important enough that someone took elaborate steps to hide it."

"What does the rest of it say, then?"

"Let me see. The Night... then twenty-six, The Poets... how promising... fourteen, Ibrahim... fifteen, The City of Stone."

"What is the City of Stone?"

"Al-Hijr was an ancient city, near the al-Ula oasis. Its people carved magnificent tombs out of rock , but they worshipped idols and rejected the Prophet Saleh, so God destroyed them with earthquakes and lightning. Let's see the next line. Dawn we already know... The Cloaked Man...The Fig Tree... The Spider. Could that be the same Spider, that will pay gold to guttersnipes for parts of my body?"

"And the last line?"

"The Friday Prayers... then one hundred and eleven, The Palm Fibre... seven, The High Place... forty-nine, the Private Apartments... and lastly, ninety-eight, The Evidence."

"What does it mean?"

"I don't know. Not all of it, at least, not yet. But it gives us a place to start. The Night is where I hunt, and I would be losing my touch indeed if I could not guess where to find Ibrahim and the Poets. Let us see what we can learn there, and perhaps then the rest of the mysteries may begin to unravel."

XVI

From the outside, there was nothing to distinguish the bath house from the many hammams to be found throughout Baghdad, in rich areas and poor. At the door, however, we were examined by hard-faced men with cudgels, who took Abu Nuwas's sword before guiding us through the steam room to a large chamber at the rear.

The room was extravagantly furnished and decorated, to the point of showiness. Rugs and cushions were strewn across the floor, gauzy curtains hung from the ceiling. All around lounged groups of young men and singing girls, drinking wine together, the girls unveiled and indecent. The curtains provided illusions of privacy, around which the guests flirted and joked and drifted. A band of musicians banged out a popular song from a discreet alcove.

The revellers pretended not to notice the arrival of Abu Nuwas. It is not done in those circles to be impressed by anything much, but I caught some of the men gazing at the Father of Locks in admiration or envy. They quickly dropped their eyes and looked away, when they saw that I had noticed them.

At the centre of all this, like a queen ant surrounded by workers, was a man in his mid-twenties. Even had he not been wearing fine clothes and a bejewelled turban, his air of languid superiority would have marked him as the prince of whom Abu Nuwas had spoken. He seemed familiar, but it took me a moment to recognise the boy I had met years before, the prince who wanted to be a poet: Ibrahim ibn al-Mahdi, younger half-brother of the Commander of the Faithful.

Abu Nuwas knelt before him.

"Peace be upon you, my lord."

Prince Ibrahim yawned.

"Spare me the formality, Abu Ali. We artists do not observe such conventions. Skill is the only rank we recognise, amongst ourselves."

"Then still I must bow before you, for your verse if not for your birth."

The prince pretended to dismiss the flattery, but could not conceal a pleased smile.

"Sit down, my friend. Everybody knows you are the greatest of us all."

Abu Nuwas placed a submissive hand on his chest, and settled himself on the only vacant rug in the prince's circle.

"Are you going to favour us with some of your poetry tonight, my prince?"

Before the prince could respond, a black man sitting beside him interjected.

"It might be a greater favour if you do not, and spare us the shame of comparing our own feeble efforts to your mighty lines."

Peeved, Abu Nuwas stared at the prince's companion, who had dared to outdo him in flattery. He was young, around the same age as the prince, with large, curious eyes. Prince Ibrahim laughed.

"Do not fall out, you two; you should be friends. You are both learned men, and sons of Basrah too. Abu Nuwas the poet, this is al-Jahiz the scholar. Al-Jahiz here has come to Baghdad at my invitation. When I heard about this phenomenon, this prodigy of learning of whom everyone was talking, I decided I simply had to meet him.

"Do you know, al-Jahiz grew up in poverty, the son of slaves, and taught himself to read and write? Once he earned a living selling fish along the canals, and now he is one of the most erudite men in the land."

Al-Jahiz seemed uncomfortable with this description, although whether he was more ashamed by his humble origins or embarrassed by the prince's praise was unclear. Abu Nuwas glared suspiciously at the newcomer.

"Are you a poet then?"

Al-Jahiz made a placatory gesture.

"No, nothing so grand. I am a mere toiler in the fields of knowledge. I reap, thresh and winnow, so that all men might benefit from the harvest. In my writing, I aim only for clarity; I leave lyricism to the likes of you. I am not an artist, like the Father of Locks; I am content to be a humble artisan. A man should know his place in this life."

Abu Nuwas, denied the argument he was seeking, looked around for other entertainment. He noticed me, observing the conversation while hovering uncertainly nearby, and snapped his fingers.

"You! Don't just stand there. Go and get me a drink."

I decided it was not the time to complain about being treated like a servant. Bowing submissively, I drifted away through the party, in search of enlightenment.

The insipid music shrouded everything, as did the diaphanous curtains. Scraps of voices whispered around him, chattering of love and dreams. They seemed like ghosts, disconnected from the recumbent bodies sprawled below. No word of conspiracy came to me, nor any way of inserting myself into their discourse.

A singing girl wafted towards me.

"Are you alone? Would you like some company?"

"No — no, thank you. I am looking for a man —"

"Oh. I see."

She turned away, ignoring my protestations that that was not what I meant, I was trying to find —

"Who is that? I know that voice. Who's there?"

An old man grasped at my coat. I recoiled, then composed myself, and crouched down next to him.

"Peace be upon you. I am —"

The old man's eyes twitched blindly, but his voice was triumphant.

"I know who you are. You are the boy Ismail, companion of Abu Nuwas."

It was only then that I recognised the poet Abbas. He was

at most a couple of years older than Abu Nuwas, but his ruined, sightless face made him look ancient. He had always been emaciated, even in the days when he was considered the most handsome man in Baghdad; now his hollow cheeks and sockets cast the shadows of a skull.

"Abbas! What happened to you?"

Abbas shook his head.

"God is punishing me, lad, for my sins. In His mercy he has left me alive to repent, but he has taken my sight, and my good looks. And the sickness is eating me away from inside."

"But how did you recognise me? It was a decade and a half ago, and my voice had barely broken then."

"There is not much left in my life, except my memories. I spend a lot of time with them, pondering them, polishing them. Those days are clearer to me now than many that have passed since then. I repent of my wrongdoing, but I am glad that I have the recollection of it. All those women..."

His face contorted in a leer. I hurried to change the subject.

"At least the prince still values your company."

Abbas cackled.

"I think they keep me round as a warning, to remind them of Judgment Day. Or perhaps as a freak, to wonder at and mock."

"But you get to hear the gossip, eh?"

"A blind man hears many things."

Without much hope I tossed out a question.

"Have there been any strangers here tonight, Abbas? A beardless man with dark skin, perhaps?"

Abbas turned his head as if to look at me.

"Why? Do you have business with such a man?"

Aware of my heart suddenly thudding in my chest. I decided that careful truth was the best course.

"I seek to prevent a conspiracy by the enemies of the Khalifate."

Abbas did not seem surprised, but smiled thinly.

"I see. It is a wise man that can tell an enemy from a friend.

You must be careful, boy. One who stands at the Righteous One's side, is chief among those who would do him harm."

"Who, Abbas? Who do you mean?"

The blind poet put a finger to his lips.

"Take this."

He handed me a necklace. The pendant was a brass plate, the size of my hand, cut into the shape of an elephant. The plate was irregularly punctured with small rectangular holes. I examined it, bemused.

"But what is this, Abbas? What does this all mean?"

Abbas cackled like an old woman.

"Hehehe. The man who would learn the truth, studies only what is revealed. Listen to the song. You will see. Only what is revealed..."

He trailed away, sinking back into his private hell. I turned my attention to the music. A singing girl had joined the band, and was trilling a recently popular tune.

"I am drawn to what hurts me, it poisons my blood,
I shake and I sweat each time I must leave her
My friends think I cannot have long to live
Love is more deadly than fever...."

I recognised the lyric. It had been written by Abbas, back when the poet was young and whole. Listening intently, I tried to find hidden secrets in the lines, chasing elusive shadows of meaning through the allusive thickets of imagery.

"So demure, the girl with the charcoal eyes
Like a trilling flute she flutters her lies.
She has driven away sleep, set my liver afire,
The night owl echoes my agonised cries.
I relished the water that flooded my sight
Twin globes drowned under liquid skies..."

Somewhere nearby I could hear Abu Nuwas holding forth to Prince Ibrahim.

"But of course a boy is to be preferred to a girl! This is not a question of inclination, but one that can be proven by rational argument. Nor is it a matter of aesthetics; for do we not use the same phrases to describe beauty in either sex? Wide eyes, full lips, slender limbs and plump buttocks: are these not the tokens of the perfection we all seek, regardless of our preferences?"

I returned to their circle, and perched quietly on a carpet. Abu Nuwas and al-Jahiz were sitting on either side of the prince, and the poet accompanied his oration with extravagant gestures, like a lawyer arguing a case.

"No, the superiority of a boy as a lover is demonstrable, and threefold. Firstly, a boy is available and desirable throughout the month. Girls, on the other hand, are unclean for days at a time, bleeding, volatile and repugnant. If I were to sell you a horse, then tell you that it could only bear you three weeks out of every four, you would call me a swindler, and rightly so.

"Secondly, women must always be paid for, one way or another; either overtly, as one buys the time of a singing girl, or less honestly but more expensively, by taking them into your household as wife or concubine, after which you must keep them for the rest of their lives, even when they age and sag and become unattractive. When a boy loses his tender charm, he will go to earn his own living, and not hang around your neck demanding to be carried.

"Third, and most importantly, women are spirits of the earth. Their place is the home, and their concern is for mundane issues, of the birth, procreation, and death of the physical body. Men, meanwhile, must tame fire, master the raging seas, and comprehend the heavens themselves. Granted, there are women of rare intelligence, and men of unfathomable stupidity. However there are also beasts that can talk, and count, and find their way home from anywhere in the world; and nobody is proposing that we take animals as lovers. Except, perhaps, ibn Khudayr."

Everyone laughed, but the reference was lost on me.

"No, as the ancient masters knew, the purest love known to humanity is that between man and boy. The boy learns, not only the ways of love, but the ways of the world; he learns how to be a man. The man is rewarded for his tutelage with the presence of beauty and the pleasures of a strong young body. And when the boy transmutes into a man, and grows hairy, gross and unreceptive, they will part as naturally as the seed falls from the tree, and the boy who has become a man will find a lover of his own, to nurture in his turn."

Abu Nuwas sat back, replete with self-satisfaction. Prince Ibrahim shouted his appreciation.

"Well said, my friend! And what say you, al-Jahiz? What is your preference, a boy or a girl? Which makes a better companion?"

Al-Jahiz stroked his beard.

"A difficult choice, my prince. I would have to say — neither. I would rather have a book."

Abu Nuwas hooted.

"A book? Remind me never to come to one of your parties. What kind of cold fish are you?"

If al-Jahiz was stung by the implicit reference to his former profession, he did not let it show.

"Yes, I will take a book, if I may choose. A book is a bottle full of learning, a cup of common sense, a jar full of jokes and gravity. It will amuse you with anecdotes, dazzle you with wonders, or correct you with good counsel, according to your mood. A book prolongs your pleasure, whets your wits, adds vibrancy to your voice, makes nimble your fingers, weighty your words, and joyful your heart. What other companion, male or female, sleeps whenever you sleep, and wakes as soon as you wake? What other companion can you fit in your sleeve?

"You mock me, Father of Locks, for choosing to spend my time with books, but to me a book is a friend, one that is never annoying, or greedy, or impatient, or dishonest. It does not interrupt when you are busy, but is always pleased to see you when you have time for it. You never have to humour a book out of courtesy, or pretend to be out when it calls. It does not become resentful if your visits are rare, but if you love it, truly love it, faithfully and honestly, it will haunt you like a shadow. And when you fall in love with a book, you need nothing else; you will be free from boredom and loneliness, and never forced to seek the company of false friends.

"It is a small thing, and light as a whisper, yet it can carry the Word of God, and the deeds of kings. It is a teacher that never fails you, that desires nothing other than to share its knowledge with you, and that continues to instruct you when your money has all gone. When your allies turn against you it remains faithful, and when your enemies surround you it stays at your side.

"If a book did nothing else for you, other than to save you from the company of other people; if all it did was to deliver you from their gossip, and their dull affairs, and their appalling manners, and their rotten Arabic, and their stupid ideas, and their woefully misguided opinions, and above all, from the need to be polite to them; if a book did nothing more than that, it would still be the best friend you ever had. That, prince, is why I choose the company of books."

Abu Nuwas was smart enough to know when it was time to be a good loser.

"You have quite converted me, man of Basrah. It is as though I have chanced upon an old flame, of whom I have been shamefully neglectful, and been mortified to discover that I am still in love."

Prince Ibrahim beamed.

"This is how it should be! Two great warriors of wit, duelling with words as weapons and learning as their armour. The Father of Locks asks for quarter, al-Jahiz. Will you grant it, or skewer him with an epithet?"

A servant appeared at my elbow with a silver platter, bearing goblets and a jug of wine. He held out a drink, but I waved it away.

"No, thank you."

The servant turned toward the prince, but on seeing Abu Nuwas he started, causing the goblets to rattle on the tray. I looked up. The man's face was round and soft, with skin the colour of chestnuts, and neither beard nor moustache. Without thinking, I cried out.

"Al-Sifr!"

The servant dropped the platter and fled. I jumped to my feet, but my shout and the crash of metal had drawn the attention of Prince Ibrahim, whose face showed his displeasure at the interruption.

"Who is this man? Is he drunk? Why is he throwing wine around?"

Abu Nuwas waved an elegant hand.

"You must forgive him, my prince. He is a congenital idiot. I feed him as an act of charity, and keep him around to amuse me with his babblings. Excuse us, my lords, I shall punish him for his effrontery."

He hustled me away to a quiet corner of the chamber.

"What do you think you are doing? The prince will —"

"Al-Sifr. He was here. Dressed as a servant."

"Are you sure?"

"He matched the description al-Mithaq gave us. And why else would he have run away, when I spoke his name? We must go after him, quickly. If we —"

"No."

Abu Nuwas placed calming hands on my shoulders.

"At best, he will have disappeared into the night. At worst, he is lying in ambush, waiting for us to pursue him. We know now that we are following the right trail. We must be patient, and careful.

"Besides, Ibrahim ibn al-Mahdi may play at being a poet, but he is a prince of the house of Abbas, half-brother to the Khalifah himself. One cannot pump him for information, then leave once satisfied as though he were a whore. We go only when he dismisses us, or retires to his bed; which, knowing his habits as I do, will not be much before dawn."

Dawn. The Cloaked Man. The Fig Tree. The Spider.

"Have you found anything out about the City of Stone?"

"No, but I know now where to find the Cloaked Man. In truth, I am a fool for not working it out sooner; he is an old friend, not only of mine, but of many here, although he does not move in these circles any more."

"Where then? Where will we find him?"

"A dark place. A dark place, on a cold morning."

***

The watery winter dawn was seeping into the city, but no brightness reached the square in which we stood. A menacing hulk eclipsed the sun, and filled the place with shadows. On the east side of the square the Matbaq prison squatted grim and silent, a warning to the citizens of Baghdad that their masters' tolerance was not to be abused.

In the square which lay before the prison gate, a man crouched in the dirt, swathed in a plain cloak of brown wool. When the call to morning prayer had faded in the air, he sang alone, a strange and unearthly song, in which the words were protracted and ornamented so that it was some time before I realised he was simply intoning the name of God, over and over again. Abu Nuwas nodded.

"The Cloaked Man. He is as renowned a landmark as the Gilded Gate, here every dawn sure as the sun."

The cloaked man now ended his song, and got to his feet. He threw his head back, and finally I recognised him.

"The Father of Madness."

Abu'l-Atahiyya, the Father of Madness, called out to the world, his eyes fixed on the heavens.

"Brothers and sisters, awake! Hear the word of God, spoken to his Prophet through the Angel Jibril:

"'By the Moon I swear, and by the Night as it flees, and by the Dawn as it glows, this is of the utmost importance: a warning to all mankind, whether they choose to press forward or hold back, that every soul is held as bond for its deeds; except those of the virtuous, who will dwell in gardens and ask of the sinners, 'What brought you to the fires of Jahannam?' And they will answer, 'We did not pray, or feed the poor, but spent our time in empty talk with empty talkers, and lived in denial of the Day of Judgement, until the inevitable overwhelmed us.' Then no intercession will save them."

Those few people who were passing through the square in the early light paid no attention to the cloaked man, or hastened their steps as they passed him. Undeterred, Abu'l-Atahiyya pressed on with his recitation.

"'What is wrong with them, that they run away from admonition, as if they were frightened donkeys, fleeing from a lion? Indeed, every man wants it set out on a scroll for him. Indeed, they do not fear what is to come. Indeed, this is a true warning, so let he who wishes keep it in remembrance. But none will keep it in remembrance unless God wills, for He is the source of all fear, and the source of forgiveness.'

"Brothers and sisters, do you hear how God sees you, and knows what is in your heart? Do you not marvel at these words, spoken to his Apostle nearly two centuries ago, but which describe you with a precision that puts poets to shame? You — yes, you, brother, scurrying away — are you not like the donkey fleeing from the lion, as you run in terror from the truth?

"But the truth will find you in the end, however fast you run. On the day when the Angel of Death comes for you, then you will know, then you will understand; but then it will be too late. Time is short, brothers and sisters. If God wills, you must keep the remembrance of these words in your heart. You must keep the remembrance of God in your heart, at every moment of every day. Only then will you be saved from the fire."

"A little fire would be welcome on this chilly morning, would you not agree?"

Abu'l-Atahiyya started at this interruption, then frowned as he saw Abu Nuwas strolling towards him.

"Ah, here comes the Father of Locks. Will blasphemy leap so lightly to your lips when you are screaming in Jahannam, my friend?"

"And peace be upon you too. Much as I enjoy our little chats about religion, I must defer that pleasure to another day. I am seeking a man, whom I believe to have business here, at dawn. A beardless man, with dark skin, like a Hindi..."

"What mischief are you engaged in now? I will play no part in the scheming of spies. If you do not wish to join me in prayer, then I must ask you to let me be."

Abu Nuwas dropped his mask of nonchalance.

"My friend, this is no time for banter or sparring. I am in great peril, and if I do not find this man, then the Angel of Death will surely find me instead."

"Then you would be better off spending your time in prayer and repentance. God willing, you may yet be saved. Is it not wiser to aim at eternal bliss, than try to eke out this existence of suffering and fear? Why must you dance with your enemy?"

"What do you know about my enemy?"

"I know him well, for he is my enemy too, although you like to boast that he is your friend. The devil Iblis, the great Shaitan, is the Enemy of all mankind."

Abu Nuwas rolled his eyes.

"Listen, Jug Seller, this is not a game. There are men all around, and women too no doubt, and children for all I know, coming at me from every direction with sharp pieces of metal to push into my flesh, and heavy clubs to bash my brains, and cords to choke my breath, and toxins to boil my guts.

"I am not asking you to commit any sin. I am not asking you to fight for me, nor to drink wine, make stupid jokes and stick your zabb in the arses of pretty boys like in the old days. But for the sake of our friendship, I beg you, please help me. This time, I am serious."

Abu'l-Atahiyya fixed him with a fierce gaze.

"And so am I, Father of Locks. So am I."

Abu Nuwas stamped his foot in exasperation.

"But you can't really believe all that rubbish!"

This seemed to me unlikely to be a successful line of argument, but Abu Nuwas persisted, heedless.

"You are an intelligent man, my friend, a man of learning and experience. Surely you cannot accept it all without question?

Are there not parts of it that worry you, parts of what you are asked to believe?"

Abu'l-Atahiyya muttered prayers under his breath.

"Do you see why people speak of you as a devil? You will not deflect me from the service of God with your sophistry."

"And are the devils not also part of God's plan? Iblis was given permission by God to tempt men into damnation. If God loves us, why would he create our Enemy?"

"Because unlike angels, men have the gift of free will. They can choose their own path, for good or evil."

"What kind of gift is that, which might destroy its recipient? Would a loving parent give his child a scorpion for a pet?"

"We are not children. We must show ourselves capable of responsibility."

"And let us consider these angels. If God is All-Knowing, why does he need two angels to follow everyone around, writing down their deeds in a book? Doesn't he know what they're going to do before they do it? In fact, the whole of human history was written at the beginning of time, if we are to believe the imams. So why does God require duplicate paperwork? Did he just have to find something for the angels to do, to keep them busy?

"Think about it, my friend. Does that sound to you like the way an all-powerful deity would organise things? Does it not sound more like a fairy story, to frighten children into behaving because there's an angel watching them?"

"God does not need to explain Himself to the mighty Abu Nuwas. You should worry less about how He conducts His affairs, and more about how you conduct yours."

"In fact, that whole business of Submission... I mean, let us accept that He exists, this Being of infinite power and knowledge, creator of the universe. Then what He decides to do, this omnipotent entity, is to fashion little figures out of mud, little dolls. He gives them the faculty of reason, of choice, then tells them that they must perform certain actions, make certain sounds, over and over again, otherwise they will be punished with infinite pain, infinitely prolonged. Can God find nothing better to do with His creation than make the little dolls sing and dance, and then hurt them beyond measure if they do not please Him?"

"You do not understand. Prayer, fasting, pilgrimage: these are merely the outward signs of devotion. It is the inward practice, the development of God-consciousness, that brings man into union with the boundless love of God."

"Poor Father of Madness. All you ever wanted was to be loved."

"And who loves you, Father of Locks? You surround yourself with sycophants and cronies, while you in turn toady to the rich and powerful. Do you imagine any of those people care for you? Does anybody love you, except your mother?"

Abu'l-Atahiyya stopped to draw in breath, as though he had shocked himself. He lowered his voice.

"I loved you once. I admired and adored you, and you did nothing but mock me, and abuse me, and lead me into evil and the peril of damnation. I have never known you to be on the side of righteousness before, Father of Locks; why should I help you now?"

There was genuine sadness in Abu Nuwas' voice.

"You know, my friend, when you talk about the inward practice, you remind me of someone else; someone else who wore a woollen cloak, and sought the boundless love of God. But in other ways she was very different to you. She never talked about the afterlife; she always said that heaven and hell alike were distractions, that all that mattered was to love God now, in this very moment. She preached by her example, not by threatening damnation. She never passed judgement on anyone, although she was more virtuous than them all. And she would never have stood by and watched, while someone she cared about suffered."

Abu'l-Atahiyya's cheeks reddened, as if he had been slapped. He stared at the ground in silence for a while. Then he mumbled:

"There is an orchard on the north side of this square. The man you described arrived at its gate a few moments ago. He looked around as though concerned about being followed, then went in."

Abu Nuwas seized Abu'l-Atahiyya's hands and kissed them.

"May God bless you, for saving the life of an old friend."

A strange look passed over Abu'l-Atahiyya's face, a look of sadness and longing. Then he turned south and west, in the direction of Makkah, and prostrated himself in prayer.

The door to the orchard stood open, and we stepped cautiously through. The trees within, olive and pomegranate, were artfully arranged so that the orchard appeared like a dense wood, and the walls that contained it could not be seen. There was no sound but the insipid tinkle of the irrigation channels that ran between the trees.

Abu Nuwas gestured, and I followed him as he wound his way through the leaves and gloom. A voice ahead caused us to halt.

"Is that you? Show yourself, Spider!"

A solitary figure stood by a fig tree. His voice was high, with a foreign accent that gave it a mocking fall at the end of each phrase. In the uncertain light of dawn, and under the shadows of the branches, it was hard to make out his features. The fat little man who walked toward him, though, was unmistakable.

"Do not call me by that name. You should address me as Chamberlain."

"Fadl ibn Rabi!"

The whisper from Abu Nuwas was unnecessary; I recognised the Chamberlain immediately. Even in our perilous situation, I could not resist a smile at the aptness of the nickname; I had been entangled in the sticky threads of ibn Rabi's plotting before. The man with the high voice showed him little respect though.

"If you are a person of such importance, Chamberlain, why are we not meeting in comfort at your diwan?"

"The Barmakid has a spy in my household. If I so much as pass water, he knows about it before I have shaken off the drops."

Cold laughter dripped from the branches.

"Your rival spies on you, and you on him. Do you ever wonder whether he might be no more than your reflection, staring back at you from a mirror?"

Ibn Rabi was unamused.

"It ill behoves an alley-creeper such as you to concern yourself with the affairs of your betters. Did you meet with the poet, as arranged?"

"I was unable to speak to him. The Father of Locks was there, and I had to flee. Could the postman ibn Idris have intercepted your message?"

"Impossible. I have arranged for someone to deal with ibn Idris."

"How can you be sure that the deed has been done?"

A thin smile was audible in ibn Rabi's voice.

"The man I hired is efficient, and fears me greatly. In any case, even if the silk had fallen into the postman's hands, nobody could have interpreted the numerals. It is simple coincidence that the Father of Locks was there. He and Prince Ibrahim drink together often."

"I wish I shared your confidence, Chamberlain. Should we change the plan?"

"No. There is no other way to reach the Khalifah. Even if you can get past his guards the swordbearer Masrur never leaves his side - what was that?"

Abu Nuwas had stepped forward involuntarily at the mention of the Khalifah, and startled a yellow bird, which fluttered toward the Chamberlain. The assassin whipped out a slender blade from a concealed scabbard, and ibn Rabi shouted out.

"Treachery! To me, men!"

There was a flurry of movement, the stamping of feet, the creak of leather and the jangle of steel. A dozen heavily armed men emerged from hiding. Yelling a curse, the assassin sprang for the wall and clambered over it.

Abu Nuwas had disappeared at the first sight of the soldiers, and I ran blindly away, dodging through the trees. The pendant Abbas had given me banged painfully against my chest, and I wrenched it off with one hand. I could hear noises all around me, scuffles and shouts, and ducked behind a bush to recover my bearings. Twenty paces away I could see the orchard gate. I took a moment to gather myself, then bolted toward it.

I had almost reached it when the Chamberlain's man stepped into my path. Unable to stop myself I cannoned into the man's chest. Arms seized my wrists, pinioning them from behind, and I was dragged out into the square, where Abu Nuwas already stood prisoner before a furious ibn Rabi.

"You! I should have doubled the reward for killing you. And the storyteller too. Al-Rawiya, I have warned you before that your inexplicable loyalty to that deviant scribbler would be your downfall. Bring them this way."

The soldiers half-marched, half-carried us toward the gate of the Matbaq. The bystanders were obviously used to seeing prisoners taken into custody, and took little heed of our plight. I noticed Abu'l-Atahiyya staring at us though, before the great gate of the prison slammed shut behind us.

We found ourselves in a small courtyard, surrounded by high walls. Sour-faced men in the blue robes of the city police stood around swinging their clubs. On ramparts above us I could see archers squinting down. The soldiers' captain addressed ibn Rabi.

"Do you want us to kill them, my lord?"

He indicated a low dais nearby, on which there were posts with chains, the wood stained black with blood. Ibn Rabi examined us balefully.

"No. They may be able to tell us something useful. Search them."

The soldiers ran expert hands over our clothes, taking the bottle of wine ibn Hayyan had given us and Abu Nuwas' sword. Ibn Rabi eyed the bottle with suspicion.

"What is that?"

The captain pulled out the stopper and sniffed at the contents.

"It is only wine, my lord, and a good one, as far as I am any judge."

Abu Nuwas was struggling in frustration.

"Chamberlain, this is madness! How can you betray your oaths —"

Ibn Rabi crooked a finger, and a soldier smashed his fist into the poet's face.

"You should remain silent, Abu Ali al-Hakami, when you do not know what you are talking about. Otherwise you risk looking a fool. It is remarkable that you still have not learnt that, at your age."

One of the soldiers held out a hand. Ibn Rabi took something from his palm, and unfolded it carefully. It was the piece of silk with the Hindi numerals on. Ibn Rabi's face turned white.

"Lock them up. I will deal with them later, when all this is over; after the Friday Prayers."

He stomped away. As the soldiers dragged us into the cold shadow of the Matbaq, I could hear Abu Nuwas sighing.

"Well, at least I was right about the message..."

XVII

We were bundled along corridors, then down a flight of stairs, our passage lit by the uncertain glare of torches. When Abu Nuwas hesitated at the top of a second stairway, they hit him in the back with a cudgel, causing him to tumble down the stone steps. At the bottom they hauled him back to his feet. Keys rattled in a lock, and I was shoved into a cell. I heard Abu Nuwas collapse beside me, then the door slammed, and all was still.

When Abu Nuwas finally spoke, his voice was low and quiet, unlike his usual confident drawl.

"I am sorry, my friend."

"What for? I do not imagine that you planned we would end up here."

"But if I had not come to find you..."

"If you had not, then Munkar and Nankir would have ripped my face off. My destiny was already tied to yours, many years ago; our fates inextricably entwined, by God, or by Ja'far al-Barmaki."

"It is generous of you, not to blame me. And I find that, in my selfishness, I am glad it is you here with me, at the end."

"Is this the end, then? It is not like you to despair. We have been in the darkness before, you and I, and we have found a way out."

"Nobody has ever escaped from the Matbaq. This is no ordinary prison, for common thieves and criminals. This is where they hide away those who pose a threat to the House of Abbas, either through their heretical beliefs, their subversive plotting, or as a result of unfortunate accident of birth. The only way out is to be pardoned, and ibn Rabi is unlikely to show us mercy. It seems he is plotting

272

with al-Sifr to assassinate the Khalifah; if we live to expose him, then not only he will pay the price, but his family too.

"I do not mourn for myself. As Abu Dujana said, I am lucky to have made it this far. But you are young, and have done nothing to deserve such misfortune."

I reached for his hand, and held it tight.

"I may be young, Father of Locks, but I am not a child. I have seen enough to know that there is no justice on this earth, save that fitfully imposed by man. Children sicken and die, snatched from the world before they have a chance to choose between virtue and vice. The poor farmer toils all year, only to have his crop eaten by locusts; the virtuous wife is barren, while the whore throws her baby into the river. Everywhere the guilty prosper and the innocent suffer. To complain of unfairness is futile. We can only hope, and strive, and pray that God will sort it all out in the afterlife."

Abu Nuwas snorted.

"God? Well, if He is truly all-powerful and beneficent, one can only wonder why he didn't make a better job of His creation in the first place."

He fell silent, and I felt sleep come upon me in the darkness. I knew I should stay awake, alert for the slightest hope of escape; but it had been a long, strange night, and oblivion was overwhelming.

I dreamed strange dreams, in the bowels of the Matbaq. I was lost in the Wazir's palace, floating down endless passages, and I should not have been there, I knew I should not be there, and the Wazir would be very angry if he caught me, because it was Friday and I should have been on my way to prayers. I tried to get out of the palace, but every turn led me back to the same room, and my legs were sluggish, unresponsive. I would never get to the masjid on time.

Now Abu Nuwas tugged at my arm, and said come this way, this is the way to the masjid, but I was looking at a mirror. I was holding the mirror in my hands, prayers forgotten, and stared into the glittering glass, falling into my reflection. I shouted to Abu Nuwas, calling him to see, that it was not my face in the mirror, but that of al-

Majousi, the little scholar from the House of Wisdom. Abu Nuwas, though, had disappeared. And then it was not al-Majousi's face after all, but the Wazir's, the long, handsome face of Ja'far al-Barmaki. Finally my sight cleared, and I could see at last, it was the face of Abu Nuwas that gazed back at me from the mirror, mouth open to speak. But no words came.

Then I was back in the dungeon, and a man was standing over me.

"Get up."

For a moment I thought I had woken, and the guards had come for me, to take me to my execution. But the man was alone, and his voice was oddly familiar. I understood that I must still be dreaming, and slowly stood up.

"Who are you?"

"I am your Mu'aqqib, your guardian angel. Don't speak a word, but come with me."

Abu Nuwas was waiting by the door. I followed him out of the dungeon and into the corridor. A soldier stood on guard there, but stared straight ahead, apparently unaware of us.

The angel gestured for us to follow. In eerie silence we retraced our steps, up the stone stairs and along the passageways. Every door stood open, every guard unblinkingly oblivious to our presence. It was not until we had emerged into the daylight, and passed through the gates to stand beneath the fig tree, that I recognised our rescuer, and realised that I was awake after all. Abu Nuwas greeted the angel cheerily.

"Yaqub al-Mithaq! Don't you have dye to weave, or wefts to warp, or something?"

"Abu Ali, I have known you for thirty years, and not for one second of that time have I found you remotely amusing."

"What a shame. I find you hilarious."

"Even so, I would not leave you to rot beneath the ground. I have lost one friend already today. That is enough."

"You know about ibn Idris?"

Al-Mithaq blinked, then smiled.

"I still have contacts, who keep me abreast of what's happening in the city. But it was your friend the Father of Madness who alerted me to your predicament. He saw them dragging you into the Matbaq, and wisely decided to come to me."

"May God preserve the demented old bugger. But the guards — how did you do that? Were they drugged?"

"That was not necessary. I am known to be the Wazir's man, and his name has not yet lost all its power. And military discipline is a wonderful thing. You can always rely on a troop of soldiers to swear blind they didn't see something that happened right under their noses. Nobody likes to break rank, you see. I demanded they give back your belongings too."

He produced the poet's sword, and the bottle of Lebanese red, which I took and stuffed into my coat. Abu Nuwas slid the sword into its scabbard.

"I am glad to see this again. It belonged to my father. But was there no scrap of silk, with ink markings on it?"

Al-Mithaq shrugged.

"That is all they gave me. Was it important?"

"Perhaps not. The Night and the Dawn have passed, for good or ill. Soon it will be time for Friday Prayers, the last of al-Sifr's appointments. We know his instructions: The Palm Fibre, The High Place, The Private Apartments, The Evidence. And now we know his purpose here. I was vain enough to believe that he had come for me, but it seems I am only an obstacle on the path to his real goal: the assassination of Harun al-Rashid."

Yaqub al-Mithaq's eyes widened.

"The Khalifah? But how can he hope to reach him? The Righteous One is guarded day and night..."

"There is a traitor at court. The Chamberlain Fadl ibn Rabi is al-Sifr's accomplice. We heard them plotting together earlier."

"The Chamberlain? But that is inconceivable!"

Something stirred in my memory.

"Abbas warned me. He said that one who stands at the Khalifah's side was chief among those who would do him harm.

Wait for me a moment."

I ran to the orchard. The gate was now locked, but I had no difficulty scaling the wall. It proved harder to locate the bush where I had concealed the necklace, but at last I spotted the brass elephant glinting among the leaves. I returned to find Abu Nuwas and al-Mithaq arguing over the meaning of the signs on the silk.

"I can see that it has guided you correctly so far, Abu Ali, but the message has not yet revealed all its secrets. What did Prince Ibrahim have to tell you about the City of Stone?"

"Well, he did seem rather baffled when I asked him —"

"And what does the rest of it mean? The Palm Fibre, The High Place and so on?"

Abu Nuwas shook his head impatiently.

"I don't know, but if the Righteous One is in danger, we must attend upon him. Then we can be there when the assassin strikes."

Al-Mithaq scratched his beard.

"The Khalifah has just returned from pilgrimage, and spent last night camped outside the city, on the Kufah road. If we hurry, we may be able to get there before he enters Baghdad."

"You are coming with us, al-Mithaq? I thought you had left the world of intrigue and espionage behind?"

"So did I. However I cannot stand by and watch a Roman spy threaten the life of the Commander of the Faithful. Anyway, you will only get yourself in trouble, without me to keep an eye on you."

So we were three in number as we approached the royal camp, a noisy confusion of tents, horses, camels and men. A festival mood prevailed among the pilgrims, now only a short ride from home after three weary months in the saddle. There was music, and laughter; but most of the men were still moved by their experience in the holy city, and their joy was good-natured and serene, not raucous or aggressive. Cheerfully they pointed the way to the Khalifah, calling out:

"Peace be with you, brothers!"

At the centre of the camp a canopy fluttered in the brisk

wind. Soldiers and courtiers milled around it, in a delicate dance of courtesy and precedence. It was impossible to see the person sitting beneath it, but the quiet intensity of the deference surrounding him identified him as clearly as any banner.

"The Righteous One."

Abu Nuwas strode off toward the canopy, but was halted by a huge black hand on his shoulder. The owner of the hand was so immense, so imposing, that it seemed impossible he should have arrived noiselessly and unseen, but I had no warning of his approach, and Abu Nuwas jumped at his touch, before recognising him.

"Ah, Masrur. I was just on my way to pay my respects to the Khalifah, and welcome him back to Baghdad."

"My master has not asked to see you, Father of Locks."

"There was a time when we were not so formal, Masrur."

"My master does not want to see you, Father of Locks."

The black man's rumbling voice was sympathetic, but firm. Abu Nuwas grasped his huge arm.

"But it is vital that I see the Khalifah! Masrur, do you know that a Roman assassin threatens your master's life?"

"There is usually an assassin threatening my master's life. Even when there is not, I like to pretend there is, just to stay in practice. Who is this assassin, Father of Locks? Where and how does he intend to strike?"

"I do not know."

Masrur raised his eyebrows, but Abu Nuwas pressed on.

"But he has accomplices here at court! I can tell you the name, the name of the traitor, the one who is to admit the killer to the Khalifah's presence —"

"What I say to you now, Father of Locks, I say as a friend. If you are about to accuse a minister or other official of treason, then you had better be able to prove it. Drunkards who shout wild slanders about prominent men do not survive long at court. Consider your next words calmly. What have you to tell me?"

Abu Nuwas chewed a finger, then sighed.

"Nothing. I have nothing to tell you. But, Swordbearer-"

He put a hand on Masrur's arm and whispered.

"Be careful around Fadl ibn Rabi."

"I am always careful, Father of Locks, around everybody. Including you."

Abu Nuwas released him, and seemed to shrink a little as he turned away. Masrur sighed.

"The Commander of the Faithful is on his way to the Gilded Gate, to lead his people in prayer. Before that he must rest, and wash the dust of the journey from his body. He has no time for such entertainment as you offer, Father of Locks. Come to him after the Friday Prayers, and I will ask if he will see you. God the Forbearing knows, he needs his spirits raised."

The Swordbearer left. Abu Nuwas was muttering fretfully under his breath.

"After Friday Prayers! By then it will be too late."

Al-Mithaq clapped him on the shoulder.

"At least we know now where the Khalifah is going. If we get to the Gilded Gate before him, we may be able to stop al-Sifr."

The camp was already disappearing around us, tents collapsing and swiftly engulfed by busy nests of servants. Horses clopped and jingled, and the pilgrims bantered and jested, hearts lightened by the prospect of seeing their wives and families again. We were swept along in their wake, and trudged once more along the dusty roads towards the city of Baghdad.

For a while we walked in silence, but as we entered the outskirts of the city Abu Nuwas grew impatient, licking dry lips and glancing around.

"I am thirsty. What happened to that wine?"

I stared at him in disbelief.

"What wine?"

"The wine ibn Hayyan gave us, the Lebanese red for the Khalifah."

"That is for the Khalifah."

"He will never miss what he does not know he is getting. If we are risking our lives to save his, he could at least provide us with a drink."

"In the name of God the Patient! Father of Locks, you have been awake all night. Your eyes are red, your clothes and breath are foul. People are trying to kill you, we are hunting a deadly assassin, and you want to have more wine?"

"I am thirsty."

"Drink some water if you are thirsty."

"Water is for washing. Give it to me, now."

I took the bottle from my coat.

"Very well, let us have wine. Al-Mithaq, would you like some wine?"

Yaqub al-Mithaq saw the poet's agonised face, and grinned mischievously.

"Thank you, my friend. That would be delightful."

He uncorked the bottle, sniffed at it appreciatively, then took a long slow draught. He wiped his mouth, and handed the bottle back to me.

"An excellent vintage. Rarely have I tasted better."

Abu Nuwas scowled.

"Very amusing. Now, if I might take my turn —"

I held the bottle at arm's length and slowly tipped it over. Abu Nuwas stared in horror, as if it were his children's blood pouring down and soaking into the dry earth.

"What are you doing?"

"It's for your own good, Father of Locks. You'll thank me some day. And if we are fighting for our lives, I want you sober."

He strode furiously up the road, and did not speak again on the way to the Gilded Gate.

We were able to see the great dome of the palace from the outskirts of Baghdad, and it served as a lodestar, guiding us to the precise centre of the Round City. At the foot of the high walls which surround the palace complex we halted, and Al-Mithaq finally broke the silence that had prevailed since the argument over the wine.

"How are we to gain access to the masjid? Only those returning from the Hajj will be admitted for prayers."

Abu Nuwas stared up at the ramparts, and answered peevishly.

"We will walk around the walls, and pray that God shows us a way."

I was unconvinced by this plan, but astoundingly God had indeed provided a way. Where a neighbouring building edged presumptuously close to the palace, creating a narrow alley, a rope of plaited fibre hung down. Abu Nuwas clapped his hands and grinned, his sulk forgotten.

"Of course! The Palm Fibre. The sura itself refers to a rope: 'a noose of twisted fibre around her throat.'"

He craned his neck to where the rope disappeared at the top of the rampart.

"Here is The Palm Fibre; and there, The High Place."

Abu Nuwas wanted to climb first, but I managed to persuade him that, as the lightest, I should lead the way, in case the rope broke under his weight. It had been some years since I had retired from burglary, and my arms and calves ached as I shinned up the side of the palace. Hands raw, I finally wriggled over the battlements and collapsed onto a walkway which ran along the inside of the parapet. At the corner I could see steps running down to the enclosed ground, where servants scurried, oblivious to my presence. On the other side of the wall, the city of Baghdad stretched away, a maze of houses, masjids, workshops and stables, streets and canals and alleys.

The rope was knotted securely around a merlon, but now it began to twitch and jerk. Abu Nuwas was making his ungainly way up the wall, feet kicking against the bricks as he relied on the strength of his arms to pull him up. When he neared the top I reached down and dragged him over by his coat. He lay panting on the walkway for a moment, then looked around.

"There are no guards."

"Good. I wouldn't like to have to explain our presence here."

"No, don't you see? The Khalifah is on his way to the Gilded Gate. Why are there no soldiers here to protect him?"

We stared at each other for a moment, then he jumped to his feet with renewed urgency. On the street below al-Mithaq was struggling to heave his portly body up the rope. We watched him jumping and grabbing hopelessly, holding on only for a moment before dropping to the ground again. Without discussion, Abu Nuwas and I began to haul up the rope, while the weaver wrapped himself around it, clinging on like a child fastened to its mother's leg. He was pale and sweating when he reached the top.

"A moment, my friends... I cannot stand."

Abu Nuwas was indignant.

"What are you complaining about? We did all the work."

I was untying the rope from the merlon.

"If al-Sifr is not already within the palace, we have removed his means of entry. Perhaps it will be enough."

"Then who is that, over there?"

Abu Nuwas pointed to a figure in tawny robes who was edging precariously around the base of the great dome.

"The masjid is on that side. From the dome, he will have a clear shot into the courtyard as al-Rashid crosses to the prayer hall."

"He carries no bow."

"What is that in his hand though? An ivory cylinder, the length of his forearm... a weapon of some kind, I have no doubt. Come on!"

We pounded along the walkway, al-Mithaq puffing at the rear, until we reached the point where the curve of the dome brought it closest to the wall. A narrow stone ledge ran around the base of the dome, at the same height as the parapet. Abu Nuwas appraised the gap, which was some six cubits across.

"We'll have to jump."

Al-Mithaq was gazing in horror at the dizzying drop to the ground below.

"Can we not take the steps down to the enclosure, and find a way up from there?"

"There is no time. Listen —"

"Allahu akbar! Allahu akbar!"

From the minaret nearby, the mu'addhin was calling the people to the Friday prayer.

"The Khalifah will be entering the courtyard at any moment. I am going in pursuit of al-Sifr. You may do as you please."

With that he launched himself across the gap. His long legs cleared the jump with ease, and he clattered against one of the copper panels of which the dome was composed. I glanced at al-Mithaq, shrugged, and hurled myself into the air. My feet landed on the ledge, but I did not have sufficient momentum and swayed backward. Abu Nuwas flung an arm around my shoulders and pulled me in. I hugged the cold metal gratefully, and Abu Nuwas grinned.

"There. Once again, I have saved your life."

With a despairing cry al-Mithaq leapt after us, landing in between us and falling to one knee. I helped him up, and we began to work our way round to the other side of the dome, Abu Nuwas in the lead. It was slow, perilous going; the stone ledge was no more than a span in width, and the copper was treacherously smooth. The wind whipped at us, tugging our clothes, as if determined to dislodge us. Step by step though we inched along, and when I dared to look down I could see over the masjid wall into the courtyard, where the pilgrims were gathering, like termites swarming below. I heard Abu Nuwas shout a wordless challenge.

The man in tawny robes was perched precariously on his haunches, gazing down at the courtyard, the ivory object clutched in his right hand. He looked up, and I stared into the horrified face of al-Majousi, the little scholar from the House of Wisdom. Abu Nuwas hissed.

"The Magus! I should have known. Why would the message be written in numerals only he understands, if it was not intended for him all along?"

Al-Majousi tried to stand, but teetered, and nearly fell. While he steadied himself Abu Nuwas hustled round, until he was within touching distance.

"Now, at last – no!"

A blade slashed past him, aimed at the scholar's neck. Al-

Majousi ducked, and the sword clanged on the copper panel. Abu Nuwas looked over his shoulder, to see Yaqub al-Mithaq, weapon in hand, steadying himself for another blow.

"What are you doing, you idiot? We need him alive, to expose the conspiracy —"

Al-Mithaq showed no sign of having heard him, but drew back his weapon to strike again. I grabbed his sword arm, and al-Mithaq lurched back, knocking me off the ledge. My feet tingled at the emptiness beneath them and I found myself dangling in mid-air, held up only by my grip on his sleeve.

For a moment I imagined myself falling, a brief rush followed by a final, agonising impact. I looked pleadingly up at al-Mithaq, but instead of helping me he jerked his arm as though trying to shake me loose. The fabric of his coat began to rip. Then I felt a hand round my waist, scooping me up. Abu Nuwas yanked me back onto the ledge as easily as though I were a child. I was still holding onto al-Mithaq's right arm, and now in a furious rage born of fear and relief I battered his wrist against the copper until his sword slipped from his grip and tumbled to the courtyard below. A despairing voice cried out behind us.

"Help me! In the name of God, help! I'm going to fall..."

While the three of us were grappling al-Majousi had seized the opportunity to get away. In his haste though he had tripped over his feet, and fallen headlong against the dome. His hands scrabbled for purchase, but he would not release the cylinder, and his legs slowly slid off, until he was clinging desperately on, his head sinking below the ledge. Abu Nuwas scrambled across to the him, and grabbed him by the arms.

"Now then, Magus, or whoever you are, we will have the truth. If I do not like your answers, I will let you fall, and your final study will be to measure the distance from here to the ground. So, tell me, where is the beardless man?"

"I don't know who you mean — I acted alone. Please — I cannot die yet — I have great work to accomplish!"

Abu Nuwas eased his grip for a second, causing the scholar

to squeal in terror.

"If you acted alone, who sent you the message? Where is al-Sifr?"

"What message? I don't understand — no, I beg you! I swear — I will show you al-Sifr, if you pull me up."

Something in his voice must have convinced Abu Nuwas, because he dragged al-Majousi back onto the ledge.

"Very well. But hand over your weapon."

He indicated the cylinder. Al-Majousi looked at it in surprise.

"But that is no weapon, it is only a manuscript. Look —"

He unrolled it, revealing a long scroll of paper covered in densely written script. Abu Nuwas grabbed the paper, gazed at it in confusion, then shoved it back into al-Majousi's hand. He helped the scholar stand up.

"Show me, then. Show me al-Sifr."

A fierce gust threatened to blow us off our feet, and al-Majousi tucked the manuscript into his coat.

"Not here. In the courtyard."

"How do you propose we get down?"

The little scholar looked surprised.

"There's a ladder, on the other side of the dome. How did you get up here?"

The ladder led down to a flat roof, from which we could easily scramble to the ground. Abu Nuwas descended first, and was waiting at the bottom, sword in hand, when al-Majousi jumped down.

"Now, Magus, quickly, and no tricks. Where is al-Sifr?"

The scholar paused for a moment, studying Abu Nuwas curiously. Then he bent down, and pressed his finger into the ground, marking a single dot in the dirt.

"There. There is al-Sifr."

"What mockery is this? I warn you —"

Al-Majousi shook with fear, but his tone was defiant.

"This is al-Sifr: this is Nothing. It is the tenth figure in the

Hindi numeral system which I showed you yesterday."

Abu Nuwas' forehead creased in bafflement.

"But — I do not understand. Nothing is not a number."

Despite his peril, al-Majousi's enthusiasm burst through.

"But it is! It is the most important number of all! Without nothing, how can there be anything? How can something be present, unless it can also be absent?"

"Very profound, but what possible use is it?"

"Look —"

He marked a short vertical line on the ground.

"That, as I told you, represents one, but also ten, and a hundred, and a thousand. Then how is one to know which it is? If there are other numbers beside it, there is no problem; if I write a figure two here, we can clearly see that the one is a ten, plus two, making twelve. But if the one stands on its own, it may mean one only, or one million. It has been the custom to leave spaces to indicate the empty places, but this can be ambiguous and unreliable.

"Now see the power of nothing. If I place two dots by the stroke, all becomes clear. There are no individuals, nor any tens, so the figure represents one hundred.

"This is the marvellous invention of the mathematicians of al-Hind, which I hope to introduce to the Land of Islam. With it, calculations that were once laborious become simple and swift, and the Hindi system far surpasses in ease both the abjad and the Roman numerals.

"When I learned that you planned to suppress the innovation, I thought to engage the Khalifah's support. I had no hope of gaining an audience, but my cousin the captain arranged for the guards to be moved from this spot, and left a ladder against the wall, so that I could get up here and throw the scroll to the Khalifah as he passed."

He pulled out the roll of paper. At its head, I could just make out the title: *On calculation using the Hindi numerals*.

"See, here, it is a treatise I have written on the subject. Please, I beg you, let al-Sifr flourish in the House of Wisdom, for the benefit and advancement of all mankind..."

"Then we have come here chasing nothing; and nothing is exactly what we have found. We stand here discussing arithmetic while the real assassin, the beardless man, closes in on the Khalifah."

Al-Mithaq had finally made it to the ground, and leaned against a wall, sickly and irritated. Al-Majousi tugged at Abu Nuwas' sleeve.

"Are you done with me, then? May I go?"

The poet seemed barely aware of his presence, but was transfixed by the marks in the dirt.

"What?"

"I have shown you al-Sifr, as I promised. Now may I go?"

Abu Nuwas waved a distracted hand.

"Yes, run along, Magus."

Al-Majousi, though, stood his ground.

"Please don't call me that. I am not a Magus. My name is ibn Musa al-Khwarizmi."

"Then go in peace, ibn Musa al-Khwarizmi. But go quickly, before I change my mind."

The scholar scurried away. Al-Mithaq coughed, and I scrutinised his ghastly pallor and sweat-speckled skin.

"Are you sick, my friend?"

"Sick? I can barely stand. My head and gut feel as though they might explode."

"We had better get out of here. Once prayers are over, this place will be swarming with guards."

"No."

Abu Nuwas shook his head slowly.

"No. I see it now. Al-Sifr was there in the message all along."

He looked up, his eyes glittering.

"Do you remember that I complained of an ink spot on the silk? It was not a stray drop, but a number, the number which is no number. It was the tenth element, the Nothing, the Void; al-Sifr. The message did not direct us to the High Place. Look —"

With his swordpoint he scratched in the dirt the "V" shape

which represented seven, then beside it a dot.

"Not the Seventh Sura, but the Seventieth: the Ascending Stairs. The Ascending Stairs which lead to the Private Apartments. We must be swift, if we are to save the Khalifah."

Without waiting for a response he turned and hurried away. I chased after him.

"Wait! I don't understand —"

He called over his shoulder.

"There is a secret staircase which gives access to the royal apartments. I have used it myself when I needed to be discreet about my visits. The entrance to the stairway is usually locked, and guarded. If I am right, though — yes."

A door stood open in the palace wall. Inside, a wooden staircase led upward. Abu Nuwas paused, and I saw an unfamiliar tension in his face. I was shocked to realise that he was afraid. Al-Mithaq came stumbling behind, barely able to speak.

"Remember, Father of Locks. Strike first... do not stop to ask questions."

The poet nodded, and set off up the stairs. The darkness was relieved intermittently by slender bars of daylight, which striped the steps where arrow-slit windows pierced the wall. I trailed a hand along the brickwork, and found that the passage was gently curving as we ascended, so that by the time we reached the top of the stairs, we must have traced a full circuit, returning to a point directly above the entrance.

There was a trapdoor above our heads. Abu Nuwas pushed it open cautiously, and we climbed into a vast round chamber, four hundred paces across. It was bright and airy, the wall studded with oriels, so that the sunlight would illuminate it at any time of day. Looking up to the vaulted ceiling, I realised that we stood beneath the same copper dome which earlier we had circled so precariously. At the centre of the chamber was a marble bath, and elaborate carpets were strewn everywhere.

"The Private Apartments. Merely to be here without permission is death."

At first I thought the chamber was empty. Then a movement caught my eye, at the opposite side. A man lurked by a curtained doorway, which I guessed must be the official entrance to the apartments. He spun round when he heard us, and cried out, a strangled shriek. I could see his face, round and fleshy, with soft, dark, beardless skin. Abu Nuwas roared and charged.

I waited for the clash of metal, but the assassin carried no sword. Instead he hurled himself at the poet's midriff, ducking under the blade. Abu Nuwas was pushed back by the impact, but brought the pommel of his weapon down hard on the man's head. The assassin released him and tottered away, swaying to avoid a wild slash.

I circled around them, hoping to come upon the assassin unseen, but Abu Nuwas waved me back furiously.

"No, Ismail! This is my enemy, and I must defeat him alone."

He feinted a couple of times, then thrust at the assassin's midriff. The man kicked high like a dancer, and his boot connected with the poet's knuckles. The sword leapt from his grip and dropped to the floor with a clang.

They both dived for the weapon, but the assassin reached it first. Abu Nuwas rolled on top of him and held down his sword hand by the wrist. With his free hand he clutched at the assassin's throat, squeezing and crushing. The man rasped out words with difficulty.

"What are you doing... al-Hasan?"

It must have been the use of his given name that startled Abu Nuwas into letting go. His friends called him Abu Ali, to the wider world he was the Father of Locks; but nobody except his mother called him al-Hasan. He sprang away and the assassin sat up, leaving the sword where it lay.

"For a clever man, al-Hasan, you are disappointingly prone to acting before you think."

Abu Nuwas stared, his eyes widening in astonishment.

"Umadha Citta? Princess? Is that really you?"

The beardless man, whom I was coming to realise was

neither an assassin nor, indeed, a man, stood up.

"Of course it's me, you idiot. Have I changed so much?"

"No, but... what in God's name are you doing here?"

"Me? I've come to save the Khalifah."

Abu Nuwas blinked in bafflement.

"Then you too are hunting al-Sifr?"

Princess Citta's brown eyes were filled with sadness.

"Oh, al-Hasan. Is that who you came looking for? How utterly heartbreaking."

"Why are you wasting time talking? Kill him... her!"

Al-Mithaq crawled into the chamber, sallow-faced and spitting with rage. Abu Nuwas ignored him though, and gaped foolishly at Citta.

"What do you mean? What do you know about al-Sifr?"

Citta folded her arms.

"Tell me, al-Hasan, this enemy of yours: why is he called al-Sifr?"

"Because we know nothing of the real man behind the disguise: his age, his appearance, his origins..."

"No. He is called al-Sifr, the Void, the Nothing, because he does not exist."

Abu Nuwas stared at her intently. Then he began to laugh, a hard and humourless sound.

"Glory to God! For a moment there I thought you were serious. I have seen him, talked to him, fought with him. You saw him too. How can you tell me he does not exist?"

"You fought with somebody. Did he ever call himself al-Sifr? Did anybody, other than you? Why do you believe that the enemy you faced was the same man, in Rome, and Aksum, and Atil-Khazaran? As for the person I saw, that could have been any concubine of my father's. I was young, vulnerable, confused."

"But Ja'far al-Barmaki told me..."

"Of course he did. Ja'far al-Barmaki invented al-Sifr. Being without honour himself, he dares not rely on it in others, and prefers to control men through their vices: through their greed, or lust, or envy. In your case it was vanity which was your weakness. He knew that he could not master you through fear alone, that in time you would chafe under his orders and seek your freedom. So he created a mythical foe to goad and oppose you, and just as the peacock attacks its own reflection, believing it to be a rival, so you dutifully chased the phantom across the world, preening and pecking at illusions.

"The Wazir used the idea of al-Sifr to manipulate you, and he used you so that he could toy with kings and nations like a child playing with dolls. If you don't believe me, ask al-Mithaq here. Everyone in the Barid knew the secret, except for you. They liked to pretend it was all real; spies are inclined to sentimentality, and the postmen loved to tell stories of Abu Nuwas and his arch-enemy the Void. You brought a tawdry glamour to what is mostly a dirty, despicable job."

"Is this true, al-Mithaq?"

The weaver, hunched kneeling on a prayer mat, stared up at him but said nothing. Abu Nuwas turned back to Citta.

"But if al-Sifr does not exist, then who is trying to kill the Khalifah?"

Before she could answer, the curtain over the doorway was flung aside and two men walked into the room. Abu Nuwas snatched up his sword, but smiled with relief on seeing the newcomers.

"Peace be upon you, ibn Hayyan. I see you managed to work out the message at last."

The Khalifah's astrologer, with Ilig the Khazar at his side, contemplated the scene in the chamber and tutted.

"Only just in time. In fact, I am very disappointed in you, Abu Ali. First you conceal from me the solution to the numbers on the silk. Now, instead of slaying the assassin, I find you chatting with her like an old friend. I have to question where your true loyalties lie."

Citta glared at Abu Nuwas.

"You showed him the message? You have betrayed me."

"Betrayed you? His allegiance is to the Commander of the Faithful and to the Wazir his master, not to any Roman spy. Now,

290

Abu Ali, if for reasons of misguided sentimentality you cannot strike down this assassin, then hand over your sword to Ilig, and he will do it."

For the first time I noticed that Ilig carried no blade of his own, here in the royal apartments; Abu Nuwas possessed the only weapon in the room. The giant Khazar reached out a hand to take it, but Abu Nuwas jabbed the point at him, forcing him back. Suspicion in his eyes, the poet swung his sword from side to side, aiming first at ibn Hayyan, then at Citta.

"Wait – I do not understand. The message on the silk, princess – that was for you?"

"Yes. The message contained instructions from my master."

"You see! She admits it. Orders from her master in New Rome, to murder the Khalifah."

"No, ibn Hayyan. My orders were not to murder the Khalifah, but to warn him, to save him from the real assassin. To save him from you."

There was silence in the chamber. Then Ibn Hayyan snorted indignantly.

"From me? What nonsense. I am a loyal and trusted servant of the Khalifah. You, on the other hand, are a foreign spy who has broken into the Righteous One's private apartments. You will not help yourself now with fantastic stories and wild allegations."

Abu Nuwas, though, had been gazing at al-Mithaq, convulsed and retching on his prayer mat, and now turned to ibn Hayyan in horrified comprehension. His voice was a whisper.

"The Lebanese red..."

In an instant the genial expression fell from ibn Hayyan's face like a mask, to be replaced by a look of cold contempt.

"So you broke your oath. I should have known. Abu Ali, you swore you would hand that bottle to the Khalifah unopened. Did you give it to al-Mithaq? Then your disobedience has cost him his life. I am sorry, Yaqub, but there is no hope for you now."

Al-Mithaq stared up at him with empty eyes. Abu Nuwas raised his sword to the astrologer's breast.

"So it is true, ibn Hayyan. You are the assassin. You sought to poison the Khalifah, and to make me complicit in your crime. Ilig, seize this traitor. We will take him to the Swordbearer."

Ilig stepped forward – then his huge arm was around my neck, pinning and choking me. I struggled and kicked, but my blows fell uselessly on his muscled body. From somewhere he produced a small bottle, and forced it between my teeth. Sensing danger, I fell still, and Ibn Hayyan smirked.

"You mocked my studies, Abu Ali; now you will learn the true power of al-khimiya. The poison in that bottle, the one in your friend's mouth, has neither odour nor taste, yet a small measure will kill a healthy man in a matter of hours, leaving no evidence of its presence. It is my greatest discovery, the perfect means to murder without being detected, the only toxin on earth that could fool the sensitive noses of the Khalifah's tasters. I call it al-zarnik."

I was gagging, but dared not swallow. Ibn Hayyan stepped closer to the swordpoint, and spoke softly.

"There is enough poison in that bottle to fell an elephant. If you draw so much of a drop of my blood, Ilig will force al-zarnik down the storyteller's throat, and he will share al-Mithaq's fate. Give us what we want though, and I will let you both go free. If you wish to save your friend, you must give us the Evidence."

Abu Nuwas nodded, his voice and blade steady.

"Of course. The Ascending Stairs; The Private Apartments; The Evidence. The final destination of our journey. But you overestimate me, ibn Hayyan. The Evidence is not in my possession."

"Then the princess still has it. You must take it from her."

Abu Nuwas turned his blade back toward Citta, who drew a small clay cylinder from her bosom, and held it out.

"You want the Evidence, al-Hasan? I have it here. Before you hand it over to the Khalifah's enemies, though, would you not like to know what it is?"

The poet glanced swiftly across at me, but said nothing.

"Then I shall tell you. It is evidence of conspiracy and treason at the very heart of government, of a plot to overthrow and murder the Khalifah; a plot conceived and led, not by any Roman spy, but by one of his most trusted ministers."

"I knew it! Ibn Rabi, that scheming, pot-bellied Spider —"

"No. Not the Chamberlain. The traitor is your master, Ja'far ibn Yahya al-Barmaki."

Abu Nuwas blinked, and shook his head.

"No. No, you cannot trick me so easily. Ja'far would never —"

"Think, al-Hasan. He lied to you about al-Sifr, as he has been lying to you for thirty years. He sent you to kill me, and sent al-Mithaq after you to make sure you obeyed. Why would he do all this unless he wanted to prevent the Evidence reaching the Khalifah?

"When you turned up at his palace, he must have thought you his salvation sent by God: the only man in his service resourceful enough to recover the message, clever enough to interpret it, and above all gullible enough to be trusted. All he had to do was resurrect your old enemy one more time, and off you trotted to do his dirty work for him."

The sword wavered in the poet's hand.

"Ja'far... it cannot be."

"Ah, how true the words of the ninety-eighth sura: 'Those who disbelieve cannot free themselves from error, until the Evidence is brought to them.' The Khalifah too found it hard to accept that his best friend would turn against him. So I came from Egypt with the Evidence, which I was to hand to the Khalifah in person, bypassing all his attendants, even Masrur. And Ja'far sent you to stop me."

The face of Abu Nuwas bore the lost, confused expression of a child abandoned by its parents.

"But why would Ja'far do such a thing? He has power, wealth, everything he could desire."

"Because he is so clever, that he believes everyone else to be a fool. For years he has overstepped his power, issuing decrees and making appointments in the Khalifah's name, releasing political prisoners without authority, embezzling gold from the royal purse. Recently he has become careless, and failed to cover his tracks. It was only a matter of time before his misdeeds were exposed. He had to strike first."

Ibn Hayyan clicked his tongue.

"The princess spins a pretty tale, but be careful that Ilig does not become weary of it. His hand may shake, and the poison spill. Either you give us the Evidence, or your friend will die. Make your choice, Abu Ali, and quickly."

I was suddenly frightened of death, afraid of the idea of poison pulsing through my blood, of those last few hours of accelerating sickness, knowing that I was doomed, still living but beyond redemption. For the first time since I met him I found myself wishing that Abu Nuwas would do the wrong thing. He looked at me, then slowly raised the swordpoint to Citta's throat. She gazed at him sadly.

"If you do this, al-Hasan, you betray your oath, your ruler, your religion, your nation. Is a single life really worth all that?"

"I am sorry, princess, but Ismail is my friend. I will not see him die for my mistakes."

He pressed the point very gently against her skin until a bright spot of red appeared. Citta sighed.

"So you are capable of love, after all. Here."

She tossed the cylinder to ibn Hayyan, who caught it and examined it greedily.

"The Wazir's seal. Yes, this must be it."

Abu Nuwas looked across at him, and in the instant his attention was distracted Citta knocked aside the sword with a sweep of her arm and seized his wrist. While they struggled, Ilig hurled me to the floor and sprang at them. The bottle fell beside me and cracked, its lethal contents trickling out. I spat violently, in case any of the poison had spilled in my mouth, then looked up to see Citta, Ilig and Abu Nuwas wrestling over the weapon.

Ibn Hayyan strolled over to them, and, after a moment's consideration, punched Citta hard in the face. She reeled back, clutching her nose. Abu Nuwas lunged at him, but Ilig had come away with the sword, and held the poet at bay. Ibn Hayyan laughed triumphantly.

"Hold these traitors here, Ilig. I will summon Masrur the Swordbearer."

"I suppose it would be futile to point out that you promised we could go free? Still, Masrur will be interested when he hears what Ja'far has been up to."

"You forget, I have the Evidence. Without it, who is going to believe you three: a drunkard, a storyteller and a woman?"

"It will be harder to explain what al-Mithaq is doing here. He may even have enough breath left to reveal who poisoned him."

"That is true. Ilig, if you would be so kind?"

The Khazar spun round and plunged the sword into al-Mithaq's chest. The weaver expired noisily, and Ibn Hayyan tutted.

"Shame on you, Abu Ali. It appears that we were unable to stop you murdering poor Yaqub before Ilig overpowered you and took your sword. Now that I come to think, it might be best if all of you were killed in the struggle, while resisting our attempts to take you into custody. It would prevent any unnecessary complications."

Princess Citta, still holding her bleeding nose, looked at Abu Nuwas and me.

"There are three of us. If we all charge at the same time, he can only kill one of us."

"There will be no more killing in the Commander of the Faithful's private apartments."

Masrur the Swordbearer appeared in the room as silently as though he had been conjured there by a jinn, and deftly plucked the weapon from Ilig's grasp. He looked around the room, at Citta, the red-faced astrologer, the sullen Khazar, and the corpse of Yaqub al-Mithaq. Abu Nuwas reached out an imploring hand.

"Masrur! You must have heard him — the astrologer just confessed to treason —"

"I heard nothing, Father of Locks, and what I see does not bode well for you. You have come armed and uninvited into the palace, and this man lies dead by your sword. But it is not for me to pass judgement in any case. You must stand before the Commander of the Faithful. He, and he alone, will determine your fate."

XVIII

In the hall of the Gilded Gate, the storyteller fell silent. A hush hung like a held breath. At last, Harun al-Rashid frowned.

"So, you are asking me to believe that your purpose was not to kill me, but to save me? That it was not you, but the Khazar who murdered the weaver? That my friend Ja'far and my astrologer were conspiring against me? That everything I believed to be true, is a lie? Where is this evidence, then, that might give substance to your improbable tales?"

"I regret to say, Commander of the Faithful, that I last saw it in the hands of ibn Hayyan. No doubt he will have destroyed it by now."

"Then you seek to make a fool of me. Masrur, take these villains outside and do not stand in my presence again unless you are carrying their severed heads."

"Forgive me, master, but the storyteller is wrong. The object of which he spoke is in my possession. I saw the astrologer trying to conceal it in his sleeve, and thought it might be important. Here it is."

Masrur opened a huge hand, to reveal a clay cylinder, exactly as Ismail had described. Harun al-Rashid stared at it.

"Well, what is it?"

"If you will permit me, master..."

Masrur snapped the clay with his fingers. Inside the cylinder was a small scroll of paper. The swordbearer knelt and presented it to al-Rashid, who unrolled it.

"This is indeed a message from Ja'far ibn Yahya, to the astrologer ibn Hayyan..."

He looked up, fury in his face.

"There is no word of treason here! It is an innocent letter, containing nothing but greetings and gossip."

He flung his staff at them in annoyance.

"Beheading is too good for these scoundrels, wasting my time with their nonsense. I want them chopped into a hundred pieces."

Ismail fell to his knees, and spoke urgently, blood trickling from the wound on his brow where the Khalifah's staff had struck him.

"Commander of the Faithful, your anger is just. I ask only that I might die obedient to your command. For was it not you yourself, my prince, who told me that the story remains unfinished until all questions have been answered? And I am sure that your shrewd mind has been puzzling over the significance of al-Hijr, the City of Stone."

Al-Rashid, who had completely forgotten about that part of the message, sat back in surprise. It would irk him for days if the storyteller died without explaining this mystery. He nodded irritably.

"Oh, very well, you may speak, but make it quick. I grow hungry."

The storyteller drew a deep breath:

"You talked of gossip, Commander of the Faithful, and in your words I found wisdom. At that moment I realised that we had misread the Hindi numerals."

"What are you babbling about?"

"There were other dots on the silk, my prince. And I understand now that the symbol of nothing, al-Sifr, might as easily fall within a number as at its end. It was not the fourteenth sura, Ibrahim, to which the message referred, but the one hundred and fourth."

"The Gossip?"

"Your knowledge of the holy book is impeccable, my prince. It was the poet Abbas, the Gossip, whom Citta was supposed to meet at the bath house, not your brother Prince Ibrahim. Our presence there scared her off, but by good fortune I had already spoken to Abbas and received from him the key to the mystery. Again, not al-Hijr, sura fifteen, but one hundred and five: The Elephant."

He took off the necklace Abbas had given him, and presented it to the Khalifah.

"Remember the words of the poet: 'The man who would learn the truth, studies only that which is revealed.' If I may suggest, my prince, that you place this pendant over the letter, and read the words which are visible through the holes?"

Al-Rashid put the scroll of paper on his lap, and positioned the brass elephant on top of it. His lips moved as he read. The silence that followed seemed eternal, but at last he looked up at Masrur, his face impassive.

"Release these men, and the woman who was taken with them. Give them each a thousand dinars in gold coin. And summon Ja'far ibn Yahya. I would like to take him hunting."

***

The square before the Gilded Gate was dotted with knots and clumps of people still chatting after prayers, and nobody took notice of Ismail, Abu Nuwas and Citta as they stood blinking in the sunlight they had never thought to see again. Abu Nuwas gazed round at the bystanders.

"Strange to think that their world has changed forever, and no one knows it yet. Whatever he may have done, I shall miss Ja'far al-Barmaki. Baghdad will be so much less interesting without him."

"Oh, al-Hasan. And to think I believed you incapable of love. You are intoxicated with it, besotted with loyalty to your master. Ja'far al-Barmaki was arrogant, manipulative and deceitful. He lied to you and used you, and would have had you killed in an instant had it suited his machinations. In the end, he broke his oath, betrayed his people and plotted to murder his best friend."

"But he did it with such style..."

Citta sighed. Abu Nuwas turned to look at her, as though for the first time.

"And you, Ummadha Citta — how did you come to be entangled in this business? Are you a postman?"

"Not exactly. You will have heard it said that the Khalifah often knew the whereabouts of his enemies when his own intelligence service did not, and that he would tell the Barid where to look for them. Where did he get his information from?"

"It was always said that he had a magic mirror. I assumed that to be a way of telling anyone who asked to mind their own business."

"And so it was, yet the truth lay within it, for those who understood. We call ourselves 'al-Minzar': the Mirror. Outsiders do not call us anything, for nobody knows of our existence, save the Khalifah himself, and the Chamberlain, who is our master. Our purpose is to watch the Barid, to monitor its activities and curb its excesses. We are the spies who spy on the spies."

Abu Nuwas glanced at Ismail.

"'*Quis custodiet ipsos custodes...*' But why would you need to seek out danger? Did I not find you a good husband, to keep you and provide for you?"

"Really, al-Hasan, did you expect me to spend my days sitting around and gossiping like a Baghdad washerwoman? I am a princess, descended from a lion. Ibn Rabi approached me first to find out what you and Ja'far had been up to. I had, by necessity, learned much about the art of subterfuge, during our escape from Serendib, and the Chamberlain recognised my talents. I have been his agent ever since."

Abu Nuwas shook his head wonderingly, then chuckled.

"Well, Ismail, at least you have a new story to tell. Men will pay good coin to hear the truth behind the downfall of the Barmakids."

"That would not be wise, I think. Al-Rashid will not want the marketplace gossiping how close he came to being overthrown."

"But how then will he explain Ja'far's arrest?"

"He is the Commander of the Faithful, Successor to the

Prophet of God. He doesn't have to explain himself to anybody."

"Of course. How ironic that you, having been present at such important events, will be unable to speak of them."

"Oh, I will tell the story, all right. Just not the real one. Listen to this..."

***

Harun al-Rashid loved no man more deeply than his friend Ja'far, but perhaps even more deeply the Khalifah loved his favourite sister, Princess Abbasah, the most beautiful and cultured woman in the Land of Islam. He longed to pass his evenings with his sister and his friend together, but he could not allow any man to look on the princess who was not her husband or close relation, without forfeiting her honour. So he secretly arranged for them to marry; but only so that they could enjoy each others' conversation unveiled and without awkwardness. He explicitly forbade the consummation of their union, lest their sons rival his own as heirs to the Khalifate.

Unfortunately the Commander of the Faithful could not command the emotions of his sister. The princess fell in love with the handsome, witty Wazir. The longer Abbasah was obliged to sit in the presence of the man who was legally her husband, but with whom she was not permitted to be alone nor to touch, the more heatedly the blood thundered in her veins.

At last she concocted a desperate plan. She knew the Wazir's mother sent a virgin slave to her son for his pleasure every Thursday, and persuaded her to send Ja'far his wife in place of the concubine. Ja'far, having taken much wine, did not recognise the princess, and enjoyed her until dawn. When morning came, and the light fell upon her face, he recoiled in horror, crying out:

'You have destroyed me, and destroyed yourself too.'

After that night he avoided her company. In time, though, she grew great with child, and the baby could not be concealed. Al-Rashid was enraged, but Abbasah refused to name the father, even when threatened with torture. However her courage was in vain, for palace gossip soon revealed the truth. And that is why the Khalifah ordered the arrest of Ja'far al-Barmaki.

***

Abu Nuwas nodded pensively.

"It's got everything, I suppose: sex, scandal, and secrets. They'll love it in the suqs. Won't the real Princess Abbasah have a few words to say about it, though?"

"I doubt it. Apparently she really did give birth to a bastard, although the father was never named. The rumour is that she and the baby were buried alive, in a hastily dug pit in her favourite rose garden."

Citta shivered.

"Poor girl. And poor, innocent child, that had no choice how it was born. But who is going to believe that Ja'far could have spent the night making love to her without once seeing her face? It's not very plausible, is it?"

Ismail shrugged.

"People will believe my story because they want to. Do you think they will worry about little things like that? It doesn't matter what really happened. Memory is an illusion, history a lie, truth is too unwieldy, too complex, misshapen and riddled with unanswered questions. It cannot live long, once exposed to human recollection; it desiccates and crumbles, like seaweed washed up onto rocks under the alien glare of the sun.

"Story, on the other hand, flourishes in every soil, in awareness and ignorance, complexity and simplicity, ecstasy and adversity. It offers elegant, compelling explanations, which please the ear and satisfy the soul. It provides a connection between what we experience, what we already believe, and what we hope to be true.

"Only God knows all and sees all. The rest of us have to snatch at what threads we can reach, and weave them into some sort of garment, to shelter us from the coldness, the emptiness, the fear."

Abu Nuwas was not listening, but instead stared away to the west, where the winter sun was sliding toward the horizon. Ismail nudged him.

"Cheer up, Father of Locks. You are free, liberated from the Barmakid's clutches. You are a postman no longer. Is that not what you always wanted?"

"Yes, but freedom is a funny thing. Now that I have it, I don't know what to do with it. I don't suppose, princess, you have any vacancies in the Minzar? No, you are right, that is a terrible idea. Perhaps I should turn to religion. Abu'l-Atahiyya makes a very good living out of preaching poverty and chastity."

"If I might make a suggestion, Father of Locks? You are a talented, successful and wealthy poet. At least, you would be wealthy, if you stopped spending gold like Abu'l-Qasim in the old story. You have your health, your senses, your limbs, your looks and your freedom. Most people would be content with that, and much less than that."

"Yes, it should be enough, shouldn't it? It really should be enough..."

Epilogue

From The History of the Prophets and the Kings, *by Abu Ja'far Muhammad ibn Jarir al-Tabari.*

That Friday after prayers, al-Rashid went hunting. He took with him Ja'far ibn Yahya, having insisted that the Wazir accompany him. The Khalifah put his hand on Ja'far's shoulder, and anointed him with precious oils by his own hand. He stayed with Ja'far all afternoon, never leaving his side, until the sunset call to prayer. Then the Khalifah embraced Ja'far, and said to him:

"If I were not spending the evening with my women, I would not be parted from you. But you should go home, drink wine and listen to music, so that you too can have a pleasant evening."

Ja'far replied:

"No, by God, there is no pleasure in drinking unless it is in your company."

Harun insisted though, and throughout the night he sent servants to Ja'far's house with delicious morsels to accompany the wine, with fragrant incense and aromatic herbs. Then he sent Masrur the Swordbearer.

***

This is the account of Masrur the eunuch:

Al-Rashid ordered me to the house of Ja'far ibn Yahya al-Barmaki, whom he had decided to have killed. When I arrived at his house Ja'far was sitting in the garden with Abu Zakkar, the blind singer, who at that moment was singing the following verse:

"Do not go far, for death is impending
       For every brave youth, this night or by morning..."

I said to him:

"O Ja'far, my message is the same as that of the poet. Death has come to you this night. You must answer to the Commander of the Faithful."

He fell on his knees and kissed my feet, begging me to let him go into the house and settle his affairs. I replied:

"There's no chance of you going into the house, but you may do what you need to here and now."

He summoned his servants, and there in the garden he dictated his will and freed his slaves. However, messengers came from my master to see why I was taking so long. So I dragged Ja'far from the house and brought him to the palace. Then I went to inform the Khalifah, who was in bed, that I had obeyed his orders. The Khalifah shouted:

"Bring me his head!"

I returned to Ja'far, and told him to prepare himself for death. He cried out:

"Oh God, oh God... My friend, he would not give that command if he was sober! Leave it until the morning, or at least go and ask him if he is sure."

So I went back to al-Rashid, but when he heard my whispered plea, he burst out:

"Sucker of your mother's rod! Bring me the head of Ja'far al-Barmaki!"

Again I approached Ja'far, and again he persuaded me to question my orders. This time al-Rashid hit me with a staff, and shouted:

"By God, if you don't come back with Ja'far's head, then I will send someone else, who will bring me his head and yours too!"

So I went, and struck off his head, and presented it to the Khalifah.

***

Ja'far ibn Yahya al-Barmaki died on the night of the first day of Safar, in the one hundred and eighty seventh year of the Islamic age. When Yahya ibn Khalid was told that the Commander of the Faithful had killed his son, he replied:

"His son will be killed in the same way."

The Commander of the Faithful ordered the body to be cut in half, and the head and two pieces of the body were gibbeted on the three main bridges of Baghdad. Later, they were taken down and burned.

The poet Abu Nuwas wrote the following lines concerning the death of Ja'far:

> We have reached our journey's end, our horses rest,
>> And the camel, and his driver, cease their sound.
> Tell the beasts, you need walk all night no longer
>> And trudge the desert wastes the wide earth round.
> Tell Death, you have done your worst, in taking Ja'far,
>> And never again will you take one so renowned.
> Tell generosity, your day is over,
>> Despair, this is your time, you are unbound.
> The light of evil day cuts through the darkness
>> as a sword cuts through to bone, and it has found
> The body of the greatest man among us
>> hanging still and rotting above ground.

The End

Author's Note

Historical fiction is a strange chimera, neither wholly fictional nor reliably historic. *The Khalifah's Mirror* is largely fantasy and speculation, but is set in a real place and time, features several real people, and takes its inspiration from real events.

One of the oddest ideas in the book, the Khalifah's magical mirror itself, is drawn directly from the historical record. The prologue and epilogue are adapted (with considerable licence) from al-Tabari's *History of the Prophets and the Kings*, the principal source for the period, written some hundred years after the reign of Harun al-Rashid. I made much use of C.E. Bosworth's translation, published by the SUNY Press. The suggestion that the Mirror might have been a secret counter-intelligence service is pure conjecture, but the Barid, the Khalifate's postal service, really did double as a spying network. (Al-Tabari describes how one Alid rebel was assassinated by the Barid using poisoned toothpaste.)

The capture and eventual fate of Amr ibn Shaddad, and the dismissal and death of the Wali of Basrah, can also be found in al-Tabari, though the Banu Jahm and the Banu Dahhak are invented. Invented too are most of the details about the culture and politics of the Khazars. The disputation itself is alluded to in ancient texts, but the truth of when, how, and at whose instigation it took place is lost in history. The rabbi's speech given here is loosely based on the *Kitab al-Khazari*, itself a later re-imagining, written in the 12th century in Islamic Spain. The Christian and Muslim arguments are a ragbag of the criticisms and slanders that proponents of the two faiths have thrown at each other over the centuries.

Princess Ummadha Citta is fictitious, although her political context is broadly accurate. The poem I have attributed to her can still be read on the Mirror Wall at Sigiriya, along with many others; my version is based on the translation by Lakshmi de Silva in *12 Centuries of Sinhala Poetry*, published by Vijitha Yapa. I must also acknowledge the Penguin anthology *Birds Through A Ceiling of Alabaster*, the source for Abbas' poems in chapter 16.

Ibn Musa al-Khwarizmi and Jabir ibn Hayyan were both real, and important enough to the history of ideas that their names have entered the English language. Al-Khwarizmi, via the eccentric transliteration of the Middle Ages, gives us "algorithm". Less flatteringly, the mysterious alchemical writings of "Geber", as the West knew him, are the origin of the word "gibberish". And of course Abu Nuwas, Harun al-Rashid, and Ja'far the Wazir all existed in fact, before entering the realm of the imagination via the *Thousand and One Nights*.

The fall of Ja'far ibn Yahya and the Barmakid family haunted the imagination of the Islamic world long after the death of all those who knew what really happened, and why. The story told by Ismail, about the tragic princess Abbasah, was the most popular explanation, and is recounted in the *Nights*. Al-Tabari though treats it with considerable scepticism; this sort of "harem intrigue" was often put forward to account for mysterious events in the lives of the rich and powerful, but is as implausible as it is appealing. More convincingly, he offers anecdotes about the Barmakids' wealth, complacency and their lax treatment of Alid prisoners. Ja'far's planned coup is entirely my invention, but none of the conventional explanations really account for the suddenness, secrecy and violence of Harun al-Rashid's action against his closest friends and allies.

I am neither a historian nor a linguist, and in writing this novel I have leaned heavily on the scholarship of others. I must thank Professor Hugh Kennedy and Robert Irwin, both for their learned and accessible writings on the history and poetry of the Abbasid Khalifate, and for their personal kindness and support. I am eternally grateful to my editor, Eric Lane, and my agent, Juri Gabriel, for their patience, wisdom and advice during the gestation of this book. Thanks are also due to Marie Lane for the cover design and typesetting, to everyone who read drafts and made suggestions, to the Pow-Wow writing group for their friendship and inspiration, to SF Said for lighting the way, and to Fionn and Oliver for making me proud. Last but most certainly not least, a huge thank you to Noah, Joseph and Karen for putting up with me.